release me

release me

A NOVEL

J. Kenner

BANTAM BOOKS   NEW YORK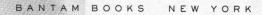

2013 Bantam Books Trade Paperback Edition

Copyright © 2013 by Julie Kenner

Published in the United States by Bantam Books, an imprint of The Random House Publishing Group, a division of Random House, Inc., New York.

BANTAM BOOKS and the rooster colophon are registered trademarks of Random House, Inc.

Library of Congress Cataloging-in-Publication Data

Kenner, J.
Release me : a novel / J. Kenner.
p. cm.
ISBN 978-0-345-54411-7
eBook ISBN 978-0-345-54412-4
1. Women professional employees—Fiction. 2. Billionaires—Fiction.
3. Secrets—Fiction. 4. Los Angeles (Calif.)—Fiction. I. Title.
PS3611.E665R45 2012
813'.6—dc23   2012038921

Printed in the United States of America

www.bantamdell.com

9 8 7 6 5

Book design by Liz Cosgrove

To Shauna and Gina . . . who know why.

Special thanks to Stefani, Kelly Jo,
and Kathleen for the early reads,
comments, and enthusiasm.

And thanks to the folks at Learjet,
the FAA, and Stars in Your Eyes
for so thoughtfully answering my
questions; any errors are my own.

release me

1

A cool ocean breeze caresses my bare shoulders, and I shiver, wishing I'd taken my roommate's advice and brought a shawl with me tonight. I arrived in Los Angeles only four days ago, and I haven't yet adjusted to the concept of summer temperatures changing with the setting of the sun. In Dallas, June is hot, July is hotter, and August is hell.

Not so in California, at least not by the beach. LA Lesson Number One: Always carry a sweater if you'll be out after dark.

Of course, I could leave the balcony and go back inside to the party. Mingle with the millionaires. Chat up the celebrities. Gaze dutifully at the paintings. It is a gala art opening, after all, and my boss brought me here to meet and greet and charm and chat. Not to lust over the panorama that is coming alive in front of me. Bloodred clouds bursting against the pale orange sky. Blue-gray waves shimmering with dappled gold.

I press my hands against the balcony rail and lean forward, drawn to the intense, unreachable beauty of the setting sun. I regret that I didn't bring the battered Nikon I've had since high school. Not that it would have fit in my itty-bitty beaded purse.

And a bulky camera bag paired with a little black dress is a big, fat fashion no-no.

But this is my very first Pacific Ocean sunset, and I'm determined to document the moment. I pull out my iPhone and snap a picture.

"Almost makes the paintings inside seem redundant, doesn't it?" I recognize the throaty, feminine voice and turn to face Evelyn Dodge, retired actress turned agent turned patron of the arts—and my hostess for the evening.

"I'm so sorry. I know I must look like a giddy tourist, but we don't have sunsets like this in Dallas."

"Don't apologize," she says. "I pay for that view every month when I write the mortgage check. It damn well better be spectacular."

I laugh, immediately more at ease.

"Hiding out?"

"Excuse me?"

"You're Carl's new assistant, right?" she asks, referring to my boss of three days.

"Nikki Fairchild."

"I remember now. Nikki from Texas." She looks me up and down, and I wonder if she's disappointed that I don't have big hair and cowboy boots. "So who does he want you to charm?"

"Charm?" I repeat, as if I don't know exactly what she means.

She cocks a single brow. "Honey, the man would rather walk on burning coals than come to an art show. He's fishing for investors and you're the bait." She makes a rough noise in the back of her throat. "Don't worry. I won't press you to tell me who. And I don't blame you for hiding out. Carl's brilliant, but he's a bit of a prick."

"It's the brilliant part I signed on for," I say, and she barks out a laugh.

The truth is that she's right about me being the bait. "Wear a cocktail dress," Carl had said. "Something flirty."

Seriously? I mean, *Seriously?*

I should have told him to wear his own damn cocktail dress. But I didn't. Because I want this job. I fought to get this job. Carl's company, C-Squared Technologies, successfully launched three web-based products in the last eighteen months. That track record had caught the industry's eye, and Carl had been hailed as a man to watch.

More important from my perspective, that meant he was a man to learn from, and I'd prepared for the job interview with an intensity bordering on obsession. Landing the position had been a huge coup for me. So what if he wanted me to wear something flirty? It was a small price to pay.

Shit.

"I need to get back to being the bait," I say.

"Oh, hell. Now I've gone and made you feel either guilty or self-conscious. Don't be. Let them get liquored up in there first. You catch more flies with alcohol anyway. Trust me. I know."

She's holding a pack of cigarettes, and now she taps one out, then extends the pack to me. I shake my head. I love the smell of tobacco—it reminds me of my grandfather—but actually inhaling the smoke does nothing for me.

"I'm too old and set in my ways to quit," she says. "But God forbid I smoke in my own damn house. I swear, the mob would burn me in effigy. You're not going to start lecturing me on the dangers of secondhand smoke, are you?"

"No," I promise.

"Then how about a light?"

I hold up the itty-bitty purse. "One lipstick, a credit card, my driver's license, and my phone."

"No condom?"

"I didn't think it was that kind of party," I say dryly.

"I knew I liked you." She glances around the balcony. "What the hell kind of party am I throwing if I don't even have one god-damn candle on one goddamn table? Well, fuck it." She puts the unlit cigarette to her mouth and inhales, her eyes closed and her expression rapturous. I can't help but like her. She wears hardly any makeup, in stark contrast to all the other women here to-night, myself included, and her dress is more of a caftan, the batik pattern as interesting as the woman herself.

She's what my mother would call a brassy broad—loud, large, opinionated, and self-confident. My mother would hate her. I think she's awesome.

She drops the unlit cigarette onto the tile and grinds it with the toe of her shoe. Then she signals to one of the catering staff, a girl dressed all in black and carrying a tray of champagne glasses.

The girl fumbles for a minute with the sliding door that opens onto the balcony, and I imagine those flutes tumbling off, break-ing against the hard tile, the scattered shards glittering like a wash of diamonds.

I picture myself bending to snatch up a broken stem. I see the raw edge cutting into the soft flesh at the base of my thumb as I squeeze. I watch myself clutching it tighter, drawing strength from the pain, the way some people might try to extract luck from a rabbit's foot.

The fantasy blurs with memory, jarring me with its potency. It's fast and powerful, and a little disturbing because I haven't needed the pain in a long time, and I don't understand why I'm thinking about it now, when I feel steady and in control.

I am fine, I think. *I am fine, I am fine, I am fine.*

"Take one, honey," Evelyn says easily, holding a flute out to me.

I hesitate, searching her face for signs that my mask has slipped and she's caught a glimpse of my rawness. But her face is clear and genial.

"No, don't you argue," she adds, misinterpreting my hesitation. "I bought a dozen cases and I hate to see good alcohol go to waste. Hell no," she adds when the girl tries to hand her a flute. "I hate the stuff. Get me a vodka. Straight up. Chilled. Four olives. Hurry up, now. Do you want me to dry up like a leaf and float away?"

The girl shakes her head, looking a bit like a twitchy, frightened rabbit. Possibly one that had sacrificed his foot for someone else's good luck.

Evelyn's attention returns to me. "So how do you like LA? What have you seen? Where have you been? Have you bought a map of the stars yet? Dear God, tell me you're not getting sucked into all that tourist bullshit."

"Mostly I've seen miles of freeway and the inside of my apartment."

"Well, that's just sad. Makes me even more glad that Carl dragged your skinny ass all the way out here tonight."

I've put on fifteen welcome pounds since the years when my mother monitored every tiny thing that went in my mouth, and while I'm perfectly happy with my size-eight ass, I wouldn't describe it as skinny. I know Evelyn means it as a compliment, though, and so I smile. "I'm glad he brought me, too. The paintings really are amazing."

"Now don't do that—don't you go sliding into the polite-conversation routine. No, no," she says before I can protest. "I'm sure you mean it. Hell, the paintings are wonderful. But you're getting the flat-eyed look of a girl on her best behavior, and we can't have that. Not when I was getting to know the real you."

"Sorry," I say. "I swear I'm not fading away on you."

Because I genuinely like her, I don't tell her that she's wrong—she hasn't met the real Nikki Fairchild. She's met Social Nikki who, much like Malibu Barbie, comes with a complete set of accessories. In my case, it's not a bikini and a convertible.

Instead, I have the *Elizabeth Fairchild Guide for Social Gatherings*.

My mother's big on rules. She claims it's her Southern upbringing. In my weaker moments, I agree. Mostly, I just think she's a controlling bitch. Since the first time she took me for tea at the Mansion at Turtle Creek in Dallas at age three, I have had the rules drilled into my head. How to walk, how to talk, how to dress. What to eat, how much to drink, what kinds of jokes to tell.

I have it all down, every trick, every nuance, and I wear my practiced pageant smile like armor against the world. The result being that I don't think I could truly be myself at a party even if my life depended on it.

This, however, is not something Evelyn needs to know.

"Where exactly are you living?" she asks.

"Studio City. I'm sharing a condo with my best friend from high school."

"Straight down the 101 for work and then back home again. No wonder you've only seen concrete. Didn't anyone tell you that you should have taken an apartment on the Westside?"

"Too pricey to go it alone," I admit, and I can tell that my admission surprises her. When I make the effort—like when I'm Social Nikki—I can't help but look like I come from money. Probably because I do. Come from it, that is. But that doesn't mean I brought it with me.

"How old are you?"

"Twenty-four."

Evelyn nods sagely, as if my age reveals some secret about me. "You'll be wanting a place of your own soon enough. You call me when you do and we'll find you someplace with a view. Not as good as this one, of course, but we can manage something better than a freeway on-ramp."

"It's not that bad, I promise."

"Of course it's not," she says in a tone that says the exact opposite. "As for views," she continues, gesturing toward the now-dark ocean and the sky that's starting to bloom with stars, "you're welcome to come back anytime and share mine."

"I might take you up on that," I admit. "I'd love to bring a decent camera back here and take a shot or two."

"It's an open invitation. I'll provide the wine and you can provide the entertainment. A young woman loose in the city. Will it be a drama? A rom-com? Not a tragedy, I hope. I love a good cry as much as the next woman, but I like you. You need a happy ending."

I tense, but Evelyn doesn't know she's hit a nerve. That's why I moved to LA, after all. New life. New story. New Nikki.

I ramp up the Social Nikki smile and lift my champagne flute. "To happy endings. And to this amazing party. I think I've kept you from it long enough."

"Bullshit," she says. "I'm the one monopolizing you, and we both know it."

We slip back inside, the buzz of alcohol-fueled conversation replacing the soft calm of the ocean.

"The truth is, I'm a terrible hostess. I do what I want, talk to whoever I want, and if my guests feel slighted they can damn well deal with it."

I gape. I can almost hear my mother's cries of horror all the way from Dallas.

"Besides," she continues, "this party isn't supposed to be about me. I put together this little shindig to introduce Blaine and his art to the community. He's the one who should be doing the mingling, not me. I may be fucking him, but I'm not going to baby him."

Evelyn has completely destroyed my image of how a hostess for the not-to-be-missed social event of the weekend is supposed to behave, and I think I'm a little in love with her for that.

"I haven't met Blaine yet. That's him, right?" I point to a tall reed of a man. He is bald, but sports a red goatee. I'm pretty sure it's not his natural color. A small crowd hums around him, like bees drawing nectar from a flower. His outfit is certainly as bright as one.

"That's my little center of attention, all right," Evelyn says. "The man of the hour. Talented, isn't he?" Her hand sweeps out to indicate her massive living room. Every wall is covered with paintings. Except for a few benches, whatever furniture was once in the room has been removed and replaced with easels on which more paintings stand.

I suppose technically they are portraits. The models are nudes, but these aren't like anything you would see in a classical art book. There's something edgy about them. Something provocative and raw. I can tell that they are expertly conceived and carried out, and yet they disturb me, as if they reveal more about the person viewing the portrait than about the painter or the model.

As far as I can tell, I'm the only one with that reaction. Certainly the crowd around Blaine is glowing. I can hear the gushing praise from here.

"I picked a winner with that one," Evelyn says. "But let's see. Who do you want to meet? Rip Carrington and Lyle Tarpin? Those two are guaranteed drama, that's for damn sure, and your roommate will be jealous as hell if you chat them up."

"She will?"

Evelyn's brows arch up. "Rip and Lyle? They've been feuding for weeks." She narrows her eyes at me. "The fiasco about the new season of their sitcom? It's all over the Internet? You really don't know them?"

"Sorry," I say, feeling the need to apologize. "My school schedule was pretty intense. And I'm sure you can imagine what working for Carl is like."

Speaking of . . .

I glance around, but I don't see my boss anywhere.

"That is one serious gap in your education," Evelyn says. "Culture—and yes, pop culture counts—is just as important as—what did you say you studied?"

"I don't think I mentioned it. But I have a double major in electrical engineering and computer science."

"So you've got brains and beauty. See? That's something else we have in common. Gotta say, though, with an education like that, I don't see why you signed up to be Carl's secretary."

I laugh. "I'm not, I swear. Carl was looking for someone with tech experience to work with him on the business side of things, and I was looking for a job where I could learn the business side. Get my feet wet. I think he was a little hesitant to hire me at first—my skills definitely lean toward tech—but I convinced him I'm a fast learner."

She peers at me. "I smell ambition."

I lift a shoulder in a casual shrug. "It's Los Angeles. Isn't that what this town is all about?"

"Ha! Carl's lucky he's got you. It'll be interesting to see how long he keeps you. But let's see . . . who here would intrigue you . . . ?"

She casts about the room, finally pointing to a fifty-something man holding court in a corner. "That's Charles Maynard," she says. "I've known Charlie for years. Intimidating as hell until you get to know him. But it's worth it. His clients are either celebrities with name recognition or power brokers with more money than God. Either way, he's got all the best stories."

"He's a lawyer?"

"With Bender, Twain & McGuire. Very prestigious firm."

"I know," I say, happy to show that I'm not entirely ignorant, despite not knowing Rip or Lyle. "One of my closest friends works for the firm. He started here but he's in their New York office now."

"Well, come on, then, Texas. I'll introduce you." We take one step in that direction, but then Evelyn stops me. Maynard has pulled out his phone, and is shouting instructions at someone. I catch a few well-placed curses and eye Evelyn sideways. She looks unconcerned "He's a pussycat at heart. Trust me, I've worked with him before. Back in my agenting days, we put together more celebrity biopic deals for our clients than I can count. And we fought to keep a few tell-alls off the screen, too." She shakes her head, as if reliving those glory days, then pats my arm. "Still, we'll wait 'til he calms down a bit. In the meantime, though . . ."

She trails off, and the corners of her mouth turn down in a frown as she scans the room again. "I don't think he's here yet, but—oh! Yes! Now *there's* someone you should meet. And if you want to talk views, the house he's building has one that makes my view look like, well, like yours." She points toward the entrance hall, but all I see are bobbing heads and haute couture. "He hardly ever accepts invitations, but we go way back," she says.

I still can't see who she's talking about, but then the crowd parts and I see the man in profile. Goose bumps rise on my arms, but I'm not cold. In fact, I'm suddenly very, very warm.

He's tall and so handsome that the word is almost an insult. But it's more than that. It's not his looks, it's his *presence*. He commands the room simply by being in it, and I realize that Evelyn and I aren't the only ones looking at him. The entire crowd has noticed his arrival. He must feel the weight of all those eyes, and yet the attention doesn't faze him at all. He smiles at the girl with the champagne, takes a glass, and begins to chat casually with a woman who approaches him, a simpering smile stretched across her face.

"Damn that girl," Evelyn says. "She never did bring me my vodka."

But I barely hear her. "Damien Stark," I say. My voice surprises me. It's little more than breath.

Evelyn's brows rise so high I notice the movement in my peripheral vision. "Well, how about that?" she says knowingly. "Looks like I guessed right."

"You did," I admit. "Mr. Stark is just the man I want to see."

2

"Damien Stark is the holy grail." That's what Carl told me earlier that evening. Right after "Damn, Nikki. You look hot."

I think he was expecting me to blush and smile and thank him for his kind words. When I didn't, he cleared his throat and got down to business. "You know who Stark is, right?"

"You saw my resume," I reminded him. "The fellowship?" I'd been the recipient of the Stark International Science Fellowship for four of my five years at the University of Texas, and those extra dollars every semester had made all the difference in the world to me. Of course, even without a fellowship, you'd have to be from Mars not to know about the man. Only thirty years old, the reclusive former tennis star had taken the millions he'd earned in prizes and endorsements and reinvented himself. His tennis days had been overshadowed by his new identity as an entrepreneur, and Stark's massive empire raked in billions every year.

"Right, right," Carl said, distracted. "Team April is presenting at Stark Applied Technology on Tuesday." At C-Squared, every product team is named after a month. With only twenty-three employees, though, the company has yet to tap into autumn or winter.

"That's fabulous," I said, and I meant it. Inventors, software developers, and eager new business owners practically wet themselves to get an interview with Damien Stark. That Carl had snagged just such an appointment was proof that my hoop-jumping to get this job had been worth it.

"Damn straight," Carl said. "We're showing off the beta version of the 3-D training software. Brian and Dave are on point with me," he added, referring to the two software developers who'd written most of the code for the product. Considering its applications in athletics and Stark Applied Technology's focus on athletic medicine and training, I had to guess that Carl was about to pitch another winner. "I want you at the meeting with us," he added, and I managed not to embarrass myself by doing a fist-pump in the air. "Right now, we're scheduled to meet with Preston Rhodes. Do you know who he is?"

"No."

"Nobody does. Because Rhodes *is* a nobody."

So Carl didn't have a meeting with Stark, after all. I, however, had a feeling I knew where this conversation was going.

"Pop quiz, Nikki. How does an up-and-coming genius like me get an in-person meeting with a powerhouse like Damien Stark?"

"Networking," I said. I wasn't an A-student for nothing.

"And that's why I hired you." He tapped his temple, even as his eyes roamed over my dress and lingered at my cleavage. At least he wasn't so gauche as to actually articulate the basic fact that he was hoping that my tits—rather than his product—would intrigue Stark enough that he'd attend the meeting personally. But honestly, I wasn't sure my girls were up to the task. I'm easy on the eyes, but I'm more the girl-next-door, America's-sweetheart type. And I happen to know that Stark goes for the runway supermodel type.

I learned that six years ago when he was still playing tennis and I was still chasing tiaras. He'd been the token celebrity judge at the Miss Tri-County Texas pageant, and though we'd barely exchanged a dozen words at the mid-pageant reception, the encounter was burned into my memory.

I'd parked myself near the buffet and was contemplating the tiny squares of cheesecake, wondering if my mother would smell it on my breath if I ate just one, when he walked up with the kind of bold self-assurance that can seem like arrogance on some men, but on Damien Stark it just seemed sexy as hell. He eyed me first, then the cheesecakes. Then he took two and popped them both in his mouth. He chewed, swallowed, then grinned at me. His unusual eyes, one amber and one almost completely black, seemed to dance with mirth.

I tried to come up with something clever to say and failed miserably. So I just stood there, my polite smile plastered across my face as I wondered if his kiss would give me all the taste and none of the calories.

Then he leaned closer, and my breath hitched as his proximity increased. "I think we're kindred spirits, Miss Fairchild."

"I'm sorry?" Was he talking about the cheesecake? Good God, I hadn't actually looked jealous when he'd eaten them, had I? The idea was appalling.

"Neither of us wants to be here," he explained. He tilted his head slightly toward a nearby emergency exit, and I was overcome by the sudden image of him grabbing my hand and taking off running. The clarity of the thought alarmed me. But the certainty that I'd go with him didn't scare me at all.

"I—oh," I mumbled.

His eyes crinkled with his smile, and he opened his mouth to speak. I didn't learn what he had to say, though, because Carmela D'Amato swept over to join us, then linked her arm with his. "Damie, darling." Her Italian accent was as thick as her dark wavy hair. "Come. We should go, yes?" I've never been a big tabloid reader, but it's hard to avoid celebrity gossip when you're doing the pageant thing. So I'd seen the headlines and articles that paired the big-shot tennis star with the Italian super-model.

"Miss Fairchild," he said with a parting nod, then turned to escort Carmela into the crowd and out of the building. I watched them leave, consoling myself with the thought that there was regret in his eyes as we parted ways. Regret and resignation.

There wasn't, of course. Why would there be? But that nice little fantasy got me through the rest of the pageant.

And I didn't say one word about the encounter to Carl. Some things are best played close to the vest. Including how much I'm looking forward to meeting Damien Stark again.

"Come on, Texas," Evelyn says, pulling me from my thoughts. "Let's go say howdy."

I feel a tap on my shoulder and turn to find Carl behind me. He sports the kind of grin that suggests he just got laid. I know better. He's just giddy with the anticipation of getting close to Damien Stark.

Well, me, too.

The crowd has shifted again, blocking my view of the man. I still haven't seen his face, just his profile, and now I can't even see that. Evelyn's leading the way, making forward progress through the crowd despite a few stops and starts to chat with her guests. We're on the move again when a barrel-chested man in a plaid sport coat shifts to the left, once again revealing Damien Stark.

He is even more magnificent now than he was six years ago. The brashness of youth has been replaced by a mature confidence. He is Jason and Hercules and Perseus—a figure so strong and beautiful and heroic that the blood of the gods must flow through him, because how else could a being so fine exist in this world? His face consists of hard lines and angles that seem sculpted by light and shadows, making him appear both classically gorgeous and undeniably unique. His dark hair absorbs the light as completely as a raven's wing, but it is not nearly as smooth. Instead, it looks wind-tossed, as if he's spent the day at sea.

That hair in contrast with his black tailored trousers and starched white shirt give him a casual elegance, and it's easy to believe that this man is just as comfortable on a tennis court as he is in a boardroom.

His famous eyes capture my attention. They seem edgy and dangerous and full of dark promises. More important, they are watching me. Following me as I move toward him.

I feel an odd sense of déjà vu as I move steadily across the floor, hyperaware of my body, my posture, the placement of my feet. Foolishly, I feel as if I'm a contestant all over again.

I keep my eyes forward, not looking at his face. I don't like the nervousness that has crept into my manner. The sense that he can see beneath the armor I wear along with my little black dress.

One step, then another.

I can't help it; I look straight at him. Our eyes lock, and I swear all the air is sucked from the room. It is my old fantasy come to life, and I am completely lost. The sense of déjà vu vanishes and there's nothing but this moment, electric and powerful. *Sensual.*

For all I know, I've gone spinning off into space. But no, I'm right there, floor beneath me, walls around me, and Damien Stark's eyes on mine. I see heat and purpose. And then I see nothing but raw, primal desire so intense I fear that I'll shatter under the force of it.

Carl takes my elbow, steadying me, and only then do I realize I'd started to stumble. "Are you okay?"

"New shoes. Thanks." I glance back at Stark, but his eyes have gone flat. His mouth is a thin line. Whatever that was—and what the hell was it?—the moment has passed.

By the time we reach Stark, I've almost convinced myself it was my imagination.

I barely process the words as Evelyn introduces Carl. My turn is next, and Carl presses his hand to my shoulder, pushing me subtly forward. His palm is sweating, and it feels clammy against my bare skin. I force myself not to shrug it off.

"Nikki is Carl's new assistant," Evelyn says.

I extend my hand. "Nikki Fairchild. It's a pleasure." I don't mention that we've met before. Now hardly seems the time to remind him that I once paraded before him in a bathing suit.

"Ms. Fairchild," he says, ignoring my hand. My stomach twists, but I'm not sure if it's from nerves, disappointment, or anger. He looks from Carl to Evelyn, pointedly avoiding my eyes. "You'll have to excuse me. There's something I need to attend to right away." And then he's gone, swallowed up into the crowd as effectively as a magician disappearing in a puff of smoke.

"What the fuck?" Carl says, summing up my sentiments exactly.

Uncharacteristically quiet, Evelyn simply gapes at me, her expressive mouth turned down into a frown.

But I don't need words to know what she's thinking. I can easily see that she's wondering the same thing I am: What just happened?

More important, what the hell did I do wrong?

3

My moment of mortification hangs over the three of us for what feels like an eternity. Then Carl takes my arm and begins to steer me away from Evelyn.

"Nikki?" Concern blooms in her eyes.

"I—it's okay," I say. I feel strangely numb and very confused. *This* is what I'd been looking forward to?

"I mean it, Nikki," Carl says, as soon as he's put some distance between us and our hostess. "What the fuck was that?"

"I don't know."

"Bullshit," he snaps. "Have you met before? Did you piss him off? Did you apply for a job with him before me? What the hell did you do, Nichole?"

I cringe against the use of my given name. "It's not me," I say, because I want that to be the truth. "He's famous. He's eccentric. He was rude, but it wasn't personal. How the hell could it have been?" I can hear my voice rising, and I force myself to tamp it down. To breathe.

I squeeze my left hand into a fist so tight my fingernails cut into my palm. I focus on the pain, on the simple process of breathing. I need to be cool. I need to be calm. I can't let the Social Nikki facade slip away.

Beside me, Carl runs his fingers through his hair and sucks in a noisy breath. "I need a drink. Come on."

"I'm fine, thanks." I am a long way from fine, but what I want right then is to be alone. Or as alone as I can be in a room full of people.

I can see that he wants to argue. I can also see that he hasn't yet decided what he's going to do. Approach Stark again? Leave the party and pretend it never happened? "Fine," he growls. He stalks off, and I can hear his muttered "Shit," as he disappears into the crowd.

I exhale, the tension in my shoulders slipping away. I head toward the balcony, but stop once I see that my private spot has been discovered. At least eight people mingle there, chatting and smiling. I am not in a chatty, smiley mood.

I veer toward one of the freestanding easels and stare blankly at the painting. It depicts a nude woman kneeling on a hard tile floor. Her arms are raised above her head, her wrists bound by a red ribbon.

The ribbon is attached to a chain that rises vertically out of the painting, and there is tension in her arms, as if she's tugging downward, trying to get free. Her stomach is smooth, her back arched so that the lines of her rib cage show. Her breasts are small, and the erect nipples and tight brown areolae glow under the artist's skill.

Her face is not so prominent. It's tilted away, shrouded in gray. I'm left with the impression that the model is ashamed of her arousal. That she would break free if she could. But she can't.

She's trapped there, her pleasure and her shame on display for all the world.

My own skin prickles and I realize that this girl and I have something in common. I'd felt a sensual power crash over me, and I'd reveled in it.

Then Stark had shut it off, as quickly as if he'd flipped a switch. And like that model I was left feeling awkward and ashamed.

Well, fuck him. That twit on the canvas might be embarrassed, but I wasn't going to be. I'd seen the heat in his eyes, and it had turned me on. Period. End of story. Time to move on.

I look hard at the woman on the canvas. She's weak. I don't like her, and I don't like the painting.

I start to move away, my own confidence restored—and I collide with none other than Damien Stark himself.

Well, shit.

His hand slides against my waist in an effort to steady me. I back away quickly, but not before my mind processes the feel of him. He's lean and hard, and I'm uncomfortably aware of the places where my body collided with his. My palm. My breasts. The curve of my waist tingles from the lingering shock of his touch.

"Ms. Fairchild." He's looking straight at me, his eyes neither flat nor cold. I realize that I have stopped breathing.

I clear my throat and flash a polite smile. The kind that quietly says "Fuck off."

"I owe you an apology."

Oh.

"Yes," I say, surprised. "You do."

I wait, but he says nothing else. Instead, he turns his attention to the painting. "It's an interesting image. But you would have made a much better model."

What the . . . ?

"That's the worst apology I've ever heard."

He indicates the model's face. "She's weak," he says, and I forget all about the apology. I'm too intrigued by the way his words echo my earlier thoughts. "I suppose some people might be drawn to the contrast. Desire and shame. But I prefer something bolder. A more confident sensuality."

He looks at me as he says this last, and I'm not sure if he's finally apologizing for snubbing me, complimenting my composure, or being completely inappropriate. I decide to consider his words a compliment and go from there. It may not be the safest approach, but it's the most flattering.

"I'm delighted you think so," I say. "But I'm not the model type."

He takes a step back and with slow deliberation looks me up and down. His inspection seems to last for hours, though it must take only seconds. The air between us crackles, and I want to move toward him, to close the gap between us again. But I stay rooted to the spot.

He lingers for a moment on my lips before finally lifting his head to meet my eyes, and that is when I move. I can't help it. I'm drawn in by the force and pressure of the tempest building in those damnable eyes.

"No," he says simply.

At first I'm confused, thinking that he's protesting my proximity. Then I realize he's responding to my comment about not being the model type.

"You are," he continues. "But not like this—splashed across a canvas for all the world to see, belonging to no one and everyone." His head tilts slightly to the left, as if he's trying out a new perspective on me. "No," he murmurs again, but this time he doesn't elaborate.

I am not prone to blushing, and I'm mortified to realize that my cheeks are burning. For someone who just a few moments ago mentally told this man to fuck off, I am doing a piss-poor job of keeping the upper hand. "I was hoping to have the chance to talk to you this evening," I say.

His brow lifts ever so slightly, giving him an expression of polite amusement. "Oh?"

"I'm one of your fellowship recipients. I wanted to say thank you."

He doesn't say a word.

I soldier on. "I worked my way through college, so the fellowship helped tremendously. I don't think I could have graduated with two degrees if it hadn't been for the financial help. So thank you." I still don't mention the pageant. As far as I'm concerned, Damien Stark and I are deep in the land of the do-over.

"And what are you doing now that you've left the hallowed halls of academia?"

He speaks so formally that I know he's teasing me. I ignore it and answer the question seriously. "I joined the team at C-Squared," I say. "I'm Carl Rosenfeld's new assistant." Evelyn already told him this, but I assume he hadn't been paying attention.

"I see."

The way he says it suggests he doesn't see at all. "Is that a problem?"

"Two degrees. A straight-A average. Glowing recommendations from all your professors. Acceptance to Ph.D. programs at both MIT and Cal Tech."

I stare at him, baffled. The Stark International Fellowship Committee awards thirty fellowships each year. How the hell can he possibly know so much about my academic career?

"I merely find it interesting that you ended up not leading a product development team but doing gruntwork as the owner's assistant."

"I—" I don't know what to say. I'm still spinning from the surreal nature of this inquisition.

"Are you sleeping with your boss, Ms. Fairchild?"

"What?"

"I'm sorry. Was the question unclear? I asked if you were fucking Carl Rosenfeld."

"I—*no.*" I blurt the answer out, because I can't let that image linger for longer than a second. Immediately, though, I regret speaking. What I should have done was slap his face. What the *hell* kind of question is that?

"Good," he says, so crisply and firmly and with such intensity that any thought I have of verbally bitch-slapping him vanishes completely. My thoughts, in fact, have taken a sharp left turn and I am undeniably, unwelcomely turned on. I glare at the woman in the portrait, hating her even more, and not particularly pleased with Damien Stark or myself. I suppose we have something in common, though. At the moment, we're both picturing me out of my little black dress.

Shit.

He doesn't even try to hide his amusement. "I believe I've shocked you, Ms. Fairchild."

"Hell yes, you've shocked me. What did you expect?"

He doesn't answer, just tilts his head back and laughs. It's as if a mask has slipped away, allowing me a glimpse of the real man hidden beneath. I smile, liking that we have this one small thing in common.

"Can anyone join this party?" It's Carl, and I want desperately to say no.

"How nice to see you again, Mr. Rosenfeld," Stark says. The mask is firmly back in place.

Carl glances at me, and I can see the question in his eyes. "Excuse me," I say. "I need to run to the ladies' room."

I escape to the cool elegance of Evelyn's powder room. She's thoughtfully provided mouthwash and hairspray and even disposable mascara wands. There is a lavender-scented salt scrub on the stone vanity, and I put a spoonful in my hands, then close my eyes and rub, imagining that I'm sloughing off the shell of myself to reveal something bright and shiny and new.

I rinse my hands in warm water, then caress my skin with my fingertips. My hands are soft now. Slick and sensual.

I meet my eyes in the mirror. "No," I whisper, but my hand

slides down to brush the hem of my dress just below my knee. It's fitted at the bodice and waist, but the skirt is flared, designed to present an enticing little swish when you move.

My fingers dance across my knee, then trail lazily up my inner thigh. I meet my gaze in the mirror, then close my eyes. It's Stark's face I want to see. His eyes I imagine watching me from that mirror.

There's a sensuality in the way my fingers slowly graze my own skin. A lazy eroticism that some other time could build to something hot and explosive. But that's not where I'm going—that's what I'm destroying.

I stop when I feel it—the jagged, raised tissue of the five-year-old scar that mars the once-perfect flesh of my inner thigh. I press my fingertips to it, remembering the pain that punctuated that particular wound. That had been the weekend that my sister, Ashley, had died, and I'd just about crumbled under the weight of my grief.

But that's the past, and I close my eyes tight, my body hot, the scar throbbing beneath my hand.

This time when I open my eyes, all I see is myself. Nikki Fairchild, back in control.

I wrap my restored confidence around me like a blanket and return to the party. Both men look at me as I approach. Stark's face is unreadable, but Carl isn't even trying to hide his joy. He looks like a six-year-old on Christmas morning. "Say your goodbyes, Nikki. We're heading out. Lots to do. *Lots* to do."

"What? Now?" I don't bother to hide my confusion.

"Turns out Mr. Stark's going to be out of town on Tuesday, so we're pushing the meeting to tomorrow."

"Saturday?"

"Is that a problem?" Stark asks me.

"No, of course not, but—"

"He's attending personally," Carl says. "Personally," he repeats, as if I could have missed it the first time.

"Right. I'll just find Evelyn and say goodnight." I start to move away, but Stark's voice draws me back.

"I'd like Ms. Fairchild to stay."

"What?" Carl speaks, expressing my thought.

"The house I'm building is almost complete. I came here to find a painting for a particular room. I'd like a feminine perspective. I'll see her home safely, of course."

"Oh." Carl looks like he's going to protest, then thinks better of it. "She'll be happy to help."

The hell she will. It's one thing to wear the dress. It's another to completely skip the presentation rehearsal because a self-absorbed bazillionaire snaps his fingers and says jump. No matter how hot said bazillionaire might be.

But Carl cuts me off before I can form a coherent reply. "We'll speak tomorrow morning," he tells me. "The meeting's at two."

And then he's gone and I'm left seething beside a very smug Damien Stark.

"Who the hell do you think you are?"

"I know exactly who I am, Ms. Fairchild. Do you?"

"Maybe the better question is, who the hell do you think *I* am?"

"Are you attracted to me?"

"I—what?" I say, verbally stumbling. His words have knocked me off center, and I struggle to regain my balance. "That is so not the issue."

The corner of his mouth twitches, and I realize I've revealed too much.

"I'm Carl's assistant," I say firmly and slowly. "Not yours. And my job description does not include decorating your goddamn house." I'm not shouting, but my voice is as taut as a wire and my body even more so.

Stark, damn him, appears not only perfectly at ease, but also completely amused. "If your job duties include helping your boss find capital, then you may want to reconsider how you play the game. Insulting potential investors is probably not the best approach."

A cold stab of fear that I've screwed this up cuts through me. "Maybe not," I say. "But if you're going to withhold your money because I didn't roll over and flounce my skirts for you, then you're not the man the press makes you out to be. The Damien Stark I've read about invests in quality. Not in friendships or relationships or because he thinks some poor little inventor needs the deal. The Damien Stark I admire focuses on talent and talent alone. Or is that just public relations?"

I stand straight, ready to endure whatever verbal lashes he'll whip back at me. I'm not prepared for the response I get.

Stark laughs.

"You're right," he says. "I'm not going to invest in C-Squared because I met Carl at a party any more than I'd invest in it because you're in my bed."

"Oh." Once again, my cheeks heat. Once again, he's knocked me off balance.

"I do, however, want you."

My mouth is dry. I have to swallow before I can speak. "To help you pick a painting?"

"Yes," he confirms. "For now."

I force myself not to wonder about later. "Why?"

"Because I need an honest opinion. Most women on my arm say what they think will make me happy, not what they actually mean."

"But I'm not on your arm, Mr. Stark." I let the words hang for a moment. Then I deliberately turn my back and walk away. I can feel him watching me, but I neither stop nor turn around.

Slowly, I smile. I even add a little swing to my step. This is my moment of triumph and I intend to savor it.

Except victory isn't as delicious as I expected. In fact, it's a little bitter. Because secretly—oh, so secretly—I can't help but wonder what it would be like to be the girl on Damien Stark's arm.

4

I cross the entire room before I pause, my heart pounding wildly in my chest. Fifty-five steps. I counted every one of them, and now that there's no place left to go I am simply standing still, staring at one of Blaine's paintings. Another nude, this one lying on her side across a stark white bed, only the foreground in focus. The rest of the room—walls, furniture—are nothing more than the blurred gray suggestions of shapes.

The woman's skin is pale, as if she's never seen the sun. But her face suggests otherwise. It reflects so much ecstasy that it seems to glow.

There is only one splash of color on the entire canvas—a long red ribbon. It is tied loosely around the woman's neck, then extends between her heavy breasts to trail down even farther. It slides between her legs, then continues, the image fading into the background before meeting the edge of the canvas. There's a tautness to the ribbon, though, and it's clear what story the artist is telling; her lover is there, just off the canvas, and he's holding the ribbon, making it slide over her, making her writhe against it in a desperate need to find the pleasure that he's teasing her with.

I swallow, imagining the sensation of that cool, smooth satin stroking me between my legs. Making me hot, making me come . . .

And in my fantasy, it's Damien Stark who is holding that ribbon.

This is not good.

I ease away from the painting toward the bar, which is the only place in the entire room where I'm not bombarded by erotic imagery. Honestly, I need the break. Erotic art doesn't usually make me melt. Except, of course, it's not the art that's making me hot.

I do, however, want you.

What had he meant by that?

More to the point, what do I want him to mean by that? Which, of course, is a bullshit question. I know what I want. The same thing I wanted six years ago. I also know it will never happen. And even the fantasy is a very bad idea.

I scan the room, telling myself I'm only looking over the art. Apparently this is my night for self-deception. I'm looking for Stark, but when I find him, I wish that I hadn't bothered. He's standing next to a tall, lithe woman with short dark hair. She looks like Audrey Hepburn in *Sabrina,* vibrant and beautiful. Her small features are alight with pleasure, and as she laughs she reaches out and touches him in a casual, intimate gesture. My stomach hurts just watching them. Good God, I don't even know this man. Can I really be jealous?

I consider the possibility, and in the spirit of tonight's theme, I deceive myself once more. Not jealousy—*anger.* I'm pissed that Stark could so cavalierly flirt with me even though he's obviously enthralled by another woman—a beautiful, charming, radiant woman.

"More champagne?" The bartender holds out a flute. Tempting. Very tempting, but I shake my head. I don't need to get drunk. I need to get out of here.

More guests arrive, and the room overflows with people. I

look for Stark again, but he has disappeared into the crowd. Audrey Hepburn is nowhere in sight, either. I'm sure wherever they are, they're having a dandy time.

I sandwich myself between a wall and a hallway cordoned off with a velvet rope. Presumably it leads to the rest of Evelyn's house. Right now, it's the closest thing to privacy I have.

I take out my phone, hit speed dial, and wait for Jamie to answer.

"You will *so* not believe this," she says, skipping all the preliminaries. "I just did the nasty with Douglas."

"Oh my God, Jamie. Why?" Okay, that came out before I had the chance to think about it, and while this revelation about Douglas is not good news, I'm grateful to be dragged so forcefully into Jamie's problems. Mine can wait.

Douglas is our next-door neighbor, and his bedroom shares a wall with mine. Even though it's only been four days, I have a pretty good idea of how often he gets laid. The idea that my best friend is another ticky mark on his bedpost does not thrill me.

Of course, from Jamie's perspective, he's a mark on *her* bedpost.

"We were by the pool drinking wine, and then we got in the hot tub and then . . ." She trails off, leaving "and then" to my imagination.

"He's still there? Or are you at his place?"

"God, no. I sent him home an hour ago."

"Jamie . . ."

"What? I just needed to burn some energy. Trust me, it's good. I'm so mellow now you wouldn't even believe."

I frown. Like a girl who collects stray puppies, Jamie brings home a lot of men. She doesn't, however, keep them around. Not even until morning. As her roommate, I find that convenient. There's nothing quite like meeting an unshaved, unshowered, half-naked man staring into your refrigerator at three in the morning. As her friend, however, I worry.

She, in turn, worries about me for precisely the opposite reason. I've never brought a man home, much less kicked him out. As far as Jamie is concerned, that makes me subnormal.

This, however, isn't the time to get into it with my best friend. But *Douglas*? She had to go and pick Douglas? "Am I going to have to avert my eyes every time I see him in the complex?"

"He's cool," she says. "No big deal."

I close my eyes and shake my head. The mere thought of being naked like that—emotionally and physically—overwhelms me. Not a big deal? The hell it's not.

"How about you? Did you actually manage to form words this time?"

I scowl. As my best friend since forever, Jamie knows a few too many of my secrets. I'd told her all about my ambiguous encounter with uber-hottie Damien Stark at the pageant reception. Her reaction had been typical Jamie—if I'd just opened my mouth and formed actual words, he would have ditched Carmela and had his way with me. I'd told her she was insane, but her words had been like tinder to my smoldering fantasy.

"I talked to him," I admit now.

"Oh, really?" Her voice rises with interest.

"And he's coming to the presentation."

"And . . . ?"

I have to laugh. "That's it, Jamie. That was the point."

"Oh. Well, okay, then. No, seriously, that's fabulous, Nik. You totally rocked it."

When she puts it that way, I have to agree.

"So what's he like now?"

I consider the question. It's not an easy one to answer. "He's . . . intense." *Hot. Sexy. Surprising. Disturbing.* No, it's not Stark that's disturbing—it's my reaction to him.

"Intense?" Jamie parrots. "Like that's a revelation? I mean, the guy owns half the known universe. I hardly think he'd be all warm and fuzzy. More like dark and dangerous."

I frown. Somehow, Jamie has summed up Damien Stark perfectly.

"Anything else to report? How are the paintings? I won't ask if you've seen any celebrities. Any celebrity younger than Cary Grant, and you're clueless. I mean, you could probably trip over Bradley Cooper and not even know it."

"Actually, Rip and Lyle are here, and they're being civil to each other despite their feud. It'll be interesting to see if the show gets picked up for another season."

The silence at the other end of the line tells me I have scored big with that one, and I make a mental note to thank Evelyn. It's not easy to surprise my roommate.

"You bitch," she finally says. "If you don't come back with Rip Carrington's autograph, I am *so* finding a new best friend."

"I'll try," I promise. "Actually, you could come here. I kind of need a ride."

"Because Carl keeled over and died from surprise when Stark said he'd do the meeting?"

"Sort of. He left to go prep. The meeting's been bumped to tomorrow."

"And you're still at the party, why?"

"Stark wanted me to stay."

"Oh, did he?"

"It's not like that. He's looking to buy a painting. He wanted a female perspective."

"And since you're the only female at the party . . ."

I remember Audrey Hepburn and feel confused. I'm most definitely *not* the only female at the party. So what is Stark's game?

"I just need a ride," I snap, unfairly taking my irritation out on Jamie. "Can you come get me?"

"You're serious? Carl left you stranded in Malibu? That's like an hour away. He didn't even offer to reimburse cab fare?"

I hesitate a fraction of a second too long.

"What?" she demands.

"It's just that—well, Stark said he'd make sure I got home."

"And what? His Ferrari's not good enough for you? You'd rather ride in my ten-year-old Corolla?"

She has a point. It's Stark's fault I'm still here. Why should I inconvenience one of my friends—or fork over a buttload of money for cab fare—when he already said he'd get me home? Am I really that nervous about being alone with him?

Yes, actually, I am. Which is ridiculous. Elizabeth Fairchild's daughter does *not* get nervous around men. Elizabeth Fairchild's daughter wraps men around her little finger. I may have spent my whole life trying to escape from under my mother's thumb, but that doesn't mean she didn't manage to drill her lessons in deep.

"You're right," I say, even though the idea of Damien Stark wrapped around any woman's finger remains a little fuzzy. "I'll see you at home."

"If I'm asleep, wake me up. I want to hear everything."

"There's nothing to tell," I say.

"Liar," she chides, then clicks off.

I slide my phone into my purse and head back to the bar—now I want that champagne. I stand there holding my glass as I glance around the room. This time, I see Stark right away. Him and Audrey Hepburn. He's smiling, she's laughing, and I'm working myself up into quite a temper. I mean, he's the reason I'm stranded here, and yet he hasn't made any effort to speak to me again, to apologize for the whole "be my decorating wench" fiasco, or to arrange a ride for me. If I have to call a cab I am absolutely going to send a bill to Stark International.

Evelyn passes by, arm in arm with a man with hair so white he reminds me of Colonel Sanders. She pats him on the arm, murmurs something, then disengages herself. The colonel marches on as Evelyn eases up next to me. "Having a nice time?"

"Of course," I say.

She snorts.

"I know," I say. "I'm a terrible liar."

"Hell, honey, you weren't even putting any effort into that one."

"I'm sorry. I'm just . . ." I trail off and tuck a loose strand of hair behind my ear. I'd curled it and pinned it up in a chignon. A few loose curls are supposed to hang free and frame my face. Right now, the damn thing is just annoying me.

"He's inscrutable," Evelyn says.

"Who?"

She nods toward Damien, and I look in that direction. He's still talking with Audrey Hepburn, but I'm struck by the certainty that he had been watching me only moments earlier. I have nothing to base that on, though, and I'm frustrated, not knowing if the thought is wishful thinking or paranoia.

"Inscrutable?" I repeat.

"He's a hard man to figure out," Evelyn says. "I've known him since he was a boy—his father signed me to represent him when some damn breakfast cereal wanted his face on their television spots. As if Damien Stark with a sugar high was the way we wanted to go. No, I landed the boy some damn good endorsements, helped make him a goddamned household name. But most days I don't think I know him at all."

"Why not?"

"I told you, Texas. *Inscrutable.*" She draws out each syllable, then punctuates the word with a shake of her head. " 'Course I don't fault him, not with the shit that was piled onto that poor kid. Who wouldn't end up a little bit damaged?"

"You mean the fame? That must have been hard. He was so young." Stark won the Junior Grand Slam at fifteen, and that had pushed him into the stratosphere. But the press had latched onto him long before that. With his good looks and working-class background, he'd been plucked out of the flurry of hopefuls as the tennis circuit's golden boy.

"No, no." Evelyn waves her hand as if dismissing the thought. "Damien knows how to handle the press. He's damn good at protecting his secrets, always has been." She eyes me, then laughs, as if to suggest she was only joking. But I don't think so. "Oh, honey, listen to me ramble. No, Damien Stark is just one of those dark, quiet types. He's like an iceberg, Texas. The deep parts are well hidden and what you do see is hard and a little bit cold."

She chuckles, amused at her own joke, then waves at someone who's caught her attention. I glance toward Damien, looking for evidence of the wounded child that Evelyn has recalled, but all I see is unerring strength and self-confidence. Am I seeing a mask? Or am I really looking at the man?

"What I'm trying to say," Evelyn continues, "is that you shouldn't take it personally. The way he acted, I mean. I doubt he meant to be rude. He was probably just off in his head and didn't even realize what he was doing."

I, of course, have moved past the snub at our meeting, but Evelyn doesn't realize that. My current issues with Damien Stark are wide and varied—ranging from the simple problem of a ride home to more complicated emotions that I'm not inclined to analyze.

"You were right about Rip and Lyle," I say, because she keeps looking in Stark's direction, and I want to head off any suggestion that we edge our way into that conversation. "My roommate is in awe that I'm in the same room with them."

"Well, come on, then. I'll introduce you."

The two stars—both polished and shined within an inch of their lives—are perfectly polite and perfectly dull. I have nothing to say to them. I don't even know what their show is about. Evelyn can't seem to wrap her head around the possibility that anyone could either not care or not know about all things Hollywood. She seems to think I'm merely being coy and is about to leave me alone with these two.

Social Nikki would smile and make polite small talk. But Social Nikki is getting a bit frayed around the edges, and instead, I reach out, snagging a bit of Evelyn's sleeve before she escapes too far. She looks back at me, her brows raised in question. I have nothing to say. Panic bubbles in me; Social Nikki has completely left the building.

And then I see it—my excuse. My salvation. It's so unexpected—so completely out of place—that I half wonder if I'm not hallucinating. "That man," I say, pointing to a skinny twenty-something with long, wavy hair and wire-framed glasses. He looks like he belongs at Woodstock, not an art show, and I hold my breath, expecting the apparition to vanish. "Is that Orlando McKee?"

"You know Orlando?" she asks, then answers her own question. "Of course. The friend who works for Charles. But where did you two meet?" She nods goodbye to Lyle and Rip, who could care less about our departure; they're back to arguing between themselves and smiling brightly at the women who sidle in close for a snapshot.

"We grew up together," I explain as Evelyn steers me through the throng.

The truth is our families lived next door to each other until Ollie went off to college, and even though he's two years older than me, we were inseparable until Ollie turned twelve and was shipped off to boarding school in Austin. I had been beside myself with envy.

I haven't seen Ollie for years, but he's the kind of friend that you don't need to talk to every day. Months can go by, and then he'll call me out of the blue, and we pick up the conversation like it had never stopped. He and Jamie are my closest friends in the world and I am beyond giddy that he's here, right when I need him so desperately.

We're close now, but he hasn't noticed us. He's talking about some television show with another guy, this one in jeans and a sport coat over a pale pink button-down. Very California. Ollie's hands are moving, because that's the way he talks, and when he flails one hand my direction, he glances that way out of reflex. I see the moment that realization hits him. He freezes, his hand drops, and he turns to face me, his arms going out wide.

"Nikki? My God, you look amazing." He pulls me into a tight Ollie hug, then pushes me back, his hands on my shoulders as he looks me up and down.

"Do I pass inspection?"

"When have you not?"

"Why aren't you in New York?"

"The firm transferred me back last week. I was going to call you this weekend. I couldn't remember when you were moving out here." He pulls me into another spontaneous hug, and I'm grinning so wide my mouth is starting to hurt. "Damn, it's good to see you."

"I take it you two know each other," the guy in jeans says drolly.

"Sorry," Ollie says. "Nikki, this is Jeff. We work together at Bender, Twain & McGuire."

"What he means is that I work for him," Jeff says. "I'm a summer associate. Orlando is a third year now, and they love him there. I think Maynard's about ready to make him a partner."

"Very funny," Ollie says, but he looks pleased.

"Look at you," I say. "My little guppy's grown into a full-fledged shark."

"Ah-ah. You know the rules. For every lawyer joke you make, I get to make two dumb blonde jokes."

"I take it back."

"Come on, Jeff," Evelyn says. "Let's let these two catch up. We'll go find our own trouble to get into."

It would be polite to tell them not to bother, but neither one of us does. We're too wrapped up in reminiscing, and I'm too happy to have Ollie beside me.

We talk about everything and nothing as we head for the door, taking our conversation outside by silent agreement. I'm completely absorbed, warmed by memories and Ollie's familiar face. But as we reach the door, I turn back and look at the room. I'm not sure why I do. Maybe it's just a reflex, but I think it's something more. I think I'm looking for someone. *For him.*

Sure enough, my eyes find Damien Stark right away. He's no longer with Audrey Hepburn. Now he's talking with a short, balding man. He's focused and attentive. But his head lifts and his eyes find me.

And in that singular moment, I know that if he asked me to blow off my friend and stay in the room with him, I would do it.

Damn him, and damn me, but I would stay with Damien Stark.

5

I wear Ollie's jacket and hold my shoes by the straps as we walk along the private beach behind Evelyn's house. I'm certain we're not supposed to be out here, but I don't care. I swing my foot through the water gaily, sending a spray of sea drops scattering. It feels mischievous. It feels *good*.

"How's Courtney?" I ask. "Is she glad you're back?" That's a dangerous question where Ollie is concerned. Courtney is his on-again/off-again girlfriend. "On again" because she's amazing and Ollie would be an idiot to do something stupid and screw it up. "Off again" because Ollie has crossed that idiot line more than once.

"She's engaged," he says.

"Oh." I can't keep the disappointment out of my voice. I should be consoling and tell Ollie he'll find someone else amazing, but all I can think is that he's screwed up.

Suddenly, he's laughing. "To me, doofus."

"Oh, thank God!" I bump him playfully with my shoulder. "I thought you'd blown it."

His expression turns serious. "I almost did. New York was hard. Being away from her. Being tempted. But no more. She's the only woman for me. Damn, Nik. How did I manage to get her?"

"Because you're a great guy."

"I'm fucked up, and you know it."

"Everyone's a little fucked up, but Courtney sees the guy underneath. And she loves you."

"She does," he says with a grin. "It amazes me every day, but it's true. She really does." He eyes me sideways. "Speaking of fucked up, how are you really doing?"

I pull his jacket tighter around me. "I'm great. I already told you." I stop walking and dig my toes into the sand. The waves come in and swoosh over my bare feet before rushing out again, leaving me sinking a bit, the ground shifting under me.

Beside me, Ollie just gives me that look. Like he knows all my secrets, and I frown because it's true.

I shrug. "It's easier now. College was fucked up for a while, but it got better." I shoot him a smile because he'd been a big part of making it get better. "And now, I don't know. But it feels good being away from Texas. Really, I'm doing fine." I shrug again. I don't want to talk right now.

I turn around and start walking. "We should get back."

He nods and falls in step beside me. We walk silently for a while, the lights of Evelyn's house growing closer. The sound of the ocean fills the space between us. It's deep and rhythmic and I feel like I could get lost in it. Like maybe I already am a little lost.

We walk about fifty more yards, then he pauses. "So how do you feel about tuxedos?" he asks, as if it's the most normal question in the world.

"I feel good about them," I say. "Tuxedos are a time-honored tradition in the world of formal wear. I have to take points off for practicality, though. Hard to surf in a tux. Doable, but hard."

He laughs. "I want you to be my best man," he says, and I get a little lump in my throat. "Courtney's cool with it," he continues, "but she thinks the pictures will look better if you wear a tux. You know, the guy side in penguin suits, the girl side in silk and satin. What do you say?"

I hug myself and blink back tears. "I love you. You know that, right?"

"That's why I'm asking. It was either that or marry you, and I think the second option would piss Courtney off." He watches me, obviously expecting me to laugh. When I don't, his expression softens. "Thanks."

"For what?"

"For being happy for me."

"I am," I say, but I'm talking from behind my Social Nikki smile. The truth is that things are changing fast, and I don't want Ollie changing, too. He's been my rock for too long. What will happen to me if that rock suddenly shifts?

But I'm not being fair and I know it.

I start walking again.

"Nik?"

I wipe away an errant tear. "Ignore me. I'm just being emotional and weird. Girls and weddings, right?"

"Nothing's changing, Nik," he says, because he's tagged the hormonal excuse for the bullshit it is. "Anything you need, anytime. Courtney won't mind."

Fear knifes through me. "She doesn't know about—"

"Of course not. I mean, she knows about Ashley," he says, but that's fair. He and Courtney had been dating when my sister's unexpected suicide had completely shattered me. She'd been more than a sister to me—she'd been my escape from the life my mother molded for me, and even though she'd already gotten married and moved away when she died, the loss had sent me spiraling down. Jamie and Ollie had been my life rafts, so of course he'd talked about it with Courtney.

"I only told Courtney that she'd died and you were grieving," Ollie says urgently. "You know I'd never share your secrets."

My relief is so intense I don't even feel guilty for thinking that Ollie would betray my confidence.

"Looks like we're not the only ones who wanted to escape the hoopla." He's looking toward Evelyn's house. There are people clustered on the balcony, backlit by the light bursting through the window. But they're not the subject of Ollie's comment, and it takes me a second to realize what he sees. When I do, I gasp.

A darkened spiral staircase leads down from the balcony to the weathered boardwalk, and there is a man sitting on the bottom step. I can't see his face—I can't see more than a dark shape. But somehow I'm certain who it is.

We approach, and he stands, and I see that I am right.

"Ms. Fairchild," Stark says, walking forward to meet us. He doesn't look at Ollie at all. His eyes are wholly on me—burning amber and deep, dangerous black. "I was looking for you."

"Oh?" I try to sound cool, but I'm anything but. "Why?"

"You're my responsibility."

I exhale a bubble of laughter. "I hardly see how. I barely even know you, Mr. Stark."

"I promised your boss I'd see you safely home."

Beside me, Ollie steps closer. He clasps my shoulder in a protective gesture. His fingers tighten, and I can feel the pressure even through the thick material of his jacket. "I'm about to head home. I'll be happy to give Nikki a lift. You can consider your responsibility absolved."

Without a word, Stark reaches out to me and takes the lapel of Ollie's jacket between two fingers, as if testing the quality of the material. His hand hovers briefly over the swell of my breast, and I am suddenly aware of how intimate the moment must appear, Ollie and I walking alone on the beach, me wearing his jacket . . .

I feel an inexplicable need to explain that there's nothing romantic or sexual between Ollie and me, and it takes a great effort to keep my mouth shut. I tilt my head up to look at Ollie. "That would be great. Are you sure it's not inconvenient?"

"It's no problem at all," he says. His hand is still on my shoulder and he increases the pressure as if urging me on. But there's nowhere to go, Stark is right there, larger than life, and the air between us is charged. If I move, I think ridiculously, I'll end up caught in his web. The thought isn't entirely unpleasant.

"I'm not looking for absolution," Stark says to Ollie. "But I do need Ms. Fairchild to stay. We have business to discuss."

I consider arguing, but I also remember his earlier comment—that if I was trying to find investors for Carl, I was doing a crap-tastic job of it. I tilt my head and nod to Ollie. "It's okay."

"You're sure?" His voice is tight. Concerned.

"Seriously," I say. "Go on home."

He hesitates, then nods. "I'll call you tomorrow," he says, but he's looking at Stark as he says it. He's gone into full big-brother mode, and I hear the message under the words. *And she better be there and fine or there's going to be trouble.*

My imagination, I realize, is running wild.

He kisses my cheek and starts to head up the spiral staircase.

"Wait," Stark calls, and Ollie pauses.

I hold my breath, wondering if I'm about to witness some testosterone-laden ritual. But all Stark does is reach out for the shoes that I'm still holding in my right hand. I hand them to him, confused until he steps closer and starts to gently ease me out of Ollie's jacket.

"It's okay," Ollie says. "I'll get it later."

But I am already out of the jacket, having moved quickly so that I can recover the distance between me and Stark.

"No need," Stark says, and his smile is bright and friendly as he hands Ollie the jacket.

Ollie hesitates a nanosecond, then takes it. He slips it on, keeping his eyes on me. "Be careful," he says, then disappears up the dark, twisting stairs.

Careful? What the fuck?

I glance at Stark to see if he is as bemused as I am, but it's clear that his thoughts have not lingered on Ollie at all. No, he's completely focused on me.

I snatch my shoes back. "Do we actually have any business to discuss? Because it seems to me that my business is downtown. With Carl. Preparing for a meeting I'll be attending in just over sixteen hours."

"The paintings," he says easily. "I believe you were going to help me?"

"Your belief system is all screwed up. I recall quite clearly declining your request for help."

"My mistake. I thought you'd changed your mind after I pointed out that I valued your opinion."

"You thought I'd changed my mind?" I repeat. "And on what did you base that hypothesis? The way I walked away from you? The way I ignored you?"

He merely quirks a brow, letting me know that all my surreptitious glances toward him and Audrey Hepburn weren't so surreptitious, after all.

He watches me, probably expecting a pithy comeback, but I'm not going to provide one. At this moment, silence is most definitely the best policy.

I tilt my head up to look at his face. The minimal illumination filtering down from Evelyn's balcony casts his features in shadows. His eyes, however, seem to absorb the light. The amber one, fiery and hot. The other one black and ringed with molten lava, so dark and deep I feel as though I could fall in and get lost. *Windows to the soul,* I think and then shiver.

"You're cold," he says, then trails a finger down my bare arm. "You have goose bumps."

Well if I didn't before, I surely do now. . . .

"I was fine when I had a coat," I say, and he bursts out laugh-

ing. I like the sound of it, so free and easy and always unexpected.

He slips out of his jacket and drapes it over my shoulders,
ignoring my protests.

"We're going back inside," I say, shrugging it off and holding
it out. "I'm fine, really."

He takes my shoes from me, but ignores the coat. "Put it on.
I don't want you catching cold."

"Oh, for Christ's sake," I snap, shoving my arms into the
sleeves. "Do you always get what you want?"

His eyes widen, and I realize I've surprised him. "Yes," he
says.

Gotta give the guy points for honesty.

"Fine. Let's go inside. Look at some paintings. I'll tell you
what I like, and then you'll do whatever you want."

He's looking at me with a somewhat baffled expression. "Excuse me?"

"You just don't seem like the kind of guy who actually takes
anybody's advice."

"You're wrong, Nikki," he says, my name sounding like milk
chocolate in his mouth. "I consider very carefully any opinion I
value."

The heat coming off him is palpable. I no longer need the
jacket. Hell, the damn jacket is stifling.

I look away, at the sand, at the ocean, at the sky. Anywhere
but at this man. I'm twisted up in knots, but that's not the problem. The problem is, I like the feeling.

"Nikki," he says gently. "Look at me."

I look without thinking, and there's no Social Nikki between
us. I'm as naked as if I'd stripped off my dress.

"That man you were with. Who is he to you?"

Blam! Social Nikki is back on duty. I feel my face harden, my
eyes grow cold. Damien Stark *is* like a spider, and I'm the foolish
insect he's going to devour.

I look away, but only for a second. When I turn back, I'm flashing the very same plastic smile that he saw on a stage six years ago. I should turn the wattage up and tell him that Ollie is none of his business.

But I don't.

I'm not certain I understand the instinct that brings the answer to my lips, but it's the one that I go with, and as soon as I've spoken, I turn my back to him and begin the walk up the stairs, my words lingering in the air behind me.

"Him? That's Orlando McKee. We used to sleep together."

6

This isn't exactly true, but it's close enough. It's a story that I can spin and weave without losing the thread of reality.

It's another layer of armor, and where Damien Stark is concerned, I need as much protection as I can get.

He is right behind me on the stairs, but they are too narrow for us to stand side by side.

"Nikki," he says, his voice like a command.

I stop and turn to face him, looking down from my position three steps above him. It's an interesting perspective. I don't think there are many people who've had the opportunity to look down on Damien Stark.

"What is Mr. McKee to you now?"

I'm probably imagining it, but I think I see something vulnerable in Stark's eyes.

"He's a friend," I say. "A very good friend."

I think that's relief on his face, and the juxtaposition of those two emotions—relief and vulnerability—make my breath hitch.

They disappear quickly, though, and his "Are you sleeping with him now?" comes out decidedly frosty.

I press my fingertips to my temple. His shifts from cold to hot to cold again are dizzying. "Am I on some sort of game show? Have you and your millions invested in a new version of *Candid Camera*? A spin-off of *Punk'd*?"

"What are you talking about?"

"You're nice, then you're ice."

"Am I?"

"Don't even pretend not to know what I'm talking about. One minute you're so rude I want to slap your face—"

"And yet you don't."

I scowl, but otherwise ignore the interruption. "And then you turn on a dime and you're all warm and fuzzy."

His brow lifts. "Fuzzy?"

"Point taken. Fuzzy is not a word anyone should use to describe you. Forget warm and fuzzy. We'll go with hot and intense."

"Intense." He murmurs the word, making it sound much more sensual than I had intended. "I like the sound of that."

At the moment, so do I.

I swallow, my mouth suddenly dry. "The point is, you're dizzying."

He looks at me with unabashed amusement. "I like the sound of that, too."

"Dizzying *and* exasperating. And impertinent."

"Impertinent?" he repeats. He doesn't smile, but I swear I hear laughter in his voice.

"You ask questions you have no right to ask."

"And you've steered this conversation in a very elegant circle. But you still haven't answered my impertinent question."

"I would have thought that a man as intelligent as you are would realize that I was avoiding it."

"A man doesn't get where I've gotten by allowing details to remain ignored. I'm both diligent and persistent, Ms. Fairchild." He has me trapped, locked tight in his sights. "When I seek to acquire something, I learn everything I can about it, and then I pursue it wholeheartedly."

I have to pause a bit to remember how to form words. "Do you?"

"I believe there's an interview with me in last month's *Forbes*. I'm certain the reporter outlined my tenacity."

"I'll be sure to pick up a copy."

"I'll have my office send you one. Perhaps then you'll understand just how persistent I can be."

"I already understand it. What I don't get is why you're so fascinated with who I'm sleeping with. Why exactly does that interest you?" I'm treading on dangerous territory, and I suddenly understand that old adage about flirting with danger.

He climbs a step, putting his body in much closer proximity to mine. "There are a number of things about you that fascinate me."

Oh my. I move carefully up to the next level. "I'm an open book, Mr. Stark." I ascend one more step.

"You and I both know that's not true, Ms. Fairchild. But someday . . ."

He trails off, and though I know better, I have to ask. "Someday, what?"

"Someday you will be open for me, Ms. Fairchild. In so very many ways."

I want to respond, but I've lost the power of speech. Damien Stark wants me. More than that, he wants to peel back the layers and learn my secrets.

The idea is terrifying, and yet also strangely appealing.

Discomfited, I take another backward step up toward the balcony, then wince. Immediately, Stark is at my side. "What's wrong?"

"Nothing. Something sharp on the step."

He looks down at my still-bare feet.

Sheepishly, I hold out the strappy sandals with the three-inch heels.

"Very nice," he says. "Perhaps you should put them on."

"*Nice?*" I repeat. "They aren't nice. They're astounding. They cup my foot, show off my pedicure, slim my leg, and lift my ass just enough to make it look damn hot in this dress."

The corner of his mouth twitches with amusement. "I recall. Truly, they are amazing shoes."

"They also happen to be my first and only purchase from my frivolous Los Angeles shopping splurge."

"Well worth the damage to your checking account, I'm sure."

"Totally. But they are an absolute bitch to walk in. And now that I've taken them off I really don't know if I can get them back on again. No, correction. I don't know if I can get them on again and actually walk."

"I see your dilemma. Fortunately, I've made a career out of coming up with solutions to such knotty problems."

"Is that so? Well, please. Enlighten me."

"You can stay here on the steps. You can go inside barefoot. You can put the shoes back on and suffer."

"Somehow I expected something better from the great Damien Stark. If that's all the brainpower it takes to become the head of a corporate empire, I should have jumped all over that a long time ago."

"Sorry to disappoint."

"Staying here won't work," I say. "For one thing, it's cold. For another, I want to say goodbye to Evelyn."

"Mmm." He nods and frowns. "You're so right. Clearly I didn't fully examine the conundrum."

"That's what makes it a conundrum," I say. "As for going barefoot, Elizabeth Fairchild's daughter does not go barefoot at social events, no matter how much she might want to. I'm pretty sure it's a genetic trait."

"Then your choice is clear. You're going to have to wear the shoes."

"And suffer? No thank you. I don't do pain."

My words are flippant and not entirely true. He stares at me long and hard, and for some reason, Ollie's parting words come back to me: *Be careful*. Then his face clears and he's looking at me with amusement once again. I about melt with relief.

"There is one more option."

"Ah, see? You were holding out on me."

"I can pick you up and carry you into the party."

"Right," I say. "I'm just going to slip these puppies back on and suffer." I sit down on the step and slide my feet into the sandals. It's not pleasant. The shoes aren't broken in, and my feet are in full protest mode. I enjoyed the walk on the beach, but I should have known that everything comes with a price.

I stand, wince a little, and continue up the stairs. Stark is behind me, and when we reach the balcony he moves to my side and takes my arm. Then he leans in so close I feel his breath on my ear. "Some things are worth the pain. I'm glad you understand that."

I turn sharply to look at him. "What?"

"I'm simply saying that I'm glad you decided to put the shoes back on."

"Even though that meant I rejected your offer to throw me over your shoulder caveman-style and cart me around the party?"

"I don't recall mentioning a caveman carry, though the idea is undeniably intriguing." He pulls out his iPhone and starts to type something.

"What are you doing?"

"Making a note," he says.

I laugh and shake my head. "I'll say this, Mr. Stark. Whatever else you are, you're always a surprise." I look him up and down. "I don't suppose you have a pair of black flip-flops hidden on your person? Because that would be the kind of surprise I could really use."

"I'm afraid not," he says. "But in the future I may have to carry a pair just to be safe. I never realized what valuable currency a comfortable pair of shoes can be."

It occurs to me that I'm in full flirt-mode with Damien Stark. The man who has been hot and cold all night. The man who bleeds power and commands an empire and could snap his fingers and have any woman he wants. Right now, that woman is me.

It's a bewildering realization, but also flattering and, yes, exciting.

"The truth is I know exactly how you feel," he says.

I gape at him, wondering if he's been reading my thoughts.

"I've always hated tennis shoes. I used to practice in my bare feet. It made my coach crazy."

"Really?" I find this tidbit into Stark's real life fascinating. "But didn't you endorse a brand?"

"The only brand I could stand."

"That's a nice little rhyme. They could have used it as the tagline."

"It's a pity they didn't have you on their marketing team." He reaches out and brushes his thumb along the line of my jaw. My stomach quivers and I exhale, a single soft moan. His eyes go to my mouth and I think that he's going to kiss me and I absolutely do not want him to kiss me and, dammit, why isn't he kissing me yet?

Then the balcony door opens, and a couple emerges, arm in arm. Damien pulls his hand back and the spell is shattered. I want to scream at the couple, and not just because I've been left feeling hot and needy. No, something's been lost. I'm liking the Damien Stark who laughs and teases in the dark. Who flirts so softly and yet so intently. Who looks at me with eyes that let me see.

But our moment is gone. And if we go inside, I'm certain his mask will go back on. I'm even more certain my own will.

I almost suggest we go back down the stairs to the beach, but he's holding the door open for me, and his face is all hard lines and angles again. I step past him into the room, something tight and sad knotting inside me.

The party is still going strong. Possibly even stronger now that the guests are on their second, third, or fourth drink. The room is stuffy, almost claustrophobic, and I slip out of Stark's jacket and hand it back to him. He runs his palm over the silk lining. "You're warm," he says, then slips it on, the movement entirely normal and inexplicably erotic.

A waitress materializes beside me, her tray full of sparkling wine. I take a flute and gulp it back. Before she can edge away, I replace my empty glass and take a fresh one.

"For medicinal purposes," I say to Stark, who has also taken a glass, but has yet to take a sip. I am not so hesitant, and I down half of my glass in one long swallow. The bubbles seem to rise straight to my head, making me a little bit giddy. It's a nice feeling, and one I'm not used to. I drink, sure. But not champagne, and not very often. But I feel vulnerable tonight. Vulnerable and needy. With any luck, the alcohol will quench the ache. Either that, or it will give me the courage to act on it.

Oh, no.

I almost toss the champagne aside. Even with the aid of tiny bubbles, I'm not going there.

As I tilt my head back to take another sip, I catch Stark's eyes on me. They're dark and knowing and predatory, and I suddenly want to take a step backward. I clutch the stem of my glass harder and stay rooted to the spot.

The corner of his mouth quirks up with amusement as he

leans in closer to me. I breathe in the clean, crisp scent of his cologne, like the woods after a rain. He brushes a strand of hair from my cheek, and I wonder why I don't melt right then.

My body is hyperaware. My skin. My pulse. I tingle all over, and every tiny hair on my arms and the back of my neck is standing up, as if I'm in the middle of a lightning storm. It's his power I'm feeling, of course, and I feel it most strongly in the increasingly demanding flesh between my thighs.

"Is there something on your mind, Ms. Fairchild?" I can hear the tease in his voice, and it irks me that I am so transparent.

That bite of irritation is good—it draws me out of the haze. And, because I'm emboldened by the champagne, I look straight at him when I answer. "You are, Mr. Stark."

His lips part with surprise, but he recovers himself quickly. "I'm very glad to hear it." I'm only halfway aware of his words. I'm too focused on his mouth. It's gorgeous, wide, and sensual.

He takes another step closer, and the storm between us grows more intense, the air full and heavy. I can almost see the sparks.

"You should know, Ms. Fairchild, that before the night is over, I'm going to kiss you."

"Oh." I'm not sure if my word is an expression of surprise or assent. I wonder what those lips would feel like on mine. His tongue forcing my mouth open. The heated exploration as hands clutch and bodies press together.

"I'm glad you're looking forward to it." His words jolt me from the fantasy, and this time I do back away. One step, then another, until the storm between us calms and I can think clearly again.

"I'm not sure that would be a good idea," I say, because fantasy is all good and well, but this can only go so far, and it's important that I remind myself of that.

"On the contrary. I think it's one of my better ideas."

I swallow. To be honest, I want him to follow through right then, but I'm saved from my foolish wish by Stark himself. Or rather, by his reputation. Apparently Carl isn't the only one who believes in the power of networking, and we're joined by a cadre of people wanting to bask in his circle. Investors, inventors, tennis fans, single women. They come, they talk, and Stark politely sends each on his way. The only constant at his side is me. Me and a never-ending stream of waiters with more champagne, chilled so as to take the edge off the fire that's building in me.

The room, however, is starting to sway a bit, and I tap Stark on the arm, interrupting his conversation with a robotics engineer who's well into hard-pitch mode. "Excuse me," I say, then aim myself toward a small bench on the side of the room.

Stark catches up to me so quickly that I imagine the engineer still pitching, unaware that his quarry has escaped.

"You should slow down," he says in a voice that suggests I'm on his staff.

But I'm not on his staff. "I'm fine," I say. "I have a plan." I don't mention that the plan involves sitting down and never getting up again.

"If it involves getting so rip-roaring drunk that you have no choice but to get off your feet by laying down, then I'd say your plan is coming along quite nicely."

"Don't be patronizing." I stop in the center of the room and glance around, taking in the collection of canvases that fill the space. I pause, then deliberately turn and look him straight in the eye. "I assume you want a nude?"

I see the heat rising, struggling to burn through his mask. I force myself not to smile with victory.

He lifts a single brow. "I thought you were disinclined to help me."

"I'm in a charitable mood," I say. "So? Nude? Landscape? Still life with fruit? I'm assuming that since we're here at Evelyn's show, you're thinking nude."

"It's certainly at the forefront of my mind, yes."

"Do you see anything here that appeals to you?"

"I do, actually."

He's looking right at me, and I think that maybe I've played this game a little too cavalierly. I know I should back off, but I don't. Maybe it's the tiny bubbles talking, but I like seeing the desire in him. No, that's not true. I like seeing him desire me.

It's a simple yet startling realization.

I clear my throat. "Show me."

"Pardon me?"

I have to force myself to sound nonchalant. "Show me what you like."

"Believe me, Ms. Fairchild, I'd be very happy to do that."

The hidden message in his words isn't very hidden, and I swallow. I opened this door. Kicked it open, really. But now I have to actually walk through it. I shift my weight, uneasy—and stumble on the damn shoe.

He catches my arm, and I gasp as the shock of his touch against my bare skin rumbles through me.

"You need to take them off before you hurt yourself."

"Not happening. I don't do bare feet at parties."

"Fine." He takes my hand and leads me toward the hall with the velvet rope. He moves slowly, allowing for my sore feet, but then looks at me with a wicked grin. "Or perhaps I should simply use the caveman carry?"

My glare changes to a gape when he unfastens the velvet rope and steps into the darkened, private hall behind it. I hesitate, then follow. He rehooks the rope, then sits on the velvet-covered bench. He looks up at me without even a hint of apology, as if he owns the world and everything in it. Then he pats the seat next to him, and because my feet hurt and my head is spinning, I sit without argument.

"Now," he says. "Take your shoes off. No," he adds, before I can protest, "we're behind the rope, so we're not officially at the party now. You're not breaking any rules."

He says the last with a grin, and I match it without thinking.

"Move sideways," he instructs. "Put your feet in my lap."

Social Nikki would protest; I slide my feet up onto his trousered legs.

"Close your eyes. Relax."

I do, and for a moment there is nothing, and I fear that he's punking me, after all. Then his fingertip traces along the bottom of my foot. I arch back, surprised and delighted. The touch is featherlight and almost tickles, and when he does it again, I release a shuddering breath. My whole body stiffens as I concentrate only on that one spot. I feel the sparks shoot through me, and realize that I'm aroused.

I clutch the edge of the bench and let my head tilt back farther. A few tendrils of hair brush the nape of my neck. The combination of sensations—his touch on my feet, the soft caress of hair—is overwhelming. My head truly is spinning now, and not from the champagne.

He increases the pressure, using the pads of his thumbs to work the soreness out of my feet, then gently strokes the sensitive spots where my shoes have rubbed. It's slow. It's intimate. It's confusing as hell.

I'm breathing hard, and I can't deny the small knot of panic that is beginning to unravel in my stomach. I've let down my guard. I've let things progress. I'm edging dangerously close to where I never, ever go—but damn me, I don't know that I have the strength to turn back.

"Now," he says.

I open my eyes, confused, and the rapturous expression on his face almost does me in.

"I'm going to kiss you," he says, and before I even have a chance to process his words, his palm is pressed against the back of my head. Somehow, he's shifted our positions, and it's no longer my feet on his lap, but my thighs, so that our bodies are close and he's bent over me, his lips pressed against mine. I'm struck by how soft his mouth is, yet firm, too. He's completely in charge. Demanding. Taking exactly what he wants—and what I'm so willing to give.

I hear myself moan, and he takes advantage of my parted lips to dip his tongue inside.

He is an expert kisser, and I lose myself in the pleasure of it. I don't know when, but at some point I realize that one of my hands is clutching his shirt and the other is twined in his hair. It's thick and soft and I make a fist around a handful and use that to leverage his mouth even harder against mine. I want to lose myself in his kiss. I want to let the fire that's spreading over my body grow. Maybe it will consume me. Maybe, like a Phoenix, I will rise again after being incinerated by Damien Stark's touch.

His tongue strokes mine, sending erotic sparks dancing through me. My skin, already so sensitive just from his proximity, now seems like an instrument of torture, because the anticipation of his touch is simply too much to bear. A low, demanding ache builds between my thighs, and I press my legs together in both defense and in an attempt at satisfaction.

He makes a growling noise and shifts me in his arms. Suddenly, his hand is on my hip and the soft material of my skirt caresses my skin as he glides over it toward my crotch. I tense, aroused and nervous, but I don't push him away. My body is pulsing, my clit throbbing, and I want release. I want Damien.

His entire body is hard against mine. He holds me close and deepens the kiss as his hand slopes down toward my sex, just slow enough to drive me crazy. I shift, leaving one leg on his thighs, but our position is awkward and my other leg slides off. I press the ball of my bare foot to the ground for balance even as I feel a rush of cool air find its way in underneath my skirt to tease my damp panties.

In this position I'm wide open and vulnerable, and Stark cups his hand over my sex and moans into my mouth. Even through the material of my skirt and the satin of my panties, I can feel his heat. He strokes me through my clothes, his fingers teasing my clit, making me so wet I think I will melt.

My skirt is hitched up, but it still covers my thighs. Even so, he's close—so close to the secrets I don't want to share, and I know that if he tries to stroke my inner thighs that I will bolt. I'm nervous. Afraid, even. But danger and fear have added an edge to my excitement. I don't think I've ever been more turned on in my life.

His fingers tease me, making a wild fever burn through me. I'm right on the edge, just a little more—

But then his hand is gone. I open my eyes, and for just an instant, his expression is warm and open, and I think that I'm the only thing in all the world that he sees. Then something alters, and his face changes as the mask clicks back into place. He shifts my position, pulling me up so that I am sitting half on his lap.

"Damien, what—"

But then I hear the voice behind me, a bright, cheery feminine voice saying, "I've been looking everywhere for you. Are you ready?"

Oh my God. Did she just walk up? How long has she been there?

I look helplessly at Damien, but he doesn't notice. He's looking over my shoulder at whomever is speaking. "I need to see Ms. Fairchild home," he says, and I shift on the bench so that I can see behind me—and find myself looking at Audrey Hepburn.

She nods at me, smiles at Damien, then turns and walks away.

Gently, he slides me off his legs. He stands, then holds his hand out for me. "Let's go."

My legs are weak—my whole body still limp from his ministrations. But I shove my feet back into my shoes and follow him without question. I'm confused and embarrassed and not entirely sure what to think.

We find Evelyn and say goodbye as we pass through the thinning crowd. She gives me a hug, and I promise to call her in a day or so. It's a promise I mean to keep.

At the door, he slips his jacket around my shoulders. We walk down the sidewalk to where a limo waits in the circular drive. A liveried driver holds open the back door, and Damien gestures for me to get inside. I haven't been in a limo since I was a kid, and I pause to take it all in. Black leather bench seats line the back and one side. On the other is a full bar, the crystal decanter and glasses twinkling from recessed lighting hidden in the polished wood of the bar. The floor is carpeted. The entire space screams luxury and money and elegance.

I sit down on the backseat so that I'm facing the front of the car. The leather is soft and warm and seems to hug my body. I glance at the door, waiting for Damien to enter.

Except that he doesn't.

"Goodnight, Nikki," he says, in the same business voice I heard him using earlier in the evening. "I look forward to the presentation tomorrow."

And then he slams the door and walks away, back to Evelyn's house and Audrey Hepburn who's now silhouetted in the doorway holding out her hand to welcome him in.

7

I am alone, and I'm angry, mortified, and embarrassed.

I'm also turned on. Thus the embarrassment.

It's my own damn fault, of course. I'd been playing with fire—and I knew it.

Damien Stark is out of my league. More than that, he's dangerous. Why could Ollie see it and not me?

But I did see it.

That hardness in his eyes. The mask he pulls down so skillfully. My first instinct was to tell Damien Stark to fuck off. Why the hell didn't I just go with that?

Because I thought I saw more than was actually there?

Because I wear a mask, too, and thought I'd found some sort of kindred spirit?

Because he's hot and so clearly wanted me?

Because part of me actually craves that danger?

I close my eyes and swallow. If this were a multiple choice test, I'd have to pick *all of the above.*

I tell myself it's just as well. At the most, Damien Stark wants to conquer me as he's conquered industry. And while I might crave the feel of his body against mine, I am now even more certain that I can never let that happen. I won't expose myself like that to a man who wants nothing more than a fast fuck—hell, I don't want to expose myself like that to anyone. I don't want to hear the questions; I don't want to make the explanations. My secrets are bound up tight inside me.

I kick my shoes off, then lean my head back and keep my eyes closed. I'm thankful the limo ride is smooth, because my head is already spinning enough as it is.

The champagne that seemed like such a good idea at the time now seems rather foolish.

I'm starting to doze off when my phone jars me awake. I jerk upright and dig into my itty-bitty purse to retrieve it. I don't recognize the number, but since I've only given my new California number to Jamie and Carl, it doesn't take a degree in statistics to figure out it's one of them calling from an unfamiliar number or a telemarketer.

I answer, expecting Jamie, since I'm sure Carl wouldn't interrupt me, not if he thinks that alone time with me is what Stark wants.

"I am so wasted," I say, because if it's a telemarketer, it just serves them right.

"I'm not surprised," replies a familiar voice that does *not* belong to my roommate. "I believe I suggested you slow down."

"Mr. Stark? How did you get this number?" I push myself back upright too quickly.

"I wanted to hear your voice." His voice is low and sensual and despite everything I've been telling myself, it curls through me like liquid heat.

"Oh."

"And I'd like to see you again."

I force myself to breathe. "You will," I say primly, because I have to nip this in the bud. "I'll be at the meeting tomorrow."

"I'm very much looking forward to it. Perhaps it would have been more prudent for me to wait and talk to you then. But the thought of you relaxed and tipsy, leaning back against the leather of my limo . . . well, that was an image I simply couldn't pass up."

My mind is in a whirl. What happened to the man who so coolly deposited me in the back of this car?

"I want to see you again," he repeats, this time more forcefully. I don't even pretend to misunderstand. He is not talking business.

"Do you always get what you want?"

"I do," he says simply. "Especially when the desire is mutual."

"It's not," I lie.

"Really?" I hear the interest in his voice. This is a game to him. *I* am a game to him. The thought pisses me off, and I'm grateful. Angry Nikki has a lot more control than Wasted Nikki.

"Really."

"How did you feel when I put you in the limo?"

I shift uncomfortably. I'm not completely certain where this is going, but I'm pretty confident that I won't like getting there.

"Nichole?"

"Don't call me that," I snap.

I hear silence on the other end of the line and I realize that I'm afraid he's hung up.

"All right, Nikki," he says, as if he knows that he's soothing a very deep wound. "How did you feel when I put you in the limo?"

"I was pissed. And you damn well knew it."

"Because I was sending you home alone in a limo? Or because I was sending you home alone in a limo so that I could keep a date with a beautiful woman?"

"In case it escaped your notice, we barely know each other. You are perfectly entitled to go out with whomever you want, whenever you want."

"And you're within your rights to be jealous."

"I'm not jealous, and no, I wouldn't be within my rights. Let me repeat the salient point: I hardly know you."

"I see. So the fact that we crave each other doesn't play into it? Nor the fact that I made you wet? That I held your cunt in my hand and made you moan?"

He's about to make me moan again, but I manage to remain valiantly silent.

"Tell me then, at what level of intimacy can jealousy rear its head?"

"I—I've drunk my weight in champagne tonight. I am not even going to attempt to answer that."

He laughs, full and genuine. I like the sound. And, yes, I like Damien Stark. He's not what I expected, but there's something compelling about him—and it's more than just the fact that he's hotter than sin and got me worked up into quite a lather. He seems perfectly comfortable in his own skin. I'm reminded of Evelyn, who so brashly told me that if her party guests didn't like the way she ran the event, they could leave. I'd been shocked—my mother would have had a coronary right then and there. But I'd also been impressed.

As far as I can tell, Damien Stark takes that attitude to an extreme.

"Her name is Giselle," he says, and his voice is soft. "She owns the gallery that's showing Blaine's work."

"I thought Evelyn was showing the work."

"Evelyn hosted the party. She's become something of a patron for Blaine. But tomorrow morning the paintings will be transported to Giselle's gallery. This cocktail date with Giselle and her husband has been on my calendar for over a week now. It's business, and not something I could get out of. But I did step away in order to call you."

"Oh." *Her husband.* "Oh."

On the one hand, I'm frustrated that I'm so transparent. On the other hand, he's calling to soothe me, and the sweetness of that gesture moves me. Of course, I shouldn't let it. I should be strong and tell him he shouldn't have bothered. Because whatever is happening between us, it needs to be quickly nipped in the bud.

"So where are you?" I ask, completely ignoring my own wise counsel.

"Sur la Mer," he says, naming a Malibu restaurant and bar that's so chic even I've heard of it.

"I've heard it's excellent."

"The food is exquisite," he says, "but it's the ambience that really sets the place apart. It's charming, but intimate. It's the perfect place to have a drink and discuss business when one doesn't want to be overheard. Or to not discuss business, for that matter."

The intimate edge has crept back into his voice, and I squirm a little. "And you're there strictly for business?"

His low chuckle rocks through me. "I assure you that a tryst with Giselle and her husband is not on the agenda. I'm not interested in men. Or in married women."

I keep silent.

"I want to see you again, Nikki. And I think you would enjoy the food here very much."

"Just the food?" In my head the words had been teasing. Out loud, they are soft and provocative. I close my eyes, trying to steady myself before I go hurtling down that slippery slope.

"Well, the coffee is good, too."

"I—I like coffee," I admit. I take a deep breath. "But I don't think it's a good idea."

"Thousands of coffee bean growers across the globe would disagree with you."

"Dinner. Coffee. A date. With you. I don't think it's a good idea."

"Really? I find it exceptionally appealing."

"Mr. Stark . . ."

"Ms. Fairchild," he says, and I can hear the smile in his voice.

"You're exasperating."

"So I've been told. But I prefer the word 'persistent.' I don't take no for an answer."

"Sometimes, that's the only answer there is."

"Perhaps. But this isn't one of those times."

I can't help but smile as I settle more comfortably back against the soft leather upholstery. "Isn't it? You forget that I'm the one who has to say yes or no, and I've already told you my answer, and I don't intend to change it."

"No?"

"Sorry. But I'm afraid you've met your match, Mr. Stark."

"I certainly hope so, Ms. Fairchild," he says.

I frown a bit as I try to guess just where he's shifting the conversation. Because I know damn well he's not giving in. To be honest, I'd be disappointed if he was.

"I asked you this once and you evaded the question. Let me try again—are you attracted to me?"

"I—excuse me?"

His laugh is low and soft. "I'm quite certain you heard me, but in the interest of fair play, I'll repeat the question. Slowly and clearly. Are you attracted to me?"

I open my mouth, then shut it again because I have absolutely no idea how I should respond.

"It's not a trick question," he says, though of course I know it is.

"I am," I finally say, because it's the truth and I have no doubt he knows it. "But so what? What straight female on this planet isn't attracted to you? I'm still not going out with you."

"I get what I want, Nikki. You should know that about me right from the start."

"And you want dinner with me? I'd think a man in your position would want something a bit more impressive. Like to colonize Mars."

"Dinner is just the beginning. I want to touch you," he says, his voice low and commanding. "I want to run my hands over every inch of you. I want you wet for me. I want to finish what we started, Ms. Fairchild. I want to make you come."

8

It is suddenly very, very hot in the limo, and I seem to have forgotten the basic steps required for breathing.

I don't think . . .

I realize the words are only in my head and try again. "I don't think that's a good idea."

"It's an extremely good idea. Hell, it's all I've been thinking about since I put you in that limo. Touching you again. Stroking you. Kissing you."

I squirm, determined to hold it together. But I am weak and well-liquored, and my determination is fraying around the edges.

"Tell me you haven't thought of it, too."

"I haven't," I say.

"Don't lie to me, Nikki. That's rule number one. Never lie to me."

Rules?

"Is this a game?" I ask.

"Isn't everything?"

I don't answer.

"*Simon Says,* Nikki. Have you played before?" His soft voice is like a caress.

"Yes."

"Is the privacy screen in place?"

I glance up. I'm at the very back of a very long limo. I can see the driver in the front, his shoulders in the black jacket, the stark white of his shirt collar. He has reddish hair, mostly hidden by a black cap. It seems to me that he is a million miles away. But he's not, he's right there, probably listening to every word we've been saying.

"He's very discreet," Damien says, as if reading my thoughts. "But why torment the man? The silver button on the console behind you controls the screen. Do you see it?"

I twist around and see a bank of buttons set into the paneling behind me. "Yes."

"Push it."

"You didn't say Simon says."

His low chuckle delights me.

"Good girl. Are you suggesting you'd rather leave it down? Think before you answer, Nikki. For what I have planned, most women would like some privacy."

I lick my lips. If I push that button I'm saying yes to so much more than the damn screen.

Do I want that? He's talking about seeing me naked. About touching me. About kissing me. About running his fingers over my skin.

I rest my finger lightly on the button, remembering the feel of his hand. Remembering how I almost let him get too close, how I almost revealed too much.

But he's not in the car. I can do this. I can lose myself to the champagne and the night and the allure of Damien Stark.

But am I leading him on? Making him think that fantasy will become reality?

I swallow again, because I don't care. I want the release. I want this man's voice in my head and the fantasy of his hands on my body. He'll deal. *He* has rules? Screw that. Right now, I'm making my own damn rules.

I press the button.

Slowly, the privacy screen rises, and I'm alone in the luxurious comfort of Damien Stark's stretch limo. "It's up," I say, but my voice is so soft I'm not certain he heard it.

"Take off your panties."

Apparently he heard it.

"What if I told you I already did?"

"I'm in public, Ms. Fairchild. Don't torment me."

"You're tormenting me," I retort.

"Good. Now take them off."

I lift my skirt and slide my panties down. My shoes are already off, so it's easy. I leave them on the seat beside me.

"They're off," I say. And then, because I'm making this into my fantasy, too, "I'm wet."

His low groan sends a spark of satisfaction running through me. "No talking," he says. "And no touching. Not unless I tell you to. That's the game, Nikki. You do what I say, and only what I say. Are we clear?"

"Yes," I murmur.

"Yes, sir," he corrects. His voice is gentle, but firm.

Sir?

I say nothing.

"Or I can simply hang up." His voice is hard, but I think I hear triumph. I frown, because I don't want to give him the satisfaction of winning this battle, but I also don't want the game to end. And I'm certain Mr. Nice to Ice means what he says.

I swallow my pride. "Yes, sir."

"Good girl. You want me, don't you?"

"Yes, sir."

"I want you, too. Does that make you wet?"

"Yes . . ." The word comes out strangled. The truth is, I'm aching now. Hot and wet and desperately turned on. I have no idea what he has planned, but I know I'll agree to anything if only he'll take this further. Take *me* further.

"Put your phone on speaker and leave it on the seat beside you. Then lift up your skirt and sit back down. I want your naked ass on the leather. I want you wet and slippery on that seat, so that when I get in that limo later tonight, I can lose myself in the scent of you."

"Yes, sir," I manage to say as I comply. The brush of my skirt against the bare flesh of my thighs is achingly erotic, but the feel of the warm leather against my naked rear makes me moan.

"Spread your legs and gather your skirt up around your waist." His voice surrounds me. His tone is low, commanding, and achingly sensual. "Lean back against the seat and close your eyes. Now leave one hand on the seat, but put the other just above your knee."

I do. My skin feels feverish.

"Move your thumb," he says. "Move it slowly, back and forth. Gentle, baby. So gently. Are you doing it?"

"Yes, sir."

"Are your eyes closed?"

"Yes, sir."

"That's me you feel. My hand on your leg. My finger stroking your skin. It's soft, and you look so beautiful spread out wide for me. Do you want me, Nikki?"

"Yes."

"Yes, what?"

My sex tightens at the growl of demand in his voice. There's something delicious about surrendering to him.

"Yes, sir."

"I want to touch your breasts, Nikki. I want to touch your nipples. I want to lower my mouth and suck until you come without me even touching your clit. Do you want that, Nikki?"

God, yes. "Only if you touch me there later, sir."

His low laugh sends ripples of awareness through me.

My clit is pulsing. I desperately want to touch myself but that's not the game. Not yet.

"I'm hard, Nikki. You're torturing me, you know that?"

"I hope so, sir, because you're sure as hell torturing me."

"Unzip your dress," he says. "Then take the hand that's on the seat and lift it to your mouth. Suck on your forefinger, baby. That's right," he says when I groan a little as I close my eyes and draw in my own finger. "That's good. Use your tongue. Suck hard, baby." I can hear the tension in his voice, and my body quakes. I'm so wet, and the leather seat is getting slippery.

"Slide your hand into your bodice and touch your nipple. Is it hard?"

"Yes."

"Stroke it," he says. "Just a tease. So light, like a butterfly kiss. Do you feel it, baby? Is it making you wetter?"

"Yes," I whisper.

"Now move the hand on your leg. Slowly—I want it to build. Do you feel it? That soft stroke?"

"Yes." I imagine that my fingers are his. That he's burning a trail up my hot, trembling body.

"That's me. My hands. I'm right there. My hands on you. On both your legs. Can you feel me, stroking the inside of your thighs, teasing you, making you hotter and wetter?"

I take my other hand off my breast and put it on my other leg. Slowly, sensuously, I stroke the inside of my thighs with soft, delicate touches. This is forbidden territory—this is where my secrets are. *But not now.* Right now, nothing is off-limits, and everything is safe.

I can lose myself in his voice. I can close my eyes and imagine Damien kneeling before me. Damien's eyes watching me. Damien's hands all over me. "Oh, God, yes."

"Spread your legs more," he says. "I want you wide open, your cunt hot and dripping for me. Do you want to touch yourself, Nikki?"

"Yes," I whisper. I feel my cheeks warm from the admission, though how I can feel a blush when my skin is already on fire is beyond me.

"Not yet," he says. I can hear the amusement in his voice. He knows he's tormenting me, and he's loving it.

"You're a sadist, Mr. Stark."

"And you comply so willingly, Ms. Fairchild. What does that make you?"

A masochist. A tremor runs through my body, tied to the erotic sweetness of my touch. "Turned on," I admit.

"We are deliciously compatible."

"When telecommunications are involved," I say without thinking.

"*Always.* Don't argue, Ms. Fairchild, or the game stops now. And that really would be a shame."

I say nothing.

"Good," he says. "I like you compliant. I like you spread wide and ready for me. I like you wet for me," he adds, as I just about melt into the upholstery. "Put your hands on the seat on either side of your hips. Have you done it?"

"I have."

The silence is ominous.

"I mean, yes, sir."

My hands are pressed to the leather. My sex is throbbing. Demanding. I squirm on the seat, but that only makes me needier.

My fingers twitch. I'm desperate to come. I swear if he doesn't let me touch myself soon, I'll—

Well, why not? He wouldn't even know.

"No touching, Nikki. Not yet."

"How did you—oh, God, are there cameras in here?" The idea is mortifying . . . and embarrassingly titillating.

"No," he says firmly. "Though at the moment I wish there were. Let's just call it a lucky guess."

That damned blush heats up again, and I squirm some more, trying to find a satisfaction that's staying painfully, frustratingly just out of reach.

"You're keeping me from an excellent Scotch and some very tasty appetizers, you know."

"I'm not the least bit sorry," I retort. "But if you're in a hurry, I know how we can finish this off real quick."

"Is that what you want? This to be over?"

"I—no," I admit. It's torture, but it's damn sweet torture.

"Did you notice the bar when you got into the limo?"

"Yes."

"I want you to move long enough to open the ice bucket and take out an ice cube. Then back here, spread wide and open for me."

"Yes, sir."

I ease out of my seat, cheating a little because I squeeze my thighs together as I do. The pressure is delicious, taking me just that much further. But frustrating, too, as I'm more aroused than I can ever remember being, and no closer to release. For that matter, I'm not sure what's coming next. *Ice cubes . . . ?*

I smile, realizing that if nothing else I trust Damien Stark to make this interesting.

"Are you settled again?"

"Yes."

"Which hand has the ice cube?"

"My right one."

"Pull down the left strap of your dress until your breast is free. Close your eyes and trace the cube around your areola. Don't touch your nipple, not yet. That's it. I can imagine your skin, soft and perfect and puckered from the cold. I'm hard, baby, I want to touch you."

"You are touching me," I whisper.

"Yes." The desire in his voice matches my own.

"Move your left hand to your thigh," he says, and I silently cheer. Had he planned this all along, or have I scored some points in his game? I tilt my head back, my hot fingers stroking my inner thigh, easing higher to where the flesh isn't smooth like Damien imagines, but instead bears the scars of my secrets.

At my breast, the ice cube melts against my flaming skin. "I'm imagining you licking the droplets off," I say. "Your tongue flicking over my hard nipple. Teasing me until you can't stand it, and then you nip it, your teeth grazing before you suck, hard, so hard until it's like a hot wire runs through me all the way to my clit."

"Jesus," he says, sounding winded. "Whose game is this?"

"I like to win," I say, but I have to struggle to speak. My hand has moved higher, and my fingers are gently stroking the soft skin where my thigh meets my sex. "Damien," I say. "Please." The ice cube has melted away.

"One finger. I'm taking one finger and sliding it over your cunt. Your wet, dripping cunt. You're throbbing, you want me so badly."

"Yes," I whisper.

"Are you wet?"

"I'm drenched."

"I want to be inside you," he says, and before he gives me permission, I slide two fingers deep inside. My body immediately contracts, drawing me in further. I'm hot and slippery, and drunk with pleasure. The heel of my hand rubs against my clit, and I can't help it—I moan. And now Stark knows my secret.

"You broke the rules," he says.

I arch back, I'm so close, but I don't dare stroke myself. Not after hearing the command in his voice. "Rules are made to be broken." I can barely croak out the words.

"Of course they are. If you're willing to accept the punishment. Shall I punish you, Nikki? Shall I bend you over and spank your ass?"

"I—" I quiver, his words making me even hotter. I've never played those kinds of games, but right now the thought of being so vulnerable to Damien Stark sets me on fire.

"Or maybe I should make you pull your hands away. Leave you hungry. Leave you wanting."

"Please no," I say.

"I should," he says. "I should leave you hanging."

I don't mean to, but I whimper a little. *Why? If I want to get off, I can just get off. My fingers work just fine, and I'm so close. So very close . . .*

But no. This is a game all right, and I'm playing with a partner. I don't just want to come. I want to come because Damien took me there.

He chuckles, fully aware of the torment he's inflicting. "Beg," he says.

"Please."

"Please, what?"

"Please, sir."

"Is that the best you can do?"

"I want to come, Damien. I want to come with your voice taking me there, and I'm so close right now I think if this limo goes over a pothole it might just send me shooting to the moon." I have lost all shame, all propriety. And I don't even care. All I want to do is explode, knowing that it's Damien hearing my screams on the other end of the phone line.

"Are you touching yourself?" There's still an edge to his voice, but it's raw now. Needy.

"Yes."

"I want to taste you. Lick your fingers," he says, and I comply, imagining my slick, wet fingers are his lips. "Tell me."

"Slick," I say. "Sweet. But, Damien, I want—"

"Hush, baby, I know. And I'm touching you now. I'm kneeling right in front of you, and you're wide open to me. You're wet and delicious, and my tongue is all over you, touching and tasting. Can you feel me flicking my tongue over your hard clit?"

"Yes," I say as my finger strokes my swollen, demanding clit.

"You taste so good, and I'm so hard. I want to be inside you, but I can't get enough of the taste of you."

"Don't stop." I'm arching up, an orgasm rising up around me like the overture of a grand opera.

"Never," he says. "But I need you to come for me now, baby. We're close now, and it's time. I'm touching you, I'm taking you over. Now, Nikki. Come for me now."

I do.

So help me, it's as if his voice takes me over the edge and I shatter like starlight against a black velvet sky, pinpoints of light bursting through me, so powerful and intense and meltingly hot.

"Oh, yes, baby," he says, his voice strained, easing me down. "That's it."

I realize that I'm gasping, and my cries dissolve into little whimpers of pleasure mixed with loss. It's over, and I'm alone in the back of a limo and the man who made me come is on the other end of a phone line somewhere.

A loose strand of hair sticks to my face and I push it off. I'm covered in a sheen of sweat. I'm spent. Taken.

I feel good.

I feel reckless.

"We're here," Damien says, and I turn to glance through the dark tinted windows. Sure enough, the limo is pulling to a stop outside my condo. I realize that when he'd said that we were close, he didn't mean my orgasm. He meant my home.

I frown, realizing I never told the driver my address. Had Damien? He must have, but how did he know where I live?

I push myself up and fix my skirt and bodice in some sort of bizarrely placed attempt at modesty. I start to ask him about my address, but he speaks first.

"I'll see you tomorrow, Ms. Fairchild," he says formally, but I think I can hear a smile in his voice.

"I look forward to it, Mr. Stark," I say, equally formal, though my pulse is pounding in my ears.

There is silence, but I know he's still there. After a moment, I hear him laugh. "Hang up, Ms. Fairchild," he orders.

"Yes, sir," I say, then press the button to disconnect the call.

Tomorrow.

Reality slams against me with the force of a tidal wave. What the hell was I thinking having phone sex with a guy I'm going to be seeing up close and personal in just a matter of hours? And not just seeing, but actually pitching to. Putting on a business presentation.

Am I entirely insane?

Yes, I think, I am.

Insane. Foolish. Idiotic.

Reckless.

I shiver.

Yes, but reckless felt so damn good.

The limo has come to a complete stop, and I see the driver approaching to open my door. I reach for my panties, intending to shove them into my purse, but then I have a better idea.

If I'm going to be reckless anyway . . .

I slip the panties under the armrest, letting the white satin and lace peek out just a little. Then I quickly zip up my dress, check that it's covering all the appropriate places, and slide to the door just as the driver pulls it open.

I step out of the limo and look up at the sky. I imagine a billion stars twinkling down at me. I grin back at them. By morning, I'll probably be wallowing in mortification, but right now, I'm going to bask. It has, after all, been an exceptionally good night.

9

I turn the key in the lock as quietly as possible, then slowly twist the knob and push the door open. I just want to get to my room and go to sleep, but Jamie is the world's lightest sleeper, so I'm not confident that I'll make it.

The condo is silent and mostly dark, the only light coming from the small nightlight I insist we keep plugged in by the bathroom. It provides minimal illumination, just enough to provide some guidance and keep the apartment from falling into pitch-black.

I consider the quiet darkness a good sign. Maybe Jamie walked down to the divey little bar on the corner next to the Stop 'n' Shop. Both the bar and the shop smell faintly of sewage and sweat, but that doesn't stop Jamie when she's in a mood for either alcohol or chocolate. I've lived here less than a week, and we've already visited the store twice (for supplies of Diet Coke and Chips Ahoy) and the bar once (for bourbon, straight up, because it's not the kind of place you trust to make a martini).

I close the door carefully and set the dead bolt, but I leave the chain dangling in the hope that my guess as to Jamie's whereabouts is right. Then I start to tiptoe to my room, just in case my guess is wrong.

Even dimly lit, the condo is easily navigable. A traditional apartment before the owners decided to go condo, it's small at only about eight hundred square feet. The main room serves a triple purpose as entrance hall, living room, and dining area. There's also a kitchen, a bathroom, and two bedrooms. The living area is on the left, and is furnished comfortably with a chair and a sofa. One long wall boasts a never-used fireplace and a mounted flat-screen television.

Just in front of the door—past the four feet or so that can be considered the foyer—is the dining area, which has a truly ugly orange Formica table and four mismatched wooden chairs. Jamie may have bought the condo when prices were down, but that didn't mean she'd been rolling in extra cash. She'd furnished it with an eye to cost, not appeal. I don't mind, but I've already told Jamie that when I can afford it, I want to paint the interior and try to make the place a little more Ikea. *Home and Garden* is completely out of the question.

The kitchen is to the left of the dining area, and is separated from the living area by a solid wall that one day I'd love to knock down and turn into a pass-through. Until then, whoever's cooking not only can't see the television, but is trapped in the claustrophobic galley-style kitchen. Between the dining area and kitchen are two stairs that seem to serve no purpose. They lead to the bedrooms—one on either side—and the bathroom, which takes up the space between.

I've gone about three feet and am transitioning from entrance to dining area when a light snaps on to my left. I turn and see Jamie in the far side of the room, curled up in the battered armchair that Lady Meow-Meow uses as a scratching post.

"You okay?" I ask, because Jamie brooding in the dark is never a good thing.

She stretches her arms and yawns, disrupting Lady Meow-

Meow who is a big blob of white fur in her lap. "I'm good. Must've fallen asleep." She shifts in the chair, then rolls her head, getting the kinks out. I eye her for signs that she's bullshitting me, but she seems genuinely fine. I'm relieved. Call me selfish, but I'm not in the mood to micromanage anyone's drama but my own.

"So?" she demands as the cat leaps down and pads to the kitchen for kibble.

I shrug, still standing there in my little dress with my shoes dangling from my fingertips and my naked tush catching a breeze under the flouncy skirt. "Tired," I say, because I need to collect my thoughts. Jamie always sees more than I want her to, and I don't want to dive into the conversation unprepared. "Wanna grab breakfast at Du-par's in the morning? I'll give you the full scoop then. But it'll have to be early." I hook my thumb toward my bedroom. "I need to go crash."

"You're really not going to tell me shit? Why the hell did I wait up?"

"You didn't wait up. You were asleep."

She waves a hand, sweeping my logic away as irrelevant.

"In the morning," I say, and before she can argue I turn and head to my room. I wait a second in case she decides to burst in after me, and when she doesn't, I peel off the dress. I stand naked for a moment, feeling the cool breeze from the air conditioner caress my still-hot skin. My favorite pajama bottoms are folded on my pillow, and I slip them on. I don't bother with underwear, and the sensation of the threadbare material against my still-sensitive sex is fantastic. I think of Damien and rub my palms lightly over my bare breasts. My nipples peak, and I'm tempted to pull out my phone and call him back.

Jesus, Nikki. Get a grip.

I don't know what Damien Stark wants from me, but the truth is that I don't care. Because it's not going anywhere. I'm not getting naked with Damien Stark. That's simply a given. But that doesn't mean I can't appreciate the fantasy he's given me, all wrapped up in silver paper with a bright, shiny orgasm.

I slide onto the bed and slip one hand down into the pajama bottoms. I'm no longer drunk, just nicely buzzed, and I can't think of a better way to drift off to sleep.

The sharp chime of the doorbell nips *that* plan in the bud, and I leap to my feet, yanking my hand out of my pants as I move like a guilty teenager caught by her parents.

"Is that Douglas?" I shout to Jamie.

"Hell no," she says. "I train them better than that."

"Then who—"

"Oh, *fuck*," she says, not in anger or fear, but in amazement. "Nik, honey, get your ass out here."

I yank on a tank top and hurry into the living room, not even willing to venture a guess as to who could be out there at this time of night.

As it turns out, it's no one. Instead, it's a huge flower arrangement parked on the doorstep. A mass of wildflowers—daisies and sunflowers and Indian paintbrushes and other flowers I don't recognize. They are beautiful and cheerful and warm and wild.

They are perfect.

Damien, I think, and it feels like my whole body is smiling. *It has to be Damien.*

Jamie bends down to snag the card and has it out of the envelope before I can reach her. I silently seethe until she looks up at me, a grin tugging at the side of her mouth.

I hold out my hand for the card, which she hands over with a gleam in her eye.

There is one word printed on it: *Delicious.* Beneath that are the initials *D.S.*

And me, the girl who never blushes, does so for about the millionth time that night.

Jamie picks up the arrangement, then carts it over to the dining table. I poke my head out the door, but there's no one there.

"Just how good a time *did* you have at that party?" Jamie asks.

"Not the party," I say, because we've reached the point where I either fill Jamie in or find a new best friend. "The ride home." I drop down onto the sofa that backs up to the wall separating the living area from the kitchen. I pull my feet up and tug my favorite purple afghan over me. I'm suddenly very tired. It's been a long and interesting day.

"No, you don't," Jamie says, plonking down on the antique cherrywood coffee table I'd brought with me from Texas. That puts her right in front of me. She leans forward, getting even more in my face. "Don't even think of claiming you're sleepy. You can't drop a bombshell like that and not explain. The ride home? So, what? You guys went up and parked on Mulholland for some late night delight?"

"He sent me home in a limo," I say bluntly, because I want to watch her reaction. "Alone."

"You are such a liar. Seriously?" she adds when she sees my face.

I nod, and then—damn me—I giggle. "It was one hell of a ride."

"Oh. My. God." Her eyes are wide. "Okay, spill. And don't give me any of that bullshit about privacy or being discreet or a lady doesn't tell. You're not your mother. I want the dirt. All of it."

I comply. Well, not all of it, but I share the high points, starting with our bizarrely cold introduction at Evelyn's and moving on to the testosterone-laden interchange between Stark and Ollie.

"I haven't seen Ollie in ages," Jamie interrupts. "The little shit. Why hasn't he called?"

She's not really interested in the answer, though, and urges me to keep going with my tale. I do. My exhaustion has faded along with my reticence. Jamie is my best friend, and it feels good to share, even if I do find myself mumbling and talking in euphemisms once I get to the part of the story that features me, my phone, Stark's commanding voice, and the backseat of a limo.

"Holy fuck," she says when I finish. It's the third time she's said it during my rundown.

"And I left the panties in the car," I add. I feel devilish admitting it, even more so when Jamie's eyes widen and she rocks with laughter.

"Holy fuck," she repeats, this time with even more enthusiasm. "So he was really in a restaurant the whole time? God, he must have some serious blue balls."

I experience a little trill of feminine satisfaction at the thought, then frown as another thought occurs to me. "How did he get flowers to me so fast? I was probably home less than ten minutes before they arrived." It's weird, the same way him already knowing my home address is odd.

"Who cares?"

It's a fair point, but I shift around on the couch so that I can see the kitchen table and the flowers. My smile blooms wide again.

"You need to toss some condoms in your purse," Jamie says.

"I what?"

"I've got a box in the bathroom. Take a few. Phone sex is the only safe sex there is, girlfriend, and he may be hot, but you don't know where that boy's been." Her mouth twitches with suppressed laughter. "Or who he's been in."

The thought is disturbing on multiple levels, not the least of which is the unpleasant twang I feel at the thought of Damien Stark in bed with another woman. I push that aside and focus on the practical. "I don't need condoms," I say, "because I'm not sleeping with him."

"Nikki," she says, and even though she's my best friend, I can't tell if that's a plea in her voice or pity.

"Don't start," I say. "I'm not you."

"Which is good, as the world can only take so much awesomeness." She grins at me, but I'm not in the mood. After a moment, her grin fades and her shoulders drop a little. "Look, you know I love you, and I'll always be on your side, no matter what."

"But?"

"But think about why you came to Los Angeles."

"I came for business." I say it because it's true. I want to learn from Carl. I want to find investors for the web-based app I've been developing. And then, once I'm confident I have the chops to actually run a business, I want to dive into the deep end of the pool.

"Yeah, yeah, whatever. I'm talking about Damien Stark. You could do a lot worse than him if you're looking for a fresh start."

I shake my head. That whole *new life, new Nikki* thing doesn't apply where getting naked with Damien Stark is concerned. "Not going there," I say firmly. "The limo was amazing, but it was on my terms. In person, all I'd be is a notch on his bedpost, and that's your gig, not mine."

"Ha! Well, you nailed me. But the rest of it is total bullshit."

"Excuse me?"

"You don't want him putting his hands all over you, fine." I wince at the way she's zeroed in on my personal neurosis. "But own up to it, Nik. Because I wasn't even at that party and I can tell that he thinks of you as more than a piece of ass." She waves at the flowers. "Exhibit A."

"So he's a polite bazillionaire. It's not like delivering flowers took more than a phone call. They probably came fast because he has a standing order for flower delivery after all his phone sex encounters." I'm being snarky, but as I speak I realize I'm probably right. The thought is not a happy one.

"No way. He wants you. Your snark. Your attitude. I mean, he flat out told you that you're not like the usual women on his arm. I Googled him, you know."

I blink at the non sequitur. "You did not. When?"

"After you told me he was bringing you home. He's pretty private—I didn't find a lot and to be honest I didn't try very hard. But it doesn't look like he dates that much. Lots of women, sure, but nobody serious except for this one socialite a few months ago, but she's dead."

"Dead? Shit. How?"

"I know. Sad, right? Some sort of accident. But that's not the point."

My head is spinning. "What *is* the point?"

"You," she says. "I mean, even if you are just a notch on his bedpost, so what? You're not a nun."

I almost ask if she was listening when I described the whole phone-sex-in-the-limo thing, but I wisely keep my mouth shut.

"And honestly, I don't think you're just a notch. I think he really likes you."

I raise a brow. "And you base this on your extensive knowledge of the man gleaned from five minutes on the Internet?"

"I gleaned it from what you told me," she says. "He wanted your opinion on a painting. He got all alpha male on Ollie's ass. He made you come, for Christ's sake. And let's not forget the foot massage. Holy crap, girl, I'd totally fuck a guy who gave me a foot massage. Hell, I'd probably marry him."

I can't help but smile. Sadly, Jamie probably isn't exaggerating.

"Not every guy is an asshole like Kurt," she says, and for Jamie her voice is surprisingly gentle. "You can't keep pretending you're wearing a damn chastity belt."

I cringe. "Just drop it. Please."

She looks at me, then bites out a sharp, "Dammit." She draws in a breath. Her eyes are sad, and I can see that she knows she's gone too far.

She stands up and moves to the fireplace. Since a fireplace in the San Fernando Valley is an absolutely idiotic concept, Jamie has converted it to a bar. Bottles instead of logs. Glasses on the mantel. She grabs the bottle of Knob Creek. "Want some?"

I do, but I shake my head. I've had enough of alcohol for the night. "I'm tired," I say, pushing myself up off the sofa.

"I'm really sorry. You know I wouldn't—"

"I know," I say. "And it's really okay. I just need sleep."

A sly smile touches her mouth, and I know that we're okay again. "I guess so. You have a meeting tomorrow, don't you? And who's that meeting with, exactly?"

"Give it a rest, Jamie," I say, but I grin as I head toward my bedroom. She's right. I do have a big meeting. With Stark. In his offices. With my boss standing right there with the two of us.

I think back over the events of the evening.

I dwell on the panties I left in the limo.

And as I collapse facedown on my bed, only one thought goes through my mind: *What the hell have I done?*

10

My arms are stretched above my head, my wrists bound by something smooth but firm. My naked body is stretched out on cool silk. I cannot move my legs.

My eyes are closed, and yet I know what binds me. A red ribbon twined around my wrists. Wrapped tight around my ankles. I struggle, but there's nowhere to go, and I don't really want to escape anyway.

Something cool brushes my erect nipple, and I arch up in surprise and pleasure.

"Hush." His voice seems to brush over me like a caress.

"Please," I whisper.

He doesn't answer, but once again I'm sweetly assaulted by a burst of cold. This time, he doesn't pull away. It's an ice cube, and he traces it over my nipple, down the swell of my breasts. I feel the trickle of water down my cleavage as the ice melts. He traces patterns on me with the melting ice, his hands never touching me, just the cold hardness that's melting against my skin.

"Please," I whisper again. I arch up, wanting more, but am stopped by my bindings.

"You're mine," he says.

I open my eyes, needing to see his face, but everything around me is gray and out of focus. I am lost in an imagined world.

I am the girl in the painting. Aroused and on display for all the world to see.

"Mine," he repeats, his body a blurred gray shape above me.

His hands on my breasts are calloused and strong, yet so tender I want to cry. He eases them down, touching every inch of me, tracing my breasts, my rib cage, my belly. I tense as he approaches my pubis, suddenly afraid, but his hands lift and settle again on the outside of my thighs. I am in heaven from his touch. Lost. Floating. Dancing in a haze of pleasure.

But then his hands shift. He takes my knees and gently forces my legs apart. And slowly, so slowly, he glides his palms up my inner thighs.

I tense, and it's no longer a pleasurable dance but a frightening maelstrom. I try to pull away, but I'm trapped, and he's coming closer to my secrets. *To my scars.*

I struggle more. I have to get away, and warning bells are ringing, echoing through the room like red-hot klaxons—

Away,

Away,

Away,

"—awake?"

I'm jolted out of my dream by the sound of Jamie's voice. "What? I'm sorry, what?"

On the nightstand beside me, my phone is screeching. Outside my doorway, Jamie is shouting.

"I said, 'Are you awake?' Because if you are, you need to answer your damn phone."

Frazzled, I reach for it, and see Carl's name on the display. I snatch it up, but the call's already rolled over to voice mail.

With a groan, I slide my legs off the bed and stretch, then glance at the phone again to check the time. Six-fucking-thirty.

Seriously? I mean, is the sun even up yet?

I'm about to call him back when the phone rings yet again, and Carl's name flashes like neon.

"I'm here," I say. "I was just about to call you back."

"Jesus Christ, Fairchild. Where've you been?"

"It's practically dawn. I was in bed."

"Well, get down here. We've got a shitload of work to do. I can't get the fucking PowerPoint to work right, and we need to print out PDFs of the specs and get the proposal packages bound for Stark and his staff. I need you on it, pronto. Unless you already signed him to the deal last night? Or was there a non-business purpose for his late night phone call to you?" There's a lascivious tone to the last that I really don't appreciate, but at least now I know how Damien got my phone number and my address.

"He called to make sure I got home okay," I lie. "But next time I'd appreciate it if you didn't give out my cell number without asking me first."

"Yeah, yeah. Whatever. Get dressed and get down here. We'll go from our office to Stark's at one-thirty."

I frown, because C-Squared occupies one corner of the eighteenth floor of the Logan Bank Building, and Stark Tower is right next door. In fact, the two buildings share a courtyard and an underground parking garage. "Isn't the meeting at two?" A snail could make the trek in thirty minutes. We should be able to manage it in five.

"I'm not leaving anything to chance," Carl says.

I know better than to argue. "I'll be there in an hour. Tops."

Jamie looks up as I rush into the kitchen to pop a bagel into the toaster. "Boss on a rampage?"

"Big time." I bend down and scratch Lady M, who's making figure eights around my legs. "And he was being oh so snarky about Damien asking me to stay last night."

"Um, hello? You did get off in the backseat of Mr. Money-bags's limousine."

I glare at her, then head for the shower while my bagel toasts. On the way, I pass the flower arrangement. I sigh. Jamie's right, of course.

I let the water get so hot and steamy it makes my skin turn red. Then I step in, tensing as those first heated drops batter my body, then relaxing as the heat oozes through me. I close my eyes and let the water sluice over me. I feel like I should be angry at myself for letting it get so out of control last night, but I can't quite work up the lather. It sure as hell wasn't the most prudent thing I ever did, but I'm a grown-up and so is Stark and there was chemistry and free will and it's none of Carl's business anyway.

Which would be all good and well if I didn't have to see the man today. Or, rather, the men. One who's a lascivious jerk. And one who I'm afraid is going to distract me and throw me off my game.

And what if he surreptitiously shows me my panties?

Enough.

I can't think about it anymore or I'll go crazy, so I focus on finishing my shower and getting dressed. I choose a black skirt, white blouse, and matching jacket. Not a suit, because this is Saturday and because I'm working in the tech field and clean jeans are about as fashionable as we tend to get, but I just can't do a meeting in jeans. The shoes are a bit of a problem because my feet ache, but I jam them into my favorite black pumps anyway. I go easy on the makeup, pull my hair back into a ponytail, and, *voilà,* dressed in fifteen minutes. I think that's a personal best.

I grab my purse and my bagel, but I don't bother with cream cheese—with my luck I'd drop it and have to go the entire day with a creamy white smear on my black skirt. Then I shout goodbye to Jamie and head out the door.

I pause immediately, realizing that I've just stepped on a large yellow envelope that someone has left on the doormat. I pick it up. It's light, with minimal bulk. A sheaf of papers or something similar. I turn it over and see that it has my name on it, along with the sticker from a local messenger service. I roll my eyes. *Carl.*

With the envelope tucked under my arm, I head to my car. If I'm going to be on time, I'll have to read it at the stoplights.

My usual commute-time entertainment is the news, but I can't stomach it today, so as I pull out onto Ventura Boulevard, I let the radio scan through static, evangelical stations, talk shows, and blaring rap music. I really need to get a new radio, the kind with a plug for an iPod. Finally the tuner lands on an oldies station, and by the time I enter the 101 freeway, I'm jamming with Mick as he and the Stones sing about not getting any satisfaction. I grin. At least last night I was one up on Jagger.

I pull into my assigned space in a remote corner of the underground parking lot exactly forty-seven minutes from the time Carl called, which probably breaks some Los Angeles speed record. I don't leave the car immediately, though, because I still haven't looked at the envelope, and if it's about the presentation, Carl's going to expect me to know the details cold.

I slide my finger under the flap and open it, then tilt the envelope sideways. A copy of *Forbes* falls into my lap, and I realize that I am grinning. There's a note paper-clipped to the outside of the magazine. *I told you I was tenacious. Read and learn.* There's no signature, but the From the Desk of Damien J. Stark stationery is a big clue.

I'm still smiling as I tuck the magazine in my oversized purse. So he's tenacious, is he? Well, I can believe that. But my decision still stands. Just like I told Jamie, I can't let this go any further.

But that doesn't mean I'm not moved by his gesture. Not only did he remember a throwaway comment from our banter at the art show, but he actually sent the magazine all the way to my house.

"What are you grinning about?" Carl demands as I push

through the glass doors into the aquarium-style conference room that is the focal point of the C-Squared offices. But he doesn't really want my answer. He's already looking me up and down, nodding, and saying, "Good. Good. You look professional, businesslike. Yeah. I'd give you money. So long as you don't screw up the slideshow."

"I won't," I say, grateful that he's not mentioning last night or Damien or late night phone calls.

Carl preps with the intensity of a criminal defense attorney preparing for the trial of the century. His organizational system is a thing to be marveled at, and in the relatively short time since yesterday afternoon he's completely revamped our presentation outline.

I ask a ton of questions and make at least as many suggestions, and instead of falling back on his asshat personality, Carl responds thoughtfully, answering my questions, considering my ideas, implementing them when they make sense, and taking the time to explain when he decides to pass on one of my proposals.

I'm in heaven. I've reviewed the specs of the 3-D modeling program enough to know that I could be a valuable member of the tech team, possibly even the team leader. But being a project leader or even a manager isn't my goal. I want to be Carl. Hell, I want to be Damien Stark. And to get there, I need to know how to pull together a kick-ass presentation that will hook an underwriter for any one of the projects I've been toying with since my last year at UT.

Today I'm going to get to see two entrepreneurs in action. Carl, who rarely fails to get financing for any project he pitches. And Damien Stark, who has never said yes to a project that didn't ultimately exceed expectations and make a fortune for both him and the underlying company.

The conference room table is littered with paper, electronic tablets, and notebook computers. While the rest of the team scurries about, Brian and Dave, the two lead programmers who had worked with Carl developing the software, bang away at the notebooks, fine-tuning the presentation slideshow and doing dry runs of the software with a staggering number of parameters.

Carl paces, his eagle eye on everyone. "We're doing this right," he says. "No fuck-ups. No slips. A well-oiled ship." He narrows his eyes at Dave. "Go order up some sandwiches for lunch, but I swear to God, if anyone goes to that meeting with mustard on their shirt, I am firing his ass right then and there."

At one-thirty sharp, Carl, Brian, Dave, and I gather our things and march mustard-free to the elevator. Carl fidgets during the entire eighteen-story descent. He looks at himself so often in the mirrored wall panels that I am tempted to tell him he makes a beautiful bride. Wisely, I keep my mouth shut.

Of course, once we cross the courtyard and enter the ultra-modern Stark Tower, I'm the one who fidgets. My nervousness exists on so many levels that I can't even rally and organize my thoughts. There's the basic flutter of nerves simply from the thought of seeing Stark again. Then there's the fear that he's going to say something during the meeting—not necessarily even something suggestive. But God forbid he should say the word "phone." Or "ice." It'll throw off my game completely.

I stop worrying long enough to sign in at the security desk, which is really more of a console, sleek and efficient. Two guards sit behind it, one typing something and the other efficiently taking and scanning our drivers' licenses.

"All checked in," the guard, whose nametag reads *Joe*, says. "You're cleared to the penthouse," he adds, handing us each a guest badge.

"The penthouse?" Carl repeats. "Our meeting's at Stark Applied Technology." The company is one of many owned by Stark and housed in this building. Tech companies, charitable foundations, companies that do things I probably haven't even thought about. I glance down at the list of business names on the backlit console. All of them, I realize, are somehow related to Stark International. In other words, all of them are related to Damien Stark. Whatever I thought I knew was wrong; I have no concept of the wealth and power that Mr. Damien Stark commands.

"Yup, all the way up," Joe is saying to Carl. "On Saturdays, Mr. Stark takes meetings in the penthouse conference room. Use the last elevator bank on the end. Here's your card key to access the penthouse."

My nervousness returns in the elevator. And this time it's not just about seeing Damien. It's about the presentation, too. I latch onto that. Work nerves are much better than sex nerves.

As Joe had said, we arrive at the penthouse quickly and smoothly. Carl and I are standing near the elevator doors when they open, with Brian and Dave behind us guiding the rolling cases that house all of our presentation materials. At first, I can only stand and gape. I'm staring at a stunning, yet comfortable, reception area.

One wall is made entirely of glass and presents a magnificent vista of the hills of Pasadena. At least a dozen Impressionist paintings line the other walls, each simply framed so as to keep the focus on the art and not the package. Each is individually lit and together they present an array of nature scenes. Verdant fields. Sparkling lakes. Vibrant sunsets. Impressive mountain ranges.

The art gives a soft, welcoming quality to the polished reception area, as does the coffee bar that stands off to one side, silently inviting guests to help themselves, and then take a seat on the black leather sofa. A smattering of magazines covers a coffee table, the topics ranging from finance to science to sports to celebrity. Off to the side, a foosball table adds a bit of whimsy.

A reception desk dominates the room, its surface cleared of everything except an appointment calendar and a phone. At the moment, it is unmanned. I'm wondering if Damien doesn't keep a receptionist working on Saturdays when a tall, lithe brunette appears in the hallway leading off to the left. She smiles at us, revealing perfect teeth. "Mr. Rosenfeld," she says, holding out her hand. "I'm Ms. Peters, Mr. Stark's weekend assistant. I'd like to welcome you and your team to the penthouse. Mr. Stark is very much looking forward to your presentation."

"Thank you," Carl says. He looks a little intimidated. Behind me, Brian and Dave are a cacophony of shifting feet and rustling clothes. They are definitely a little intimidated.

Ms. Peters leads us down a wide hallway to the right and into a conference room so huge that NFL teams could practice there. It's then that I realize that the penthouse office takes up a full half of the top story. The elevator rose in the center of the building, and the side we're on is roughly shaped like a rectangle, with the reception area in the middle, the conference room on one side, and Stark's office on the other.

But that means that there is an entire half a story behind us. Does Stark's office flow into that space as well? Is some other CEO subletting from Stark?

I'm not sure why I'm so curious, but I am, and so I ask Ms. Peters about the building's layout.

"You're right," she says. "The office area of the penthouse takes up only half the square footage. The rest of the space constitutes one of Mr. Stark's private residences. We call it the Tower Apartment."

"Oh," I say, wondering how many residences Damien Stark has. I don't ask, though. I've already pushed the bounds of nosiness.

Ms. Peters points out the hidden wet bar built into one wall. "It's fully stocked. Help yourself to orange juice, coffee, water, soda. Or if you need it to calm your nerves, you're more than welcome to have something stronger." She says the last with a smile, her voice full of humor. But honestly, at the moment I'm thinking that a double shot of bourbon might be just the ticket.

"I'll leave you to set up," Ms. Peters says. "If you need anything, just buzz me. Mr. Stark is finishing a call. I expect he'll join you in ten minutes."

It turns out to be twelve. Twelve long minutes during which I alternate between working feverishly to set up our showcase and worrying nervously about how I'll react when I see him again.

And then the twelve minutes are over and Damien is striding into the conference area. The moment he enters the space, the air shifts. This is his territory, and though he doesn't say a word, power and authority seem to cling to him, and the two men who enter behind him are little more than afterthoughts. Every movement is controlled, every glance has purpose. There can be no doubt that Damien Stark is the one in charge, and I feel a strange little surge of pride that this exceptional man not only wanted me, but has touched me so intimately.

He's wearing jeans and a tan sport coat over a pale blue shirt. The top button is undone, and the ensemble gives him a casual, approachable quality. I wonder if he dressed that way on purpose in an attempt to make his guests more at ease. Just as quickly, I realize that of course he did. I can't imagine that Damien Stark does anything without fully understanding the impact his actions will have.

"Thank you all for meeting here. On the weekends I like to work out of the penthouse. The change of pace reminds me that it's time to kick back a little." He turns to his two companions and introduces them as Preston Rhodes, the new head of acquisitions, and Mac Talbot, a new member of the product acquisition team. Then Stark shakes Brian's and Dave's hands, taking the time to chat briefly with each. They still look nervous, but I think that he's soothed them enough that neither of the boys will botch the presentation by pushing a wrong button with a shaky finger.

He greets me next. Acceptable, polite, professional. But when he pulls his hand away, there's the slightest curve of his finger, so that he gently strokes my palm. Maybe it's my imagination, but I choose to take it as an acknowledgment that last night happened, but that today is only about the presentation.

All that in one little touch. I smile, and as I take my seat at the table, I realize that I'm much calmer. Whether he intended it to or not, Stark's touch has soothed me.

Finally, he shakes Carl's hand and greets him as if they're the best of friends. They chat about vintage LPs—apparently Carl collects them—and the weather and the traffic on the 405. His intent is clear—he's putting Carl at ease, and he's done it so skillfully I can't help but admire his technique. Finally, Stark takes a seat at the conference table, but not at the head. Instead, he sits opposite me, his long legs stretched out. He gestures to the head of the table and tells Carl to begin whenever he's ready.

I've seen the presentation so many times that I mostly tune it out, focusing instead on Stark's reaction. The technology really is amazing. Video footage of athletes is analyzed using a series of proprietary algorithms that translate anatomical movement into spatial data sets. Stats from each player are mapped against the data. Then, taking into account the player's particular body structure and metrics, the software provides concrete suggestions for improving performance. But what is truly revolutionary is that those suggestions are demonstrated in holographic form so that the athletes and their coaches can see the actual position adjustments necessary for improvement.

Every article I've read about Stark mentions how brilliant he is, but today I get to see that intellect in action. He asks all the right questions from theoretical to applied to marketing and sales. When Carl raves and crows instead of letting the product speak for itself, Stark shuts that down so skillfully that I don't think Carl even notices. He's direct and to the point, efficient without being rude, firm without being patronizing. The man may have made his original fortune on a tennis court, but as I watch him, I have no doubt that business and science are in his blood.

Stark asks questions of all of us, including Brian and Dave, who gape and mumble but manage to articulate responses under Stark's easy but firm control of the conversation.

He turns to me next and asks a technical question about one of the key equations at the heart of the primary algorithm. I can see Carl out of the corner of my eye, and I'm pretty sure he's about to have a heart attack. This question is very firmly outside of my job description. But I've done my homework, and I use the virtual whiteboard to show Stark the mathematical underpinnings of the equation. I even go so far as to address the anticipated consequences of a few hypothetical adjustments that Stark suggests. At the head of the table, Carl sags in relief.

I've obviously impressed my boss. But what's more satisfying is that I've impressed Stark. I can't say the satisfaction rises to the same level as last night, but it comes pretty damn close.

When the meeting finally wraps up, I can tell that Carl is having a hell of a time playing the cool, calm professional. He knows too well that the whole thing went over fabulously. Stark's interested in the product and impressed by the team. In this business, it doesn't get much better than that.

We're just about to start the round of goodbyes and handshakes when Ms. Peters steps in, her expression tightly efficient. "I apologize for interrupting, Mr. Stark, but you asked me to inform you if Mr. Padgett returned to the building."

"He's here now?" I watch as Stark's expression shifts from casual and calm to hard and dangerous.

"Security just called up. I assume you'd like to speak to them?"

Stark nods, then turns to face us. "I'm afraid you'll have to excuse me. There's a situation that demands my attention. I'll be in touch next week." He glances at Ms. Peters. "If you could see our guests out?"

"Of course, sir."

His eyes meet mine, but they are unreadable. And then he

steps out of the conference room and disappears down the hall. The sense of loss from his departure surprises me, but I say my goodbyes to his colleagues, then turn my attention to helping Brian pack one of the cases, all the while afraid that everyone in the room can read my expression.

After Ms. Peters has put us on the elevator and the door has firmly closed, Carl does such a funky little jig that I can't help but laugh. "That was great," I say. "Thank you so much for letting me be here for this."

Carl spreads his arms in a magnanimous gesture. "Hey, we're a team. And we all kicked some ass." The elevator doors open onto the lobby, and Carl swings his arms jovially around Brian's and Dave's shoulders. They valiantly try to move with their boss and still drag the rolling cases. I'm about to take pity on them when I hear my name.

I look up and see Joe the security guard gesturing toward me. "Ms. Fairchild? If you have a moment?" He's holding a phone to his ear.

"Yes?" I say, hurrying to the guard desk.

Joe holds up a finger in a *just a moment* gesture. I glance sideways at Carl, who's looking at me with an unmistakable *what the fuck?* expression. I shrug, just as clueless as my boss.

Joe says something I can't hear, then hangs up the phone. "You're wanted upstairs, ma'am."

"Upstairs?"

"Back in the penthouse," he says. "Mr. Stark would like to see you."

Behind me, I see Dave and Brian nudge each other. *Great.* Apparently Carl shared his suspicions with the staff. Maybe by tomorrow there'll be an interoffice memo.

"Now's not a good time," I tell the guard. "I'm on my way to a team meeting."

"Mr. Stark was very insistent."

I bet he was. An unpleasant heaviness starts to settle over me.

I spent most of my life being told exactly where to be, where to stand, what to do, and when to do it. I squeeze my right hand into a tight fist and force myself to smile at Joe. "I'm sure he'll find something else to occupy his time this afternoon. But if he calls my office, I'll be happy to work him into my schedule next week."

Joe's eyes are wide, and his mouth hangs open a little, as if his jaw is made of rubber. I have the feeling nothing like this has happened before. People don't say no to Damien Stark.

I toss my shoulders back a little, liking the new Nikki. "Shall we?" I say to Carl and the boys.

Carl frowns. "Maybe you—"

"No," I say. "If he wants to talk about the project, we can all go back up." In the distance, I hear the *ding* of an elevator, the sound punctuating my resolve.

"And if it's not the project he wants to see you about?" Carl asks, looking at me hard.

I stare back, just as coolly. "Then he doesn't need to see me, does he?" I stand firm, daring Carl to send me up there. He did it once at the party. If he does it again in the lobby of Stark's building, it really isn't going to be pretty.

After a moment, he nods. "Come on. Champagne's waiting."

Joe has been eyeing us warily, and now that we're moving toward the exit, he becomes animated. "I'm going to need to call Mr. Stark's office," he says. "He's expecting you upstairs."

"It's all right, Joe."

I recognize the voice before I see the man—it's Stark, of course, and he emerges from the elevator bank looking calm and polished. Just seeing him sends a jolt of awareness through me. It's like the fight or flight response. With Stark, I think it's a little bit of both.

He passes by the security desk and shakes hands with my good buddy Joe and the second guard before continuing on toward me and Carl and the boys.

"Ms. Fairchild," he says, my name sounding soft and decadent on his lips. "My decorator sent over some portfolio pages from local artists. I was hoping to get your opinion on a few of the pieces."

"You didn't find something you liked last night?" Carl asks.

"I wouldn't say that," Stark answers, his eyes on me. "But I'm still not satisfied."

Fortunately, Carl is looking at Stark. Otherwise, he might notice that my face has undoubtedly turned a dozen shades of red.

"I apologize for the short notice—you probably have a team meeting planned?—but I'd like to get this matter put to bed."

My mouth goes dry at his choice of words.

"No plans," Carl lies, waving his hand casually. "It's Saturday. I was just about to wish everyone a good weekend and congratulate them on a job well done."

"Then you don't mind if I steal Ms. Fairchild again." He takes a step closer to me, and as is always the case with Damien Stark, I can feel the effect of him in the air between us.

"Not at all," Carl says. "I'm sure she'll be very helpful." The last is said with a tone that I really don't appreciate, but since I'm going to accept Stark's invitation and not return with my co-workers, I can't really complain.

Yes, despite my earlier resolve I'm going up to the penthouse with Stark.

Why? Because of the way the air has fired between us.

Because of the way my flesh is tingling merely from his proximity.

Because he came down here and so boldly demanded it.

And, finally, because even though he wants a piece of my ass, all Stark's getting today is a piece of my mind.

11

Stark takes my arm and leads me back toward the elevator bank. I'm hyperaware of his touch, but I try to ignore it and hold on to my irritation.

We stop in front of an elevator next to the one I rode up in with the team. The doors open the moment Stark inserts his identification card into a slot so well camouflaged it looks like part of the granite. We step onto the elevator and I jerk my arm free. "What do you think you're doing?" I demand.

"Hold on," Stark says as the doors close behind us.

"No, I'm not holding on. You don't get to just snap your fingers and expect me to—" The ground bursts upward, and I stumble forward, clutching at Stark as I try to steady myself. He slides an arm around my waist and pulls me closer. My pulse kicks into overdrive, and I know damn well it's not from the velocity of our ascent.

"I meant hold on to something," he says. "This is my private elevator. It goes straight to the penthouse, and it goes there quickly."

"Oh," I say stupidly. My irritation is fading, diluted by the intense power charging the air between us. It's magnetic . . . and like a magnet it has the power to erase. Thoughts. Memories. Emotions.

Hold on a minute. . . .

I press my palms flat against his chest and use him as leverage to push myself back up. When I'm righted, I move my hands from his chest to the elevator's interior railing. I hold it tight, just in case.

"He knows," I say, firmly and without further explanation. "Dammit, Stark, you can't just waltz into the lobby and pluck me up like a flower."

"Speaking of, I hope you liked the flowers. I had considered something more exotic, but you remind me of daisies and wildflowers."

"That's not the point."

"What?" His brows lift in mocking amusement. "Ms. Fairchild, I'm surprised. Such a well-bred young lady, and you don't even say a simple thank-you?"

"Thank you," I say coldly.

"And for the record, I didn't pluck you. Though I would be more than happy to remedy that oversight anytime you wish."

I fight to keep my ire up even though he has begun to amuse me. "I don't appreciate being treated like a puppy who's been told to heel," I snap.

Some of the amusement fades from his eyes. "Is that what you think?"

"I—" *Shit.* I close my eyes and draw in a deep breath. I don't like being ordered around, but at the same time, Stark isn't my mother, and maybe I'm not being fair. "No," I say. Then, "I don't know. But dammit, Damien," I continue, as I try to shift myself back to solid ground, "think about how it looks. He *knows*."

"So you said. Carl, you mean? And what exactly does your boss know? I assure you that I didn't tell him anything." He eyes me, the amber one alight with amusement, the dark one firm and steady. "Did you say something?"

"Don't be obtuse," I say. "He knows that something is going on between us."

"I'm very glad to hear you say that something is."

"*Went,*" I correct quickly. "That something *went* on between us."

He says nothing. It's a good plan, that silence. I, however, am not so strong.

I clear my throat. "It, um, was fun," I begin, but close my mouth tight at his burst of laughter.

"Fun?"

I can feel my cheeks heat. He has me blushing again, and I don't like it. "Yes," I say primly. "Fun. A lot of fun, actually. A rollicking good time that I will probably replay over and over again as I lay in my bed alone and touch myself until I come." I'm staring hard at him, my voice matter-of-fact, my words like a lashing.

The amusement fades from his face, replaced by heat and desire. I suddenly want to take it back. My temper has made me take it one step too far.

"Fun," I repeat and square my shoulders. "But it's not happening again."

"Isn't it?" He takes a single step toward me—and the elevator chimes as the car glides to a stop.

"No," I say, then draw in a sharp breath as he leans closer. I anticipate his touch, and then find myself disappointed when it doesn't come. All he's done is press a button on the control panel. Behind us, the opposite set of doors slides open. I turn and find myself looking into the foyer of Damien Stark's Tower Apartment.

"No," I repeat, not sure if I mean the apartment or a repeat performance or everything all mixed up together. Considering my senses and emotions are all in a tumble, I think the latter is the best guess.

"Why not?" He straightens, but now he's standing even

closer than he was before. I'm having a little trouble breathing and I'm suddenly so warm that little beads of sweat have gathered at the nape of my neck. Honestly, it's a little hard to think.

"This isn't a good idea," I say as he takes my hand and leads me into the apartment. The entry hall is elegantly furnished, but inviting and comfortable, much like the offices on the other side of the elevator. A wall directly opposite the elevator blocks my view of most of the apartment.

A massive flower arrangement on a low, glass table dominates the foyer. Curved benches surround the table, and I imagine Stark's dates sitting there to adjust shoes, check purses. It's not an image I like.

The wall itself is almost completely covered by a huge painting, this one of a field of flowers so exquisitely rendered that I almost believe I could step into the canvas and lose myself in that world.

"Your home is beautiful," I say. "It tells a lot about the man who lives here."

"Does it?"

"He likes flowers."

Stark smiles. "He likes beauty."

"Did you pick out the floral arrangement?"

"No," he says. "Though Gregory knows my taste."

"Gregory?"

"My valet."

Valet? I was raised in a family with quite a bit of Texas oil money, but nobody in my family ever had a valet.

"The painting is beautiful. But I'm surprised to see a pastoral scene in your home."

"Are you?" He sounds genuinely surprised. "Why?"

"You're so intent on a nude for your new place." I shrug. "I just wouldn't have pegged you for flowers and trees and all that stuff."

"I'm a man of mystery," he says. "But to be honest, the decision to hang a nude in the Malibu property is a relatively new one. You might say that inspiration struck me at Blaine's show. Of course, unless I'm able to acquire what I want, the wall will stay bare."

He's looking hard at me as he speaks, and though his tone sounds perfectly conversational, I can't help the shiver of awareness that tingles up my spine.

"Did you have some portfolio pages you wanted to show me?" I ask, forcing my voice to stay cool and businesslike. "If not, I should be going. I'd like to enjoy my Saturday."

"I'd be happy to suggest some very engaging activities," he says.

I keep my lips pressed together, and Damien laughs. "Ms. Fairchild. How your thoughts do wander. . . ."

I flush and have to force myself not to snap out a curse.

"Come on in," he says, his voice still light with humor. He heads toward the passage leading into the main section of the apartment. "I'll make you a drink and we can talk."

I hesitate, wanting to tell him we can park ourselves on the bench right there and chat about whatever pictures he wants. But I'm curious. I want to see where he lives—one of the places, anyway. And so I allow him to lead me into a stunning living room filled with contemporary furniture. Steel and leather, but highlighted with enough pillows and lamps and pottery to make it seem warm and inviting.

The most stunning feature is the wall of windows, beyond which stretches an urban panorama.

Damien nods to a wet bar that occupies a corner of the room. I follow him and sit on a bar stool, my back to the window. The placement of the stool in proximity to the window makes it seem as though I'm floating in space. It's exhilarating, though I have to wonder if it wouldn't be a bit unnerving after a few drinks.

"I like your smile," Damien says as he steps behind the bar. "What are you thinking about?"

I tell him, and he laughs.

"I've never thought about it," he admits. "But I promise to keep you fully tethered to me. No sailing into space." His grin turns wicked. "Not unless it's me who's sending you there."

Oh my. I squirm a little on my stool, thinking that maybe I should have insisted we stay in the foyer.

"Wine?" he asks.

I tilt my head. "I'd prefer bourbon."

"Would you?"

I lift a shoulder in a casual shrug. "My mother used to pound into my head that a proper lady only drinks wine or feminine mixed cocktails. Never hard liquor. My grandfather was a whiskey kind of guy."

"I see," he says, and I have the feeling he sees more than I've actually told him. "I think I may have just the thing." He bends down, disappearing beneath the bar. A moment later he appears again, setting the bottle on the bar, pulling down a highball glass, and pouring me two fingers of liquor without another word.

I take the glass, a little in shock, because surely I'm not seeing what I think I'm seeing. "Glen Garioch?" I ask, reading the name off the bottle. I take a tentative sip. It's exceptionally smooth with a woody flavor and floral undertones. I close my eyes to savor it, and take another sip. "What year is this?" I finally ask, fearing I already know the answer.

"Nineteen fifty-eight," he says nonchalantly. "Excellent, isn't it?"

"Nineteen fifty-eight? Are you serious?" This whiskey was my grandfather's idea of the holy grail. Only three hundred fifty bottles of the Highland whiskey were put out onto the market, and I happen to know that a single bottle retails at about twenty-six hundred dollars. And here I am, drinking it on a Saturday afternoon without a trumpet or a big band or a press release to mark the occasion.

"You're familiar with this particular label?"

"Yeah," I say. "Basically we're drinking gold."

"Why would I offer you anything but my best?"

He's poured himself a glass as well, and now he walks around the bar. I think he's going to sit on the stool next to me, but he doesn't. He simply leans against it, which means that he's a few inches closer to me . . . and between Damien Stark and me, inches can be dangerous.

I tell myself it's to quell my nerves and take another sip, then wait for Damien to say something else. He's quiet, though, watching me. I begin to feel a bit self-conscious under his unabashed inspection.

"You're staring," I finally say.

"You're beautiful."

I look away. It's not what I want to hear. "I'm not," I say. "Or maybe I am. Does it matter?"

"Sometimes," he says, which is the most honest answer I've ever heard to that particular question. "It matters to me."

"Why?"

"Because I like looking at you. I like the way you hold your shoulders back. The way you walk as if the world is yours for the taking."

I shake my head a little. "That's just years of walking with a book on my head, and lectures from my mother, and endless etiquette classes."

"It's more than that. I like the way you wear your clothes, as if you understand that it's you and not the cloth that matters. You are beautiful, Nikki, but it's because of what you exude as much as it is the standard of beauty that we see in pageants and on magazine covers."

"What if everything you see in me is a lie?"

"It's not," he says.

I take a slug of my whiskey. "Maybe you're not as smart as you think you are, Mr. Stark."

"Nonsense. I'm fucking brilliant. Or haven't you heard?" His grin is wide and boyish and I can't help but laugh. And then, before I even have time to catch my breath, the boyish expression is gone, replaced with one of fire and need. He moves fast, and before I can blink he's twisted my bar stool so that my back is to the bar and he has a hand on either side of me. I'm caged in, trapped in Damien's heat. "I am smart, Nikki," he says. "I'm smart enough to know that you feel it, too. This isn't just heat, it's a goddamned conflagration. Not chemistry, but nuclear fission."

I'm flushed and breathing hard. He's right—so help me, he's right. But even so . . .

"There's nothing good about an atomic reaction," I say. "And the blast destroys everything it touches."

"Bullshit." The word comes out hard. He's right in front of me, and I can feel the anger coming off him in waves. "Goddammit, Nikki, don't do that. Don't play those kind of games with me. Don't make this complicated when it should be so damn simple."

"Should be?" I repeat. "What the hell does that mean? Nothing is simple. Am I attracted to you? Hell yes. But you don't even know me."

I stifle a sigh. Sometimes I wonder if I even know myself, or if all those years of being molded by my mother—being told what to eat, what to drink, who to date, when to sleep, and all the other *Mommie Dearest* bullshit—had sucked Nikki right out of me.

But no. No, I fought to keep the core of myself, even if I do keep it buried deep.

I look fiercely at him. "You don't know me," I repeat.

The intensity with which he looks back at me almost makes me stumble. "But I do."

Something in his voice makes me feel exposed. He has me on

edge again, and I look away, not liking the way he seems to be shining a spotlight on me.

It takes me a moment to gather myself, and when I do, I tilt my head just enough to look up at him. "We're not taking this further, Mr. Stark. Absolutely not."

"I don't accept that." His voice is a low growl that rumbles through me, weakening my resolve.

I don't say a word. I can't seem to form one.

"I liked it," he continues, as he traces his fingertips down the sleeve of my jacket. "You liked it. I'm not seeing a sound basis for cessation, Ms. Fairchild."

I force myself to make a coherent sound. "I like cheesecake, but I only have it rarely. And I know it's bad for me."

"Sometimes bad is good."

"Bullshit. That's what people say to alleviate their own guilt or justify their own weakness. Bad is bad. A is A."

"I didn't realize we were discussing philosophy. Shall I counter with the teachings of Aristippus? He held that pleasure is the highest good." His fingertip traces my collarbone. "And I want to be very, very good with you."

I shiver from his touch, allowing myself one brief moment to savor the pleasure of basking in the glow of Damien Stark. Then I turn away, so that I'm speaking to the air, not to the man. "This isn't going anywhere." My voice is a whisper. My voice is the sound of regret. "It can't."

"Why not?" I hear the gentleness in his voice and wonder how much of myself I've inadvertently revealed.

I don't say a word.

He exhales, and I can feel the frustration rolling off him in waves. "Ultimately, your free will is your own, Ms. Fairchild. As is mine."

"Yours?"

"I'm free to try to convince you otherwise."

The space between us is so thick that it's a wonder I can breathe the air. "You won't convince me," I say, but not as forcefully as I want. "I have a job with someone you're going to invest with. I've already gone further than I should." I suck in a fortifying breath. "But it has to stop now. I'm not risking my professional reputation any more than I already have."

"Why not work for me?"

The retort is so quick that I can't help but wonder if he's already considered the possibility. "Not happening," I say.

"Give me one reason why not."

"Um, gee, let me see. Maybe because I don't want to be the poster child for sexual harassment?"

The change in his face is instant and disturbing, and I am left with no doubt that I've angered him. My immediate instinct is to slip off the stool and scoot away, but I remain rooted to the spot. No way am I giving him the satisfaction of backing down.

"Did you feel harassed last night?"

"No," I admit. As much as I'd like to take the easy way out, I can't lie to him.

I see the relief wash over his face, banishing the anger. Or was it fear? I'm not sure, and it doesn't matter. Right now, I see only desire.

"I thought about you last night," he says. "Giselle and Bruce will probably never have me out for drinks again. I was terrible company."

"I'm so sorry to have ruined your evening."

"Hardly," he said. "And the ride home—I think that was the first time in my life I wanted a drive to be longer. Me, alone in the back of the limo, surrounded by the scent of you."

He doesn't mention the panties. I wonder if he's found them. And if he hasn't . . .

Oh, dear. Who else does he let use that limo?

I feel my cheeks warm, and from the way his eyes crinkle with amusement, I know that he's noticed.

"I imagined undressing you," he says, reaching for the top button on my blouse. He pops it open effortlessly. "I pictured you naked." *Pop*, another button. "You're beautiful," he whispers.

With the side of his thumb, he gently strokes the swell of my breast and the lace of my white satin bra.

My breath catches in my throat. I open my mouth to tell him to stop, but no words come out.

His hands find the bra's front clasp, and as efficiently as he unbuttoned my blouse, he's released me from my bra, which hangs limp from my shoulders. His groan is low and needful and desperately arousing. I want nothing more than to close my eyes and surrender, but I can't, I can't—

"Damien, please."

He lifts his eyes to mine. He's breathing hard, and there's longing in the hard angles of his face. "Free will, Nikki. Tell me to stop, and I will. But tell me fast, because I'm going to kiss that damnable mouth of yours, and goddammit, Nikki, I'm doing it to keep you quiet."

Faster than I can react, his mouth covers mine. Claiming me, marking me. Making me his. My mind goes blank, all thoughts dissolving, replaced only by pleasure and the need to be claimed by this man. To open my mouth and take and be taken.

Blindly, I grope for him, my fingers clutching at his hair, pulling him closer. It's as if all my protestations have been nothing but a sham, and now that they've been beaten aside, the pressure of emotion—of *need*—that's been building inside me has to burst out, wild and hot and desperate and demanding. The kiss lasts either seconds or an eternity, I'm not sure. But when he releases me, I suck in air, craving oxygen because I am light-headed and weak.

This is my chance, and I know it. Tell him to stop now, and he will. Tell him to leave me alone, and he'll walk out of my life.

I throw myself at him. Wanton. Willful. I'm risking everything, but right then I don't care. All I can feel is the fire.

Our mouths clash as I draw him in, and he's right there, tasting me, his low moan of pleasure making all my risks worthwhile.

He breaks our kiss roughly, then closes his mouth on my neck. I gasp and arch back, and as I do, his hands slide into my shirt, cupping my breasts, and then his mouth is there, suckling, drawing me in until my nipple is a tight pearl against his teeth. I realize he's tugged me closer, so that my ass is barely on the bar stool and his thigh is wedged between my legs. I'm bucking against him because the pleasure has shot like a hot spark from my breast to my sex.

"Baby," he whispers, as he comes up for air. His fingers quickly finish unbuttoning my shirt, and his hands ease down to my waist, leaving my skin hot and prickly in his wake. He slides me off the stool so that I am standing in front of him. I'm damp from the heat of my desire, and my body aches all over, craving his touch.

"So soft," he says, as he untucks my shirt and brushes his fingers lightly over my skin. His fingers skim around the waistband of my skirt, then slowly unzips it. It falls a bit, hanging loose around my hips. "So damn beautiful."

The awe in his voice unnerves me, and cold fingers of trepidation creep in beneath the fog of pleasure.

I tremble, not sure if it's from my fears or from his touch. "Reach back," he orders. "Hold on to the stool."

"Damien . . ." I hear the protest in my trailing voice, but my actions don't match my words. I do as he says, my hands clutched tight, my back arched, my head tilted back with pleasure.

He opens my blouse fully, so that the thin material hangs limply on either side of me, and I feel the gentle flutter of the edges against my bare flesh. He brushes his mouth over my nipples, and I groan, wanting to feel him suckle me, but he's only teasing, and with each soft, feathertouch of a kiss upon my nipple, I feel my sex tighten and throb. I want him—I want him desperately. And yet I don't. And all I can do is hold tight to the stool and try to ride out the storm, afraid all the while that I will shatter and break.

"Did you know you glow?" he asks. He is trailing kisses down my cleavage, to my belly, to the waistline of my skirt. I tense, afraid he's going to slide the skirt the rest of the way down over my hips and leave me exposed in the tiny bikini panties I put on that morning.

He doesn't, though, and I glory in the brief reprieve. Instead, he pulls me roughly to him, then shifts our positions, so that he is the one leaning against the bar, and I am in front of him. "Turn around," he says roughly, but doesn't wait for me to comply. Instead he turns me, and I feel his mouth tug at my earlobe even as one of his hands closes over my naked breast.

His other hand snakes around my waist, and he pulls me tighter against him. I gasp, both in surprise from the quick motion and from the pressure of his denim-clad cock against the swell of my ass.

"Damien," I whisper, my voice a plea. But whether I'm begging him to stop or continue, even I don't know.

His mouth is at my ear, his voice so carnal, so full of lust, it makes my clit throb. "I'm going to fuck you, Nikki. Pleasure? We're going to blow the roof off pleasure. I'm going to make you beg for it. I'm going to claim you. I'm going to tease you. I'm going to torment you. And you're going to come for me like you've never come in your life."

I can barely breathe I'm so turned on by the power of his words. And as he's talked, his hand has been snaking down under the waistband of my skirt, over my panties to cup my swollen, dripping cunt.

"You're so wet," he whispers. "Oh, baby, you're soaking."

I make some sort of rough noise in my throat. Maybe a response, I'm not sure. I'm shifting my weight shamelessly, wanting to feel his fingers against my swollen clit. What was it he'd said about making me beg? I was on the verge right then.

He roughly yanks my panties to the side, and in what feels like one movement, he slides two fingers into me. "Tell me you like that." His voice is rough, demanding.

"Yes. God, yes." My vagina spasms around him as his fingers move in and out, finger-fucking me, teasing my clit, and sending me higher and higher until I'm close, so close, so close.

I cry out as he pinches my nipple, and the delicious pain triggers my release. I come in violent, shuddering waves, his fingers still inside me, my body trying to draw him in, to keep him there, to hold on to the moment.

"Nikki," he whispers, gently pulling out of me. He turns me around—I am a limp rag—and his mouth closes over the tender nipple. He suckles it, pinching and pulling at the other one, the sensation of near-pain keeping my sensitive sex throbbing. Slowly, he kisses his way down my cleavage, my belly. I'm still in my skirt, and as his tongue dips into and out of my belly button, I hear the rough scrape of his palms over the raw silk of my skirt.

I am jelly. I am lost in a haze. I am floating.

But even here in my new heaven, that low rumble of fear is growing. I know what's coming, and even though I want it— want him—I don't think I'm strong enough yet to stand it. But maybe . . . maybe . . .

He wants you. *Your snark. Your attitude.*

I cling to Jamie's words, hoping, even as Damien whispers that I'm beautiful, beautiful, so very, very beautiful. "I have to taste you," he says. "I want to lick all of that sweetness up and then kiss you. I want you to know how fucking amazing you taste."

His hands have reached the hem of my skirt, and now his

fingers graze along my stockings as he pushes the skirt up, up until he's reached the band of my thigh-high stocking, and I'm no longer breathing and holding so tight to his shoulders that I fear I may break a bone.

And then his hands are on my flesh, rising above the tops of the stockings, and he's stroking the soft inner thigh, and I know the hard, swollen ugliness he'll feel as his hands climb higher and higher. I tense, fighting shame and fear and pain and memories. They beat their way in, through the haze of lust and desire. Through the sweet moment of being in Damien's arms.

I try to battle it back, the voice in my head that tells me to run. I don't want to run. I want to try. I want to stay and I want to feel and I want to get lost in Damien's touch. I'm so hot and I almost believe what Jamie has said about him wanting me, me, *me*.

But then he whispers the one word that destroys everything. The one word that makes the fantasy disappear.

"Perfect," he says. "Dear God, Nikki, you're perfect."

12

I jerk away, twisting sideways and banging my thigh against the side of the bar as I shove free from Damien's embrace.

"I'm sorry, I'm sorry," I say. I don't look at him. "I have to go. I'm sorry." I yank my skirt down and reach back to zip it. My fingers shake as I button my blouse. I don't bother with my bra, but hold my jacket closed with one hand as I hurry toward his foyer.

"Nikki—"

There's pain and confusion in his voice, and I feel like shit because I'm the reason it's there and he doesn't deserve this. I should have cut this off sooner. Hell, I should have cut it off last night.

"I'm sorry," I say again, even though it's lame. I'm at the elevator, and the doors open the instant I press the button. I'm relieved; I was afraid I'd have to wait for it. But then I realize that Damien is on the premises, so of course his elevator is going to be parked wherever he is.

I step inside and stand erect until the doors shut tight. Then I melt against the glass panel and let the tears flow. I have fifty-seven floors to get them out of my system. No, sixty, because my car's on the third parking level.

When the car eases to a stop, I hastily wipe my face and stand up straight, sliding my mask back into place as I fluff my hair and flash a quick smile at the mirror. *Perfect.*

But my act isn't necessary. There's no one waiting when the doors open. Still, I keep the mask on and the act up as I make the long walk across the Stark Tower side of the parking structure to the area beneath the bank building wherein C-Squared is housed. My car is on the far side, and I'm walking fast now, because I can feel the cracks all over me. I'm going to shatter soon, I know it, and I need to be in my car when I do.

It's right there, parked opposite the stairwell. The whole corner is dark and despite being open, it makes me twitchy. I reported it to the property manager my first day, but so far they've yet to put in a new bulb. Once again, I remind myself to ask Carl for another assigned space, because this corner is too damned creepy.

I hurry to the car and shove the key in the lock—because my Honda's almost fifteen years old, and I don't have a keychain remote. I yank the door open, then slide inside, letting the familiar sounds and smells surround me. I tug on the heavy door and the instant it slams shut, I lose it. Tears stream down my face, and I alternately clutch and pound on the steering wheel. Hitting and slamming and pummeling until the heel of my hand is red and raw and sore. I'm shouting, repeating a chorus of "no, no, no," but I don't even realize it until my voice fades, raw and raspy.

Finally my tears are spent, but my body doesn't seem to realize it. I convulse, hiccuping painfully as I try to breathe in and out and gather some control.

It takes a while, but I finally quit shaking. My hand is unsteady as I try to insert the key into the ignition. I can't manage.

Metal scrapes against metal. I drop the key ring. Fumbling, I bend down to pick it up again, only to whack my forehead on the wheel. I clutch the keys tight and curse, and pound my fist against the wheel one more time.

The tears are welling again, and I breathe deep. It's too much, too fast. The move, the job, Damien.

I want to crawl out of my own skin. I want to escape. I want—

I grab a handful of my skirt and thrust it up so that the material is gathered at my hips, exposing a triangle of panties and my bare thighs above the stockings.

Don't.

Just a little. Just this once.

Don't.

But I do. I spread my legs and press the key into the soft flesh of my inner thigh. Once upon a time, I kept a knife on my key ring. I wish I still had it. *No. No, I don't.*

The key's teeth bite into my skin, but it's nothing. Mosquito bites. I need more if I'm going to keep the storm at bay—and it's that realization of my need that hits me like a slap in the face.

Oh, God, oh, God, oh, God, what the fuck am I doing?

Before I can talk myself out of it, I shove open the door and toss the keys out into the dim parking garage. I hear them skitter across the asphalt. I don't see where they land.

I sit there breathing deeply, telling myself that's not who I am. I haven't cut for over three years. I fought, and I won.

I'm not that girl anymore.

Except of course, I am. I'll always be that girl. I can wish all I want, and I can run across the country, but those scars don't go away, and they won't stay hidden forever.

I guess I learned that the hard way. That's why I ran from Damien, isn't it? And that's why I'll keep on running.

A wave of loneliness crashes over me, and I think about what

Ollie said. About how nothing would change. About how I could call him anytime I needed him.

I need him now.

I reach into my purse and pull out my phone. I have Ollie on speed dial and I punch in the number. It rings. Once. Twice. On the third ring, a woman's voice answers. *Courtney*.

"Hello? Hello, who is this?"

I forgot to give Ollie my new phone number. I'm not in his contacts, and she has no idea who's on the other end of the line.

I hang up, breathing hard. After a moment, I dial another number. This time, Jamie's voice mail answers.

"Never mind," I say, forcing a cheer into my voice that I don't feel. "I'm going shopping and thought you might want to meet up. But no big."

I hang up thinking that shopping sounds like a damn fine idea. Retail therapy won't cure the world's ills, but it works pretty well to take your mind off them. On that point, at least, I agree with my mother.

I take a deep breath, then another. I'm calmer now, ready to go. Ready to crank the radio up on a classic country station and let George Strait sing about how his problems are so much worse than mine.

I glance out my window, but don't see the keys. With a sigh, I push open my door and get out of the car, adjusting my skirt as I do. I'd thrown them hard, so they're probably yards away near the dark green Mercedes or the massive Cadillac SUV. The only flashlight I have is the app on my iPhone, and I hope it'll be enough.

My heels click on the asphalt as I cross the garage to the Mercedes. The area with the Mercedes and the Cadillac isn't as dark as the corner with my car, but it's still dim, and I frown as I contort my body and shine the light, trying to look under the two cars without getting down on my knees and putting huge runs in my stockings.

It takes a while, but after circling the cars twice, I finally see the keys hidden in a shadow behind the Mercedes' back tire.

I snatch them up, then freeze when I see movement in my peripheral vision. There, near the stairwell by my car, I see the shadow of a man.

"Hello?"

The shadow doesn't move, and I shiver, unnerved by the sensation that he is watching me.

"Hey," I call. "Who's there?" I stand, debating whether I should move forward—toward the shadow and the car—or whether I should start walking back toward Stark Tower and get a security guard to escort me.

I hold up my phone. "I'm calling security. You might want to take a hike."

At first, the man doesn't move. Then the shadow moves backward and is absorbed by the deeper darkness. A moment later, I hear a metallic creak, followed by the heavy thunk of the stairwell door slamming shut.

I shiver and hurry to my car. Right then, all I want is to get out of there.

By the time I arrive at the Beverly Center in West Hollywood, I've had my fill of George Strait and have twirled the dial back to the classic rock station. I'm jamming to Journey as I pull into a space right near the brightly lit escalator that leads into the fashionable mall.

Jamie hasn't called me back, and to be honest, I'm grateful. I'm feeling centered again, the Hyde to my Jekyll buried deep once more, and the thought of rehashing the whole day with Jamie just seems overwhelming. I don't want to think about it. I don't want to push those buttons or tug on those triggers.

And I really don't want to think about the way I ran from Damien Stark.

What does he think about me now?

No. Not going there.

I get out of my car, lock it tight even though no one in this part of Los Angeles would be caught dead with my piece of shit vehicle, not even a criminal, and head into the mall, my thoughts on makeup and shoes and purses. Thoughts of Damien Stark are not allowed.

The escalator moves me up, up, up, like I'm rising out of a dark hell into the light of a shiny bright heaven. Beautiful people are everywhere, and we are alike in our plastic-ness. Me, the people, even the mannequins in the windows. We're all hiding behind our masks, strutting our stuff, pretending to be perfectly perfect.

Beautiful clothes call to me like sirens from window displays, and I dip in and out of the stores like flotsam moving with the tide. I pull things off racks. I try them on. I twist and turn in front of three-way mirrors and smile politely when the sales-clerks tell me how *darling* an outfit is. How it makes my legs look so, so sexy. How I'll turn heads everywhere I go.

I put them all back.

In Macy's, I find a display of colored T-shirts, along with some cotton drawstring pants in a blue and white pinstripe material. I buy the pants and two T-shirts, also blue and white. I carry my little bag to the Starbucks and order a coffee loaded up with cream and a blueberry muffin. Comfort clothes, comfort food.

I sit by the window and watch the world go by. Once again, I'm caught without my camera, and I wish I had it. It's been like a security blanket since Ashley gave it to me for Christmas during my freshman year of high school. I'd like to capture some of these passing faces. They are mysteries, all of them. I watch them and try to guess their secrets, but it's impossible. I have no clue. She might be having an affair. He might beat his wife. The clean-cut teen might have shoplifted a pair of lacy underwear. There's no way for me to know, and that hollow, empty question mark lifts my spirits. If I can't look at them and read their secrets, then they can't know mine, either. I am a mystery, too. To them and, I hope, to Damien Stark.

I'm not proud of the way I burst out of his apartment. I know I owe him an apology. I probably owe him an explanation, too, but that will have to wait. I need to come up with something plausible. Stark may not be able to guess my secrets, but I'm certain he will know if I lie.

I finish my muffin and stand up, taking the rest of my coffee with me. As I do, the full import of my thoughts hit me. *I'm planning to see Damien Stark again.*

The thought twists through me, trepidation mixed with anticipation. And a tiny bit of fear mixed in there, too. Will he even want to see me again? More important, will he accept that this thing between us has to come to an abrupt and permanent end?

Of course he'll accept it. Wasn't he the one who said it was my decision? Who'd put the power very firmly with me?

I'd blown it, though. I'd forgotten the depth of my own weakness, and it's never safe to think that you're stronger than you are.

My thoughts have propelled me through the mall back to the escalator. I take it down to my parking level and climb back in my car. I feel better even if I don't feel whole. But it's good that I've made the decision about Stark. I will see him, and I will apologize. But not yet. A few days. Maybe a week. I need time to get centered again. Time to grow strong.

Because Damien Stark is like crack to me. Seductive and very, very addictive.

13

Jamie's car is parked in her spot when I get back to the apartment, and I'm glad. With luck, she won't have plans for the evening. It's Saturday, and on the drive over the hill I decided that we should do the whole best friends hanging out thing. Maybe a hike in the hills above Studio City, then hit the showers, get dressed up, and do dinner and drinks in some trendy Los Angeles hot spot. After all, I'm still new in town. Los Angeles and I are still in the honeymoon phase.

I'm not overtly planning on telling her the details of my day, but I know that after a few glasses of wine I'll probably reveal all. The thought cheers me, actually. I've had my few hours to brood. Now I want to dish with my best friend and let her remind me that as screwed up as I might be, I'm not the biggest head case in the world. That's Jamie's special talent. No matter how many knots I twist myself into, she's the one who can unravel me. She and Ollie. I suppose that's why they're my best friends.

I circle the building, then take the stairs two at a time to 3G, our unit.

The door's unlocked, and I throw it open and stomp inside.

"Dammit, Jamie, why not just post a sign on the door inviting every whack job in the city to waltz right in and—*oh.*"

She's home, all right. Sitting on the couch, the television blaring out an old episode of *Jeopardy!* And sitting right next to her is Damien Stark.

At least he was sitting when I first burst through the door. Now he's standing and moving toward me. Jamie shifts position, pulling her feet up onto the couch and raising herself up so that I can't help but see her face over Damien's approaching form.

OMG, she mouths. *He is so fucking hot.*

Yes, he is.

He's still wearing jeans, but the sport coat and button-down shirt are gone, replaced with a simple white T-shirt that accentuates his broad shoulders and strong, tanned arms. I imagine those arms holding a racquet. Then I imagine them holding me.

Then I clear my throat.

Damien grins, and although I know he's barely thirty, this is the first time he's looked so young. Almost boyish, like a guy you'd hold hands with as you walk across a college campus. I catch the scent of him as he comes closer. A musky cologne. Or maybe that's just the man. I'm not sure. All I know for certain is that I'm desperately aware of him. Desperately aware of my own body. His scent, apparently, works on me like pheromones.

"You're here," I say stupidly.

"I'm here," he says.

"Right." I look around the condo that has become so familiar to me over the last few days. Right then, it looks like alien territory. I set my bag down on the ground, then ease myself off to the galley-style kitchen. With the wall separating the kitchen from the living room, I'll have a moment of privacy to gather myself.

Except he follows me, then leans up against the refrigerator. I turn away from him toward the sink, but I can feel his eyes on me as I grab a glass from the dish drainer and fill it with water.

"So, how come you're here?" I ask brightly, then chug the whole thing down. Only after I've refilled the glass do I turn to look directly at Damien.

His eyes are locked onto me, holding me in place. "I wanted to see you," he says. From his expression, though, I know what he's really saying: *I wanted to see if you're okay.*

I smile, understanding that his discretion means he hasn't told Jamie what happened. "I'm good," I say. "I went shopping."

"And what woman wouldn't be good after that?"

I raise my brows. "Stereotypical, much?"

He chuckles. "If the shoe fits, Ms. Fairchild."

"Mmm." I try to fight my grin, but lose the battle.

Jamie sidles in from the living room, a vicious grin on her face. Her eyes dart between the two of us. She's in pajama bottoms and a cheap white tank top covered with paint. "I am so freaking late," she says. "I have totally got to run." She practically sprints for the door. "You two be good."

"Jamie! What the hell?" I make a motion with my hand that vaguely indicates her outfit.

"I'm just going next door," she says.

"Douglas?" I hear my voice rise. She is *not* going over there again. Especially since I know the only reason she's popping over to Mr. Mark On Her Bedpost is because our apartment is now too crowded by one.

"Just a friendly chat," she says. "Cross my heart," she adds, then makes the appropriate motions. Like that's going to make a difference. But she yanks open the door and slips out before I can stop her, and I blurt out a curse contemporaneously with the sound of the door slamming shut.

"We don't like Douglas?" Damien asks.

"Douglas is bad for her," I say. I look him in the eye. "Please tell me that's a concept you understand."

"It is," he says. "I'm also familiar with a number of corollary concepts."

"Such as?"

"Maybe Douglas isn't bad for her at all. Maybe there's just something about him that frightens her. Or you."

"You're very smart, Mr. Stark."

"Thank you."

"But that doesn't mean you know everything."

His mouth twitches, and I feel a little trill of pleasure. I've managed to zing Damien Stark. I wonder how many people can say that?

The humor in his eyes fades quickly, though. "Nikki," he says, his voice as soft and soothing as velvet. "What are you afraid of?"

My stomach twists into knots as I turn away from him and use a hand towel to dry the already dry dishes in the drainer. "I don't know what you mean," I say to a coffee cup.

"Yes, you do," he says. He moves like a cat, so I don't hear him come up behind me. But I feel the change in the air even before he speaks. Even before his hand rests lightly on my shoulder. "You bolted." Gently, he turns me around, then brushes my cheek with his fingertips. "Do I scare you?"

God yes, and in so many ways. Not the least of which is that Damien Stark terrifies me precisely because I feel safe with him. And I can't become complacent. It's when those walls come down that your heart gets shattered.

"Nikki?" His brow is furrowed. He looks miserable, and I can't stand the thought that I'm the cause.

"No," I say, and even though it's not the truth, it's also not a lie.

"Then why?"

"I . . . I was embarrassed."

"Were you?"

I glance at the floor. The pull of Damien's touch is so intense that I'm having a hard time thinking. And this is a danger zone. I need to keep a clear head. "Yes," I insist. "I said no, but then you made me so hot that I forgot myself, and when I was able to breathe again I just ran."

"Bullshit." There's disappointment in his voice. And, I think, a little bit of anger.

I swallow.

He takes a step toward me, and I take a corresponding step sideways, easing away down the length of my kitchen counter. *Clear head. I need a clear head.*

He exhales, and I can sense the exasperation. "I don't like seeing fear in your eyes."

"You're going to be my knight in shining armor?"

The corner of his mouth lifts into an ironic smile. "I think I'm a bit too tarnished for the job."

I can't help but grin. "I guess you'll have to be a dark knight, then."

"I'll fight whatever dragons you want me to," he says with a seriousness that belies my teasing tone. "But you don't need a knight. You're strong, Nikki. Hell, you're exceptional."

I conjure up the Social Nikki smile. "Is that a line you give to all the women you date?"

"Date?" I hear the hardness creeping into his voice. "I've escorted a lot of women around this town, and I've fucked a hell of a lot of them. But I didn't date them."

"Oh." I'm not sure if I'm surprised or angry or sad or relieved. True, I need to end this with Damien; I need to protect myself and my secrets. But that implies that there is something to end, and now I fear that I was right all along—I'm just a conquest. A fast fuck before he moves on. And all that bullshit Jamie said about him wanting *me* was exactly that—bullshit.

Damien is watching my face, but I can't get a read on his expression.

I turn back around and pick up an already dry bowl and start attacking it with the dishrag I'm still holding. "So that's it? You just fuck them and dump them?"

"That's a bit harsh," he says. "*Dump* suggests they wanted something more, and I'm quite certain that all they wanted was to be photographed on my arm and have a bit of fun in my bed."

"All of them?" I keep my back to him. This conversation has turned surreal.

"I've gone out with a few women who wanted more. I disentangled myself from those women. And no, I didn't sleep with them."

"Oh." The dish is bone dry, but I'm still moving the rag over it. "So you just don't do relationships?"

"Not with them."

"Why not?"

His hand closes gently on my shoulder and I feel the now-familiar heat. "Because none of them was the woman I wanted," he says as he turns me so that I have no choice but to look at him. His eyes are dark and intense, his voice is like a caress. My heart pounds in my chest, and breathing has suddenly become difficult. I think about the way he looked at me six years ago, that one glance that inspired so many fantasies. But that's not what he means; I know it can't be.

"But you did date someone not too long ago," I say, then immediately regret the words when I see his expression darken. Nice turning to ice.

For a moment, I don't think he's going to answer. Finally, he nods. "Yes," he confirms. "I suppose I did."

So was she the woman you wanted? The question seems to hang in front of me, but I can't say it out loud.

The silence thickens and I feel like an idiot for mentioning the woman in the first place. Finally, I lick my lips. "I heard that she died. I'm so sorry."

His face is hard, his jaw tense with the effort of holding in a strong emotion. "It was tragic." His voice sounds unnaturally tight.

I nod, but I don't pursue it any longer. I don't know why he told me that he didn't date at all when it's so clear that this woman meant something to him, but I'm not going to push. Considering the secrets I'm keeping, I can hardly fault him for holding on to a few of his own.

I'm tired now, though, and I want to be alone. I want to find Jamie and go to the corner store and get ice cream and cookies. I want to watch sappy old movies and sit on the couch and cry.

I want Damien Stark out of my head.

Mostly, I want to try to forget the way his touch makes me feel, because I need to abandon even the fantasy of Damien Stark. It's too raw, too real. And despite the fact that I know I have to, the thought of pushing him away rips right through my heart.

I pull out Social Nikki and smile brightly as I toss my dishtowel on the counter. "Listen, it was nice of you to come by to check on me. But I'm fine. Really. And I'm actually in a little bit of a hurry. I don't mean to be rude, but . . ." I trail off, looking meaningfully at the door.

"Do you have a date tonight, Ms. Fairchild?"

"No!" I blurt out the word, then immediately regret it. If I did have a date—if I was already seeing that special someone—I'd have the perfect excuse for brushing off Damien Stark.

"Where are you going?"

"What?" I blink, because that's not the polite way to play the game. Then again, I haven't yet seen evidence that Stark follows the traditional social norms. Why I thought he'd start now . . .

"If you're not going on a date, then where are you going?"

I can hardly tell him about my new cry-on-the-couch plans, so I fall back on a version of my original itinerary. "As a matter of fact, I'm going to grab a smoothie and then go hike Fryman Canyon Park."

"By yourself?"

"Well, I could take the Royal Guard, but I think they're busy."

"It's going to be dark soon."

"It's not even six yet. Sunset's not until eight-thirtyish."

"The sun may not dip below the horizon until then, but there are foothills involved. And once the sun starts to sink, it gets dark fast."

"I'm only going to take a few shots of the view and the sunset. Then I'm coming back. I promise you I won't let the boogeymen get me."

"They won't," Damien says, "because I won't let them. I'm coming with you."

"No," I say. "I appreciate the concern, really I do. But no."

"Then don't go at all. Let me bring the sunset to you."

I can't argue with that, primarily because I have no idea what the hell he's talking about. "What?"

He leaves the kitchen, then comes back in view with a brown paper–wrapped package. From the size and shape, it's obviously something framed. "It reminded me of you."

"Really?" A little trill of pleasure swirls through me.

He puts the package on the kitchen table. "I had intended to give it to you earlier, but you were called away so quickly that I didn't have the chance."

I smirk, but if this is his way of extracting an explanation from me, it is not going to work.

"Maybe I should be grateful," he says. "This way I get to see where you live."

"I haven't really put my stamp on it yet. Jamie's taste runs to Early American Garage Sale."

"And yours?"

"I'm much more refined. I go for Mid-Century Flea Market."

"A woman who knows her own mind. I like that."

From the way he's looking at me, I'd say he likes it very much. I clear my throat and glance at the package. I know I should tell him that I appreciate the thought, but that I can't accept it. But

I'm curious to know what's inside it. And I'm warmed by the mere fact that he brought me a gift.

"May I?"

"Of course."

I leave the safety of the kitchen counter and venture to the table. I keep a chair between us, but even that is too close. I can feel his presence, that sense of the air thickening with awareness. I have to work hard to keep my hands steady as I slide my finger under the tape and start to peel back the wrapping.

I see the frame first and know that this is no ordinary trinket. It's simple, but made with incredible craftsmanship. But it's the canvas that truly takes my breath away. An Impressionist sunset that conveys both realism and a heightened sense of reality, as if the viewer were looking at the horizon through the lens of a dream.

"It's stunning," I say, and I can hear the awe in my voice.

I turn to look at him and see pure pleasure reflected in his face. It strikes me that he's been silently anticipating my reaction. Nervously, even. The thought delights me. Damien Stark, worried about what I'd think about his present. "Evelyn mentioned you were enjoying the sunset."

The statement, so casually made, sends another frisson of pleasure through me. "Thank you," I say, the simple words too small to hold the fullness of my feelings.

There's something familiar about the painting, and it takes me a moment to realize its frame matches the ones that lined his reception area. I remember the array of canvases, including the two stunning sunsets.

"Is this from your office?"

"It was. Now it has a new home with a woman who appreciates its beauty."

"Didn't you?"

"Beauty should be shared."

I shift the painting so that I can prop it safely against the wall. And when I do, I see the faded label on the frame. "A Monet? This is a copy, right?"

"It's an original," he says. "If it's not, I'll be having some very stern words with Sotheby's."

"But . . . but . . ."

"It's a sunset," he says firmly, as if that should quell all my protests. "And it reminds me of you."

"Damien . . ."

"And, of course, this gift isn't nearly as precious as the one you left for me in the limo." His eyes sparkle and his grin is devious. I feel a tug of heated pleasure between my thighs.

"Oh," I say.

He reaches into his pocket and pulls out a bit of white satin. Slowly, with his eyes never leaving mine, he lifts the panties to his face and breathes in deep. I see his eyes darken with lust and feel a corresponding tug of longing between my thighs. I clutch the back of the chair to steady myself.

"They made the ride from the restaurant to my house much more enjoyable." His voice slides over me. I want to wrap myself inside it, but all I can do is shake my head.

"Please," I beg. "Please don't start."

For a moment, I think he's going to argue. Then he slips the panties back into his pocket. I swallow, thinking of them there, with him. I wonder if he'll ever give them back. I hope that he doesn't.

We lock eyes, and for a moment it's as if the air has been sucked out of the room. Then he moves toward me, and suddenly I can breathe again as the real world rushes back in around me.

I raise my hand to ward him off. "Damien, no."

"I assure you, Ms. Fairchild, your messages here and at my apartment have been well received." His expression tightens, but I see the humor around his eyes and relax a little.

"Oh. Good. That's good." I take a deep breath. "It's just that you look—"

"How?"

"A bit like the big bad wolf."

"And would that make you Little Red Riding Hood? I may want to devour you, Ms. Fairchild, but I promise you that I'm capable of controlling my urges. Most of the time, anyway."

"Of course. I'm sorry. You just make me . . ."

"What?"

"Skittish," I admit.

"Do I? Interesting." He looks pleased by the thought. I frown, feeling exposed.

"Listen, thank you for the painting. It's amazing."

"But you can't accept such an extravagant gift?"

"Hell no. I love it." And I love that he wants me to have it. "I'm perfectly happy to keep it if you really want me to have it. Despite, well, you know . . ."

I trail off, and he laughs. "Good. I was afraid that since you're in the habit of denying yourself things that you so obviously want . . ."

Zing. Well, he definitely got me with that one.

"Actually, I was going to say that good manners would require me to offer you a drink." I smile sweetly. "But I'm not going to, since I'm hoping you'll leave."

"Because I make you skittish?"

"Pretty much," I confess.

"I see."

Apparently he doesn't, though, because he's still standing there in my apartment.

"Well?" I ask.

"Well, what?"

I sigh. "Well, are you going to go?"

His eyes widen with surprise. "I'm sorry. I didn't realize you wanted me to. I thought you were speaking hypothetically."

Now it's my turn to laugh. And as I do, I realize I'm not feeling quite so skittish anymore. "I'm going to have a drink. Of course my bourbon's probably not up to your exacting standards. But if you'd like one anyway . . ."

"So I can stay?" He looks very smug and self-satisfied. And sexy as hell.

"I guess you'll have to. We only have two highball glasses, and if you take the drink with you, Jamie will get pissed off."

• "Wouldn't want to disturb the subtle inner-workings of roommate relations. I accept your invitation."

"Straight up? Or over ice?"

"However you're having it is fine."

I fetch the bourbon from the living room and bring the bottle to the kitchen to pour. "It's a trade-off," I say when I pass him a glass with a few ounces of bourbon and two cubes of ice. "I like it slightly chilled, but if you savor it too long the ice melts and it gets watered down."

"Then we'll have to drink fast," he says, then tilts his glass and tosses it back.

"Sorry, dude. I've already done the wasted thing with you. I'm going to sip mine."

"A shame. You're entertaining when you're drunk." His hand slides into his pocket.

"No way. Don't even go there."

He smiles back at me, and it's a nice moment. Just me and Damien Stark kidding around in my kitchen. Who would've thought?

He pours himself another glass. "I do have one more reason for coming here tonight," he says. "I wanted to check on you, and I wanted to give you the painting. But there's something else, too. I have a proposition for you."

I let the words sink in, trying to analyze my feelings about them. *Proposition.* That could mean so many things. Something to do with C-Squared. With me. With me and Damien.

I swallow. The best course—the safest course—is to thank him for the present and tell him that I don't even want to hear this latest twist. And yet . . .

And yet I want to. I'm playing with fire, and I know it.

But the sad truth is that part of me wants to get burned.

"I'm listening," I say, and then I toss my bourbon back, too. I'm not sure what it is that I'm trying to prove to him, but I meet his eyes with satisfaction.

"Another?" he asks dryly.

"Why the hell not?"

He pours me the drink, then moves close to hand it to me. I stay rooted to the spot. I can feel his heat. I could reach out right then and run my hand over his chest. I could watch as my skin cracked and burned from the fire that is Damien Stark. I don't, but I have to clutch my glass hard against the impulse.

"I've scoured Los Angeles and Orange County. I've looked at the online collections of galleries all over the country. I haven't found what I'm looking for."

"For your new house. We're talking about the artwork you want to hang in the house you're building?" Of all the possibilities, this is not one that would have occurred to me.

"I've finally figured out what I want, and yet it doesn't exist. Not yet, anyway."

He's eyeing me with such deliberate intensity that I start to feel nervous under his gaze.

"I'm not really following you."

"As I said, I have a proposition. You."

"Ah. Um. I'm still not following you."

"I want a portrait. Of you. I want a nude."

My mouth opens, but I can't quite form words.

"The view is from behind. You're at the foot of a bed, facing a window that looks out over the ocean. Sheer curtains billow around you, caressing your skin. You stand at an angle, so we can see the swell of your breast, the barest hint of a nipple. But your face is turned away. Your identity is a secret. It's known only to me. And, of course, to you."

His words crash over me like waves, their pull as strong as the tide. I feel the tug of them between my thighs, and the unmistakable wetness as well. I want this—to be on display, and not just for Damien's pleasure, but for all the world to see. Anonymous, and yet known. It's not the kind of thing a girl like me is supposed to want. It's wild and wanton and even though I know Damien would say that it's art and it's beautiful, there's no denying that it's a little bit naughty, too. The pretty princess up on display.

Except that's not who I am. And that's sure as hell not *what* I am.

Damien is watching my face with the same intensity I saw in his boardroom. "Good," he says. "You're not discounting the idea outright. I want this, Nikki. I can already picture how it will look on my wall."

I don't look at him, but trail my fingertip over the countertop. "You think you know what you'd be getting, but you don't."

There's silence, and I peek up at him. He's taking me in, his eyes moving slowly over me. "Don't I?"

My breath hitches as he moves close, then reaches out to slowly stroke my cheek, his movements suggesting that I already am a work of art, fragile and beautiful and perfect.

The thought makes me flinch and I jerk away. "No," I say. "Not happening." I summon a teasing grin. "Maybe we should just find you a nice poster. Like the *Hang in there, Baby* kitten. That would be charming."

My weak attempt at humor doesn't even faze him. "Name your price, Ms. Fairchild. Tell me what you want."

"What I want?" What I want is to be like him. Strong and confident and capable.

But I'm not ready to reveal that much of myself. So I give him the standard line. "I want a family," I say. "I want a satisfying career." And with a tossback to my years of pageant training, I add the pièce de résistance. "I want world peace."

His eyes seem to burn into me, cutting through all my bullshit.

And then he's right there, his hands on my waist. He pulls me roughly toward him, and I tilt my head back to look into his eyes. What I see makes me shiver. Makes me *want*. I feel the flesh between my thighs throbbing. I remember the feel of his hand there, of his fingers inside me, and my muscles clench in need.

It's burning hotter and hotter, and I'm afraid I won't be able to turn back. More, I'm afraid I won't want to.

I keep my face motionless, thinking that I'm revealing nothing.

"I *can* give you what you want, Nikki," he says, and his voice is so gentle that I begin to think I've won. Maybe Damien does see what no one else does. Maybe he sees through my mask.

The thought both terrifies and excites me. Slowly, I shake my head, then manage an insolent smile. "Will you be orchestrating world peace today or later this month?"

"I'll pay you for the portrait," he says, his words seemingly a non sequitur. "I'll pay you. I'll pay the artist. I'll arrange a studio space. You're a businesswoman, Nikki. Isn't that what you ultimately want? Your own business?"

I gape at him, too surprised that he knows this to respond. Who the hell has he been talking to about me?

"This is a chance to kick-start your career."

I shake my head, ignoring the small knot inside me that is excited by his proposition. "I'm a businesswoman, not a model."

"You're *my* model. And everyone has a price."

"I don't."

"No?" He steps closer, his body full of challenge and confidence. "One million dollars, Ms. Fairchild. You get the cash, and I get you."

14

One million dollars. The words surround me, tempt me, and it's that temptation that pushes me to react.

I lurch back out of his grasp, then lash out and slap him hard across the face.

He looks at me, his eyes burning with something I don't recognize. Then he grabs my wrist and pulls me to him. His arm is around my waist, my wrist still clutched tight in his hand so that my arm is twisted painfully behind me. His body is hard against mine, and all I'm aware of is Damien. In that moment, I'm totally his, and we both know it. He can hurt me. He can have me.

My body quivers with desire. My lips part. I'm breathing fast. I don't understand my reaction to him. It's primal. Fierce. I am overwhelmed by the urge to simply surrender.

No.

I focus on his face. "I think you should leave." I'm not sure how I manage to keep my voice steady.

"I'll go," he says. "But I will get my painting." I start to snap out a retort, but he presses a finger over my lips. "I'll get it because I want it—because I want *you*. And I'll get it because you want it, too. No," he says before I can speak. "Remember the rules. Don't lie to me, Nikki. Never lie to me."

And then he's kissing me. He releases my arm and buries his fingers in my hair, tilting my head back as his mouth covers mine. I moan as his tongue roughly explores my mouth, and my arm snakes around his neck. I don't know if he's pulled me closer or if I've moved against him, but I can feel the hard press of his erection against my thigh. He's right, damn him. He's right. *I want this, I want this, I really shouldn't want this.*

Then he releases me, and I feel so loose and weak I'm surprised that gravity doesn't suck me down to the ground. He shoots me one final, smoldering look and then strides to my door. He opens it and disappears over the threshold before my heart rate has returned to normal.

I reach out and clutch the back of the dining table chair, then slowly lower myself until I'm sitting. I bend forward, my elbows on my knees, wanting to hate him for the offer he made and for the things he said. True things, but they're a truth I wish I could ignore. That I *will* ignore.

I don't know how long I sit there, but I'm still at the table when Jamie waltzes in, hair mussed and no bra. I'm certain she was wearing a bra when she left; I would have noticed if she'd been sitting half-naked with Damien.

"Douglas?" I ask. I hadn't heard the familiar bang and thump, but I'd been a bit preoccupied.

"God no," she says, and for a moment I'm relieved. I have no theory as to how she misplaced a bra, but at least I know she wasn't out grabbing a fast fuck. "Kevin in 2H," she says, and my relief turns cold and icy.

"You fucked him?"

"Trust me, that's all he's good for. The guy's really not a brain trust, and we don't have a lot in common. Well, except for an excess of energy."

"Jesus, Jamie." My problems seem petty and stupid compared to the complete randomness of Jamie's conquests. "Why sleep with him if you don't even like him?"

"Because it's fun. Don't worry. He's not going to go all stalker on me. We both know it's a no-strings kind of thing."

"It's dangerous, *James*," I say, the nickname from our childhood signaling that this is a Serious Conversation.

"Bullshit, *Nicholas*," she counters. "I told you. He's not the dangerous sort."

"I'm not talking about only him. But just because you think he looks nice doesn't mean he's not a whack job. And how do you know you won't catch something? Were you careful?"

"Christ, already. Are you my mom? Of course I was careful."

"Sorry. I'm sorry." I move the five feet into our living room and flop onto the sofa. "You're my best friend. I worry. I mean, you do these guys, and then they're out of your life." I frown, thinking of Damien. "Do you ever think about dating?" I ask, more harshly than I intend.

"Do you?"

I struggle to remain level. "This isn't about me."

"No, but it could be. I fuck around. You don't fuck at all. It's like we're that Emily Dickinson poem."

I stare at her, utterly confused.

"The candle," she clarifies. "You burn at one end, and I burn at the other."

I can't help but laugh. "That makes no sense whatsoever."

She shrugs. Sometimes Jamie is profound. Sometimes she's not. She doesn't much care either way. It's one of the reasons I love her, and one of the things I admire about her. No matter what else she might be, at the end of the day, Jamie is always Jamie.

Not so, me.

Or Damien Stark, I think.

I wonder if that's why I find him so alluring.

"That smile isn't for me," Jamie says. "And I seriously doubt it's for Kevin or Douglas. So let's see . . . hmmm . . . could you be thinking about the sexy hunka hunka billionaire who just left our little shack of a condo?"

"I could be," I admit.

"So what was the present? More important, why aren't you two in your bedroom fucking your brains out?"

"We're not dating," I say.

"Like you have to date to fuck?"

"He wants me to pose for a nude portrait," I say, though I hadn't intended to tell her a thing. "And he's willing to pay me one million dollars to get it."

She gapes at me. I have actually flummoxed Jamie Archer. This is a first.

"A million dollars? Seriously?"

"Yup."

"So? Are you thinking about it?"

"No," I say automatically. "Of course not."

But even as I say the words, I know I don't mean them. I *am* thinking about it. About being naked on that canvas. About Damien Stark standing in his living room and looking up at me.

A shiver runs through me. "Let's go," I say.

Jamie cocks her head. "Go? Where?"

"Out. It's Saturday. There will be dancing involved. And drinking. Definitely drinking."

"Are we celebrating?" There's a knowing lilt to her voice.

"Maybe." I shrug. "But maybe I just want to dance."

"We should call Ollie and Courtney," she says once we've both changed and are back in the living room. I look up from where I'm checking my purse for all the necessities of a night out. "He called earlier, by the way. I forgot to tell you."

"Oh, hell. Did he want me to call him back?"

She shrugged. "He was just calling to check on you. Make sure Damien Stark didn't eat you up last night. Little did he know."

My cheeks warm. "You didn't tell him?"

"All I said was that you got home safe. That Stark put you in a limo and sent you home. I didn't share the dirty details. Should I have?" There's a mischievous gleam in her eye. "I bet Ollie would like that story."

"No," I say firmly. "No."

"So do we call them?"

"Why not?"

Courtney declines since she has to wake up early to go to some conference in San Diego, but Ollie is up for meeting us. We start out at Donnelly's, a pub near the house he's renting in West Hollywood, and move on to Westerfield's. "Don't worry," Ollie says as I eye the long line behind the red velvet rope. "I promise we'll glide right in."

I assume Ollie has some sort of suck with the guy at the door, but it turns out that my friend is relying on Jamie and me. The bouncer looks us up and down, and Jamie gives him her best *I'm so hot it should be criminal* look. "In," the guy says, and I can feel his eyes on my ass as we enter the dark, thrumming venue.

"This is crazy," I shout. "We can't even talk."

"Then dance!"

Jamie takes my hand and Ollie's and drags us onto the dance floor. I can feel the bass reverberating through my chest, and after a moment, I allow myself to get lost in the wild, pulsing sensation. Ollie and Jamie have both had a few more drinks than me, and they're totally into the music, doing a little bump and grind number that I'd worry about if I didn't know what good friends they are.

No, I think, what good friends *we* are. I ease my way between the two of them, hook my arms around their shoulders, and proceed to laugh my head off as we try to coordinate some sort of move that doesn't end up with the three of us falling on our asses. It's fun, but I'm sure we look ridiculous. I don't care, though. I'm in the midst of a total attitude adjustment. I'm there with my two best friends. I'm in Los Angeles. I have a great job. I've had two amazing orgasms in the last twenty-four hours, and I've fielded an offer worth one million dollars. Honestly, days like these don't come along that often.

"Drinks are on me," I say, realizing that I'm more than a little parched.

The bar is all the way in the back of the room, and when I arrive there, I realize why. It's infinitesimally quieter here, which means that the bartender doesn't have to know how to lip-read in order to hear the drink order. I'm standing there waiting to get the drinks back when Ollie approaches, his hair stuck to his forehead and his face red from the efforts of keeping up with Jamie on the dance floor.

"She wear you out?" I ask.

"Never," he says, and there's a devious little gleam in his eye. "She hit the ladies'. Thought I'd come find you. There's something I want to talk to you about."

"Okay." I frown, because this is hardly the best location for a heart-to-heart. "What's up?"

"Stark," he says. "I got the impression from Jamie that things between you two might be heating up."

I make a mental note to strangle Jamie.

"They're not," I say, not sure if I'm telling the truth or telling a lie. It's the first time I can remember not being completely honest with Ollie, but for the moment, I want to keep my complicated feelings about Damien Stark to myself.

"Yeah?" he says. "Well, good. Because I was worried about you."

Alarm bells ring in my head. "Really? Why?"

He lifts a shoulder in a shrug. "The way he looked at you at the party. The way you looked back."

"Okay, yeah, there was heat," I admit. "But why is that a problem? Why did you tell me to be careful?"

He runs his fingers through his hair, and the damp strands curl even more. It gives him a mussed, sexy look.

"Just stay away from him, okay? The guy's dangerous."

"Dangerous how?"

Ollie shrugs. "You know. He has a temper, for one thing."

"That's hardly news," I say. "He was famous for it during his tennis days. That's how he messed up his eye." During a fight with another player, Damien had been hit in the face with a racquet. According to the stuff I'd read, he'd been incredibly lucky that he'd suffered no permanent or debilitating injury, but the pupil of his left eye is now permanently enlarged. "But that was a long time ago, and he's not a competitive athlete anymore. Is that seriously what you're concerned about?"

But Ollie just shakes his head as Jamie bounces up to the bar and grabs his arm. "I'm taking him back," she says.

I watch them slide back onto the dance floor. *Dangerous*.

He's dangerous, all right. But somehow I don't think Ollie means it the same way that I do.

"Seriously, Jamie," I say, as she turns down yet another twisting, winding, darkened Malibu street. "Can't we just go home?" We are completely lost. The street signs have apparently been hidden by elves. I'm sure it's to keep the riff-raff out. And we, of course, are firmly among the riff.

We parted ways with Ollie over an hour ago after having eggs and toast and an ocean of coffee at Dukes on Sunset. Only after he'd gone did Jamie tell me that we were going on a mission to find Stark's new Malibu house. "One of the articles I read said it had beach access. And I used to hang with this guy from Malibu, so I got to know the roads pretty well."

I, of course, protested that she was insane. But I didn't protest too loudly. I admit I was curious. And even though I doubted we could find the place, driving around Malibu in the middle of the night seemed just crazy enough to be fun.

Now, however, I am getting tired and a little bit carsick.

"We might as well go home," I say. "We're never going to find it."

"We will," she insists, pulling over long enough to squint at the map she's pulled up on her phone. "If it has beach access there aren't that many streets it can be on. And it's not like there's a lot of construction going on right now, especially not for the square footage that a guy like Damien Stark will want. When we get close, we'll see it."

"Yeah, but that's part of the problem, isn't it? I mean, this isn't some two-thousand-square-foot house in suburban Texas where you can just wander through the framing and drywall. Even if you find it, there's going to be a fence and probably security."

"I just want to see," she says, edging back out onto the road. "Don't you? I mean, you can learn a lot about a guy from his taste in buildings, right?"

I don't answer. She and Ollie have made me think, and the truth is that I don't know a lot about Damien Stark. I know what the public knows. And I know a few truly intimate details. But the man himself? How much have I seen of the real Damien Stark?

I glance sideways at Jamie, and then the words are out without me even making a conscious decision. "Ollie says Stark is dangerous."

"Yeah," she says, surprising me. "He told me. He's worried about you."

"I'm fine," I say, sliding down in the seat and putting my bare feet up on the dash. I'm not going to pursue this. Ollie is just being overprotective. "Dangerous how?" I ask, ignoring all my wise counsel. "I'm not buying his line that it's all about Stark's temper."

"Temper? I don't think so. He wouldn't say exactly. I figure he knows something from work. Bender, Twain & McGuire reps Stark, you know. Their corporate department handles all his business stuff, and I guess the rest of the firm handles, you know, everything else."

"Oh." I consider that. "Attorney-client privilege?"

"I guess," Jamie concedes. "I mean, I don't think Ollie has worked on any of Stark's stuff directly, he's too junior. But he's probably seen files and heard the partners talking."

"But he didn't give you any idea what it's about?"

"Well, no. But it's pretty obvious, right?"

Not to me. "Obvious?"

"That girl. The one who died." She pauses at a stop sign and shifts in her seat long enough to glance at me.

"The one you said he dated? What about her?"

"I read a little bit more about it." She shrugs as I gape at her. "I was bored and I was curious. Anyway, she was asphyxiated. The coroner officially ruled it an accident, but I guess her brother's been hinting around that Stark was involved. . . ." She trails off with another shrug.

I feel cold. "He's saying that Damien killed her?" I try to process the thought, but it won't fit into my head. I don't believe it. I can't believe it.

"I don't think he's gone that far," Jamie says. "I mean, if Damien Stark's a murder suspect, that would be all over the news, right? And it really isn't. I just found a few comments on some crap-ass gossip sites. Honestly, I didn't think anything of it. A powerful guy like Stark must field all sorts of nutcase rumors." She drives in silence for a moment, and I watch as a frown creeps onto her face.

"What?"

"Nothing."

"Dammit, Jamie, what?"

"I was just thinking about Ollie. If it is just Internet bullshit, then why would he know any of this? But if there's really something to it, then Stark's lawyers must be all over the brother, you know? Threatening libel or slander or whatever the hell you call it. And a guy like Stark is probably pretty good at controlling the press, right?"

I remember that Evelyn said almost exactly the same thing and feel a little queasy. "I guess. Is that what Ollie told you?"

"No, no. He didn't say anything specific." She shrugs. "He's just worried about you. But honestly, Nik, it's probably nothing. Just the crap uber-rich guys have to deal with."

"So who's the girl?"

"Some socialite type. Sara Padgett."

Padgett. I remember Ms. Peters coming into the conference room during the meeting and mentioning that name.

Without warning, Jamie slams on the brakes and I lurch forward against my seat belt. "What the hell?"

"Sorry. I think I saw something on that street we just passed." She thrusts the car into reverse and careens backward on the winding canyon road.

I swivel in my seat, terrified that I'll see headlights approaching. But the road is dark, and we make the turn safely. By the time I'm facing forward again and ready to chew Jamie out for being so damn reckless, my anger is forgotten, pushed out of my mind by the sight of the incredible structure rising in front of me.

"Wow. Do you think that's his?"

"I don't know. It's not as big as I thought it would be," Jamie says. She pulls the car over to the side of the road, and we both get out and walk to the temporary chain-link fence that has been put up around the structure. A small metal plate identifies Nathan Dean as the architect. "It's his," Jamie says. "I remember that name from one of the articles. But shit, Stark is rolling in money. Shouldn't this be a mansion?"

"No," I say. "It's perfect."

As bazillionaire houses go, it probably is small. I'm guessing it's about ten thousand square feet. But it seems to rise from the hills as opposed to being plunked down on them. Any larger and it would overwhelm. Smaller, and it would be lost. Though still unpainted and raw, the stonework only half-finished, the overall essence of the home is clear. It suggests power and control, but there's also warmth and comfort. It's inviting. It's Damien.

And I think it's spectacular.

From our spot on the road, we stand slightly above the building. Guests will enter by a driveway that slopes down, giving the illusion of entering a private valley. There are other houses nearby, but none will be visible from the property itself.

All that is visible, in fact, is the ocean. The house is finished enough that I can tell there are no windows on the side facing inland. I can't see the side facing the ocean, but after seeing Damien's apartment and his office—and after hearing his description of the portrait he wants painted—I have no doubt that the west wall is made entirely of windows.

"A million dollars," Jamie says, and then whistles. "It's like winning the lottery."

She's right. A million dollars is everything to me. A million dollars is start-up capital. A million dollars changes my entire life.

Yeah, but there's that little problem. . . .

I slide my hand down the inner seam of the jeans I'd pulled on for our night on the town. Through the denim, I can barely feel them, but if I close my eyes I can easily picture the thick, brutal scars that mar both my inner thighs and my hips. "He wouldn't be getting what he thinks he's getting."

Her grin is wicked. "*Caveat emptor*, baby. Buyer beware."

And that's why I love Jamie.

I turn back to the house and try to imagine myself standing in front of those windows. The curtains. The bed. Everything as he described it—and Damien Stark with his eyes on me.

My whole body quickens at the thought, and I can no longer

deny how much I want this. Damien Stark has thrown me off-kilter, and part of me wants to punish him for it. At the very least, I want to regain the upper hand. Although perhaps "regain" is the wrong word. Where Damien is concerned, I'm not sure I ever had it.

"*Caveat emptor*," I repeat. And then I squeeze Jamie's hand and smile.

15

On Sunday, I am forced to face the most basic truth of my life: If I don't spend a few hours washing clothes, I'll be going to work naked.

"Carl would like it," Jamie says, when I tell her why laundry is my plan for the day.

"I'd rather not test that theory. You coming?" I have a laundry basket tucked under my arm and am leaning against her bedroom door. She looks around at the mishmash of clothing strewn across her floor and says cautiously, "I think most of this stuff is actually clean."

I shudder. "How is it that we're friends?"

"Yin and yang."

"Do you have any auditions next week?"

"Two, actually."

"Then rewash all that stuff, and I'll help you fold and iron. Because you are not going to an audition covered in cat fur." As if she can tell that I'm talking about her, Lady Meow-Meow lifts her head. She's curled up on a pile of black material that looks suspiciously familiar. "Is that my dress?"

Jamie flashes a guilty smile. "One of the auditions is for Sexy Girl in Bar and there's three lines of dialogue. I was going to have it dry-cleaned."

"Yang," I say wryly. "Come on. Let's go see if the machines are free."

The laundry room is connected to the pool deck, and once both our loads are going, we snag two lounge chairs. As I'm settling in, Jamie runs back upstairs without explanation. A few minutes later she returns with a tote bag slung over her shoulder and a bottle of champagne in her hand.

"We have champagne?"

She shrugs. "Got some at the store yesterday." She lifts her shoulder and glances down at the tote. "And orange juice." She untangles the metal cage, then places her thumbs and deftly wiggles the cork. A moment later, I'm jumping at the sound of the *pop* and then the *twang* of the cork slamming into the metal sign prohibiting glass in the pool area.

"Awesome," I say. "Did you think about cups?"

"I thought of everything," she says proudly, and proceeds to unpack the juice, the cups, a bag of chips, a jar of salsa, and a small plastic bowl.

"I love Sunday," I say, taking the mimosa that Jamie hands me and holding it up in a toast.

"No shit."

We settle down on our lounge chairs, sipping and talking about nothing in particular. Fifteen minutes later, I've finished my drink, Jamie's finished three, and we've made a blood pact to go to Target that very afternoon and buy a coffeemaker that brews coffee instead of swill.

That's apparently all the conversation Jamie can stand, because she closes her eyes, tilts back her head, and starts to soak up the sun.

I, however, am antsy.

I shift around on the lounge for a few minutes, trying to get comfortable. Then I give it up and go upstairs to fetch my laptop. I've been fiddling with a pretty simple iPhone app, and I run what I've coded so far through the simulator before settling into the fun part. But in the end I spend only a half hour or so with coding, declaring objects, synthesizing properties, and creating various subclasses. The day is just too lazy for even easy programming work. Besides, the glare from the sun makes it hard to see the screen. I shut down my computer and head back into the apartment, this time returning with my camera.

The pool area is not beautiful, but the cracked concrete and splashes of water make for some interesting close-ups. A flowering plant I don't recognize grows near the fence, and I grab a few petals and toss them in the pool, then lay on my stomach, trying to get a shot of only flowers and water, with no hint of concrete from the pool or the deck.

After a few dozen shots, I turn my attention to Jamie, trying to capture on film the way she looks at peace, in such contrast to her usual frenetic persona. I actually get some amazing shots. Jamie's got the kind of face that the camera loves. If she ever gets a break, I think she has a chance of actually getting work as an actress. But getting a break in Hollywood is about as common as, oh, being offered a million dollars for your portrait.

I almost laugh out loud. Now *there's* someone I'd love to photograph. I close my eyes and imagine light and shadow falling across the angles of that amazing face. A hint of stubble. A slight sheen of sweat. Maybe even his hair slicked back after a dip in the pool.

I hear a faint noise and realize it's me, moaning softly.

Beside me, Jamie stirs. I sit up straighter, trying to shake off the fantasy.

"What time is it?" The question's rhetorical, as she's picking up her phone to check the time even as she asks. I glance at the display. Not quite eleven. "I told Ollie he should come hang with us today," she says, her voice a little groggy. "I mean, it must suck with Courtney out of town, and I thought he had a good time last night, didn't you?"

"He looked to be," I say. "But you're the girl who can force anyone to have a good time on a dance floor."

"Ha! I was *so* not forcing him. That boy may not admit it, but he likes to dance." She peels off her T-shirt to reveal a pink bra that she apparently assumes will pass as a bathing suit top. "Do you think he'll come?"

I shrug. As much as I love Ollie, I don't really want brunch company. Going out would mean getting dressed. Staying in would mean cooking. "Call and ask."

"Nah. It's no big deal. If he comes he comes." She sounds suspiciously nonchalant.

I take a sip of my mimosa and shift on the chaise so I can see her better. "He wants me to wear a tux at the wedding," I say, stressing the last word. "Because I'll be his best man. When he gets married."

"Oh please, Nikki. I am not banging Ollie. Quit worrying."

"Sorry," I say, but I'm genuinely relieved. "Sometimes I think you need these little reminders."

"But were you serious about the tux? Because that's just so eighties. Or maybe the seventies? When did *Annie Hall* come out? That's the movie where Diane What's-Her-Face wore the men's clothes, right?"

"Diane Keaton," I say. "*Annie Hall*, and it's classic Woody Allen from 1977. Honestly, James, it won Best Picture. How can you not know this? You're the one who wants to work in Hollywood, not me."

"I want to work in Hollywood now. Not before I was born."

I'm sure there's a great comeback lurking out there—something about *Saw: Part 27*—but before I can articulate it, my cell phone rings. Jamie shoots me a smug look, satisfied to have gotten the last word.

I glance at the caller ID, silently swear, then push the button to answer the call. "Mother," I say, forcing myself to sound glad to hear from her. "How did you—" I see Jamie's guilty expression and know exactly how she got my number. I cough and backtrack. "How did you get so lucky to call when I actually have time to talk?"

"Hello, Nichole," she says, making me cringe. "It's Sunday morning. You should be at church trying to meet a nice man, but I had a feeling I'd catch you at home." For my mother, religion is on par with *The Bachelor*.

I can tell she's waiting for me to say something, but I never know what to say to my mother, and so I stay quiet. I'm actually proud of myself for managing the feat. It's taken a lot of years for me to reach this level of defiance. And being fifteen hundred miles away helps, too.

After a few moments, she clears her throat. "I'm sure you know why I'm calling." Her voice is low and serious. Have I done something? What could I have done?

"Um, no?"

I hear her suck in air. My mother is a stunningly beautiful woman, but there is a small gap between her two front teeth. A scout for some New York modeling agency once told her that the gap added character to her beauty, and if she wanted a career as a model, all Mother had to do was pack her bags and move to Manhattan. My mother eschewed the idea, stayed in Texas and got married. A proper lady was interested in a husband, not a career. But she never got the tooth fixed, either.

"Today is Ashley's wedding anniversary."

I feel Jamie's hand close over mine and realize that I'm clenching the arm of the chaise so tight it's a wonder the metal doesn't crumble. How typical of my mother to remember my dead sister's anniversary when she hardly ever bothered to remember her birthday when Ashley was alive.

"Listen, Mother. I have to go."

"Are you dating anyone?"

I close my eyes and count to ten. "No," I say, but an image of Damien fills my mind.

"Does that no mean yes?"

"Mother, please."

"Nichole, you're twenty-four years old. You're beautiful—assuming you haven't gotten even bigger in the hips—but you're not getting any younger. And with your—well, we all have flaws, but yours are so extreme, and—"

"Jesus, Mother."

"I'm simply saying that at twenty-four you need to be thinking about getting on with your life."

"That's what I'm doing." I lock eyes with Jamie, silently pleading for rescue.

Get rid of her, Jamie mouths.

Like that's easy . . .

"Mother, seriously, I have to go. There's someone at the door." I cringe. I'm a terrible liar.

Jamie scrambles off her chaise and sprints to the far side of the pool. "Nikki! Some guy's at the door! Holy fuck, he's gorgeous!"

I clap my hand over my mouth, not sure if I'm mortified or thrilled.

"Well, I'll let you go, then," my mother says. I can't tell if she actually heard Jamie. I think I hear a tiny bit of excitement in her voice, but I might just be imagining it. "Goodbye, Nichole. Kiss-kiss."

That's all it's ever been. Never *I love you.* Just *kiss-kiss,* and then she hangs up before I can even answer.

Jamie flops back down beside me, looking far too impressed with herself.

"Oh. My. God," I say. "Are you nuts?"

"That was priceless," she says. "Honestly, I wish I could have seen your mother's face."

I maintain my stern expression, but secretly I agree.

"Come on," Jamie says, standing up and gathering her things. "Let's go move our stuff to the dryer. And I'm still hungry. Wanna do pizza and a movie? How about *Annie Hall*? I hear it won an Oscar."

Jamie's not the least bit interested in *Annie Hall*, and she dozes off about fifteen minutes into the movie. To be honest, I'm not entirely sure if she's asleep or in a food coma from the six slices of pepperoni pizza she consumed within minutes of the delivery guy's arrival at our door.

Me, I love the movie, but that doesn't mean I've been paying attention. No, I've been thinking about Damien Stark. About his offer, the one that my mother would *so* not approve of.

The one I think I've decided to accept. I just need to ask Damien a couple of questions.

Be careful.

He's dangerous.

I don't believe it. Not really. Not the way Ollie means. But I need to know for sure.

Butterflies dance in my belly as I grab my phone off the charging station by the sofa and pad barefoot to my bedroom. My laundry, I realize, is still in the dryer. But my panties can wait.

I scroll back through my incoming calls and find his number. I hesitate only a second, and then I dial.

"Nikki," Stark says, before the first ring dies out. He sounds relieved to hear from me.

"What happened to Sara Padgett?" The question bursts out of me. I have to ask while I have the nerve.

I can feel the chill coming off Damien all the way through the phone line.

"She died, Nikki. But I believe you already knew that."

"I want to know how," I say. "And I want to know about the two of you. Your security got all riled up yesterday when someone named Padgett showed up. And if I'm going to—"

"What?"

I suck in a breath. "If I'm going to consider your very generous offer, I need to understand the kind of man I'm dealing with."

"Jesus." For a moment I hear only traffic noise. He must be in his car.

"Damien?"

"I'm here. This is bullshit, Nikki. You know that right?"

"No," I say. "I don't know shit because you're not telling me anything."

The words, when they come, sound grudging. "Sara Padgett and her brother, Eric, inherited a controlling share of an interesting little company called Padgett Enviro-Works from their father. The company had made their father quite wealthy, but it lost its edge after he passed away, and started spiraling downward. Eric was failing at management and Sara wasn't interested in the company at all. I saw an opportunity for growth and made an overture to buy their shares of stock."

He pauses as if waiting for me to comment, but I stay silent. I want to hear where this is going.

After a moment he continues, his words flat, as if he's reading from notecards. "They both declined my offer, but Sara asked if I would escort her to a charity function. I agreed. One thing led to another and we continued to see each other."

"Did you love her?"

"No. She was a friend. Her death was a horrible shock."

"It was an accident?"

"I can only imagine so. Apparently it looked like autoerotic asphyxiation that went very, very bad. The coroner ruled it an accident and that was that."

I run my fingers through my hair. I believe what he's told me—but I'm also certain that he hasn't told me everything. I consider just dropping it, but I can't. I have to know. "But there's more, isn't there? That's not the whole story."

"Why do you say so?"

"I—someone—I mean, a friend is worried about me." It's only fair he knows, right? "About me and you. He thinks you're dangerous."

"Does he?" Right then, the tone of Stark's voice sounds very, very dangerous. I close my eyes and hope that I somehow haven't gotten Ollie in trouble. Surely he can't know this is coming from Ollie. Can he?

"That's not the point," I say. "What else happened?"

"Her brother," he says flatly. "Somehow, Eric is convinced that I tied her up, choked her, and left her for dead, accidentally killing her. And he's just itching to go sell his story."

"Oh." I lick my lips. "That's horrible." No wonder he doesn't want to talk about it.

"So that's that. What do you think, Nikki? Am I dangerous?" The words are harsh. Angry. I'm thinking this may not be the best time to discuss his proposal.

"I'm really sorry. I shouldn't have brought it up. It's none of my business."

"No, it's not." Again, that pregnant silence. And then one sharp curse. "Dammit, Nikki. I'm the one who's sorry. Of course you'll hear rumors. Of course you have a right to ask questions. Considering what I'm asking, you can ask all the questions you want."

"You're really not mad?"

"At you, no. At Padgett—well, let's just say he's on my list."

I decide not to ask what list that might be.

"I hope you're still considering my offer," he says. "I very much want for you to say yes. I'm hoping it won't take too much longer for you to reach a decision."

"I've already decided," I blurt.

He's silent for so long, I think he hasn't heard me.

"Tell me," he finally says.

I swallow and nod, even though of course he can't see me. "I have conditions."

"So we're negotiating. Excellent. What are your terms, Ms. Fairchild?"

I've rehearsed this in my mind and my words spill out like a thesis presentation. "First of all, you need to understand that I'm doing this for the money. I need it, I can use it, I want it. So please keep that in mind. Your million dollars color all of my terms."

"I understand."

"I get paid no matter what, even if you end up not liking the painting."

"Certainly. The money is your fee. It has nothing to do with my satisfaction with the painting."

"You can't sell it. Not to anyone. It's either yours, or it's destroyed."

"So far your terms are satisfactory."

I pause and draw a breath because we're getting to the key points. "The artist has to paint me. *Me.* Not some artistic representation of me, but the real me."

"You are what I want, Nikki," he says, with the same tone of voice he'd used when he'd put his fingers inside me. *Tell me you like this.*

Yes. God, yes.

I cross and uncross my legs as I sit on the side of the bed. "Just making sure we understand each other, Mr. Stark. Once I take my clothes off, that's it. What you see is what you get."

"Be careful, Ms. Fairchild. You're making me hard."

"Dammit, Stark, I'm serious."

"Oh, I'm serious, too. Believe me."

I mutter a soft curse and hear him chuckle on the other end. "So we agree?" I ask, probably too sharply.

"To your terms? Absolutely. Of course, I have a few deal points of my own to address."

"Deal points?"

"Certainly. You've changed the original terms with a counteroffer. It's my privilege to do the same."

"Oh." I hadn't thought he'd change the original deal, but I realize now I should have.

"And let me be just as clear as you were, Ms. Fairchild. This is no longer a negotiation. These are my final terms. You agree, or you don't."

"Um, okay." I lick my lips and squirm some more. I'm suddenly very interested in what he has to say. "So what are the terms?"

"From now until the painting is completed, you're mine."

"Yours?" The word tastes like chocolate in my mouth. "What exactly does that mean?"

"What do you think it means?"

I open my mouth, but nothing comes out. I try again. "That I belong to you." My voice is a whisper. Hell, it's a prayer, and I'm surprised by how turned on I am by his words. I mean, I'd moved to LA to take control of my life, but here I am getting hot at the idea of putting myself in Damien's hands.

"What else?" he asks.

"That I do as you say." I slip my hand down between my legs and into my shorts. I'm wet, slick, and hot.

"Yes," Damien says. His voice is hard, tense. He's on edge, too, and that knowledge makes me even more turned on.

"And if I don't?"

"You studied science, Ms. Fairchild. Surely you're aware that every action has an equal and opposite reaction."

"Oh." I slide my finger over my sensitive clit, then gasp, not expecting the fast, hard tremor that shoots through me in release.

"You like that, Ms. Fairchild?" he asks.

My cheeks flame. I'm not sure if he means his terms or my orgasm. I draw myself up. "What if I don't agree?"

"Then I don't get my painting, and you don't get your million."

"Why make me agree? I've already said I'll pose."

"Because I can. Because I want you. Because I don't want to court my way up to our first fuck. And because I don't want to play games."

"Isn't a game exactly what you're playing?"

"A fair point, Ms. Fairchild. But I want this on my terms."

"You say you want me, but you don't. You say you want my portrait, but you won't."

For a moment, I hear nothing. Damien Stark is trying to figure out my angle. "You're wrong," he finally says.

"I don't think so. And that's why my terms are important. You call it off—the painting, this game—and I still get my money."

"Is that an agreement?"

"It's a condition."

"Very well. I accept your condition."

"And we don't start now. We start at the first session with the artist."

"You're a tough negotiator, Ms. Fairchild. But I accept your proposed commencement date."

I roll my eyes. He's getting weary of my tweaks to his deal. Well, too bad. "And it's not open-ended," I add. "For all I know, you're paying the artist by the hour, and he'll take a year to complete it. One week, Mr. Stark."

"One week?" He doesn't sound happy.

"That's my best offer. And, of course, you'll have to work

around my day job. But my evenings and the weekend are yours."

"Very well. One week. Now, do we have a deal?"

I want to say yes. Instead, I say, "What—what exactly do you want to do with me?"

"So many things, but mostly I want to fuck you. Hard and fast and very thoroughly."

Oh my.

"I—will it be kinky?"

He chuckles. "Would you like it to be?"

I don't know. "I'm not—I mean, I haven't ever." I feel my cheeks start to burn furiously. I've been out on a horrible number of first dates, courtesy of my mother, but have had only two real boyfriends. The first was more experienced than I was, and by that I mean that he'd dated a college girl even though we were in high school. But unless a fast fuck on top of his parents' pool table counts, there was nothing remotely kinky about our relationship. As for the second, there was definitely pain with Kurt, but only the emotional kind.

All in all, the types of things Damien might be talking about are outside my realm of experience.

Stark seems to understand my hesitation. "I want to give you pleasure," he says. "That's all I want to do. Will we do things that are kinky? You may think so. But I also think you'll like it."

I tremble, surprised by how much I want to know what things he wants to do with me. Under my tank top, my nipples are hard. Between my legs, my sex throbs. *I think you'll like it.* Yeah, I think so, too. Assuming we get that far. Assuming he doesn't call off the deal once he sees me naked.

I close my eyes wishing things were different. Wishing *I* was different.

"Take a chance, Nikki," he says softly. "Let me show you how far I can take you."

I draw in a breath, then let it out slowly. I remember our game in the limo. "Yes, sir," I finally say.

He sucks in air sharply. I've surprised him, and the thought thrills me. "Good girl," he says. Then, "Dear God, I want you now."

Me, too. "The first session, Mr. Stark," I say, but the tremble in my voice gives me away.

"Of course, Ms. Fairchild. I'll send a car for you tomorrow evening. I'll text you when it's on the way. Stay in tonight and relax. I want you refreshed. And open your door. There's something for you on the mat."

On my mat?

"Sweet dreams, Ms. Fairchild," he says, then clicks off before I can ask what he's talking about.

I hurry from my bedroom, passing Jamie who's still napping on the couch. I open the door to find a small box wrapped in silver paper.

I don't even bother taking it into the apartment, just tear off the paper and lift the lid. There's a stunning ankle bracelet inside. Diamonds and emeralds set in platinum and strung on a delicate chain. It sparkles in my palm, the weight negligible.

Beneath the bracelet, I find a handwritten note. *For our week. Wear this. D.S.*

Our week? He must have just written this. Must have just been *here,* outside the apartment.

The realization sends a shiver up my spine. I unclasp the latch, bend down, and hook it around my ankle. Then I stand up and look defiantly out toward the street.

I see a car, red and sporty and obviously expensive. I can't see through the tinted windows, but that doesn't matter. I am certain that it's Damien.

I watch, silently daring him to come to me. Or maybe I'm begging? I honestly don't know. But the car door doesn't open. The car doesn't move.

Our time hasn't begun.

Finally, I have reached my limit. I turn and go back into the apartment. I close the door and sag against it, feeling warm and edgy. But I'm smiling. Because out there in the world, Damien Stark is waiting for me.

16

I wake up when the sun coming through the blinds hits my face and I realize I forgot to set an alarm. Except for the diamond and emerald ankle bracelet, I'm naked under the covers. My hand is cupped between my legs, and I'm slick with desire.

I'd fallen asleep thinking about Damien, and I think I must have dreamed of him, too.

I roll over and grope for my phone—then immediately panic when I see that it's already after seven.

Shit.

Any lingering erotic fantasies dissolve. If I don't hurry, I'm going to be late for work.

I take a longer shower than I should, but I need it. The water is near scalding, and it pounds at my body, dissolving fantasies and desires. I need to be in work-mode now; Damien Stark has no place in my head.

I don't have time to blow-dry and style my hair, so I towel-dry it to dampness, then comb it out. It will air dry on the drive, and I can brush it out into its natural waves as I'm making the trek from my crappy parking place to the elevator.

Traffic is a bitch, and by the time I finally pull into that crappy parking place, I'm a bit bitchy myself.

I sling my bag over my shoulder, grab my brush, then furiously brush my hair as I stomp to the elevator on two-inch heels.

The receptionist, Jennifer, looks wide-eyed at me as I pull open the glass door to the C-Squared offices. I frown and do a quick mental check of my outfit, but as far as I can tell, everything is buttoned and zipped.

"Is he in?" I say. "I have an idea about tweaking one of the algorithms." Jennifer probably doesn't care, but it's one of those ideas that hits you like a blast furnace, and I want to talk it out with Carl and then get Brian or Dave crunching the numbers.

"He didn't call you?" Jennifer squeaks. "I thought for sure he would call you."

Something's very weird. "Why would he call?"

"He—oh, shit. Here. He said to give this to you." She hands me a thin envelope.

I don't want to take it, but I do. It seems to weigh a thousand pounds. "Jennifer," I say very slowly. "What is this?"

"It's your check. And that's your stuff." She cocks her head to indicate something behind her. For the first time, I notice the copy paper box filled with my personal things. Jennifer bites her lower lip.

"I see." I square my shoulders. "You never answered my question. Is he in?" I am not going to cry or lose my temper in front of Jennifer. But I am damn well going to talk to Carl.

She nods, then shakes her head. "No. I mean, yes, he's here. But he said he wouldn't see you. I'm sorry, Nikki, but he was really, really clear on that. He said that if you didn't just take your stuff and go, that I'm supposed to call security."

I feel numb. *This is shock. I'm in shock.* "But why?"

"I don't know. Honest." Jennifer looks like she's in physical pain, and even though I want to melt into the carpet, I feel sorry for her. And pissed at Carl. What a fucking coward to make the receptionist fire me.

"He didn't say anything?"

"Not to me. But I think it has something to do with the pitch."

"The pitch?" My voice is a squeak. "But it went great."

"Really? Because Stark called first thing this morning and told Carl he wasn't going to invest."

My stomach roils. "You're serious?"

"You really didn't know?"

"I really didn't." *But I think I know why I was fired.*

I'm in a weird kind of fog as I take my stuff down to my car. I drop the box in the trunk, but I don't get in the car. It's only when I'm halfway across the parking level that I realize I'm on my way to Stark Tower.

Since it's not the weekend, I don't need to sign in with Joe. But I stop by the security desk anyway since I have no idea what floor the reception area for Stark International is on.

"Thirty-five," Joe says.

"Thanks. Do you happen to know if Mr. Stark is in today?" I am amazed at how calm my voice sounds.

"I believe so, Ms. Fairchild."

"Great," I say, surprised he remembers my name.

I hurry to the proper elevator bank and drum my fingers on my leg as I wait for the car to arrive. Finally, it comes and I pile on with a half dozen other people. The car seems to stop at every floor, until I'm the only one left for the final leg of the journey. The car stops on thirty-five, the doors glide open, and I step out into another well-appointed reception area, my heart pounding so hard I'm surprised I haven't cracked a rib.

A young woman with curly red hair smiles at me from behind a polished desk. "Ms. Fairchild? Welcome to Stark International. If you'll follow me, I'll take you to Mr. Stark's office."

"I—what? Oh . . ." I am a stuttering mess. This isn't what I'd scripted when I rode up. I'd intended to demand to see him, refusing to leave reception until he spoke to me and explained himself. And for that matter, how does this woman know who I am?

I would ask her, but she's already leading me through a set of frosted glass doors. We've entered yet another reception area, this one done in a contemporary style. There are photographs on the wall featuring waves, mountains, tall redwood trees. There's even a close-up of a bicycle tire, a winding road visible through the spokes. Each is artistically composed, with such precise and startling perspectives, that I'm certain they were all taken by the same photographer. I shove my irritation aside long enough to wonder who took them. Damien, perhaps?

Another girl sits behind another desk. This one is a brunette, with a short pixie cut. She also smiles at me. "Ms. Fairchild," she says as she pushes a button on her desk. "You can go on in."

The woman who escorted me leads us forward as a set of beautifully polished wooden doors swing open in front of me revealing the impressive form of Damien Stark. Today, there's nothing casual about his outfit. He speaks into a headset as he paces behind his desk in a perfectly tailored double-breasted suit in a dark pewter over a crisp white shirt. The outfit is pulled together with a red tie and onyx cuff links. The sheen from the material reflects some of the light coming in from the window behind him, making Stark look like he's radiating heat and power. It's an outfit meant to intimidate and impress, and I have to admit that it works.

"Go ahead and have a seat," my escort says. "He'll be with you in a moment." Then she's gone, the doors swinging shut behind her.

I don't sit, but stand right in front of his desk, my arms crossed over my chest. I want to hold on to my anger, but it's hard, because Stark is right there, and I've already learned that just being in the same room with him makes my head go all fuzzy. I think it's because when I'm close to him, all the air seems to vanish.

"I'm looking at the quarterlies right now," Stark says, snatching a sheaf of papers from his desk. It's huge, and every inch of desktop is covered with papers. From where I stand, I see neat stacks of magazines—*Scientific American, Physics Today, Air & Space,* even the French *La Recherche.* Charts and graphs are spread out in the middle, both marked up with handwritten notes made with red and blue pencil. A stack of correspondence rests on the far side of the desk, the corner of the pile held down with a battered copy of Isaac Asimov's *I, Robot.*

"I'm not interested in excuses," Stark continues. "I'm interested in hard, cold numbers. Yes, well, tell him that the time to ply me with projections was when he pitched the project in the first place. And the time for excuses is never. If he can't live up to the schedule we agreed to, then I'll put in my own team. Hell yes, I have that right. No? Well, have him read the contract again. Then we'll talk. Fine. No, I think this conversation is over. All right, then."

He clicks off, and turns to me, and it's as if I'm watching a computer graphic of a man shifting into the form of another. The executive seems to melt before me, leaving only the man. Albeit one insanely sexy man in a tailored business suit that probably cost more than Jamie's condo.

"What a wonderful surprise," he says as he crosses the room, his long strides bringing him right in front of me. He looks so cool, so fucking *innocent* that the anger that had been fading spews back up like hot lava out of a volcano.

"God*damn* you," I snap as I lash out and slap him hard across the cheek, shocking myself as much as him.

The way his expression shifts from pleasure to shock to anger and then, finally, to confusion would be amusing if I didn't feel so sick to my stomach.

"Oh, God," I say. "I'm sorry." I'm speaking from behind my hand, which I've pressed to my mouth. "I'm so, so sorry."

"What the fucking hell?" he asks. His body is rigid and his eyes are burning. The amber one seems to hold some compassion, but the dark black one looks like it could suck me down, down, down. *Dangerous,* I think. *Ollie's right. That temper is dangerous.*

"Carl fired me. Don't even pretend like you didn't know."

"I didn't," he says. The tension leaves his body. "Fuck, Nikki, I swear that I didn't, though I probably should have expected it." He reaches for my hand, and I'm numb enough that I let him take it. He presses his lips to my fingertips, and the contact is so gentle and sweet it makes me want to cry. "I'm so sorry."

"Why did you say no? The proposal was amazing. The product is amazing. You were impressed—I know you were. And now Carl thinks that I snubbed you or fucked you or otherwise got under your skin enough that you want to get back at me through him."

"He told you that?"

"He hasn't told me shit. He didn't even have the balls to fire me himself. But I'm not an idiot. I know what it looks like and what he must think."

"You have gotten under my skin," he says. "But that's not why I said no."

"Then why did you? I mean, come on, Damien. It's a damn good product."

"It is." He pulls a small device out of his pocket. It takes me a second to realize it's a remote control. He pushes a button and the room grows dark as the lights dim and the windows shift from clear to opaque.

"What are you—" But I don't bother to finish the question. A menu appears on a drop-down screen. Damien scrolls down to select one entitled *Israeli Imaging 3IYK1108-DX.*

A moment later, a grainy image appears. It's difficult to see everything, but it's clear that what Damien's showing me is a product similar to the one Carl pitched.

"An Israeli company called Primo-Tech has already received a patent on a similar product. They have a marketing plan in place, and they're deep into beta testing. They expect to roll out the full product next month."

I shake my head. "Carl doesn't know anything about this."

"No? Well, maybe he doesn't. Or maybe he was hoping that I would invest so that there would be enough capital behind his product to beat Primo-Tech in the marketplace."

I look at him. Carl can be a shit, but surely he wouldn't do that. Would he?

"I don't play those kinds of games, Nikki. When I invest, it's because I have a clear path in the market. I said no to C-Squared because of the Primo-Tech product. It has nothing to do with you."

I nod. "I'm glad to hear it."

"Would you like me to explain that to Carl?"

"Hell no. I don't want to work for a man who jumps to those kinds of conclusions."

"Good." He looks me up and down, a smile tugging at the corners of his mouth.

"What?"

"Nice suit."

It's an innocent compliment, but it doesn't sound innocent at all. I notice that the lights in the room are still dim and bite my lip in nervous anticipation.

"Not that I like to see you unemployed, but this works out well. Your day job was interfering with my plans for you."

"Oh." My mouth is dry. I swallow. "Yes, well, I'm hardly joining the ranks of the idle masses. I'll need to find a new one."

"Why?"

"I have this thing about eating and paying my rent. I'm just wacky that way."

"In case you forgot, you'll have a cool million in a week. For that matter, if you need money now, I'm happy to advance you a portion."

"No, thanks. That money's going into the bank. I'm not spending a dime until I'm ready."

"Ready?"

I shrug. I know Damien could help me launch a start-up, but I'm not ready to share that dream with him. Not yet.

"Secrets, Ms. Fairchild?" His voice is playful. He moves closer, so that I have to tilt my head up to look at him. "Shall I beg you to tell me what you intend for my money?"

"*Your* money, Mr. Stark? I don't think so. I'm earning every last penny."

"Oh yes," he says. His low, sensual voice curls through me. "You most definitely are."

His thumb grazes my lower lip and my breath hitches. Beneath my thin blouse, my nipples are stiff against the lace of my bra. I want to draw his thumb into my mouth and suck on it. I want to slide my tongue over it and listen as Damien moans. I want to feel his hands on me, our bodies pressed together, his erection straining against the expensive weave of his tailored slacks.

I want it, but I don't take it.

Instead, I back away. "Our time hasn't started yet, Mr. Stark," I say.

His eyes burn with dark fire, and then he laughs, the sound as smooth as fine whiskey. "You're a tease, Ms. Fairchild."

"Am I? Well, I guess you'll have to punish me."

He sucks in a sharp breath, and I flash a seductive smile. I'm playing a dangerous game, but right then I don't care. I feel powerful, and I like it.

"Nikki . . ." His voice is raw and needy and I feel the quickening in my belly, the tightening in my thighs. I want his hands on me, and I feel my resolve weakening.

I'm saved by the sharp buzz of his intercom. "Mr. Maynard on line two."

"Thank you, Sylvia."

He holds up a finger, signaling me to wait, then taps his earpiece. "Charles," he says. "Give me an update."

He listens for a moment. "No," he says, and I'm certain that he's just interrupted Mr. Maynard. "You know damn well that I'm not interested in playing games or idle threats. I will file a defamation action if this goes any further. Make sure he understands that. Yes, of course I realize that. No, Charles, I'm not concerned about how difficult our case might be, I'm interested in stopping the son of a bitch. Well, then I guess you'll just have to bill me for all those extra hours, sounds like a win-win as far as your firm is concerned." His expression hardens. "Well, if he digs that up, then I'll really have to play hardball." He listens for a moment, then frowns. "No, you know she wouldn't. You took care of the new facility?" He nods, his expression weary. "Just make this go away, Charles. That's what I'm paying you for."

He hangs up without saying goodbye. I can feel his tension.

I'm tense, too. I'm certain the call was about Sara Padgett and her brother. "Do you want to talk about it?"

He looks at me, but it's as if I'm not even here. "No. It's just business."

I press my lips together, forcing myself to keep silent. After a moment, he seems to shake it off. He smiles slowly, then reaches for my hand. "Come with me."

Hesitantly, I twine my fingers with his. "Where are we going?"

"Lunch," he says.

"But it's not even ten yet."

His grin is boyish. "That should be just enough time. . . ."

17

We take Damien's private elevator down to the parking level, and when the doors open, I recognize the red sports car from last night. I glance sideways at Damien. "Nice car. Looks familiar. Probably a lot of them in Los Angeles, huh?"

"Hundreds, I'm sure," he says dryly.

I don't know much about cars, but I can tell this one is sweet. It's cherry red and polished to a mirror shine. The windows are tinted as dark as a limo. It's so low to the ground that I'm afraid my ass will get bruised if we hit a pothole. It's sleek and beautiful and definitely the kind of toy I'd expect a billionaire to own.

"What?" he says, seeing my smile.

"You're predictable, that's all."

His brows lift. "Am I?"

"What is this, some kind of fancy Ferrari? I mean, what billionaire doesn't own a Ferrari?"

"Ah, it's much worse than that," he says. "This is a Bugatti Veyron. It costs about twice as much as a Ferrari. Nine hundred eighty-seven horsepower, a W16 engine, top speed of two hundred fifty-three, and she'll go from zero to sixty in under three seconds."

I force myself to look unimpressed. "In other words, you don't own a Ferrari?"

"I own three." Before I can react, he grins and presses a soft kiss to my forehead. "Watch your head getting in. She's low to the ground."

He opens my door, and I slide in. The all-leather interior smells amazing, and the seat hugs me like—well, I don't know like what, but I could get used to it.

"Where are we going?" I ask, as he gets in behind the wheel.

"Santa Monica."

The beachside town is maybe thirty minutes away, and that's only if we hit a ton of traffic. "Oh. So we're having an early lunch?"

"The Santa Monica Airport," he clarifies. "That's where I keep the jet hangared."

"Of course it is." I lean back in the seat and decide I'm either going to have heart palpitations or just go with it. The latter seems healthier. And more fun. "And we're taking the jet where?"

"Santa Barbara," he says.

"Really? With this car, I'd think we'd just drive."

"If I didn't have a meeting at three, we would." He presses a button on the steering wheel and the car fills with a dial tone, then begins to ring.

"Yes, Mr. Stark?"

"Sylvia, I'm taking the Bombardier out. Call Grayson and get her ready and put in a flight plan for me to Santa Barbara."

"Of course. Shall I arrange for a car to meet you at SBA?"

"Yes. And let Richard know I'm coming. We'll be dining on the terrace."

"Consider it done. Enjoy your lunch, Mr. Stark."

He clicks off without saying goodbye.

"She sounds efficient."

"Sylvia? She is. I expect only two things from my employees, loyalty and competence. Sylvia excels at both."

I am, I realize, slightly jealous of Sylvia and her pert smile and pixie cut hair sitting right there outside Damien's office every single day. It's a stupid, petty emotion and I'm ashamed to even entertain it. I console myself with an even pettier truth—that I'm the one he's taking to lunch.

"Looks like traffic is with us," he says as he pulls onto the relatively clear Interstate 10. He hits the accelerator, and I immediately see that he didn't lie. The car is sweet and it rockets up to sixty before I even have time to draw in a breath.

"Wow," I say.

Beside me, he's grinning like a teenager. "I'd really open her up, but the cops tend to get testy."

"Why buy a car like this if you can't drive her fast?"

He glances sideways at me. "Spoken like a true pragmatist. I didn't say I never drive her fast. But I'm not willing to risk your life—or the lives of any of the other commuters stuck out here on the 10."

"I appreciate the courtesy."

"But if you're interested, we can take her out to the desert one day and I'll show you what she can do."

"Show me? I can't drive her?"

He eyes me with interest. "You know how to drive a stick?"

"I bought my Honda my second semester at UT," I say. "It had decrepit upholstery, primer instead of paint, and a standard transmission. I replaced the upholstery, painted it on the cheap, and learned how to work a clutch." I'd been damn proud, too. When my mother had cut off the flow of money, she'd also taken my BMW. I'd wanted wheels, and I'd scraped together just shy of fifteen hundred dollars to get the Honda. It was a total piece of shit, but it was all mine, and it's still chugging along.

"In that case, maybe you can drive her." I hear the heat in his voice. "If you're very, very good."

"To have all this power beneath me?" I say, pitching my voice low and breathy. "I think that's incentive."

Beside me, Damien groans. "Jesus, Nikki. I thought we were trying to avoid a traffic accident."

I laugh, feeling sexy and powerful. It's one hell of a nice feeling.

Despite not going close to three hundred miles per hour, it takes almost no time to get to the Santa Monica Airport. Damien pulls up in front of a hangar beside a futuristic-looking jet with wings that seem to extend forever from the belly of the plane and bend upward at ninety-degree angles at each end.

"Wow," I say. I glance around and see an older man with graying hair and a beard striding toward us. "Is that Grayson? Is he the pilot?"

"That is Grayson," Damien says. "And he's the mechanic, flight guru, and all-around grease monkey. Good morning, Grayson. She all ready to go?"

"That she is. Great day for it, too."

"Grayson, this is Nikki Fairchild, my date for the afternoon."

"It's a pleasure," he says, shaking my hand.

"How long have you been flying?" I ask him.

"Over fifty years," he says. "My dad used to take me up in his Cessna when I was a little thing and let me control the stick." He passes a clipboard to Damien, along with something that looks like a test tube. "She's fueled up and ready, but I know you're going to give her your own once-over."

"My bird, my responsibility."

He takes the clipboard, then walks to the plane. He checks the pressure in the tires, then circles the jet, pausing occasionally to open something so that liquid can drip into the tube.

"What's he doing?"

"Checking for water in the fuel and for fluid in the lines," Grayson says. "I've been prepping planes for him for five years now, and he's never once not double-checked me."

"Isn't that a little annoying?"

"Hell, no. It's the sign of a good pilot, and Damien Stark is a damn good pilot. I ought to know. I'm the one who taught him."

"Pilot," I repeat, as Damien returns and passes the tube back to Grayson. "You're flying?"

"I am," he says. "Ready?"

I glance at Grayson, who chuckles. "You're in good hands."

"Very good," Damien says, but I have a feeling he's not talking about flying. Or, at least, not about flying in jets.

The access stairs are already down, and Damien gestures for me to go first. I climb up and find myself in a cabin so fine it makes commercial first class look like prison. I aim myself at one of the seats, only to feel Damien's hand on my arm holding me back. "We're going left," he says, and I follow him into the cockpit. Still polished and shiny, but this is a workplace, not an area to kick back with music and a cocktail.

He gets me settled into my seat, then gives the belt a tug, making sure I'm nice and snug before seating himself. "Why not let Grayson fly?" I ask. "Isn't it a shame to forgo all that luxury and have to do all the hard work?"

"I have comfortable chairs and cocktails on the ground. Flying is where the thrill is."

"All right," I say. "Thrill me."

His grin is wolfish. "I intend to, Ms. Fairchild. In the air, and when we're back safely on the ground."

Oh . . .

He puts on a headset and checks in with the tower. Then we're taxiing to the runway and Damien is maneuvering the plane into position. "Ready?" he asks, and I nod. I hear the power build before I feel it, and then suddenly we're moving, racing down the runway. Damien's hands are on the wheel, firm and in control. And then he pulls back and I feel the ground fall away beneath us. I'm leaning back in my seat and we're flying.

I gasp. "Wow." I'm no stranger to commercial airplanes, but

somehow the whole experience is different when you're sitting in the copilot seat.

We climb for a while, with Damien talking back and forth with the tower. Then we level off. When I look out, I see the California coastline far below us, and the mountains rising in the distance. "Wow," I say again, then rummage in my purse for my iPhone. I take a few snapshots, then turn to Damien. "I wish I'd known we were going to do this. I'd love to get some real shots."

"I doubt you could get anything decent through the glass. Grayson keeps it clean, but it's still going to cause some distortion."

He's right, and I feel a little better about the missed opportunity.

"Do you shoot digitally or on film?" he asks. Now that we're in the air, it's surprisingly quiet.

"Film," I say. "My camera's pretty old."

"Do you develop your own film?"

"No." I shudder involuntarily and hope that Damien won't notice. Of course, he does.

"I didn't realize that was such a loaded question."

"I'm not crazy about small, dark spaces," I admit.

"Claustrophobia?"

"I guess. It's being enclosed in the dark, mostly." I lick my lips. "And locked rooms. I don't like feeling trapped." I look down and realize I'm hugging myself.

He reaches over and presses a gentle hand to my thigh. I close my eyes and concentrate on steadying my breathing. It's easier now that I have his touch to center me.

"Sorry," I finally say.

"You don't have anything to apologize for."

"I should be over it. It's stupid. Just childhood crap, you know?"

"Things that happen in childhood stay with you," he says,

and I remember what Evelyn said about shit being piled onto him when he was a boy. Maybe he does get it. And right then, I want to share. I want him to see that there's an explanation for my quirks. Maybe I think that without a reason, I just look weak, and I don't want to seem weak to Damien Stark.

Or maybe I just want him to truly know me.

I don't know, and I don't want to wallow in self-analysis. I just want to say the words. "My mother had me competing in pageants from the time I was four," I say. "She was strict about a lot of things, but the one we battled the most on was me getting my beauty sleep."

"What did she do?" he asks. His voice is gentle, but clipped, as if he's holding on tight to control.

"At first, she just told me lights out at whatever time she set for my bedtime. Always at least two hours before my friends. I was never tired, so I'd go to bed, turn out the lights, then pull out a flashlight and play with my stuffed animals. When I got older, I'd read. She caught me one too many times."

He doesn't say anything, but I can feel the heaviness in the air between us. He's anticipating my next words.

"She started searching my room. Taking away my flashlight. Then she moved my bedroom to an interior room so that I didn't have a window, because there was some light that crept in from a streetlamp, and she'd read somewhere that you can only truly sleep well if you're in pitch-black." I lick my lips. "And then she put a lock on my door. From the outside. And had an electrician move the light switch to the outside, too." I'm damp with sweat, wondering if I should have started talking about it, because even though the sky is bright outside the windows, the darkness feels like it's pressing in around me.

"Your father did nothing?" The anger in Stark's voice is palpable.

"I don't know my dad. They divorced when I was a baby. He

lives somewhere in Europe now. I almost told my grandfather once, but I never quite worked up the courage before he died."

"That horrific bitch." He spits out the word, and though I completely agree, I can feel social niceties rising to my lips, as if I have to find excuses for my mother.

I tamp them down. "My sister tried to help." I smile as I remember the way Ashley used to shine a light under the crack in my door and read me stories until I got sleepy. At least until our mother found out.

"She didn't have to have her beauty sleep, too?"

"She didn't win enough, so my mom eventually quit entering her in pageants." The freedom had given Ashley time. It had given her back her life. I had adored my big sister, who'd always been my guardian angel, but I'd been incredibly jealous, too. I used to think she was the lucky one.

And then she'd killed herself.

I shiver. "I really don't want to talk about it anymore," I say.

He doesn't acknowledge my words, but after a moment he speaks again. "I thought I knew a bit about photography, but I guess I know less than I thought. I always assumed some light was allowed in."

I glance sideways at him, grateful for his discretion. He's stepped away from my personal issues with the dark, but kept the thread of our original conversation. "At a certain point in the process, yes," I say, letting my fears and memories fade under the weight of a subject I love. "And a red or amber safelight is common when making black and white prints because most of the papers are sensitive only to blue or blue-green light. But if you're working with color like I usually do, then the prints need to be kept in total darkness until they're properly fixed."

I shrug. "It's really not a big deal. Access to a darkroom is expensive and doing your own developing eats up a lot of time. One of these days I'll get a digital camera, but in the meantime,

I send my film out and get back a contact sheet along with all the pictures on disk. Then I sit down and play with the images in my native environment."

"The computer?" he asks, grinning.

"Ever since I got my first one at age ten," I confirm. I don't tell him that the computer was my escape. I could turn it on and tell my mother I was doing homework, then lose myself in games and later in writing my own code. For a week or so, I'd even used the screen as a nightlight, but my mother caught on. My mother never missed a thing.

"Doing photographic work on the computer is like holding magic in your hand," I say. "I mean, I could take a picture of you and then find stock footage of the surface of the moon and make it look like you're standing in space." I grin wickedly. "Or I could put your head on the body of monkey."

"I'm not sure that would show me off to my best advantage."

I have to agree. "No, it wouldn't."

"That's one of the apps you have for sale, isn't it?" he asks.

I blink, surprised he knows about that. I've designed, coded, and am selling three smartphone apps across various platforms. I designed them while I was at UT, though not for any particular class. Turns out there's actually a market for apps that allow you to paste a headshot onto a provided stock animal photo, then share the new image across various social media.

"How did you know about that?" I ask. That app is reasonably popular, but it's not bringing in so much money that it would be on Stark's radar.

"I make it a point to know everything I can about the things I care about." He's looking at me as he speaks, and there's no mistaking that he means me and not the app. I don't know why I'm surprised. Damien never misses a thing, either.

I smile, feeling flattered but also exposed. I can't help but wonder what other things he knows about me. How deep has he looked? Considering the resources at Damien Stark's disposal, he could have looked pretty damn deep, and that truism gives me pause.

If he notices my mood this time, he ignores it. "I've always thought of science as magic, too," he says, returning to the thread of our conversation. "Though not just computer science."

"I was pretty impressed with your questions during the pitch," I say. His questions had covered the technical aspects of the software design as well as the anatomical components, reflecting an understanding of both tech and basic anatomy. "What did you study in college?"

"I didn't go to college," he says. "For that matter, I didn't go to school. I had private tutors from the time I was ten. My coach insisted, and my father agreed."

An unfamiliar edge sharpens his voice, and although I want to know more, it's clear I've stumbled upon a sore subject. "So, do you know much about photography?" I ask, grappling for a shift in the conversation. I remember the photos in his reception area. "Did you take the pictures outside your office?"

"I know just enough to be dangerous," he says lightly, and I'm glad of the change in mood. "And no. I tried to find photos that represent my hobbies. Those are done by a local photographer. He has a studio in Santa Monica, actually."

"He's very skilled. His use of contrast and perspective is stunning."

"I agree, and I'm flattered you thought I might be the photographer."

I shift in my seat to look at him better. "Well, you are a remarkably talented man. And very full of surprises."

His decadent grin is pure Damien, promising more surprises to come, and I feel an answering tingle between my thighs.

I drop my eyes and clear my throat. "Your hobbies, huh? So there were photographs of the ocean, some mountains, redwoods, and a bike tire. I'm guessing sailing, skiing, I have no idea, and biking."

"Not bad. The ocean represents diving and the trees are for hiking. Other than that, you got it right. Any of those appeal to you, Ms. Fairchild?"

"All of them," I admit. "Although I've never tried diving. Not many opportunities in Texas."

"California has excellent diving," he says. "Though a wetsuit is a bit cumbersome. I much prefer the warmer waters of the Caribbean. There," he says, pointing out the window.

It takes me a second to switch gears, but then I see that he's pointing to Santa Barbara.

"I'll need to put her into the landing pattern soon, but why don't you take control for a bit."

"What?" I clear my throat and try that again without squeaking. "I'm sorry, but *what*?"

"It's easy," he says, releasing his hold on the wheel. He reaches over and takes my hand. The contact burns through me—why do I feel this man's every touch so intensely? Right then, I wish I didn't, because he's putting my hands on the wheel and I'm supposed to keep this plane in the air, and he's making it really hard to concentrate.

"Oh, fuck," I say as he lets go of my hand. "Shit, Stark! What am I supposed to do?"

"You're doing it. Just keep her steady. Push in, we descend. Pull out, we climb. Go ahead, pull out gently."

I do nothing.

He laughs. "Go on. Give it a try."

This time I do, and then gasp with pleasure as the plane responds to my command.

"I like that sound," Damien says. "I think I need to hear that sound on the ground." He puts his thumb on my cheek and strokes it softly. This time, I try very hard not to make a sound. "There you go, baby. Okay, steady it out."

His hand grazes down my neck and rests on my shoulder. He squeezes it lightly. "Good job."

My breathing is coming fast, and I'm not sure if it's the ex-hilaration from the flight or from the man. "I am flying," I say. "I am really flying."

"Yes," he says. "And you will again."

We're the only guests on the terrace dining area at the Santa Bar-bara Pearl Hotel on Bank Street. We're just a few blocks from the ocean, and from where we sit, we can see the pier at Stearns Wharf and, in the distance, the Channel Islands rising like sea creatures from the water.

I'm sipping a white chocolate martini, and I'm pleasantly full after a lunch of raw oysters and stuffed salmon. "This is amaz-ing," I say. "How did you find this place?"

"It wasn't difficult," he says. "I own the hotel."

I don't know why I'm surprised. "Is there anything you don't own, Mr. Stark?"

He reaches out and takes my hand. "At the moment, every-thing I want is mine."

I take a sip of the martini to hide my reaction.

"Don't worry, Ms. Fairchild. I take very good care of the things I own."

My cheeks flush, and I'm suddenly very aware of my body, especially the parts below my waist. I savor the feeling, because the truth is that I'm a little afraid he's going to want to back out of our deal once he gets a full view of the condition of the mer-chandise.

A man in a tailored suit steps onto the terrace and approaches us. He's carrying a white shopping bag, which he hands to Damien. "This just arrived for you, Mr. Stark."

"Thank you, Richard."

As Richard leaves, Damien passes me the bag. "I believe this is for you."

"Really?" I put the bag in my lap, peer into it, and gasp. It's a Leica, shiny and new.

I look to Damien and see his wide, delighted grin. "You like? It's digital. Top of the line."

"It's wonderful." I laugh. "You're amazing, Mr. Stark. You just blink and things happen."

"A bit more than a blink, but it was worth the extra effort. How else will you get shots of the beach today?"

I stand and walk to the edge of the terrace. "I can see the ocean from here, but not much of the beach."

"The view will be better when we're walking on it."

I lift my foot and show off my pumps with the two-inch heels. "I don't think I'm dressed for the occasion."

The ankle bracelet sparkles in the sun. He runs his finger over it, the heat from his skin radiating over mine.

"It's beautiful," I say.

"Beauty for beauty," he replies. "The emeralds match your eyes."

I smile, delighted. "I'm feeling showered with gifts lately."

"Good. You deserve to be. And that's not a gift," he says, brushing his finger over the bracelet. "It's a bond . . . and a promise." He's looking right at me as he speaks, and my cheeks heat with a blush.

"I don't want to miss walking on the beach with you," I admit. My words come out a whisper. "I can go barefoot."

He chuckles. "You could. But have you looked under the camera box?"

"Under?" I go back to the table and pull out the box. Sure enough, there's something else there, wrapped in blue tissue paper. I look at him, but his expression gives nothing away. Slowly, I pull out the tissue paper. Whatever's hidden is flat and firm. I peel back the paper until I reveal a pair of black flip-flops. I look up at Damien and grin.

"For walking on the beach," he says.

"Thank you."

"Anything you want. Anything you need."

"Not everything can be bought," I say.

"No," he agrees, and he's looking hard at me. "But I stand by my promise."

His words twist deliciously inside me, and I'm saved from answering by our waiter's entrance. We return to the table for coffee and a chocolate lava cake that is so perfect I wish I'd let Damien order two instead of insisting that I only wanted a few bites.

"What else did you do this weekend?" I ask him.

"I worked."

"Earn another billion?"

"Not quite, but the time was profitable. And you?"

"Laundry," I admit. "And we went dancing Saturday night."

"We?"

"Ollie," I say. "And my roommate, Jamie."

His expression is tense. Is that jealousy? I think maybe it is, and I'm just petty or vain or something enough to be a little bit glad of that.

"Shall I take you dancing this week?"

"I'd like that," I say.

"Where did you go with Jamie and Ollie?"

"Westerfield's," I tell him. "It's that new place on Sunset close to the St. Regis."

"Mmm." He looks thoughtful. I'm guessing that loud clubs aren't his thing.

"Too wild for you?" I ask. "That harsh beat? Those bright lights?" I know he's only thirty, but he usually seems so much older. I wonder if he belongs to a ballroom dancing club. Surely they have those in Los Angeles. I consider the idea, thinking of all the movies I've watched with Fred Astaire and Ginger Rogers. Yeah, I could handle dancing like that in Damien's arms.

"Did you like Westerfield's?"

"I did. But, you know, I just left college, and Austin has a lot of clubs. So the loud music and the heavy beat don't really—" I stop, suddenly aware of the amused expression on his face. I feel my shoulders slope as I figure it out. "You own the place, don't you?"

"As a matter of fact, I do."

"Hotels. Clubs. What happened to your little technology empire?"

"Empires are often widespread," he says. "I believe there's strength in having a varied portfolio. And my empire is not little at all."

"I pegged you wrong," I admit.

"Did you?"

"I was picturing us as Fred and Ginger. When you take me dancing, I mean. But I'm okay with a nasty little bump and grind, too." I give him my most flirtatious smile and am shocked at myself for doing so. I blame it on the martini. Well, the martini and the man.

He smiles enigmatically, then stands and crosses the terrace. I see him fiddling with something on the wall. A moment later, I hear music. It's "Smoke Gets in Your Eyes," one of my favorite Astaire and Rogers numbers. He returns to me with his hand out. "Ms. Fairchild, may I have this dance?"

My throat constricts and my pulse races wildly as he pulls me up and into his arms. I'm not a good dancer, but with Damien leading I feel like I'm floating. We glide over the terrace, his hand on my back as light as a feather. And when the music ends, he pulls me close and bends me backward, smiling down at me with devilish intent.

I'm breathless, my chest rising and falling in his arms. His lips hover over mine, and I find myself unable to think of anything but the way his lips would feel pressed against mine. The touch of his mouth. Of his tongue.

"Is there something on your mind, Ms. Fairchild?"

"No."

He lifts an eyebrow, and I hear his voice in my head. *No lies.*

"I just—I was just wondering."

"Wondering what?" He eases me up, and our bodies are pressed close. Hips touching. My breasts against his chest, my hard nipples revealing my arousal. "Tell me," he whispers, his lips grazing my ear and making me shiver with desire.

"I was wondering if you were going to kiss me."

He turns his head slowly, then looks me in the eye. I want to lose myself in the heat I see there, and my lips part in anticipation of a kiss.

"No," he says, and then he takes a single step away from me.

I blink, confused. *No?*

His smile is wicked. "No," he repeats. And that's when I understand. He's punishing me for pulling back in his office. "Our week begins when you arrive for your first sitting."

"Tonight?" I ask.

"At six."

I nod, disappointed but excited.

His hand slides down the curve of my ass over the thin material of my skirt. "And, Nikki," he adds, "don't bother wearing underwear. You really won't need any."

I swallow and realize I'm already wet with anticipation.

Oh. Fucking. My.

18

I hang the Leica around my neck, but we leave the rest of our stuff with Richard and exit the back door of the hotel, following a path that takes us past the pool, an outdoor dining area, and then the tennis courts. Two couples are playing doubles, laughing and teasing each other as they miss most every stroke.

"Not a lot of hotels have courts," I say. "Was that your idea?"

"The courts were here when I bought the place," Damien says. It may be my imagination, but I think he's begun to walk faster. I, however, am slowing down. There's a bench just off the courts, and I pause there, my hands on the backrest. I'm looking at the players, but I'm imagining Damien on the court. His legs taut and tanned. His broad shoulders and strong arms. His jaw tight with determination.

After a moment, I feel him come up behind me. "We should go," he says. "I want to show you the wharf, and I need to be back in the office by three."

"Oh. Sure. I forgot." I take his hand and we continue walking, leaving the hotel grounds and then strolling past the charming stucco houses on Mason Street.

"Do you miss it?" I ask, as we turn right off Mason into a small, green park. Ahead of us is the beach and the Pacific Ocean, shining blue-green in the afternoon sun. "Tennis, I mean."

"No." His answer is flat, without any hesitation or guile. Even so, I don't quite believe him, and I say nothing, hoping that he will elaborate. After a few more moments, he does. "At first, I loved it. But after a while, the fun went out of the game. There was too much baggage."

"The competition?" I ask. "Maybe you could get the fun back if you just played. I'm terrible, but we could hit a ball around sometime."

"I don't play anymore," he says. His tone is hard and firm, and doesn't mirror my light suggestion at all.

"Okay." I lift a shoulder in a casual shrug. It's obvious I've touched a nerve, and I'm not quite sure how to get the flirtatious, laughing Damien back. "I'm sorry."

He looks at me sideways, then exhales, as if in frustration. "No, I'm the one who's sorry." He smiles, and I see the ice start- ing to melt, revealing nice underneath. "It's just that I'm done with tennis. Like you're done with pageants. You don't compete anymore, do you?"

I laugh. "Hell no. But there's a difference. I never thought it was fun." *Dammit,* I should have kept my mouth shut. I don't want him icing over again.

But he's not icy at all. He's looking at me with interest. "Never?"

"Never," I say. "Well, maybe when I was little I liked the dressing up. I honestly don't remember. But, no, I don't think I liked it even then. I can't remember feeling like anything other than my mother's personal Barbie doll."

"And dolls don't have a life of their own," he says.

"No, they don't," I say, pleased that he understands so well. "Did your parents push you to play?" I'm edging up against a sore point, but I want to get to know this man better.

We've reached the end of the park, and he takes my hand as we cross Cabrillo Boulevard. We reach the beach and walk in silence toward the surf. I've pretty much decided that I'm not going to get an answer when Damien finally speaks.

"At first I liked it. Loved it, actually. I was so damn young, but even then I loved the precision and the timing. And the power. Damn, I could hit that ball. It was a crappy year—my mother was sick—and I took out all my frustration on the court."

I nodded. I got that. When I was younger, I lost myself in the computer or behind a camera. It was only when that stopped being enough that I started cutting. Somehow, everyone finds a way to cope. I think of Ashley and bite back a frown. They find a way—or they don't.

"I started staying after school and the gym teacher coached me, but pretty soon he said that I'd blown past him. My dad worked in a factory and I knew that we couldn't afford a coach, but that was okay. I was a kid, only eight, and I just wanted to play for fun."

"What changed?"

"The teacher knew my mom was sick and that we couldn't afford lessons. He mentioned me to a friend, and before I knew it this local pro was working with me, free of charge. I loved it, especially when I started winning tournaments. You might have noticed that I'm slightly competitive."

"You? I'm flabbergasted." I take off my flip-flops and dangle them from my fingers so that I can kick my toes in the surf. Damien is already barefoot, having left his shoes with Richard at the hotel. I don't think many men could walk barefoot on a beach in a tailored suit and look damned sexy doing it, but Damien does. It was like a reflection of his confidence. That whatever he wanted, he would simply take.

Like me.

Pleasure trills up my spine, and I smile. Despite its rather crappy beginning, this is turning out to be an exceptional day.

There are a few people on the beach, but it's a weekday and not very crowded. Even so, the sand has been picked clean, and I can't find one decent shell, just bits and pieces, but the ripples that the water leaves as it surges in and out are beautiful in their precision. I drop the shoes so that I can take the lens cap off and focus, wanting a shot that includes the ridged sand and the white froth of the waves.

Damien waits until the shutter clicks, then hooks his arms around my waist. I feel the light pressure of his chin against my head. "Will you tell me the rest?" I ask. "What changed for you?"

"Success," he says darkly.

I turn in his arms. "I don't understand."

"I got good enough to attract a bastard of a professional coach." His tone is so low and biting it gives me chills. "He made a deal with my father—he'd train me for a percentage of my prize money."

I nodded; his first professional coach had been in the Wikipedia article I'd read. They'd worked together from the time Damien was nine until he was fourteen. That's when his coach had committed suicide. Apparently he was cheating on his wife.

I can't help but think of Ashley, and I don't want to raise those kinds of ghosts for Damien. Instead, I ask, "Did competing make it shift from fun to work?"

Damien's face darkens and the change is so quick and so dramatic that I actually look up to see if something overhead cast a real shadow. But it is just him. Just the reflection of his own emotions. "I don't mind hard work," he says flatly. "But everything changed when I was nine." There's a harshness in his voice that I don't understand. It occurs to me that he hasn't answered my question.

"What happened?"

"I told my father I wanted to quit, but I was already earning prize money, and he said no."

I squeeze his hand. Once again, he's evaded my question, but I don't press. How can I when evasion is an art I know well?

"I tried to get out again about a year later. I was playing all over the country by then, internationally, too. I was missing so damn much school that my dad just hired tutors. I focused mostly on science, and I loved it. I read everything I could on every subject, from astronomy to physics to biology. And fiction. Man, I ate up sci-fi novels. I even secretly applied to a private science academy. They not only accepted me, they offered me a full scholarship."

I lick my lips. I've figured out where this is going. How could I not see the way the story was developing? We are so alike, he and I. Our childhoods ripped from us and driven by the whims of a parent. "Your parents said no."

"My father did," Damien says. "My mother had died a year earlier. It was—" He draws in a breath, then reaches down to collect my shoes. We start walking down the beach again, heading for the massive pier that makes up Stearns Wharf. "I was ripped up the year she died. Numb. I let it all out on the court. All the anger, the betrayal." His jaw is tight with the memory. "Hell, it's probably why I played so damn good."

"I'm sorry," I say, and my words sound hollow. "I knew you were attracted to the sciences. All anyone has to do is look at the businesses you're in. But I never realized it was a lifelong fascination."

"Why would you?"

I tilt my head up to eye him. "You're not exactly a blank slate, Mr. Stark. In case you haven't noticed, you're something of a celebrity. You've even got a Wikipedia page. But there's nothing on it about turning down a scholarship to a science academy."

His mouth tightens into a thin line. "I've worked hard to keep my past off the Internet and away from the press."

I think about what Evelyn said about Damien learning to

control the press at a young age. Apparently, she was right. I wonder what other bits and pieces of his life Damien Stark has kept close to the vest.

I lift the camera and look through the viewfinder, aiming it first at the sea, and then at Damien, who puts up his hands as if to ward me off. I laugh and snap a few images in quick succession. "Bad girl," he says, and I laugh more.

"You bought the camera," I say. "You have no one to blame but yourself."

"Oh, no," he says, and he's laughing now, too. I dance backward as he lunges for me. I'm happy to see him smiling again and the melancholy of visiting the past fading from his eyes. I lift the camera and take another set of shots.

"And she keeps piling on the punishment," he says, following his words with a *tsk-tsk* noise.

I let the camera hang from its strap as I raise my hands in mock surrender. "I'm a free agent today, remember."

His grin is positively devilish. "I may not be allowed to act on it," he says, "but that doesn't mean I can't keep a list for future reference."

"Oh, really?" I snap another picture of him. "If I'm going to be punished anyway, it might as well be worth it."

His expression is all heat and promise. "I assure you I'll be very thorough."

"Of course, I don't think you're being very equitable. I mean, fair is fair. You're going to have a portrait of me. I think I should have some photos of you."

"Nice try," he says. "But the punishment stands."

I ease in close to him and slide my arm around his neck. Only the bulk of the camera is keeping us apart, and I'm suddenly enveloped in the heat of him. I lift myself up on my tiptoes so that I can whisper in his ear. "What would you say if I told you I was looking forward to it?"

He stands completely still, but as I ease back, I see a single muscle in his cheek twitch. It's not much, but it's enough. I've surprised Damien Stark. More than that, I've turned him on.

With a light laugh, I skip back, overflowing with feminine self-satisfaction.

We've reached the wharf, but we don't go out onto it. Instead, we turn around and head back down the beach toward Bath Street and the hotel. As we walk, I take a few snaps of the Channel Islands, then manage to get an excellent shot of two seagulls flying so close together they look like one creature. We've almost returned back the length of the beach when Damien settles on a bench. I think I see a sand dollar and squat in the sand in front of him.

"I'm looking forward to tonight, Ms. Fairchild," he says, his voice ripe with quiet urgency. He's looking right at me, and I see the heat in his eyes that has become familiar to me. "It's hard to be so close to something so precious and know you don't yet possess it."

"Possess?" I repeat.

His grin is slow and confident. "Possess. Have. Hold. Enjoy. Control. Dominate. Pick your verb, Ms. Fairchild. I intend to explore so very many of them."

I lick my lips. "Now you're breaking the rules."

"Oh, I don't think so." He lifts his hands. "No touching. No demands. You're not mine yet." He glances at his watch. "Not for a few more hours," he adds, and I have to stand up. My legs are too weak, my body too tingly, to let me remain squatting in the sand.

"Totally free for now," I agree, but I'm thinking about those hours. About what will happen when they pass.

"So I have no authority now," he says, his eyes roaming over my body. "I can't tell you to touch yourself. I can't insist that you lie naked in the surf and slide your fingers over your cunt. I can't take you back to the pool and ease you in, then suck on your nipples while the water washes the sand from your body. I can't slide my fingers inside you and feel how slick you are, how much you want me."

His eyes are locked on mine, and my breathing has become shallow. My skin glistens with sweat, and not from the heat of the sun. I'm standing at least three feet from him, but it's as if he's right there. As if we're connected. As if his hands are moving over my body in time with his words. And, dammit, I *do* want to touch myself. It takes all my willpower to keep my hands at my sides. Even then, my thumb is brushing the outside of my thigh, the motion slow and sensual. It's all I have, and I'm clinging to it even as I cling to his words.

"I can't take you into the hot tub and turn you around so that I can fuck you from behind while the water jet strokes your clit. I can't clutch your breasts and fuck you harder while you come for me, exploding all around me. And I can't make love to you on a balcony under the stars."

Make love . . .

My heart flutters.

"I can't, Nikki," he continues, "because you're not mine yet. But I can soon," he says. "Soon I can do whatever I want with you. I hope you're ready."

I swallow. I hope I am, too. Dear God, I hope I am.

When we exit the plane in Santa Monica, there are two cars waiting. Damien's sleek red expensive car with the unpronounceable name and a Lincoln Town Car. A short man in a cap stands by the Town Car. He inclines his head when I glance at him.

Damien presses his palm to the small of my back and steers me toward the man. "This is Edward, one of my drivers. He'll be taking you home."

"You're going back to your office?"

"I'm so sorry to cut our afternoon short, but it can't be avoided."

"No, no. Obviously you have work to do. It's just that my car is in the parking garage. Why don't I ride back with you?"

He presses a kiss to my forehead as Edward opens the Town Car door for me. "I would love the company, but your car is at your apartment."

It takes me a second to process. "What? How did it get there?"

"I arranged it."

"You arranged it," I repeat. I'm not angry so much as baffled. No, actually, I'm angry. I feel the tension boiling up inside me. "You just did that without asking?"

He looks perplexed. "I thought you'd appreciate it."

"That's micromanaging my life and putting your sticky fingers all over my property." I can hear my voice rising and force myself to tamp it down.

"I think you're overreacting."

Am I? I think about my mother and how much her fingers in every aspect of my life irritated me. Am I projecting my issues with my mother onto Damien? Or has he actually crossed some line? I'm not sure, and it bugs me that Elizabeth Fairchild is still haunting me from fifteen hundred miles away.

I run my fingers through my hair. "Sorry," I finally say. I slide into the back of the Town Car and look back out at him. "You're probably right. Just ask first next time, okay?"

"I was trying to help," he says, another nonanswer, but he's closing the door and that's that.

Well, damn.

Edward climbs into the driver's seat and takes off toward my apartment. But the truth is, I'm not ready to go home yet. "You can just drop me on the Promenade," I say, referring to the shopping street in Santa Monica. "I'll either catch a taxi home or have my roommate pick me up."

"I'm sorry, Ms. Fairchild," he says, guiding the car onto the entrance ramp to the 10. "My instructions are to take you straight home."

Oh, for Pete's sake!

"Instructions?" I echo. "Don't I get a say?"

Edward looks up, and I meet his eyes in the rearview mirror. The answer is clear: *No.*

Dammit.

I pull out my cell phone and call Damien.

"Hey, baby." His voice is low and sensual and now I'm even more angry—this time at myself for letting the caress of his voice shift me from my mission.

I rally and speak very firmly and clearly. "Would you please tell Edward that he doesn't have to take me straight home? He seems to be under the impression that you were giving orders and not just telling him a destination."

The pause before he answers is ominous. "You need to be ready at six. It's already past two. You need to rest."

"What the fuck?" I snap. "Are you my mother?"

"It's been a long day, baby. You're tired."

"The hell I am." Except he's right. I am. Not that I'm about to admit it to him.

"No lying," he says. "Remember."

"Fine," I say sharply. "I am tired. I'm also pissed. See you tonight, Mr. Stark." I click off without waiting for an answer, then flop back in my seat and cross my arms over my chest. I close my eyes just for a second, but when I open them again, it's because Edward has pulled up in front of my apartment. I must have been asleep for almost an hour.

I exhale, bemused and frustrated.

Edward opens the door for me, reminds me to be ready at six, and then gets back behind the wheel. He doesn't drive off, though, and I realize he's waiting for me to safely make it to my door. I stomp up the stairs, jam my key in the lock, and shove the door open—and am immediately confronted by the sight of a high-quality tote bag with *Third Street Promenade* silk-screened on the side, along with the logo for a local street fair. I know, of course, who sent it, but I can't imagine how he pulled it together so fast.

"It just came for you," a male voice says, and in the split second before I recognize that it's Ollie, I jump. "Sorry, I didn't mean to scare you." He gets up from the armchair tucked in the far corner of the living room and comes toward me. I notice he's barefoot. He's left a magazine in the chair—*Elle*. Apparently he's been reduced to reading my and Jamie's coffee table fare.

"Just came?" I say.

"About five minutes ago. I put it on the table for you. It doesn't weigh a thing."

I've crossed to the table while he was talking, and I immediately see why it's so light. It's filled with nothing but crumpled tissue paper. On top is an envelope. I break the seal and pull out a card with words written in ornate calligraphy: *I am jealous of your time away from me. I owe you a shopping trip. D.S.*

My smile is as refreshing as a cool breeze. Somehow, he always knows the right thing to say—and manages to say it with incredibly efficiency. Once again, I can't help but wonder how he got this to me so fast. The man must have staff all over the city.

I slide the card back into the envelope and tuck it back into the tissue paper; I don't want Ollie to see.

"Who's it from?" he asks.

"Long story," I answer, then change the subject. "So what happened to you yesterday? Jamie said she invited you over."

"Yeah, well, you know. I had stuff to do around the house, and then Courtney came back early from the conference, so we did the engaged-couple-hang-out thing."

"What's she doing today?"

"Work," he says. "Same old, same old."

"Right." I put my bags down on the table and go into the

kitchen for a bottle of water. As I'm taking a long swallow—I'm parched from alcohol and altitude—I realize what's wrong with Ollie's statement. "Why is she at work and you're not?" I ask as I head back into the living area.

"Deposition ended earlier than I expected," he says. "So I decided to come hang here."

"That's great. You didn't come to see me, did you? Sorry I wasn't here. Starting tomorrow, though, you might actually find me at home during the day." It's a hefty hint, but he doesn't take it.

"No, I popped by to see Jamie. You know, to make up for blowing off her invitation yesterday."

"Cool." I flop down on the couch next to him. "So where is she, anyway?"

"Um, the bathroom. She's taking a shower. I think she's going out in a bit. I told her I'd hang out for a while and watch some screen, but now I think I'm getting hungry." He stands. "Why don't we go grab something?"

I shake my head. "I'm stuffed. You go on."

"At least come sit with me. I'm just going around the corner to the Daily Grill."

He's already at the door. For someone who was casually vegging a moment ago, he's certainly eager to get food. "Do you want me to make you something? We have a ton of leftover pizza."

"Nah. I'm craving their burger. You coming?" He has the door open now.

I think about the camera and the pictures I want to dump into Photoshop. And then I think that Ollie is one of my best friends. "Sure," I say. "Just give me a sec."

I grab my sack and head toward my bedroom, but I pause long enough to tap on the bathroom door.

"Don't be coy," Jamie says. "Just come on in."

The shower's running, but Jamie's voice is clear, and I imagine she's probably got her leg propped up on the toilet seat as she shaves. Since we haven't been shy with each other since ninth grade, I open the door. I'm not at all surprised to see her leg slathered with shaving cream. I am surprised by the expression on her face. It's one of complete and total shock.

Everything clicks into place.

"Hey, Nik! Why are you home in the middle of the day?"

"What the hell do you think you're doing?" I snap. "He's engaged. Off limits. Jesus, Jamie."

"I—" But she doesn't finish. Just grabs a towel and wraps it around herself.

"Shit." The curse bursts out of me. "Shit, damn, *fuck*." I am not an expert curser, so that's pretty brutal for me. "Did you fuck him?"

Her lips are tight together, but she gives just the tiniest nod.

I leave the bathroom and slam the door behind me. Ollie is still standing by the door, and I can tell from his expression that he either overheard our conversation or is smart enough to have figured out the gist of it.

"Jesus, Ollie," I say.

He looks contrite. Hell, he looks beat up. "I fucked up, Nik. What can I say?"

I exhale. I'm furious, but this is Ollie and I love him and I have to be there for him. For him, and for Jamie. *Oh, God. Jamie.* "It had to be Jamie? You couldn't have fucked someone I don't love? You guys are my best friends—I don't want to be in the middle of this."

"I know. I do. I'm sorry. Look, come get some lunch with me. I'll—we can talk. Or not talk. Just come, okay?"

I nod. "I'll just have a tea or something. I had a huge lunch with Damien."

"Damien," he repeats, and I force myself not to wince. I hadn't meant to mention Damien's name. "Christ, Nik. He's bad news."

"Don't you dare," I say, and I have to work to keep tight control on my voice. "Don't you dare give me that shit. You can't stand here and tell me you don't like Damien Stark. You can't toss something like that at me and stand there like you've got the moral high ground beneath your feet, because you so do not."

"You're right—you're right." He runs his fingers through his already untidy hair. "Listen, I'm just gonna get a burger and head back to the office. We should talk tomorrow, okay? You can berate me about Jamie all you want. And maybe I'll even have some shit to tell you, too."

"About Damien?" I ask coldly.

He hooks his thumb at the door. "I'm going to just—I really am sorry."

I don't bother saying anything else. I watch him go, and then I take my stuff and stomp off to my room. My mood is vile, and twice I pick up the phone and think about calling Damien. But what would I say? *Hi, you want to paint me and you're paying me to be your plaything and so I thought I'd call you and dump my friends' problems on you?* Somehow, that just didn't seem right.

Jamie's still in the bathroom, most likely because she's either avoiding me or working up the courage to talk to me. Honestly, I'm not in any hurry.

I boot up my laptop and use the cord from the Leica's box to download the images into Photoshop. The first one that loads is the rippled image of the wave-battered beach. It's crisp and clean and makes me think of escape. As if I could step into the froth that the camera has captured and let the tide tug me out to sea, away from everything and everyone.

Except I don't want to get away from everyone. . . .

I open another image, and find myself looking at Damien. I've caught him in motion, and I think that's appropriate. When I think of Damien Stark, he's always moving. He's a man who makes things happen. He's action personified, and I've managed to catch that, along with something else. *Joy.*

He'd been turning toward me when I snapped the picture, and his face fills my screen. His lips are parted with the beginning of a laugh, and the afternoon light is reflected in his eyes. His expression is wide open and he's completely in the moment. My chest feels heavy with emotion. I've seen him smile and laugh and smirk and tease, but only in this captured moment have I truly seen exultation.

I press my fingertips to the computer screen and touch Damien's face. Damien, so strong and yet so injured.

I think of the scars that mar my body and pull up my feet so that my heels rest on the desk chair. Then I hug my knees tight. Damien may not have taken a knife to his skin, but I know that he's scarred, too. But when I look at his face—at the euphoria in this image—it's not the injuries I see, but the man who survived them.

After a few minutes, I hear the bathroom door open and Jamie's soft footfalls on the carpet. They pause outside my door and I tense, but she doesn't knock and a few moments later I hear the click of her door. I wait a minute, and then head for the bathroom for a shower. I feel gross, soiled by my friends' dirty laundry. I want to stand in scalding water and let it wash the grime off me.

I take off my clothes and get in without waiting for the temperature to adjust. At first it's ice cold, and I want to scream from the shock. Then the heater kicks in and I close my eyes, taking it, wanting to slough off the outer layer of myself.

I squirt some of Jamie's strawberry scented bodywash into my hand and rub it all over myself, including my inner thighs. I slow down as I feel the raised flesh beneath my fingers.

Damien's going to see them tonight.

I squeeze my eyes shut, thinking about how stupid I've been. I'd been planning on turning his little game around on him.

Making the revelation of my scars some sort of triumphant fuck you instead of the reminder of how weak I've been. Of how much I let the pain take over.

But I no longer want my scars to be a weapon. I no longer want to risk losing this week with Damien. I've lost so much already today.

I stand there in the shower, my shoulders shaking as I cry, and hot tears snake down my cheeks to mix with the scalding water that beats down upon my damaged skin.

19

I am standing on a cliff, the waves crashing far below me.

I look down. Damien is there, his arms outstretched, his head back. He's calling to me. You're mine, he says. Jump to me. I'll catch you.

Jump,

Just jump,

Just jump . . .

I wake with a start as the timer on my phone blares. I'd closed my eyes after my shower intending only to lay in bed for ten minutes. Thankfully I had the foresight to set the timer for an hour just in case. It's almost five—Damien will be here in just over an hour.

I don't bother dressing in anything fancy. After all, I'm just going to be taking my clothes off again. I frown and tell myself it will be okay. He won't want the painting once he learns the truth, but he won't be cruel. Damien might be ice sometimes, but he's not cruel.

I pull on jeans and a Universal Studios theme park tank top I bought last year when I'd flown out to visit Jamie. I slide on the flip-flops, check my hair in the mirror, and decide that I look passable. I'm not wearing makeup, and I feel a bit naked without it. One of those sad truths that annoys me, since I only feel like I need makeup every time I step out into the world because my mother drilled into my head that a woman shouldn't leave the house without first putting her face on.

Really, Mother? Because I'm pretty sure that faces aren't actually removable.

Yet despite my quick dip into the land of sarcastic comebacks, I still bury myself under cosmetics every day of the week. I console myself with the knowledge that most girls do the same. It's not a mother thing, it's a feminine unity thing. Or, better, it's a me thing.

But I've done enough pageants and photo shoots to know that artists often like their subjects to start out as blank canvases. So here I sit with a naked face to match my soon-to-be-naked body.

I spend the next half hour at my computer fixing up my resume. I shoot it off to Thom, the headhunter who got me the job with Carl. I include an email explaining the situation so that he understands why I'm looking for a new job after less than a week at the first one. With luck, he won't decide I'm a problem client and cut me loose. With even more luck, he'll get some new interviews lined up this week.

I still have a few minutes, so I decide to work on some code. But instead of pulling up my template, I find myself typing Damien's name into a search engine. I'm not looking for anything in particular. I just want to know more. Instead of satisfying me, the bits and pieces of himself Damien has tossed my direction have only whetted my appetite.

Not surprisingly, I get about as many hits as the man has dollars. His tennis career, his industrial empire, his philanthropic causes. His women. Though I'm still desperately curious about his youth, I can't fight the compulsion to narrow the search to Damien and the women he's been photographed with. I click on the link that shows me images only, then sit back as an array of beauties fill my screen, each on Damien Stark's sexy but enigmatic arm.

Damien has rarely been photographed with the same woman twice, which matches what he told me. I find one girl and click back to the original source of the image. It's a celebrity gossip blog, and the woman is identified as Giselle Reynard. When I look closer, I recognize her as Audrey Hepburn with much longer hair. Some of the tension leaves me. I already know that Giselle is married.

There are also a number of pictures that show Damien with a wide-eyed blonde identified as Sara Padgett. Several of the captions reveal that Sara was found asphyxiated. And though none come out and claim that Damien was involved, there are enough hints that I have to wonder if these photos and captions are Sara Padgett's brother's doing, and if this is the kind of stuff that Damien is pushing Mr. Maynard to fight.

I press my finger to my monitor and touch Damien's face, but my eyes are on Sara. Did she kill herself on purpose? Or was she really trying to get off and died accidentally? Either way makes me sad. I've felt so lost and helpless that I hurt myself in order to feel real, but I never crossed that line into desiring death. On the contrary, I was trying to find that pulse of life inside me.

I close out the website. I'm already melancholy, and this is not the way to feel better. Instead, I go to YouTube and watch old Ginger Rogers and Fred Astaire dance clips. I start with "Smoke Gets in Your Eyes."

Fred is just dipping Ginger when there's a knock at my door. I shut my laptop, grab my purse, and head for the front of the apartment. Already my pulse has quickened and my body is more aware of the space it's occupying, as if readying itself to share that space with another human being.

I pause, take a deep breath, and reach for the doorknob.

I tug the door open expecting to see Damien, and am surprised to find Edward. "Oh," I say. "I thought—"

"Mr. Stark apologizes," Edward says. "He got held up."

"I see." I follow him to the car, each of my steps weighed down with disappointment—and with a rising anger. Not at Damien, but at myself. I've been letting myself get lost in girlish fantasies, and I've lost sight of the larger picture. I'm something Damien bought, like his hotel or his jet or his car. I'm not his girlfriend or his lover. Not really. I'm simply *his,* and that's okay because I agreed to it and I'm getting paid for it. But I can't start thinking that a tantalizing arrangement has some semblance to reality. This is a game to him, and I came in as a willing player, negotiating hard for the terms I wanted.

I got them, too. And I remind myself of that important fact. It may feel as though Damien has all the power, but he doesn't. I kept a little bit of control—and I'll walk away with a million.

The grounds are dotted with workmen when we arrive. They're hauling dirt, planting flowers, clearing rocks. Another crew works on the stone facade on the eastern-facing wall. At least I assume it faces the east. As far as I'm concerned, anything that looks out on the California ocean is west and the opposite is east.

For a moment I fear that there are workmen inside, too, because I never added privacy to my conditions. I assumed that only Damien and the artist would be there. But now, seeing these men . . .

Surely Damien wouldn't ask me to stand naked in front of the world?

Don't be so sure.

But when Edward opens the door for me and leads me in, I see that my fears are unfounded. The place is silent except for the soft strains of music coming from somewhere in the back.

The house is not yet finished, but the shell is firmly in place. The walls still need painting, the wood needs to be finished. Light fixtures are missing, with only a few dangling wires indicating where they will go. But the grandeur of the home is obvious. The ceilings soar. The floors are stunning, even though I can see only bits and pieces under the protective brown paper. And the marble staircase and twisted iron handrail look like something out of a five-star hotel.

I follow Edward up that staircase, and the change when we step onto the third floor landing is astonishing. There is nothing raw or half-complete about *this* area. The wood floors are polished to a shine, and accented by thick, expensive area rugs. The walls are painted in a pale rose, and I imagine that the space glows at sunset.

The entire room is stunning and inviting. It's obviously meant for entertaining, despite the fact that the focal point is a giant bed. It's been put there for my benefit, I'm certain, and I squeeze my thighs together in an attempt to stall the blood that is rushing to my sex.

The room appears to be missing a wall, but I quickly realize that the wall is made of glass partitions that have been pushed aside and hidden, like pocket doors taken to the extreme. I step outside and find myself on a stone balcony that looks out over the ocean. It's closer than I expected considering how twisting and turning our drive was, and I can actually hear the crash of the waves.

"Mr. Stark will be right with you," Edward says, and then he bows and leaves, and I'm left to explore on my own.

Part of me wants to stay outside and feel the sea breeze on my hair and listen to the ocean crashing beneath me. But I want to see the room. I go back inside and stand by the bed. It is positioned at an angle to the wide-open wall, and in that area sheer drapes have been hung from the ceiling. They flutter now in the breeze. An easel stands a few feet away, and I know that this area has been staged. For me. I tremble at the thought and run my hand over one of the bedposts. It's old-fashioned, iron polished to a reflective sheen. Sturdy and yet sensual. *Like Damien.* Strong. As if this bed has demands of its own.

Oh . . .

The bed has no spread, only blue-gray sheets, rumpled to give it a slept-in quality. I wonder if Damien has slept here and I move to sit on the side facing the ocean. A gust of wind catches the drapes and they blow in, brushing my arms, bare in the souvenir tank top. I close my eyes and lie back, no longer wondering why Damien isn't here yet. He wants me lost in my thoughts with this bed and this breeze and the gossamer feel of the silky drapes on my skin.

"I like that view."

I know that voice, and I don't move. I stay on the bed, but allow a smile to creep onto my face. "Then why don't you come enjoy it?"

A moment later, I feel the mattress shift. I keep my eyes closed as his thumb strokes my lips, then traces downward between my breasts to the waistband of my jeans. "I told you not to wear underwear," he whispers.

"I didn't," I say.

In the silence, I think I can hear his smile.

I keep my eyes closed as he unbuttons my fly and unzips my jeans. They fit loose, and his hand glides easily inside. My trimmed pubic hair is already damp, and by the time his fingers slide over my vulva, I'm slick with desire, my hips rising off the bed to meet his touch, my clit throbbing with anticipation.

"Mmm," he whispers, sliding two fingers inside me, the sensations so surprising and arousing I bite my lip to keep from crying out. "And no more jeans. I want you only in skirts. No underwear. A garter if you want stockings. I want you accessible. Anytime, anywhere."

My sex clenches around his fingers with excitement, and he

moans softly. "God, you're so responsive." He pulls his fingers out of me, and I want to whimper from the loss. "Keep your eyes closed," he says, and then I feel his fingers on my lips. "Suck," he orders, and I draw his finger inside. It is slick with the taste of me, and I shift on the bed, squeezing my thighs together, sucking hard on him as I try to reach satisfaction.

Slowly, he pulls his fingers free.

"Damien," I whisper.

"Mine," he whispers, the word telling me everything I need to know. I'll come when he's ready for me to. The knowledge is arousing in itself—and damn frustrating, too.

I feel the press of his mouth against my breast. He sucks me through the tank top, and I arch up to meet him, then cry out when his teeth nip at my tender nipple. My eyes fly open and I find Damien Stark grinning playfully down at me. "Well, hello. I take it you like the bed?"

I sit up, trying to present a prim and calm facade. "Is it yours?"

"No," he says. "Not the way you mean. It's for the portrait. And this week. That means it's yours, I suppose." His eyes skim over me, and I shiver under his inspection. "Or ours."

I swallow. "Well, you've staged a lovely room. I'm sure the portrait will be wonderful. When is the artist getting here?"

"He's already here," Damien says, then laughs when my eyes go wide with horror. "Don't worry, he's in the kitchen. I don't do public sex." He nips my ear. "I do everything else, though," he whispers, and I feel my body flush as I wonder just what "everything else" could mean.

"Blaine," he calls. "Why don't you bring your coffee in here."

"Blaine?" I ask. "I thought you didn't care for his work."

"On the contrary. I think his skill is exceptional. He conveys an intense eroticism. I simply wasn't impressed with his models or with the staging. I want that same erotic allure, but without the trappings. I'll tie you up, Nikki, but I won't put a picture of it on my wall."

Tie me up . . .

I nod stupidly. He keeps knocking me off kilter.

A moment later, Blaine comes in carrying a mug of coffee and I quickly button my jeans and get off the bed. He's more casual than he was at Evelyn's party, just Dockers and a black T-shirt. He smiles in a wide, friendly greeting. "Great to see you again, Nikki. Are you nervous?"

"Hell yes," I say, which makes him laugh.

"Don't worry. I'm like a doctor. Purely clinical."

I raise my brows.

"Okay, that's not entirely true. But I appreciate beauty, and I get off on capturing it. It's personal, but it's not. Does that make sense?"

"It does," I say, thinking of my photographs.

"We have to trust each other. Work for you?"

"I'll try."

"And just so you know, I signed Damien's agreement."

I have no idea what he's talking about, and my confusion must show on my face.

"The confidentiality agreement," he clarifies. "I'm not allowed to talk about you or the sessions. And once it's done, I'm not allowed to reveal who the model is."

"Really?" I look to Damien, who nods. He turns and points to the wall opposite the ocean. It isn't a full wall, in fact it's not really a wall at all. There's a huge fireplace, with a great expanse of stone rising above it, hiding the chimney, I presume.

"It will hang there," he says. "You'll be looking out on the ocean. You'll see the sunset every night."

I nod. "Where's the canvas?" If it's going to fill that space, it must be huge. But there's nothing but an oversized sketchpad on the easel.

"Tomorrow," Blaine says. "Today's about getting us familiar

with each other. I sketch your curves, you stand there and look fabulous."

"I think you have the easier job," I say dryly.

"Hell yeah, I do," he says, and we both laugh.

"I'm still nervous," I admit.

"Totally normal," Blaine says.

I look desperately toward Damien. My skin is clammy and my pulse is pounding. Why on earth did I think this would be easy? I'm going to be standing naked in front of a stranger. Holy shit. "Do you have any wine?" I blurt.

He brushes a chaste kiss over my lips. "Of course."

He disappears behind the fireplace, and returns quickly with three glasses and a bottle of Pinot Grigio. He passes me a glass first, and I drink half of it in one swallow. The men look at each other with amusement and I defiantly swallow the rest.

"Okay," I say, then reach for the bedpost to steady myself. "Yeah. I think that's better." I hold out my glass, but Damien pours only a tiny bit.

"I want you standing, not passed out," he says, but he's smiling indulgently. He squeezes my hand. "The first moment is the hardest."

"And you know this because of the many times you've posed naked?"

"Touché," he says. "Take your time."

"By the window," Blaine says, and I'm grateful for the businesslike tone in his voice. "Close to the drapes. Damien, where'd you put that robe?"

There's an antique trunk at the foot of the bed, and Damien opens it and pulls out a red silk robe.

"Just put it on the bed—the far side so it's not in my composition. Yeah, that's right. Okay, Nikki, right there. Do you want to put the robe on in the bathroom and then come in? Easier to just slip it off your shoulders."

I run the drape through my fingers. "No," I say. I take the

hem of the tank top and pull it defiantly over my head. The cool air assaults my bare breasts, and my nipples feel hard and heavy. I don't look at Damien. Instead, I look out at the ocean.

"Oh, man," Blaine says. "That's great. Your profile is amazing. And you have the most beautiful breasts. Stay like that," he says as he starts to walk the room. "I just want to find the right place."

After a few moments, he's settled in and though I should be more relaxed all I can feel is the tension building inside me, getting tauter and tauter every time he says I'm beautiful. Every time he praises my soft, perfect skin.

I'm holding my eyes wide open, trying not to blink, trying to imagine I'm part of that ocean. That I am the tide, coming in and out, in and out.

"Can you do the jeans now?" Blaine asks, and his voice startles me so much that I jump.

"Nikki?" Damien's voice is soft.

"I—sure." I put my hands on the button and unclasp it, then start to ease the jeans down over my hips. My fingers are on my skin, and I feel the scars, raised and ugly.

I freeze, take a deep breath, and try again.

But I can't do it. I open my mouth to say something—to ask for more time, a moment alone, something. But no words come out. Instead, I'm suddenly sobbing, my body shaking and my legs unable to hold me up. I sag to the floor and bury my face in the soft material of the drapes.

Damien is immediately at my side. "Shhh," he whispers. "It's okay. We'll take it slow. It's hard, I know. Revealing yourself like that. It takes courage, but you can do it."

I shake my head and let him pull me into his arms. I press my face to his shoulder and he holds me close. My breasts are pressed tight against his chest, the cotton of his T-shirt soft against my nipples. His palm strokes my back. But there's nothing sexual. He's comforting me, holding me, and I feel warm and safe.

"I can't do it," I whisper when the sobs slow enough to let me speak. "I'm sorry, but I can't."

I pull away. My body is still shaking, and I have the hiccups. "I thought I could. I don't know what I thought. That it would be revenge against you. Against the world. I don't know."

I'm babbling, and he's looking at me with such concern and sympathy that I think my heart is going to break.

"I'm sorry, Damien," I say. "I can't take your money. And I can't do this."

20

I scramble out of his embrace and snatch my shirt off the floor. I pull it on, then stand up, brushing my tears away with the back of my hand.

I fasten my jeans and look around for my purse and camera bag. They're on the floor by the foot of the bed, right where I left them.

I hurry that way and sling my purse over my shoulder. I briefly register that Blaine is gone. I'm grateful he didn't make a show of leaving, even though I'm embarrassed I melted down in front of him.

"I—I can call a cab if you want. Or Edward can—" I cut myself off, closing my eyes. My entire body feels warm. I'm burning up with embarrassment.

Damien has risen to his feet and he's standing by the bed, watching me. I can't read his face, but I know he must be furious.

"I'm sorry, Damien. I'm so sorry." How many times can I say it? Will it ever not sound hollow? "I'll wait outside."

I hurry toward the stairs, my head down.

"Nikki . . ." His voice caresses my name, and I hesitate, but then move on.

"*Nikki.*" This time, my name is a command. I stop, my back stiff, and turn to face him.

He is right there, and he brings his hands to my shoulders, his eyes on my face. His expression is dark. "Where do you think you're going?"

"I have to leave. I told you. I can't do this."

"We have a deal," he says, his eyes burning into me. "You're mine, Nikki." His hand slides behind my neck, tugging me toward him. With his other hand, he lifts my tank top and cups my breast. "Mine," he repeats.

The warmth of his hand fills me, and I gasp. I want him, but I can't do this. I can't . . .

I shake my head. "I'm breaking the deal."

"I don't accept that."

Anger pierces my embarrassment and shatters my desire. "Fuck what *you* accept. I'm saying no."

His thumb makes lazy circles on my nipple.

"Stop it."

He doesn't. "What are you afraid of?"

"I'm not afraid." *This,* I think as desire knots through me. *The way I feel. Where this will lead . . .*

No, I'm not afraid. I'm fucking terrified.

"Bullshit." He pulls me close and takes my mouth with his, kissing me roughly and then pushing me away. "I can taste the fear on you, baby. Tell me. Dammit, Nikki, let me make it better."

I shake my head. I have no words.

Slowly, he nods. "All right. I won't hold you to our deal. But at least let me see what I'm losing."

My head jerks up to look at him. "What?"

"I wanted a portrait. And I wanted the woman. Naked, Nikki. Naked and open in my bed. At least let me see what I'm missing out on."

The anger that's been growing bursts out like gasoline thrown on a fire. "Are you fucking kidding me?"

He is perfectly calm, his eyes flat and focused on me. "I'm not. Take your jeans off, Nikki. Let me see you."

"You son of a bitch." I blink, and a tear streaks down my cheek. I wanted my scars to be a weapon? Well, they're damn well going to be. Angrily, I rip open the button of my jeans and yank the zipper down. I wriggle out of them until the denim is pooled at my feet. I kick off the damn flip-flops and stand there, my legs spread slightly. There's no way he can miss the welts on my hips and inner thighs. "You goddamn son of a bitch."

I don't know what I expect, but Damien drops to his knees. His face is about level with my hips, and he gently rubs the pad of his thumb over the thickest scar on my hip. I'd cut too deep, and I'd been too scared to go to the emergency room. I'd closed the wound with duct tape and super glue and kept pressure on with an Ace bandage wrapped tight around me. I'd kept my secret, but the scar was vile. Even now, years later, it's still slightly pink.

"Oh, baby." His voice is soft, like a caress. "I knew there was something, but . . ." He trails off, his other hand tracing the scars on the inside of my thighs. "Who did this to you?"

I close my eyes and tilt my head away, ashamed.

I hear his soft exhale and know that he understands. I force myself to look back at him.

"Is this what you were afraid of? That I'd learn about these scars? That I wouldn't want you?"

A tear is clinging to the end of my nose. It falls and lands with a plop on his arm.

"Sweetheart . . ." I hear my pain in his voice. And then he leans close to me and runs his tongue over the inside of my left thigh. Over my flesh, over my scar. I can't believe this is real, but it is. He's not running. He's kissing me there, so sweetly, and then he takes my hands and pulls me down until I'm kneeling in front of him.

I'm a mess, tears spilling, my nose running. I'm hiccuping and it's not easy to breathe.

"Shhhh," he says, and then he's gathered me in his arms. I cling to him as he carries me back to the bed and lays me down, naked except for my tank top, which he very slowly pulls off.

I cross my arms over my chest and tilt my head to the side, not looking at him.

"No," he says, and eases my arms to my sides. He takes some pity on me, though, and doesn't make me look at him.

Slowly, he explores my scars, as if I am a road map, his finger tracing over each of them. He speaks soothing words, and there's no horror in his voice. No disgust. "This is what you were trying to hide. Why you've run from me. Why you wanted to be painted exactly the way you are."

He doesn't wait for me to answer. He already knows.

"You're a goddamn fool, Nikki Fairchild." The harshness in his voice makes me turn my head. I look at him, expecting anger or disgust or exasperation. What I see is desire.

"I don't want an icon. Not on my wall, not in my bed. I want the woman, Nikki. I want you."

"I—"

He presses a finger over my lips. "Our deal is on. No arguments. No exceptions."

He eases off the bed and goes to the window, then pulls down one of the drapes. I hear the rattle of the ornate clips that have connected the material to the bar.

"What are you doing?"

"What I want," he says as he ties the end of the drape to the bedpost. "Raise your arms."

My pulse quickens, but I comply. Right now, I don't want to be in charge. I don't want to control. I want to be swept away, to be taken care of.

Gently, he twists the drape around my wrist, then weaves it through the bedposts before repeating the process with my other wrist. Finally, he ties the loose end off on the other bedpost.

"Damien."

"Hush." He kisses the soft skin of my wrist, then trails his lips down my arm, my shoulder, then over the curve of my breast. His mouth closes over my right nipple, and he sucks hard, making the areola pucker and tingle as he twists and strokes my other breast. Hot threads seem to crisscross my body, tracing from my breasts to my clit. My sex is throbbing, and I bring my legs together, trying to quell some of the building pressure.

He lifts his head and grins at me, and his expression is so devilish that I'm certain he knows exactly how I'm suffering. Then he sets off on his trail of kisses once more, moving down my stomach, to my navel, to my pubic bone, and then—oh, yes, oh, please.

But he shifts his attention, sitting up and putting his hands on my knees. "Spread your legs, Nikki."

I shake my head, and he chuckles, then stands up and rips down another drape.

"What are you doing?"

"You know."

"Damien, no. Please, no."

He pauses and looks at me. "Do you know what a safeword is?"

"I—yes. I think so."

"No doesn't always mean no. But the safeword always means stop. If I go too far, that's what you say. Do you understand?"

I nod.

"What do you want your safeword to be?"

My vocabulary has entirely left my mind. I look around the room, as if something will leap out at me, then gaze out at the ocean. "Sunset," I say finally.

His mouth curves into a smile, he nods, and then he ties the drape to the post at the foot of the bed. I swallow and watch him.

Slowly, he reaches for my right foot, easing my legs apart. He looks at me, and I see the question mark in his eyes.

"Will you hurt me?"

His eyes dart to my scars. "Do you want me to?"

"I—I don't know."

"Do you know what passion is?"

I blink, confused.

"Most people think it only means desire. Arousal. Wild abandon. But that's not all. The word derives from the Latin. It means suffering. Submission. Pain and pleasure, Nikki. *Passion*." The flash of heat that burns across his expression is unmistakable. "Do you trust me?"

"Yes," I say without hesitating.

"Then trust me to take you where you've never gone before."

I nod, and he looks at me with such naked desire that warm satisfaction fills me. Gently, he binds my ankle, then moves on to the other. When he's done, I'm spread-eagled on the bed, naked and helpless and undeniably turned on.

"You're mine, Nikki. To touch. To soothe. To pleasure." He tenderly cups my sex. I'm slick and hot and he groans with desire. "I want you, Nikki. I want to bury myself in you and fuck you hard. I want to hear you scream when you come. Tell me you want it, too."

"Yes, oh, yes." I've wanted it since he first touched me. Wanted to feel him inside me, filling me, claiming me.

He sits beside me on the bed, still in jeans and T-shirt. He trails his index finger up my stomach to my breasts. Slowly, he circles one, then the other. "Should I make you beg for it?" he teases.

"I will," I say, utterly shameless.

His expression is devious. "I want you hot, I want you desperate."

I swallow. "I already am."

"We'll see," he says. Then he reaches for the robe and pulls off the sash. Without his eyes ever leaving mine, he puts it over my eyes.

"Damien?"

"Shhh."

He ties it behind my head. I think of the word—*sunset*—but I keep it to myself. I want this. I want to *feel*, and how much more will I be able to if I can't see?

The bed shifts, and I realize he's no longer beside me. I bite my lower lip, but I refuse to call out. He's playing a delicious game with me, and I fully intend to hold my own. He's taken me full circle, I realize, from fear and shame, to excitement and arousal. I don't think anyone but Damien could do that, and whatever he has planned for me now, I trust him.

I jump as something cold and wet hits my breast.

"Ice," I whisper.

"Mmm." But he doesn't speak, because he's licking the water off, his mouth hot against my nipple. He traces the cube down my belly, and my muscles jump and twitch from the cold and from excitement. His mouth follows, his tongue, his lips. He leaves a hot trail down my body. I tug against the sash that binds my wrists, wanting to touch him, wanting to rip off the blind-fold. And yet I don't want to, either. There's something exciting about being so totally at his mercy. Of seeing just where this will lead.

My legs are spread wide, and I can feel the cool night air against my soaking wet sex. I shift my hips, partly to try to quell the growing need and partly as an invitation. Either that or a demand. I want him in me, and I want it now.

"Getting anxious, Ms. Fairchild?"

"You're a cruel man, Mr. Stark."

His laugh suggests that I don't yet know just how cruel, and then I feel the bed shift again. One finger stays on my belly, but I don't feel the rest of him. And then—oh, God, yes—I feel his warm breath against my sex followed by the brush of his cheek against my inner thigh.

I almost come right then, and my hips buck up involuntarily.

"Please," I whisper. "I'll beg. Damien, I'll beg."

"I know you will, baby." His mouth is right there, and then I feel the sharp flick of his tongue and I cry out from the almost painful pleasure that shoots through me. "But you're not ready yet, not quite yet."

"I think you're wrong about that," I grump and draw another laugh.

It's stifled, though, by his mouth on my inner thigh. I squeeze my eyes closed tight behind the sash as he brushes his lips over my scars, kissing his way down my leg, worshipping me with his mouth. I feel his tongue dart out and tease the back of my knee, and I learn in that moment just how sensitive that part of a body can be.

I'm still twitching from the electrical sensations that buzz over my body when he reaches my feet.

"You have lovely toes, Ms. Fairchild," he says. "I don't have a foot fetish, but if I did . . ." He trails off, and his mouth closes over my big toe. He sucks on it, gently at first, and then harder until I'm squirming again, feeling the corresponding tug all the way in my cunt. I'm throbbing, but I know better than to beg. Damien's not done with me yet.

He moves his attention to my other foot and licks each of my toes gently. Then he kisses his way back up my leg. By the time he reaches the soft skin between my thigh and my vulva, I am completely lost in a haze of pleasure.

At least, I think I am. When he closes his mouth over me and grazes my clit lightly with his teeth, I am wildly, hotly, intensely proven wrong. There *are* still heights, and Damien is taking me there.

He has an expert tongue, and it swirls over my clit, soft and gentle, but with a building intensity. My eyes are squeezed shut behind the blindfold, my breath coming in short gasps. I twist against the bindings that hold me. I am lost, I am nothing but pleasure. A vibrant white scream of pleasure concentrated between my thighs.

And then—oh, yes, oh, my—the world seems to explode, and I'm bucking against him, and still he's sucking and pulling and tonguing me and I'm climbing higher and higher until finally, finally, the world settles back around me and my chest is rising and falling with the power of the explosion.

"Now," Damien whispers, and I realize he's above me. His mouth closes over mine, slick with the scent of me. The thick head of his penis is pressed against me, and he thrusts inside. "Oh, baby," he says. His hand slips down between our bodies, and I feel his thumb on my sensitive clit. My body trembles again, and I gasp as my muscles clench, drawing him in even more. "There you go, that's right. Are you sore?"

I manage to croak out a no.

"Good," he says, and I feel him withdraw just a little, then slam back into me. He said he was going to fuck me hard, and he is, and I'm lifting my hips to meet him, because I want him deeper now, deeper and harder. I want all of him, and, dammit, I want to see him.

"Damien," I say. "Damien, the blindfold."

I'm afraid he's going to ignore me, but then his fingers brush my temple and he pulls it off. He's above me, his face hard but his eyes showing nothing but pleasure. His mouth curves into a gentle smile, and then he kisses the corner of my mouth. The frenzied fuck slows to a sweet, sensual rhythm that is all the more devastating because he's drawing it out, making it last. It can last forever as far as I'm concerned.

And then I see the tension building in his body, his muscles tightening, his body stiffening against mine. He closes his eyes and I watch as he arches back, and then I feel the sweet pressure as he explodes inside me.

"Christ, Nikki," he says as he collapses against me.

I want to press my body against him, but I'm still trapped. "Damien," I whisper. "Untie me."

He rolls over and smiles at me, warm and languid. At some point he put on a condom, and he takes it off and drops it in a small trash bin by the bed. Then he moves quickly to undo the drapes. I didn't get to enjoy watching him strip, but I'm very happy with the view now. He may not have played tennis professionally for years, but the man still has an athlete's body, long and lean and so damn sexy.

"Come here," he says roughly once I'm untied. He pulls me close to spoon against him, my back against his chest, my ass against his magnificent cock. His fingers stroke the outside of my thigh, and his lips graze my shoulder. "I liked taking you tied up," he says. "We may have to try more of that."

"More?"

"Have you ever heard of Kinbaku?"

"No."

His hand slides over my thigh to rest on my sex. His fingers stroke my hair lightly. "It's ropes," he says. "But they're for restraint as much as for pleasure." His fingers ease between my thighs, and I gasp, amazed that I already want him again so desperately. He rubs his finger over my clit and whispers, "It's all about the placement of the ropes."

"Oh." My voice is breathy.

"Would you like that?"

"I—I don't know." I swallow. "I liked this," I admit.

His fingers slide easily inside me and I moan. "Yes," he says. "I could tell."

He's teasing me for being aroused, but I can feel his cock

twitching against my rear. He's getting hard again, and I wriggle my butt a little, hoping to speed up that process.

"My, my, Ms. Fairchild. You are a naughty girl."

"Very," I say. "Fuck me again, Mr. Stark."

He bites my earlobe, just hard enough that I squeal. "On your knees."

I look back at him. "What?"

"On your knees."

I obey.

"Spread your legs."

I do. I've never had sex like this—who am I kidding, I've never had sex like anything I've done with Damien. I feel exposed. And, yeah, I like the feeling.

He is behind me, and he runs his palms over my ass, then bends to kiss my cheek. "Sweet," he says. He slides his fingers between my legs, stroking my sex, the sensation of his touch beyond delicious.

He brings his hand up, and I feel his thumb at my anus. I bite my lower lip. "No," I whisper.

"No?" he repeats, increasing the pressure and sending a shock of amazing sensations through me. "Not sunset?"

I gasp, and he laughs. "No," he repeats. "You're right. Not now. Not yet." He slides his finger between my ass cheeks, and I draw in air, overwhelmed by the sensations. "But soon, Nikki," he says. "Because there is no part of you that isn't mine." Swiftly, he thrusts two fingers into my vagina even as the pad of his thumb presses against my ass. My muscles contract, wanting to draw him in, and there's no denying the intensity of my arousal. Even if I admit it only to myself, I want to experience everything with Damien. Every last thing.

"Put your arms down," he says, "so you're resting on your elbows. That's right."

I'm on the mattress, my head low, my ass high. Yeah, exposed is right. But I don't have time to think about my position, because Damien's touch grows more intense. He's leaning over me, one hand stroking my nipple as the other plays with my cunt, dipping in and out, in and out. "You make me so hard," he says.

I hear the rip of a condom packet, and then, a moment later, the pressure of his cock against me. This time, he does fuck me hard and, dammit, I don't want it to end. The pressure of his thrusts moves us across the bed, and I reach out, grabbing hold of the iron bedframe to hold myself in position, meeting him thrust for thrust, losing myself in the sensation and the sound of our bodies meeting.

I feel when he gets close, and as he does, his hand returns to my clit, stroking and teasing and bringing me closer and closer. "Come with me," he demands. "I'm coming, baby, I want you to come with me, too." He explodes inside me, and that's all it takes to bring me over the edge with him, the universe showering stars down on the two of us.

Spent, we collapse together on the bed, a tangle of arms and legs.

When my body is functioning again, I prop myself up on an elbow and brush his cheek. He looks rumpled and sexy and very well-fucked, and I get a nice little knot of satisfaction in my belly.

He looks at me and smiles.

I grin flirtatiously. "That was nice," I say. "Can we do it again?"

21

"Nice?" he repeats. I can tell he's trying to sound offended, but the crinkling around his eyes gives away his mirth. "That wasn't just nice. That was rocket ship to the moon. That was fucking amazing. *Guinness World Records* quality. Hell, that fuck was a thousand times better than those shoes you were wearing the night we met."

"I wasn't sure you remembered."

He runs his fingers through my hair and sighs. "I remember everything about you."

Considering how well he knew the details of my education, he may not be exaggerating. "You didn't remember the pageant."

"The Dallas Convention Center. You wore a fire engine red ball gown and a turquoise bathing suit. You were also about ten pounds lighter, and you were eyeing the mini-cheesecakes with the kind of lust that makes a man hard."

I laugh. "Yeah, I probably was."

He strokes my breasts and my hips. "The curves are an improvement."

"I think so, too. But my mother about had a heart attack

when I told her I wasn't going to count carbs or calories anymore." I grin at him. "I can't believe you really remember all of that."

"You were the only contestant who seemed alive to me, and that was despite the fact that everything you were doing was a lie. Or maybe because of it."

"A lie?" I prop myself up on my elbow, fascinated. "What do you mean?"

"Exactly what I told you at the time. You didn't want to be there. You felt like a kindred spirit."

"You were right. That was my last pageant. After that one, I finally managed to get free." I frown. "Kindred spirit? You said that because you wanted out of tennis, didn't you?"

His expression darkens. "Hell yes."

I hope he can't see my sadness. I remember the emcee introducing him at the pageant, announcing that Damien Stark had just won the US Open. He had so much talent, and the joy had been ripped away from him. I'm certain there's more to it than the story he told me, and I wonder if he'll ever tell me the full truth.

He strokes my cheek, and I smile. "We both got out," I say, forcing myself away from melancholy. "And now we're both free to explore other options."

His expression turns devious as his hand creeps down. "Let me show you what I want to explore."

I gasp as he slides his fingers inside me.

"Too sore?"

I am, but I don't want to admit it. "No," I whisper.

"I'm very glad to hear it." He lays me back, then eases his body on top of mine. His weight feels delicious, the pressure safe. Like he's holding me close and protecting me. His mouth brushes mine in a flurry of soft kisses that start at my lips and then trail down my neck before he eases back up to press a kiss to my ear. "I thought we'd try something new," he says. "Or, rather, something old."

"Old?"

"Plain, old-fashioned missionary position. Spread your legs, baby," he says, then groans in satisfaction when I do. The wide head of his cock presses against me, but he doesn't enter. Instead he moves just slightly, teasing us both.

My breath comes in fluttering gasps, and just as I'm about to break down and beg, he thrusts inside me. I gasp, arching back, grimacing from both pain and pleasure.

"I think someone broke the rules," he murmurs as he finds his rhythm and eases in and out of me. "I think you lied when you said you weren't sore."

I grin up at him, mischievous. "Maybe I did. Maybe it was worth it."

"I'll go nice and easy," he says, and he does, moving so slow and deep that it's almost like torture as the crescendo builds, higher and higher until I finally explode in his arms, limp and open to him. His orgasm follows quickly, and he clutches me, slamming hard into me, then collapsing against me.

"There's something to be said for traditional," I murmur, and beside me, Damien laughs.

For a few minutes, we just lay in the dark listening to the ocean. Then Damien takes my hand. "Let's get cleaned up and eat."

I'm not about to argue with either of those, so I slide back into the robe and follow the stunning view of a naked Damien past the fireplace to the rest of the third floor. It's also been finished out, and there's a tricked-out, restaurant-sized kitchen—"just a small one for parties"—a still unfurnished bedroom, and the most amazing bathroom I've ever seen. It's at least twice the size of Jamie's condo. The ceiling is over thirteen feet high, and it's made entirely of glass. Right now, it's a dark void, but if

Damien were to turn off the lights, I imagine that the stars would twinkle above us.

One wall is lined with a granite countertop that has two huge sinks. On either side of each is a vanity area. An electric razor is at the far sink. Along with a toothbrush and a bottle of after-shave. On the closer sink, there is another toothbrush, still in plastic. There's also a small box. Curious, I open it, and find foundation, powder, and a variety of eye shadows and liners, all in my favorite colors.

"How did you know to get all of this?"

"I'm a man of many resources," he says.

I frown. Why didn't he just ask me what brand and colors I wore? I'm feeling a bit under a microscope, with nothing quite my own. It's the way my mother always made me feel, but Damien is not Elizabeth Fairchild, and I'm afraid that I'm over-reacting.

"What's wrong?"

"Nothing." I don't quite manage a smile.

"Your makeup preferences and shoe size are in the Macy's gift registry," he says gently.

"Oh." I shake my head, feeling like a fool. "I forgot. I did that for last year's birthday." I take a deep breath and look him in the eye. "Thank you."

"You're very welcome."

I run my finger over the cool countertop. "I can't believe how amazing this floor is. The house isn't even finished yet."

"I made sure to complete the areas that mattered for this week."

"Oh. When did you do that?"

"After you agreed. It's remarkable how fast things can be accomplished when the price is right."

"You didn't have to do this for me."

"I didn't want to bring you to a construction site." He reaches out his hand and I take it. He leads me to the back of the bathroom, past the shower with at least a dozen showerheads and a tub the size of a swimming pool.

There's only one closet, but it's huge. We step inside and I see that it's been divided down the middle with something that resembles a kitchen island, but has bureau-style drawers on either side. There's a remote control on top of the island. He picks it up and presses a button. I hear water start to run in the tub.

The right side has a few white shirts, some jeans, some slacks, and something in a garment bag. A tux, I presume. On the whole, it's pretty thin. In contrast, the left side of the closet is packed full. Robes. Dresses. Skirts. Blouses. And shoes. Hundreds of shoes. "Mine again?" I ask, raising a brow.

"I think you'll find it all fits."

"You know, shopping is part of the fun."

"And I've already promised you a spree. In the meantime, you have plenty to choose from."

I roll my eyes. "What's in the island? Underwear?"

"No." His mouth twitches. "I thought we were clear that underwear isn't needed."

"But when I'm home—I mean, I'm going to have job interviews this week, I hope."

"No underwear," he repeats. "Not this week. Not unless I specifically tell you to."

I consider arguing, but I don't. It would be for form only. The truth is, the idea excites me. Being naked beneath my dress. Knowing that it's because it pleases Damien. Thinking of him every time a breeze caresses my sex.

"Bra?" I ask.

He eyes the curve of my breasts under the red robe. "No," he says, and my nipples peak with arousal. He notices, and I see the answering excitement in his eyes.

"People will be able to tell," I say.

"Let them," he says. "Come on." I follow him to the tub. "Too hot?" he asks.

I dip my hand in. It's hot, but not unbearable. "Not even close."

"Really?" He looks intrigued, and turns down the cold water tap until it is only a trickle.

"Is that bubble bath?" I ask, pointing to a built-in dispenser.

"Go ahead."

I press the button, and a floral-scented gel squirts into the water right beneath the tap. Bubbles immediately form. "Now that's a bath," I say, laughing. "Can I get in?"

"Of course."

I drop the robe and climb in. Already conveniently nude, Damien follows. He eases his back against the side and then settles me in between his legs. I feel his cock, soft now, against my rear. I shimmy a little, and it twitches.

"Tease," he murmurs. He squirts some liquid soap into his hands and begins to bathe me, caressing my arms with suds, then my breasts, then dipping down to stroke between my thighs. I close my eyes and lean back, feeling him get hard against me, feeling my body opening for him again. I just had him—and now I really am a little sore—but I still want. Dear God, how I want.

His fingers tease me, gently making circles around my clit, making me squirm. "I'm not going to fuck you again," he whispers. "And I'm not going to make you come."

I shift position, silently protesting.

"Tomorrow," he says. "Anticipation. It's a good thing."

"You're mean," I say.

"Baby, you ain't seen nothing." He grips me at the waist and eases me around, so that I'm kneeling on his lap in the tub. Considering he's just told me he's not going to fuck me, it's one hell of an interesting position since the length of his cock is hard between us. I slip my hand down and stroke him. Soft, teasing. He feels like velvet on steel, and I want him inside me. Boldly, desperately, I want him. "You're not going to fuck me," I say softly. "But that doesn't mean I can't fuck you."

As I ease my hips up, I see the look of heated surprise on his face.

"Oh, no," he warns.

"Oh, yes," I say, positioning his cock beneath me, then lowering myself onto him, fast and hard. I clutch his shoulders, arch my head back, and ride him.

"Jesus, Nikki." His voice is a desperate groan and he grabs my hips, taking over the work of pistoning us together. I'm learning his body, and I can see how fast he's building. I move harder, faster, pushing him along. "Oh, Christ, I'm going to come."

He explodes inside me, then pulls me close as he breathes hard, his entire body going limp. "That was . . . unexpected," he says. "And pretty damned amazing," he adds, making me feel hot and sexy and powerful.

He strokes my cheek. "You didn't use a condom."

I look away, weirdly shy. "I assumed you were clean. You are, right?"

"I am," he says. "But that's not the only issue."

"I'm on the pill," I admit. I don't tell him that it's more for cramps than for birth control.

"Good," he says. "In fact, that's excellent."

I ease off him, and curl up beside him in the rapidly cooling water. He holds me close, then shifts our position and stands, reaching to pull me up. I let him help me out and dry me off with the kind of thick towel I've only seen in spas. Then he holds the robe for me and ties the sash around my waist. He dries himself off next and pulls on a simple cotton robe. "Come," he says, then leads me to the bed.

He opens a trunk and pulls out two pillows and a light comforter, which he spreads over the sheets. He holds the sheet open in an obvious invitation, so I start to slide in. "Take the robe off," he says, and I do, untying the sash and then letting the soft material fall off my shoulders to pool at my feet.

"Don't fall asleep on me," he says, after he's tucked me in. "I'll be right back."

I roll over and look out at the ocean. The windows are still open, and the cool night air is blowing in, but it's warm under the comforter. The sky is black, and the ambient light is minimal enough that I can actually see the stars twinkling above.

After a moment, I feel the mattress shift as Damien sits beside me. He has a tray with wine, cheese, and grapes. I grin and ease myself up to a sitting position, the pillow propped against the cool metal of the bedframe.

"Open your mouth," he says, then feeds me a grape when I comply. "You're beautiful, Nikki," he says. "Do you believe me?"

"When you say it, I do."

My legs are under the covers, but he rests his hand on them. "How long?"

I don't pretend to misunderstand. "I was sixteen when I started," I say. "My sister got married and moved out. And Mother kicked the pageant stuff into overdrive. It sounds petty, I know, but Ashley was the only person who kept me centered. Without her around, I got so frustrated I'd take the crowns out of the trophy case and bend them. Not so much that Mother noticed. Just enough so that they weren't perfect anymore." I shrug. "I guess I graduated from crowns to my own skin."

"Why cutting?"

"I don't really know. It's a compulsion; it just felt like that was what I needed. Either cut or float off into some black hell. I felt so disconnected, like my life didn't belong to me. The pain gave me an anchor. Now, I think it was something my mother couldn't touch. Then, I just knew it helped. It's hard to explain." I shrug. I want him to understand, but I don't really understand myself, and I don't like talking about it.

"I get it," he says.

I look at him, wondering if he's just being polite, but I see genuine comprehension in his face.

"Sixteen," he says thoughtfully. "But when I saw you compete at eighteen, there were no scars."

"My hips," I say. "I kept all the cuts on my hips at first. Easy enough to hide, even in a pageant dressing room."

"What changed?" He's holding my hand, gently stroking my fingers.

"Ashley," I admit. "When I was eighteen, she committed suicide. Her husband had left her—my mother had been appalled. Said Ashley must have done something to drive him away. I guess Ashley thought so, too, because her suicide note said she was a failure." I swallow, appreciating the way he's squeezing my hand in support. "That was the first time I realized how much I hated my mother. But I still didn't have the courage to tell her to fuck the pageants. So I sliced up my thighs." My smile is ironic. "That's a lot harder to hide."

"Did she get you help?"

"No. First she went on and on about how I screwed up her plans and embarrassed her. Then she told me I was a selfish bitch because I was throwing away all that prize money and scholarships and probably even a husband."

Damien says nothing, but I can see the burn of temper in his eyes and the tightness across his body. He's holding in an explosion, and the fact that his wrath is on my behalf gives me the strength to continue.

"She told me I destroyed all her hard work, and she didn't know why she'd spent years bothering with a ridiculous little fool like me. She said I'd ruined my body and my future. I guess part of me believed her, because even once I was in Austin at school, I still cut."

He hands me a glass of wine, and I take it gratefully. "I was scared and alone and overwhelmed. But I did see a counselor, and things started to get better and finally I stopped." I take a sip. "My mother has money," I admit. "Nothing like you have, but she inherited the family oil business when my grandfather passed away, along with a pretty hefty bank account." I don't mention that Mother's ineptitude drove the company into the ground and she ended up selling it. Now she's living on what's in the bank, and the fortune is shrinking every year because she hasn't got a clue how to manage it and refuses to hire an advisor. That's one of the reasons I'm determined to learn how to run a business before I actually have a business to run.

"Anyway, Mother cut me off financially after I declared my majors. Science wasn't what she wanted for her little girl. But that was the best thing for me, because suddenly I didn't have her looking over my shoulder. I didn't have to be perfect. I didn't quit immediately, but it started to get better, and after a while I didn't need to cut anymore."

My words have been pouring out of me. It's more than I've ever told anyone. Even Jamie and Ollie only learned the truth in small doses. But it feels good to get it out, even though the price is the growing ferocity I see in his eyes.

Still, I haven't told him everything. . . .

He puts our glasses on a table by the bed and moves the tray with the food out of the way. Then he pulls me into his arms, so that my head is resting on his shoulder. Slowly, his fingers trail up and down my arm. "I understand, baby. I promise you, I understand."

I squeeze my eyes tight. I believe him.

"But what aren't you telling me?"

I blink at him. "I—how do you know that?"

"The way you ran from me," he says simply.

I ease out of his embrace and roll over on my side.

He presses his palm to my shoulder. I close my eyes.

"What if I say 'sunset'?" My voice is a whisper.

His fingers tighten, then relax. "If you need to." He reaches over me and takes my hand, then twines his fingers with mine. "Or you can just hold tight."

I don't know where to begin, so I start with the easiest. "I never slept with Ollie," I say. "Not the way you understood me, anyway."

He is silent, and so I continue, telling my story to the night sky and to Damien. "It was about a week after Ashley's birthday, a few years after the suicide. I'd mostly stopped cutting, but sometimes—well, sometimes I needed it. But I was getting better. Ollie knew. And Jamie. And they were helping me."

"What happened?"

"I got drunk. I mean wasted drunk. My mom had called and given me some head trip. I missed Ashley something fierce. And I was dating this guy. Kurt. We'd been going out for months, and it had taken me a while, but we started sleeping together, and he would tell me how he didn't mind the scars, that I was beautiful, that it was about me, not my scars or my tits or any of that stuff. Just me and him and our connection. And I believed him and, honestly, the sex was good. We had fun together."

I suck in a deep breath to give me courage to continue. "But this night, we both got wasted. Honestly, I don't even know how he managed to get an erection. But he did, and we did, and afterward he looked at my legs and he"—my voice breaks with the memory— "he told me I was lucky I had a pretty face and such a sweet pussy because I was one totally screwed-up bitch, and my scars made him want to puke."

I take deep breaths, keeping my eyes on the sky and my fingers tight in Damien's hand. Even now, the memory makes me feel sick. I'd trusted Kurt, and he'd completely ripped me apart.

"I went to Ollie," I continue. "He knew about my scars and he was my friend and I knew he was attracted to me. And I tried to seduce him."

"He wouldn't sleep with you," Damien says.

"He wouldn't fuck me," I clarify. "But he took off my jeans

and he told me that for some of those scars he remembered what I'd been through, and he told me that he thought I was strong. That he didn't want me cutting anymore. That I was better than my mother and I needed to forget assholes like Kurt and finish school and get the hell out of Texas. Then he held me until I fell asleep."

I manage a watery smile. "I thought he got me through it. Guess I still have some issues to work through, huh?"

I've put a light note in my voice, but Damien doesn't respond to it.

"Damien?" I roll over to look at him, then immediately sit up. He looks angry, like he's barely holding in his fury. I take his hand. "He's ancient history."

"He will be if I ever meet the fucker. What's his last name?"

I hesitate. Considering Damien owns half the universe, I think better of saying it. "No. It's all in the past. I'm over it," I lie.

He eyes me but I look back blandly. "What about the other men you've slept with?"

I frown, surprised by the question. "There haven't been any others. Just my first when I was sixteen—some prep school idiot my mom fixed me up with. And then Kurt." I shrug. "It's okay, though. I mean, I dated and fooled around, but mostly I've been focused on school. I haven't been sitting in an ivory tower wondering why no one's unlocking my chastity belt. And I own a really nice vibrator."

The last makes him burst out laughing. "Do you?"

I can't believe I said that. I consider lying and telling him it was a joke, but instead I just nod.

"Well, maybe someday you can show it to me." His hand slides over my bare ass, and I have to admit that his suggestion sounds pretty tempting, though I'm not sure I'd have the nerve. Then again, where Damien is concerned, I seem to be able to find the nerve for a lot of unexpected things.

"And after Kurt?" Damien asks. "Did you cut anymore?"

"No. There were a few times I really wanted to, but no."

"The garage?"

I remember the figure of a man as I searched for my keys. "That was you?"

"I was worried about the way you left."

"I was scared of what you'd think. You were . . . I wanted you, but you were about to see them, and—"

He presses a kiss to my forehead. "I know, baby. Did you cut yourself?"

"I thought about it," I admit. "I even jammed my keys into my flesh. But did I cut?" I shake my head. "No. I didn't."

"And you won't." His voice is hard, earnest. He presses his palms to my cheeks, cupping my face. "You asked if I'll hurt you," he says. "There are a lot of things I do—things I want to do with you. And if there's pain, it's only to bring more pleasure. Okay?"

I nod.

"I won't draw blood. That's not my thing. But even if it was, I wouldn't do it with you. Do you understand that?"

I swallow and nod. I'm slightly embarrassed—this is starting to feel like a counseling session. But at the same time, his words and his concern are making me feel cherished. Like I'm more than just the girl in his bed for the week.

"Do you still need the pain?" he asks.

"I didn't think so," I say. "But then in the car—I wanted it, but I fought it."

"If you need it, you tell me." His voice is hard. Urgent. "Do you understand?"

I nod and curl up close to him and let him stroke my hair. Because I also hear what he doesn't say. That if I need to feel grounded—if I need the pain to feel centered and real and *here*—then Damien is the one who'll stand at my center. Whatever I need, he'll give.

I shiver a bit. I've never been so exposed to another person, not even Ollie, not even Jamie. And I've never felt more taken care of.

"And what about you, Damien?" I finally ask. "What do you need?"

He looks at me, and for a moment, I think he's going to tell me the secrets he's kept buried deep inside. That he's going to give me a clue as to what really makes Damien Stark tick. Considering how much I opened up, it only seems fair. But then his expression shifts and I see only a playful spark in his eye.

"You," he says, and then he closes his mouth over mine.

22

"Blondie, I swear you are on fire today." Blaine grins at me as I stand in the red robe with the morning light creeping in through the open windows. "So you think you're good? We can take it slow again if you need to."

"I'm good. Thanks. Damien told you why I freaked?" I'd asked Damien to explain to Blaine that my meltdown yesterday didn't have to do with posing as much as it had to do with what Blaine would be painting.

"He did, and I'll tell you exactly what I told him—except for the fact that your scars mean you've been hurting, I am one-hundred-percent cool with having them in the painting. Some models, especially the professional ones, it's like painting air-brushed people. Give me something raw any day. Honest, Nikki. I'll do you right."

"I believe you." I shift a little, and rest one hand on the foot of the bed, my palm cupping the ball at the top of the bedpost. With my other hand, I reach for the drapes. "Something like this, maybe?"

"I'm not sure," Damien says from beside me. His hands close

over my waist and he shifts me toward the window. "Maybe if we set up a fan outside? Really get the drapes billowing?"

"You'll need to put back the two you took down," I say with a smirk.

"Huh?" Blaine says, and Damien laughs.

"What do you think?" Damien directs the question toward Blaine and sidesteps my comment about the drapes.

"You're the boss."

"And you're the artist."

Blaine raises an eyebrow and smirks at me. "That's a first. According to Evelyn, our benefactor doesn't take direction from anybody."

"I'm not taking direction," Damien says. "I'm asking your opinion. I didn't say I would accept it."

Blaine studies me, circles me, and finally moves me a few inches to the left. Then back to the right. Then slightly at an angle.

He stands back, his chin in his hand, and looks at Damien, who moves me a few inches forward. Then shifts me to a slightly different angle.

"Boys!" I'm beginning to feel like the paid chattel I am.

"Actually, that looks good," Blaine says. "Stay there. I think I'm having a moment of brilliance."

I try hard not to move, while at the same time looking sideways at him.

"How do you feel about a reflection?" Blaine asks Damien, then brushes past me before Damien can respond. "I swear, this is going to be amazing." He pulls out one of the window panels, leaving the wall mostly open except for one pane of glass in front of me. "You see? I'm right, aren't I?"

He moves back toward the humongous canvas he's propped up against a table. He shifts a bit as if looking for something, then points. "There. Her reflection on the glass, the breeze, and the woman herself facing out. It will be stunning."

"Her face?" Damien asks.

"Hidden. Probably looking down. And the reflection will be muted. Nothing graphic. Trust me. It will look exceptional."

"I like it," Damien says. "Nikki?"

I force myself not to turn to face him, in case that messes up the composition. "I have a say?" I ask playfully. "I thought you bought me lock, stock, and barrel."

"Stocks are tempting," he growls, moving into my line of sight. He glares at Blaine. "Yes. I want the reflection. I want as much of her as I can get. I haven't had enough this morning."

My cheeks flame because that's a rather private joke. We'd been in the shower when Blaine had pounded on the front door. And not just getting clean. I'd been about to follow up my breakfast of fruit and cheese with a delicious serving of Damien. But Blaine's arrival put a damper on that—and I'm afraid it left Damien a little grumpy.

I smile sweetly again. "By the way, isn't it Tuesday? Aren't you supposed to be out of town?" I remember Carl saying that the original meeting was bumped to Saturday because Damien would be away on business at the time of the originally scheduled slot.

He looks at me blankly, and then his face clears. "No," he says. "I have no plans outside of the office today."

"Oh." It takes me a second, but I figure out what he'd done. He wanted to see me sooner rather than later, and he'd lied to Carl to make that happen.

"Somebody broke a rule," I say. "No lying."

His grin is pure evil. "I never said the rule applied to me."

Blaine laughs, and so do I. But some small part of me can't help but cringe. *I never said the rule applied to me.*

I know he's teasing, but at the same time, I'm certain he means it. The rule *doesn't* apply to him. Has Damien been lying to me? Maybe not maliciously, but simply because he can? Because sometimes it's easier?

I think about the questions he's avoided, the times he's shifted our conversations. Is he just being a guy? Silent and unsharing? Is he simply inscrutable?

Or is he hiding something?

I recall what else Evelyn said. About how after Damien's rough youth she couldn't blame him for being closed off. For being a little damaged.

I think about the Damien who's held me and kissed me and laughed with me and teased me. I've seen a lighter side of Damien Stark. A side that most people don't know. But have I yet to see the dark?

"Yo. Blondie!"

Blaine's voice pulls me from my thoughts. He's motioning for me to move again. I do, and then finally—*finally*—settle into what Blaine deems the perfect pose.

Damien slides in to press a kiss to my forehead. "Tonight," he says. "I have meetings all day, but I'll text you with the details. Edward's ready to take you home whenever you're done."

"I could keep her here all day," Blaine says. "She's a fabulous subject."

"All day?" I squeak. I've been posing for no time at all, and my muscles are already stiff.

"I said I *could*," Blaine clarifies. "I think Mr. Big Shot Businessman will fire me if I tire you out or keep you too long."

"I certainly will," Damien says. He lowers his voice. "I have plans for her." His voice curls around me, running through me, sending blood pulsing to all sorts of interesting places.

"*There* you go," Blaine says. "I like that color on your cheeks, Blondie."

I can't move, of course, but I'm seething as Damien leaves, chuckling softly as he descends the marble staircase.

After he's gone, Blaine is a whirlwind of activity, in constant motion, looking, sketching, giving orders, adjusting lights. Despite the overtly erotic nature of his work, he's actually a hoot to work with, and as far as I can tell there's not a dark bone in his body.

"Evelyn's dying to see you again," he says when we're finally wrapping up. "She wants the gossip on Damien."

I slip the robe back on and tie the sash around my waist. "Really? I get the feeling she's the one who has all the gossip. On Damien and on everybody else."

"Sounds to me like you've got my lady nailed."

"I really do need to give her a call," I admit. "I've been wanting to see her, too. Maybe we can see each other tomorrow."

He gives me an odd look and shakes his head. "Get out of here, Blondie. You're messing with my concentration."

"Oh." I'm not sure how the conversation slipped away, but maybe Blaine is just showing off an artistic temperament. "You're sure it's okay if I go? I mean, how can you paint me if there's no me to paint?"

"It's amazing how much of painting from life doesn't actually require the living to be present." He makes a shooing gesture with his paintbrush. "Go. Edward's probably bored out of his mind."

"He's just waiting out there?" I had assumed I'd need to call him or something.

I get dressed quickly, then grab my stuff and hurry down the stairs, but before I do I also grab the Leica and take a few quick shots of the room, of the painting in progress, and of Blaine. "This kind of thing doesn't happen to me often. I'm keeping a record."

"Blondie," Blaine says, "I know the feeling."

Edward isn't at all put out by how long I've taken. Apparently he likes to sit in the Town Car and listen to audiobooks. "Last week it was Tom Clancy," he says. "This week, Stephen King."

On the ride from Malibu back to Studio City, Edward listens to his book and I listen to my thoughts. Or I try to. There's so much going on in my head—Damien, my job search, Damien, the portrait, the million dollars, Damien, Jamie and Ollie. And, oh yeah, Damien.

I lean my head back, half-dozing and half-thinking, and before I know it, Edward has pulled up in front of the condo and is walking around to open the door for me.

"Thanks for the lift," I say as I climb out.

"It was my pleasure. And Mr. Stark asked me to be sure you got this. He said to tell you it's for this evening." He hands me a white box tied with a piece of white twine. I take it from him, surprised to find there is essentially no weight to the box at all.

I'm curious about the box, but I'm more curious about my job prospects, so I toss the box on the bed as I enter my room, where I immediately fire up my computer and pull up my resume. This probably qualifies as anal, but I don't want to call Thom, my headhunter, without having my resume in front of me. What if he has a question about the exact date one of my apps went on sale? What if he needs to know the title of the research paper I presented during my summer internship two years ago. What if he wants me to change the font and then resubmit the thing?

As soon as I've printed a copy, I dial Thom's direct dial. "I know you just got my resume yesterday," I say, "but I wanted to check and see if you'd had any nibbles."

"I've had more than a nibble," he says. "I've had a bite."

"Seriously?" A sudden image of Damien asking why I didn't just go work for him pops into my head. "Wait. With who?"

"Innovative Resources," he says. "Familiar with them?"

"No," I admit, sagging a bit with relief. I'm having a perfectly lovely time lost in my fantasy with Damien. But while silk sashes and blindfolds may get me hot in the bedroom, I don't think I want to bow to the amount of control Damien would demand in the boardroom. "What kind of bite?"

"They want to schedule an interview. They're short-staffed

and they're busy. They'd like to see you in the office tomorrow afternoon. Can you make it?"

"Absolutely," I say, certain Blaine won't mind. If I set the interview for two, that should be plenty of time to get in a full session, return to Studio City, get changed, and make it to wherever Innovative is located.

Thom promises me that he'll set it up, and that he'll pull some information on the company and send it over so that I can prep. I hang up the phone, drop the professional attitude, and do a wild dance out of my bedroom and out into the hall. I pound on Jamie's door, but she's not there, so I take my dance into the kitchen, pop the top on a Diet Coke, and go wild. Because it's a celebration, I even dig into my secret stash and pull out the frozen Milky Way I keep hidden behind the ancient TV dinners.

Heaven.

I'm heading back to my room with my frozen chocolate bar sticking out of my mouth when I see the Monet still on the floor by the kitchen table. Jamie had promised she'd help me hang it—after making repeated lame jokes about needing to buy a stud finder so that it could get nailed—but so far we'd made no progress in that direction. I want it in my room, though, so I take it with me back to my bedroom. I clear a spot on my dresser, then prop it up in front of the mirror. Now, when I look at myself, I see me standing over an Impressionist sunset. Not a bad way to live, when you think about it.

In the mirror behind me, I see the reflection of the white box that Edward gave me. For this evening, he'd said. I turn to look at it, lift it, shake it a little.

I use a pair of nail scissors to clip the twine, then pull the top off the box. Inside, there is a piece of cloth and a strand of pearls. I peer at it for a second, confused, then hook a finger under the pearls. They rise, bringing the lace with them.

Panties.

A thong, to be specific. And the pearls are, well, in the thong part.

I leave them on my pillow and snatch up my phone. He's probably buying the universe or something, but I text him anyway: Got ur present. V pretty. I wonder abt the comfort factor, tho.

His reply comes almost immediately: This from the woman who can't walk in her shoes?

I scowl and type fast with my thumbs: U raise a good point. But shldn't a man who can buy continents & small planets hve better sense?

I imagine his grin as his reply comes: Trust me. You'll find my gift very satisfying. Did you read the card?

What? My reply is simple: ???

Under the thong. Read it. Follow it. Don't break the rules.

And then, just moments later: Must go buy a large planet. Until tonight.

I laugh, grinning like an idiot as I toss my phone back on the bed and pull the box toward me. Sure enough, I find a card tucked into the tissue. I read it, and then I pick up the panties again. I run the strand of pearls between my fingers, breathing just a little bit harder than before as tiny beads of sweat gather between my breasts and my body warms all over.

I close my eyes, and I picture the words Damien wrote:

Wear this tonight. I'll pick you up at 7.
Cocktail attire.
You'll want to touch yourself. Don't.
*That's **my** privilege.*

D.S.

23

I will never doubt Damien again.

I'm dressed by six-thirty. By seven, I'm so desperately turned on that I wonder how these panties can be legal. They're most definitely not practical. I grab a sparkling water and sit on the couch trying to read, but mostly I just press the water to the back of my neck because every time I move, the pearls make me hot, and if I'm not careful I'm going to melt before Damien picks me up.

Or I'll break a rule.

Except, dammit, simply breathing is making me crazy. I imagine Damien's voice in my ear, telling me how hot I'm getting, how tormented he knows I am, how wet I'm going to be for him, and how I absolutely, positively cannot do anything to release this pressure growing inside of me.

Oh, to hell with it.

I'm wearing a black garter and black stockings, and as I lean my head back against the couch, I trail my fingers up my thighs. It's only cheating a little if I pretend it's Damien's hand, right? And after all, it's not like he needs to know. . . .

My fingers slide over the pearls, but I don't touch myself. I only touch the strand. It moves, just like it does when I walk, and the sensation is amazing, like tiny rockets shooting through my body, raising me up. I'm so wet I can hardly stand it, and I imagine Damien's hands on my thighs, his mouth leaving a trail of kisses up my leg, his tongue flicking gently over me.

I moan softly—then jump guiltily from the sharp knock at the front door.

"Coming!" I call, and the irony *really* isn't lost on me.

I straighten my skirt, take a deep breath to hopefully smooth my face and hide my secret, then hurry to the door.

I open it to find Damien standing there, looking so sexy in a tux that I think I might just come without the benefit of pearls or fingers or anything except the sight of this man in front of me.

"You look amazing," he says, then moves his finger in a twirling motion. I comply, spinning with enough force so that the skirt of my deep purple cocktail dress flares out. It's a vintage dress that I've loved for years, with a fitted waist and a plunging neckline. Sexy, and yet at the same time it has a Grace Kelly kind of class. It makes me feel stunning, so it's easy to smile and accept the compliment.

"You're not so bad yourself," I say as he bends down to brush a soft kiss over my lips—a kiss he punctuates with a not-so-soft squeeze to my ass.

"Careful," I say. "Much more of that and we won't be leaving this apartment."

"Oh really? Why is that?" he asks innocently.

I smile sweetly, then grab my purse. I press a hand to his shoulder and lift myself up on my tiptoes so that my lips are right by his ear. "Because your little present is making me so hot that all I can think about is you inside me fucking me hard."

I ease back, keeping the breezy smile pasted on. His expression no longer looks so innocent. With smug satisfaction I glide past him out the door. "Coming?" I ask from the threshold.

"Apparently not yet," he growls, then follows me.

He's brought the limo, and I swallow when I see the familiar backseat. My attempts to be cool may be harder than I imagined.

I nod to Edward, who is holding the door open for us, then slide in, the pearls moving with me. I can't control the little gasp of pleasure that escapes me, but I settle into my seat and try to look nonchalant.

Damien eases in next to me and rests his hand on my knee. "Did you say something, Ms. Fairchild?"

"No. Nothing." I clear my throat. It feels very, very warm in here. "So, where are we going?"

"It's a charity function," he says.

"Mmm." I am *so* not interested. I'm also *so, so* aroused. Playing coy might be fun, but the fun is starting to turn into self-torture. "What charity?" I ask. "Any chance you could just write them a very big check and we can go to the house? Or your apartment? Or right here? Here is good, actually."

What started as a grin on Damien's perfect lips has turned into a full-blown chuckle. He reaches for the console and pushes the button to raise the privacy screen. "As a matter of fact, here is very good."

Oh, thank God . . .

"I think you have something to tell me, Ms. Fairchild." His eyes are dark and hungry.

I shift away from him, which considering the pearls isn't the best idea. He sees my reaction and the corner of his mouth twitches. He's enjoying my torment, the rotten bastard.

"Well?"

"I—I don't know what you're talking about."

He slides closer to me and takes my hand. He guides it to my thigh, then eases my skirt up just enough to reveal the band of my stocking. "You glow when you're aroused," he says. "I've told you that before. It's an incredible turn-on."

"Oh." The word slips out of me like a wisp of cloud.

"Did you do this, baby?" he asks, guiding my hand higher. Tracing over my scars, finding that soft, tender spot where my thigh meets my sex. "Did you touch yourself before I came over?" He slides my hand over my sex. I'm slick with desire. He guides me to the pearls, then curves my fingers so that I'm caressing them as he moves my hand up and down, up and down. "Did you play with your clit? Did you think of me?"

"Yes," I whisper, as his hand continues to control my finger.

"Did you read my note?"

"Yes." I squirm as our joined hands continue to tease me. I am desperately, achingly hot for him.

"Yes, what?"

I fight not to smile and end up gasping. "Yes, sir."

"What did it say?"

"Not to touch myself." I tilt my head so that I'm looking straight into his eyes. My skin is burning, my dress clinging to me from the sheen of sweat our heat has generated. "You said that was your privilege."

"And why is it my privilege?"

I'm so desperate for him I can barely speak. "Because I'm yours."

"That's right." Slowly, he thrusts two fingers inside of me. I bite my lip so as not to cry out, silently begging him to just fuck me right then.

He doesn't. Instead he pulls out, then gently takes both our hands away, sliding out from under my skirt. I actually whimper. "You broke the rules, Ms. Fairchild. What happens to girls who break the rules?"

I shift my hips, letting the pearls continue the work that our hands were doing. "They're punished."

He casts his eyes down toward my crotch. "I think you better sit still, Ms. Fairchild."

"Damien," I beg.

He bends over and slides his hands down into the bodice of my dress. His fingers find my very erect, very sensitive nipples, and twists them. Not hard enough to hurt—but just barely. I gasp as a fresh wave of pleasure breaks through me.

"Do you like that?"

"Oh, yes."

He keeps one hand on my breast. With the other, he pulls out the lacquered chopstick I'd used to hold up my hair. It falls in loose curls to my shoulders. He runs the strands through his hands and breathes in the scent of my shampoo.

"I'm crazy about your hair," he says, then takes a handful and tugs my head back so that I'm looking up at him. His mouth brushes over mine. My lips are parted, ready for his kiss, but he's only teasing me. Torturing me.

"You're so cruel," I say.

"Oh, but I'm not," he says, his lips brushing over my cheek, my temple as he speaks. "Tell me, Ms. Fairchild. What should your punishment be? What should I do to a naughty girl who touches herself when she's not supposed to?"

I think about what he whispered to me the last time I was in this limo. About how he might have to punish me. About how if he was there, maybe he'd have to spank me. He'd been teasing—playing—but I'd heard real desire in his voice—and that had made me even wetter.

I lick my lips and turn my head so that I'm looking right at his face. "Maybe you ought to spank me."

His eyes grow so dark I think I could get lost in them. "Jesus, Nikki."

I wriggle off the seat and lay myself over his legs, my hips on his thighs. Slowly—deliberately—I raise my skirt. The pearls of the thong are tight between my ass cheeks, and the lace of the garters is pulled down tight to my stockings. But my ass is otherwise bare.

"Go ahead," I whisper. "Punish me."

I'm even wetter now, my cunt pulsing in anticipation. I can't believe I'm doing this.

His palm strokes my rear, and I close my eyes. His touch feels amazing.

"Nikki," he says. "Is this what you need?"

I open my eyes and see the slightest hint of worry beneath the desire. I think of my scars. Of my promise to him that I no longer need the pain.

"No," I say. "But it is what I want."

I watch as the worry fades to pure, erotic heat. "You've been a bad girl, Ms. Fairchild," he says, his voice sending shockwaves through me.

"Yes, sir, Mr. Stark."

His palm strokes my ass, then I feel a quick flash of cool air before his hand stings my rear. I cry out, more from surprise than from pain. He rubs me again, his fingers sliding down between my cheeks to find where I'm slick and wet for him. I hear his groan as my vagina clenches around him when he roughly thrusts two fingers inside me. "Oh, baby," he says, then withdraws his hand and lands another smack on my ass.

This time, I don't jump, but I do gasp, sucking in air while I keep my eyes closed, imagining the white of my rear turning slightly pink from the punishment he's delivering.

"Do you like that?"

"Yes," I confess.

"Hardly a punishment if you like it." *Smack*. "But I like it, too." *Smack, smack*.

I am in serious distress now, not from pain, but from such intense arousal that if Damien doesn't fuck me right then and there, I'm probably going to lose my mind.

One more smack and I cry out for him to stop. He hesitates, probably not certain if I meant to call out our safeword, but I use the break to shift my position until I'm straddling him and my fingers are on the fly of his tux. "Fuck me," I demand. "Fuck me now or don't ever think of fucking me again."

He laughs, then pulls me close and kisses me hard. I have his cock out and the pearls shoved to one side and I don't wait for him because I am truly, totally, completely shameless at this point. I lower myself on him, taking him in, pressing my palms to the roof of the limo so that I can take him harder and deeper. He holds my waist and I ride him, everything disappearing around me except the sensation of pleasure and the feel of Damien's cock filling me and my sore ass rubbing against the fine material of his tux.

"Oh, God, Nikki, those pearls," he says, and even through the haze of passion, I have to laugh. He's getting an interesting stroking, too. And I smile as I explode, my muscles clenching, milking him, making him come, too, until I collapse forward, my arms around his shoulders, and we breathe together, spent and sated.

"Serves you right," I whisper, and Damien, now soft inside me, laughs.

Damien pushes the button for the intercom and tells Edward to circle the block until he says otherwise. Apparently we'd arrived at the party.

Funny how I hadn't noticed.

Once he and I have adjusted our clothes and otherwise tried to make it look like we haven't been having sex in the back of a limo, Damien gives the order to return.

"Your lipstick is smeared," he says, sounding amused.

"Gee. I wonder why?" I have a compact and a lipstick in my purse, and I use some of the bar napkins to do a quick removal before I reapply. I'm about to twist my hair back up when Damien takes my wrist.

"Leave it," he says. "The way it falls on your shoulders is incredibly sexy."

I toss the chopstick aside and fluff my hair. I peer out the window at the tony Beverly Hills hotel that is hosting the event. "So no skipping out, huh?"

"I'm afraid not."

A valet opens the doors, but Damien helps me out. He presses his hand lightly to the small of my back and guides me inside.

The hotel is amazing. It's nestled in the hills and so exclusive that I've never even heard of it. The reception desk is in its own building, and we walk across the Saltillo tiles to a set of French doors open in the back. There's a tricked-up golf cart waiting for us. We get in and are whisked toward the event building. I spend the ride gaping in wonder at the grounds. Private bungalows are nestled away from the public areas but still close enough that guests can walk to the pool, the hiking trails, or any of the five-star restaurants that dot the premises.

The stucco event center sits beside a tennis court. It's surrounded by birds of paradise and palm trees and suggests California in the twenties. The inside is less California traditional and more Beverly Hills money. The walls are light wood, the floor a polished stone. An inviting bar dominates one entire wall, and two others are lined with floor-to-ceiling windows that open out onto a stone patio with a massive fire pit. Gambling stations fill the space. From where we stand near the entrance, I can see roulette, craps, and blackjack.

Waiters mingle with trays of finger foods and drinks. Every corner is filled with clusters of people laughing, talking, gambling, and generally having a good time. A banner over the entrance reads: S.E.F.—Five Years, Five Million Children. And Growing.

"What is S.E.F.?" I ask Damien, but we're moving again and he doesn't hear me.

"Do you want to play?" he asks, stopping a woman in a Vegas-style outfit with a money changer.

"Sure. How does it work?"

"We buy the tokens and play for prizes. All the cash goes to the educational foundation."

I glance up at him—I'm pretty sure I just figured out what the "S" stands for. "Stark Educational Foundation?"

"You're a very bright woman, Ms. Fairchild." He hands the girl two hundred dollar bills and she trades them out for tokens.

"I have a twenty in my purse."

"And I won't object if you spend it. It's a very good cause. But we can start with these." He hands me half the tokens. "Where to?"

Since I am terrible at blackjack and never learned how to play craps, I head to the roulette table.

"The lady feels lucky," Damien says to the operator, a petite redheaded woman who looks to be barely sixteen.

"On your arm, Mr. Stark? I guess she is."

As it turns out, it's Damien who's lucky. After half an hour, he's quadrupled our money, despite the fact that I keep losing it. "I give up," I say, taking a drink from a passing waitress. "Do you want to mingle?"

"Of course." He takes my arm and we move away from the table and into the crowd.

"I think our dealer—is she called a dealer?"

"In the States, yes," Damien says. "If we were in Paris, you could call her a croupier. What about her?"

"I think she has a bit of a crush on you."

He pauses to look at me. "Does she? And why do you think that?"

"She kept looking at you. But don't get any ideas. She's far too young for you."

"Actually, she's older than she looks."

I look up at him, surprised. "You really do know her?"

"Hell yes. She's one of our most successful foundation recipients," he says. "She grew up in a shithole of a town in Nevada with a mom who used the child-support check to buy meth. Now Debbie's a freshman at UCLA majoring in chemistry."

"That's wonderful. What exactly does the foundation do?"

"We identify kids with an aptitude for science who, for whatever reason, aren't able to access the opportunities. Most come from families like Debbie's, but we have a few who are bound by their own circumstances. One young man is a quadriplegic. He thought his dream of college was over after the accident that left him paralyzed. He's working on his Ph.D. from MIT now."

I feel tears prick my eyes, and I lean over to kiss his cheek. "Excuse me," I say, then slip away from him to one of the girls in the Vegas outfits and change my twenty dollars. It's not much, but right then it's everything.

Damien is smiling when I return. He says nothing, but he does take my hand and squeeze it.

We do the mingling party thing for a while, but then he pauses. "I see someone I'd like to speak with. Are you okay on your own for a few minutes?"

"I think I can tough it out," I say. He brushes a kiss over my lips and I am left alone. I don't mind, except that I don't really know anybody. I glance around, searching for a familiar face, and am rewarded when I actually see one. *Ollie*. I take a step in that direction, only to see that he's being intercepted by Damien.

A little knot of fear forms in my stomach. Why on earth would Damien want to talk to Ollie? I can think of no reason other than Ollie's repeated mentions to me of his fear that Damien isn't good for me and his hints that Damien has some serious skeletons in his closet. But I've never let on that Ollie's mentioned that kind of stuff. Have I?

Suddenly I'm very afraid that I talk in my sleep.

I consider interrupting them, but that would be too neurotic, and so I force myself to turn in the opposite direction. I do, and am thankful to see another familiar face—Blaine. He sees me at the same time and holds out his arms. I slide into them and accept his vigorous hug.

"There she is, my favorite model."

"You didn't tell me you'd be here." I tilt my head and glare. "Is Evelyn here? Is that why you looked so coy when I mentioned getting together with her?"

"Busted," he says. He raises his hand and waves, and a moment later, Evelyn is by our side.

"I see her all the time," Blaine says as he takes his leave of us. He winks at me. "*All* of her. You two talk." He gives Evelyn a passionate kiss and, from the way she squeals, a little bit of a grope, too. Then he saunters off, Evelyn watching him go.

I start to speak, but Evelyn holds up her hand. "Hang on, Texas. I want to watch the view." After a moment, his formal-wear-covered tush disappears in the crowd, and she turns to me with a sigh. "I'm almost sixty years old, and I'm only just now getting the best sex of my life. I swear, the universe isn't fair."

"Then again, maybe the universe is very good to you," I say, and she laughs.

"Well, look who's a glass-half-full kinda gal. You're right, Texas. I like the way you think."

I've never considered myself particularly optimistic, but maybe I am. Honestly, I really like this woman.

"I've been hearing nothing but good things about you, young lady," she says. "Guess it was a rom-com, after all. Or are we talking NC-17?"

I feel my cheeks heat. "Could be," I admit.

"Good for you. Hell, good for you both. That boy . . ." She shakes her head in an almost grandmotherly fashion.

"What?" I want to sit her down and demand she tell me everything she knows about Damien. Unfortunately, that kind of interrogation is generally considered uncool.

"I saw the way he kissed you just now. Gentle, but I swear he looked like he could eat you up."

Her words are like cotton candy to me, sweet and delicious.

"He's usually so closed off. It's wonderful to see him opening up to you."

"It is," I say, even though I am completely clueless and desperately curious. Opening up to me? Hardly. I'm learning that Damien is closed even tighter than I'd thought. Considering how much I've exposed myself to him, I'm feeling a little bit sick to my stomach. I don't show it though. Social Nikki is in full form tonight. "He's overcome so much," I add, hoping she'll respond with something that gives me a clue about the dark things in Damien's past.

"Now you see what I meant by inscrutable." She sighs. "It doesn't matter that so much has been swept under the carpet. These things haunt you. How could they not?"

"I know," I lie. *What was swept away?*

"See? That's why I think you're good for him. Hell, a year ago, you'd have to drag him to his own fund-raiser. Tonight he waltzed in here with you on his arm looking like he owns the world."

"Well," I say, "he pretty much does."

"True. Shit, I'm not anywhere near drunk enough for tonight. Let's go find one of those skinny bitches with the trays of drinks."

I follow her because I want to talk more and learn more, but we're soon sucked into the crowd and the rolling waves of conversation.

When Damien finds me ten minutes later, I've lost Evelyn and am discussing Humphrey Bogart movies with a guy who looks to be twelve but who swears he's the hottest new director of horror films.

Thankfully, Damien leads me away.

"Everything okay with you and Ollie?"

He gives me a sharp look, but nods. Then he traces the pad of his thumb along my lower lip, which has fast become one of my erogenous zones. "I think I need to taste you," he says, tugging my hair to tilt my head up to him. We're interrupted, though, by a tall thin man with salt-and-pepper hair.

"Charles," Damien says coldly. I have a feeling the ice is because of more than the interruption.

"We need to talk," the man says. He turns to me. "Charles Maynard. I'm terribly sorry to intrude."

"Oh, no. It's okay." Because, really, what else can I say?

Maynard leads Damien away and as soon as he does, Ollie sidles up to me. "Hey. I've been wanting to talk to you."

"I've been here all night." I hear the frost in my voice, but can't seem to control it.

Ollie either doesn't hear it or he ignores it. "I know. But I wanted you alone."

"What is it?" I'm sure I sound exasperated, but I'm not interested in another cryptic comment about how Damien's not right. for me.

"I just wanted to say I'm sorry. About what happened with Jamie, I mean. It was stupid and—"

I hold up my hand. "You guys are both adults. But you're also my friends. And you're engaged." I reach out and take both his hands in mine. "I don't want you to screw up a good thing. And I really, really don't want to get caught in the middle."

"I know. I know," he says. "It was a one-time thing. Stupid, but it's over."

I'm not sure I believe him, but I also don't want to talk about it. So I just nod and change the subject. "What did Damien want?"

"Oh, that." He tugs his hands away and shoves them into his pockets. "He thanked me. For, you know. Being there for you. After that stuff with Kurt."

I feel my cheeks warm. "It meant a lot to me."

He looks at me and shakes his head. "Don't you thank me, too. You know there's nothing I wouldn't do for you."

I look around the room and find the back of Damien's head. "He's a good guy, Ollie," I say. "Are you starting to see that?"

"Sure," he says, but there's something odd in his voice.

"What?" I demand. "What is it about Damien Stark that bugs you so much? Is it all the shit Sara Padgett's brother is stirring up?"

He exhales loudly, and I'm certain that I've nailed it. "Oh, hell, Nik. Stark's a celebrity. He's not up on billboards, but that's what he is, and there are always shitstorms around celebrities. Eric Padgett's just the latest guy tossing wads to see what sticks."

I peer at him. "And that's it? That's all that's bugging you?"

Ollie straightens his tie, a sure tell that he's hiding something. "Yeah. Yeah, that's it. Listen, I see a client. I'm going to catch her, okay?"

I grab his wrist. "Wait. What aren't you telling me?"

"Nothing."

"Jesus, Ollie, this is me. What aren't you saying?"

"I—oh, hell, fine." He runs his fingers through his hair, then takes my arm and leads me to a quiet corner. "Honestly, I wasn't even sure if I was going to say anything to you. I mean, maybe it's nothing."

I force myself to stay quiet and wait.

"I mean, he seems like an okay guy."

"He is. Now tell me."

Ollie nods. "You need to keep this to yourself, okay? It's attorney-client stuff. Privileged. I could get fired. Hell, I could lose my license."

I nod, suddenly nervous. "Okay."

"Well, I haven't worked directly for Stark, but I hear things. Whispers. Impressions. You know."

"No," I say. "I don't."

"Oh, hell, Nikki. I've just heard enough folks talk about the guy that I was worried about you. So when I had the chance, I did some snooping."

"Snooping? What does that mean?"

"Jamie told me what he said to you at Evelyn's party. About you turning down MIT and Cal Tech."

"So?"

"So why would he know that? Those opportunities came in when you were done with college. It's not like you put that on a fellowship application."

I frown. He has a point. "Go on."

"The Stark files are in a locked filing room a few floors up. Access is incredibly tight. But Maynard needed something fast—not for Stark, but for another client with files in the same locked room—and he sent me up to get it. I sort of took advantage of the opportunity."

"What did you do?"

"The firm administers the fellowship, so the applicant files are there. I found yours and took a peek."

"And?"

"And there was no mention of MIT or Cal Tech."

I laugh. "It was incredibly sweet of you to jeopardize your career because you're worried about me, but I could have told you that. I keep copies of all my fellowship applications."

"But you wouldn't know that your file was flagged."

"Flagged?"

He nods. "The only one. I checked them all."

"What does that mean?"

He shakes his head. "I don't know. But for some reason you were singled out."

I cock my head. "Oh, come on, Ollie. I'm sorry you don't like Damien, but you can't be serious. So there's a flag on my file. Big deal. Maybe it's because I'm allergic to penicillin. Or because I'm the most photogenic fellowship recipient and they were going to do some sort of publicity thing. Or because I'm the only one who moved to LA and I got added to some local mailing list. Hell, you don't even know that it was Stark who flagged my file.

Maybe it was your boss. Or some legal assistant who has a thing for the former Miss DFW."

His expression turns defensive. "I know, I know. I told you I wasn't sure it was worth mentioning. But don't you think it's weird? Your file is not only flagged, but he knows all sorts of personal shit about you?"

I shake my head. "Personal shit? Like where I was accepted to grad school is a state secret? Come on, Ollie. Get a grip." Even as I speak, though, I can't help but remember how Damien knew my address and phone number, not to mention my makeup preferences. But each of those had a simple explanation.

"Just think about it," Ollie says. He waves at someone, then meets my eyes. "Promise?"

I stay silent. He sighs, then walks away, disappearing into the crowd. I remain in the corner, trying to sort out my emotions. I'm confused—that much I know for sure. And I'm edging toward anger. But whether it's directed toward Damien or Ollie, I'm not certain.

Antsy, I step outside. There's a flagstone path that runs along the perimeter of the building and I follow it until I'm in front of the tennis courts. I pause, looking out over the court and imagining a young Damien playing, exuberant and happy as he chases the ball. It's a nice fantasy, and it erases the last bits of angst from my mind. Let Ollie worry if he wants to; I know better.

I can tell Damien's behind me before I hear him. It's as if he's so powerful that the air shifts to let him pass. I turn and find him looking at me. For a moment, I'm afraid he's going to be irritated—after all, he made it clear that he was done with tennis, and yet here I am. But he looks calm and happy, and when he comes forward, he kisses my head and cups my ass. "Watch it, bub," I say, and he laughs.

"Hiding out?"

"Yup. And thinking."

"What about?"

"You," I admit. I nod toward the court. "I was imagining you playing." I hold my breath, hoping my admission won't irritate him.

"I presume you were imagining me winning," he says dryly.

I laugh. "Always."

"Good girl." He captures my mouth with his, and his kiss is wild and deep and intense. He's not touching me intimately—his hand has moved to my back and the other is on my arm—but I feel as though he's inside me, filling me, stroking me.

I moan in protest when he breaks away.

He takes a step back. "See you inside, Ms. Fairchild."

I raise my brows. "You just came out here to tease me?"

"I came to tell you I'm giving a speech in about fifteen minutes. If you're inclined to, come in and join me."

"A speech? I wouldn't miss that." I look back at the court and the empty night spread out before me. "I'll be right behind you. I want to stay here with the stars a little bit longer."

He squeezes my hand and leaves, disappearing around the curve of the building. I sigh and realize that I am absolutely happy at that moment. Ollie's fears seem a million miles away.

I let the feeling settle over me, then turn to head back inside as well. A tall man with a caterpillar of a mustache and a wrinkled suit is walking from the opposite direction, coming toward me. I don't think anything of it, but as I get closer, his words startle me. "You the one Stark's banging?"

I stop, certain I must have heard wrong. "Excuse me?"

"You got money? Be careful. He'll fuck you and he'll use you, and when he tosses you away, he'll be richer for it."

My mouth is dry and my legs are struggling to hold me up. I can feel my underarms getting sticky. I don't know who this man is, but I know that he's dangerous and that I need to get away. I glance around quickly and see a sign for a restroom just across the walkway, almost hidden by the landscaping.

"I—I have to go." I turn fast and hurry that way.

"I know that bastard's secrets," the man shouts after me. "I know about all the goddamn bodies. You think my sister's the only one he's fucked up?"

Eric Padgett. It has to be Eric Padgett.

My heart is pounding as I jerk open the door to the ladies' room. The automated lights turn on and I hurry inside. There are multiple stalls, so it's not the kind of restroom that you would normally lock. The door does have a bolt, though, and I turn it immediately. As soon as I do, the lights wink out.

I suck in air, fighting rising panic. *Calm, Nikki, calm.* The lights went out with the door. Presumably, the idea is that when the janitor locks the door from the outside, the lights are turned off. So just turn the bolt again to unlock it.

I try, my hand shaking because at least here in the dark I'm away from Eric Padgett. But I have to get out. I have to open the door.

The bolt won't turn.

No. No, no, no.

Okay. Okay, I can deal with this. The bolt turns off the lights, but there must be a switch inside, too. Because otherwise someone might get stuck inside in the dark. I am a living, breathing, panicking case in point.

I fumble near the door, trying to find it, but I don't have any luck. My breathing is coming faster and shallower. *Stop it. Think.*

Right. Think.

Oh, fuck. I've forgotten how to think.

I breathe. That, at least, I can manage, though not without some difficulty. I'm still clammy with panic and I want to pound on the door and scream. But Eric Padgett is out there, and I think that he's scarier than the dark and—

Okay, maybe he's not.

I slam my fist against the door. "Hey! Hey! Is anyone out there? Hello!"

Nothing.

I pound again. And again and again and—

"Nikki?"

"Damien?"

"Oh, shit, baby, are you okay?"

I am so not okay I cannot even begin to say.

"I'm fine," I manage.

"The door won't open. Can you unbolt it?"

"No. It's stuck." But as I'm speaking, I'm grasping the thing and turning and it flips open like a well-oiled machine. The second it clicks, Damien pushes the door open. I'm not sure if I run to him or if he comes to me. All I know is that I'm in his arms and I'm sucking in air and I'm apologizing over and over and over.

He waits for me to calm down, then cups my face. "You don't have a thing to apologize for," he says.

"I'm so glad you came back. Why did you come back?"

He gives me a fifty-dollar token. "I thought you might want to play a bit before my speech."

For some reason, that makes me tear up. I lean against him. "It was Padgett," I say.

"What?" Alarm and anger color his voice.

"He didn't say his name, but I'm sure I'm right." I describe the man and repeat what he said.

Damien's face is as hard as I've ever seen it. He shifts me in front of him, then his hands roam over my body. "He didn't hurt you?"

"No," I say, my own fears fading under Damien's blatant anger and concern. "No, he didn't even threaten. But he scared me anyway, and that's why I ran."

"If you see him again—I don't care if he's three blocks away and you're not quite sure—you tell me. Okay?"

I nod. "Yes. Of course."

He takes my hand. "Come on. I'm going to make my speech, and then I'm taking you home."

I follow him in, and stand by the podium as a polished woman in Chanel thanks us all for showing our generous support to the Stark Educational Foundation, then introduces Mr. Damien Stark himself.

The room bursts into applause, mine included, and I watch as the man who now consumes my days and nights steps up onto the podium. I listen as his powerful, confident voice talks about helping children. About finding those who need a hand. About pulling them up from the muck and giving them the chance to shine.

His eloquent words extinguish the last embers of panic. Now my eyes are brimming with tears of pride. Maybe this man does have secrets and skeletons. But right now, I'm seeing his heart. And I like what I see.

24

The ocean shines in the morning light as I stand naked in the window under the steady gaze of two men. Blaine's professional inspection, and Damien's heat-filled gaze that makes my nipples peak and my thighs quiver despite the fact that there's another man in the room.

It's awkward—and yet I feel powerful, too.

"It's a crime you look so hot," Blaine says. "I feel like hell."

"That would be all the wine you had," I tease.

"Actually, that would be all the vodka," he counters. "Why the devil I told you to be here at eight, I really do not know. Oh, wait. Yes, I do. Because the morning light on your skin makes you glow."

I can't help it—I have to turn to Damien. I see my own amusement reflected in his face, and I know we're both thinking about how he says that I glow when I'm aroused.

Damien's eyes graze the entire length of my body, the inspection so intense that I think I really will start to glow right then. When his eyes meet mine again, there is undeniable heat there.

And here I am stuck like a statue while a second man stands on the far side of the room.

Damien clears his throat. From his expression, I think he's regretting the current arrangement, too.

Blaine looks between the two of us, his expression overly innocent. "Problem?"

"I'm going to go for a bike ride before I go to the office," Damien says. I display a great deal of restraint and manage not to laugh. Of course, I'm the one standing naked in front of a terrace. He gets to go work off his sexual energy. I get to stew in mine.

"Depending on how long you ride, I may have left by the time you get back," I say. "Today's my interview, remember?"

"Of course," Damien says. He moves toward me.

"Go ahead," Blaine says with a wave. "Say goodbye properly. I'll go make coffee or something." He disappears into the kitchen area, and I grin.

"I really like him," I say.

"Mmm," Damien agrees, pulling me into his arms. His clothes are cool against my bare skin, and he keeps one arm around me as we both move to the canvas. It was covered when I came in, and I'm curious about the way the painting's progressed. Blaine's accomplished a lot in a short time, and there's no doubt that's me sketched on the canvas, my back straight, my head high. I wasn't certain how I'd feel about the portrait, but I'm starting to think it's going to look pretty damn good.

"I'm jealous of the way he touches you," Damien says, so softly I can barely hear him.

I look questioningly at him. "Blaine's never touched me."

"No," Damien says. "But he's bringing you to life." He pulls me into his arms and buries his face in my hair. "That's my job," he murmurs.

"And you do it very, very well."

He nuzzles my hair. "We can send Blaine out for doughnuts and I'll forget the bike ride."

"No way, dude." I laugh and push him playfully away. "I'm

on a schedule today, remember. I need time to get dressed, read
some of the research on the company. All those girl-looking-for-
gainful-employment kinds of things."

"I'll hire you right now. Gainful-employment conundrum
solved."

"No. A million times no."

"Can't blame a guy for trying. Go." He pulls me in for a
long, slow kiss. "I'll see you on the flip side."

"Yes," I say. "You will."

I spend three solid hours at Innovative Resources, and I'm pretty
sure I meet every person who works there from the janitor on up
to the owner of the company, Bruce Tolley.

I'm a wreck at first, nervous and fumbling. But I slide into a
groove pretty quickly, and Mr. Tolley and I get into a conversational rhythm. He seems sharp—and everything I've read about
the company suggests that my impression is correct. More important, he doesn't display any of Carl's egotistical and bizarre
management traits.

In other words, Bruce is interested in the work, not my tits or
my ass.

I really can't help but like the guy.

As we talk, he takes me through the offices, pointing out the
cafeteria, the employee gym, the break rooms, and even a supply
closet. Honestly, it seems like overkill for a first interview. Or it
does until we wrap it up at the front conference room and he
extends an offer.

I, of course, tell him that I'll have to think about it, which I
do for a grand total of three seconds before enthusiastically ac-
cepting.

I manage not to break into a song and dance routine while
I'm still in the building, but once I'm outside, I swing my way
around a signpost, then pull out my iPhone and call Damien.

I'm completely bummed when I get his voice mail.

Undaunted, I send a text: Got it! Start next week! XXOO

His reply is immediate: Knew you would. Congrats. XXXOOO. P.S. Did you break any rules? Ps or Bs?

It takes me a second to translate, but when I get it, my cheeks heat: No panties, and I thought of you. No bra, and I kept my jacket buttoned.

He comes back right away with: Perfect on all counts.

I type back another one: But now I'm all wound up. Lack of Ps and adrenaline rush. Are you free?

This time the reply takes a full minute to come through: Wish I was. I know how to unwind you.

I grin and type: You could call me right now. You do some pretty good unwinding by phone.

His reply makes me smile even wider: I could, but in a meeting in Century City with some execs from Tokyo. Not sure they would understand. Back in office soon. Will see you later. All of you, baby. In the meantime, imagine me, touching you. . . .

No problem there—imagining Damien's touch has become one of my favorite pastimes. Right behind actually experiencing his touch.

When I get home and find Jamie in the apartment, I feel less cheated that Damien is unavailable. Jamie is, of course, sufficiently enthusiastic, and I get to hang on to my new job high.

"So what should we do to celebrate?" she asks.

"A movie?"

"No way. I want the dirt on you and Mr. Moneybags. Sushi?"

"Perfect."

Since I am fed up with heels and skirts and tailored blouses, I head into my room to change into jeans while Jamie does the same. I hesitate before pulling them on, then toss them aside. I put on a denim skirt and sandals—and no underwear. Even when Damien isn't around, rules are rules.

The bra's easy. I pair my skirt with a backless halter and call it a fashion choice. "You almost ready?" I call to Jamie.

"Five minutes," she promises, then, "Hey, did you see today's paper?"

"Why?"

"It's on the coffee table. The Life and Style section. Check it out."

I shrug, then settle onto the couch and pick up the paper. I flip through, but nothing much catches my attention until I get close to the end. And then what catches my attention is me.

Or a picture of me. Me with Damien to be precise.

It's an article on the Stark Educational Foundation and the charity event. A double-page spread with candid shots of the guests. I smile as I scan the photos, looking for Blaine or Evelyn or Ollie.

I don't find them, but I do see Giselle. And my fingers stiffen when I see the man she's standing next to—Bruce Tolley.

What the—?

Damien didn't tell me he knew my new boss. But maybe he doesn't. Maybe it's just a coincidence that Bruce is standing with Giselle.

My attempt at self-delusion is quickly foiled when I glance at the caption. Turns out Bruce is Giselle's husband. The husband that Damien had cocktails with the very first night we met. And Damien hadn't said a word when I told him I was interviewing with Innovative, or just now for that matter.

What the bloody hell does that mean?

Nothing good, that's for damn sure, and I feel a little queasy as this oddity roils around inside me, mixing with Ollie's fears.

Shit.

I grab my cell phone and start to call him, but I end the call before I finish dialing. This isn't a phone call kind of conversation. For better or worse, I'm heading to him.

"James," I shout. Now that my mind's made up, I'm not going to hesitate. "I've got to go. Sorry about the sushi."

I don't wait for her to answer, and as the door's slamming behind me, I hear her surprised, "What? What?" echoing behind me.

My mind is either too blank or too full during the drive to Stark's office. All I know is that there's not a coherent thought in my head. When I get to Stark Tower, I ask Joe if Stark's back, and am told he's not.

"Fine," I say. "I'm going to wait for him in the penthouse. Tell him Ms. Fairchild wants to see him the minute he returns."

Joe looks a little taken aback, but I just march to the elevator, leaving him to call up and relay my demands to Stark's overly efficient staff.

The elevator that opens isn't the one I rode up in with Carl and the boys. It's Stark's private elevator. I assume that Sylvia has sent it down for me and step on, feeling powerful and in control. Yes, indeed, Stark is about to get a piece of my mind.

My exuberant purpose fades a little when the elevator doors open not on the office, but into Stark's Tower Apartment. Suddenly I feel a little intimidated.

I consider staying in the elevator and pushing the alarm button until the opposite set of doors open, but I don't go through with it. Instead, I step out into the apartment and take a deep breath. As I do, the elevator doors close behind me.

My breath hitches, and I turn and press the call button again, feeling suddenly, weirdly nervous.

The doors don't open.

Apparently, I'll be staying here until Stark returns.

Right. Okay. No problem.

I've been here once, so I head on in, then grab myself a Diet Coke out of the refrigerator behind the wet bar. I take it into the living area and try to sit and wait, but I can't. I'm up and pacing in seconds, too full of nerves and anger to sit still.

I know I shouldn't, but I explore the apartment. Then again, why the hell shouldn't I? Stark knows all sorts of shit about me. At the very least, I want to know what his bedroom looks like.

I'm surprised when I find it, and yet I'm not. It's a simple room. One wall showcases a low wooden dresser with clean lines and recessed pulls. Another wall is dominated by a pair of elegant French doors that open onto a bathroom. As is Damien's style, a third wall is made entirely of windows looking out over the expanse of Los Angeles. The fourth wall features a bed.

Unlike the bed in the Malibu house, this one has no frame. It's low to the ground and is made up with crisp white sheets. A deep blue blanket is tossed across it, but other than that there is no spread or cover. There are two pillows, also encased in white. And although there is no headboard per se, a section of the wall has been paneled in what looks like a deep mahogany. It acts as a faux headboard and ensures that the bed is the room's focal point.

It's simple and elegant and yet there's something a little sad about the room. It's like a mask, I think. Revealing only what Damien wants to be revealed.

I wonder what women he's brought here, and then I shiver a little, because I have not been one of them and somehow, that makes me feel special.

"Nikki?"

I jump. I'd been so preoccupied I hadn't registered his approach. I turn to face him. He's leaning casually against the hallway wall. He's in suit trousers, but he's removed the jacket and tie, and the first two buttons of his shirt are undone. He looks deliciously sexy, and I want to slap him for distracting me from my purpose.

I don't speak, and I see the concern edge onto his face. "Is everything okay? What's happened?"

"Why didn't you tell me about Bruce?"

His brows rise. He actually looks surprised by the question. "What should I have told you?"

"Are you fucking kidding me? Shit, Damien, you're the reason I got the offer."

"I pulled strings so that Bruce knew you were in the market," he says sharply. "But that's it. You got it because you're damn good at what you do. Because your credentials are stellar. Because you're smart and hardworking and you deserve it."

I cock my head and look at him, because that is a load of bullshit. "And how exactly do you know all that about me? From watching me pose naked? From fucking me?"

"I see *you*, Nikki."

"Yeah, well, maybe that's because you've been looking for such a long time."

His eyes narrow. "What are you talking about?"

"At Evelyn's party, for one. You were so pissed at me for being Carl's assistant. You gave a better rundown of my credentials than I could. How did you know so much about me? It wasn't in my fellowship file. So how, Damien?"

"I've followed your academic career. I've talked with your professors. I've watched you blossom."

"I—" He's knocked me off kilter with the matter-of-fact nature of his confession. "But why?"

He says nothing.

"Damien, why?" I hear panic creep into my voice.

"Because I want you," he finally says, and the heat in his voice curls through me so vividly that the panic fades and I have to force myself to concentrate. "I have since I met you at the pageant."

My mind is spinning. "But—but why not say something back then?"

His small smile gives away nothing. "I can be a very patient man when the goal is worth waiting for."

"I—" I don't know what to say. My mind is spinning with

questions. I want to ask why he's so certain I'm worth it, but the best I can manage is, "Why me?"

The corner of his mouth quirks up. "I told you that, too. We're kindred spirits. And you're strong, Nikki. There's a core of strength and confidence in you that's damn sexy."

I don't meet his eyes. As he always does, he understood the heart of my question. "Have you not noticed the scars?" I ask. "I'm not strong, I'm weak." And I can't shake the fear that it's because I'm weak that he wants me. Damien likes to be the one in control, after all.

"Weak?" He's staring at me like I've gone a little crazy. "The hell you are. You're not weak, Nikki. You're powerful. You're a survivor. When I hold you, I can feel the power in you. It's like holding a live wire."

He moves closer, then cups my face gently in his palm. "*That's* why I want you, baby. I'm not weak, either. Why would I want a woman who is?"

I tremble. He sees in me what I find so attractive in him. Power. Confidence. Ability.

But are those really my traits, or is he only seeing the Nikki I show the world? Or is that Nikki part of me, too?

"You know so much about me, and I hardly know you," I say. "Do you know this is the first time I've even seen your bedroom?"

"There's not much to see."

"That's not the point." I tilt my head to look up at him, and find his eyes fixed hard on my face.

"Nikki, I need to know that we're okay."

I have to fight not to nod. I so desperately want everything to be okay between me and Damien. But it's going to take more than just wants and wishes. "Will you try?" I ask. "Try to share more with me?"

"I've shared more with you than I have with any woman," he says.

I think about what he's told me about his dad and his tennis career. "I know. I just—I just really want to know *you*. Does that make sense?" I don't say that I know he has secrets in his past; it is those secrets I want him to share. I force myself to smile brightly. "Unlike some people, I don't have the resources to find out on my own."

"I thought you had Wikipedia," he deadpans.

I make a face, and he bends down to kiss my nose. It's playful and erotic and I realize that my fears have evaporated. Has he soothed them? Or am I simply unable to think clearly when I'm close to this man?

"It's not easy for me," he says, the intensity of his words surprising me. "I've never wanted to share the bits and pieces of my life before."

"Do you want to now?" My words are a whisper, as if truly voicing them will kill that little bit of hope.

He strokes my cheek, making me tremble. "Yes."

The relief that floods my body has a sensual, fiery quality. "Then you'll try?"

"I'll try," he confirms. He steps into the bedroom, then holds out his hand. "Come with me."

I put my hand in his, feeling the familiar tingle as my skin brushes his. He leads me to the window, then takes my hands and presses my palms against the glass. He stands behind me, his arms around my waist, the strong length of him tethering me to the earth as the darkening city opens up in front of me.

"Nikki." His voice is low and needful, and my body responds automatically. My breasts feel heavy, my nipples are tight nubs. Between my thighs, my sex quivers. I want him. Dear God, how I want him.

"Why?" I whisper. "Why does everything fall away when I'm with you?"

"Because there's nothing else," he answers. "Nothing but you and me."

He keeps one arm around my waist, but removes his other hand. He trails his fingers up my leg, then pushes up my skirt until it's bunched around my waist and my bare ass is pressed against his trousers. I feel him against me, his erection straining against a piece of cloth that is undoubtedly worth more than my car.

"Please," I say. I want it fast and hard. I want to feel the passion that burns between us. I want it to erase all the doubts I'd come in with until there truly is nothing but me and Damien and the world outside. "Please fuck me."

"Oh, God, Nikki." His voice is a groan, and I hear him fumbling with his trousers. I feel him shift behind me, and then the press of his erection like velvet steel against my bare rear. "Spread your legs."

I do, and he slides his fingers over my cunt, stroking me, teasing me, making me writhe against him. But this isn't what I want. I want him inside me. I want him *now*, and I tell him so.

He takes my hips and positions himself. I ease up onto my toes, then lower myself as he thrusts inside, but I have no control in this position. It's all Damien, thrusting deep inside me, the power of his strokes pushing me forward. My palms are still on the glass, and with every stroke I'm pressed closer and closer, the wide void calling me, and nothing but Damien keeping me there.

I take one hand off the glass and reach down to stroke my clit as Damien fills me.

"That's it, baby," he whispers. The world is getting dark outside, and I can see our reflections now in the glass. I meet his eyes as the orgasm rockets through me, making me clench tight around him, drawing him out, making him come in deep, long spurts inside of me.

I gasp, shaken by the power of the orgasm, my body still pressed slightly forward, my hips still high, and Damien's cock still deep inside me.

"Look outside," Damien whispers. "What do you see?"

"It's sunset," I say playfully as I look over my shoulder to once again meet his eyes.

He presses his mouth to my ear, and there's nothing playful in his tone. "Never, baby. Between us, the sun is never going down."

"No," I whisper, feeling safe and satisfied. "Never."

25

Because Damien has to spend the next day in San Diego and Blaine is off dealing with some sort of gallery crisis in La Jolla, I'm back at my apartment before eight in the morning, and am surprised to find Jamie already awake.

"What the hell?" she says, by way of greeting. "You just vanished into thin air."

"I know," I say. "I'm a terrible roommate, but I'll make it up to you. Breakfast. My treat."

"And you'll tell me everything?"

"Swear," I say. And I cross my heart for effect.

We end up at Du-par's on Ventura Boulevard, and after I tell her about Bruce and about what Ollie said and about Damien's explanation, she proves that she is in fact worthy of best friend status by siding with me one hundred percent. "Ollie's like an overprotective brother. And Damien's just too damn hot to stay mad at. Besides, it's not like he told Bruce to hire you. He just told Bruce about your resume."

"Exactly," I say. And since Damien and I worked through our issues rather thoroughly last night—as my soreness this morning can testify to—I shift the conversation. "This is my last week among the unemployed," I say. "Wanna catch a movie?"

We end up seeing two, because what's the point of being a lazy bum if you don't do it up right, then head back to the apartment in a popcorn-and-soda-induced haze.

Jamie immediately heads to her room to change into pajamas even though it's not yet four. I'm about to do the same when I'm stopped by a sharp knock at the door. "Hang on," I say. If it's Douglas, I'm totally shooing him away. For that matter, Ollie will get shooed, too.

It's neither. It's Edward.

"Ms. Fairchild," he says, and though he keeps his professional face on, I see the smile in his eyes. "Mr. Stark asked me to deliver a personal apology that he wasn't able to spend the day with you in celebration of your new job."

"He did?" I bite back a grin. We'd done a bit of celebrating last night. Celebration sex. Make-up sex. We'd pretty much run the gamut.

"And may I extend my congratulations on your new job as well?" Edward adds.

"Thank you," I say. "But he really didn't need to send you. He already congratulated me when I saw him last night."

"Yes, but I'm to deliver your gift. Or, rather, deliver you to your gift."

I narrow my eyes at him. "What are you talking about?"

"I'm afraid I have very specific instructions that forbid me from actually telling you."

"Oh. Um, okay. Let me just tell my roommate."

"Ms. Archer is invited as well, of course."

"Really?" This was getting interesting. I give a shout toward her room. "Hey, James. Change of plans. We're going . . . somewhere."

She pops her head out of the door, while still only half in her

T-shirt. She tugs it down, and peers at Edward. "Huh? Where are we going?"

"Edward won't say. But it's a present. From Damien."

"And I'm invited, too?"

"Absolutely," Edward says.

"How fab is that? Well, shit," she says to me, "I'm not turning down a mystery present from a guy with billions. That's just not something I'm programmed to do."

"Fair enough. I guess we're going," I add to Edward.

Jamie switches the pj bottoms out for jeans, and we grab our purses and follow Edward down to the limo. I wonder if Damien requested it, or if Edward decided to drive the limo instead of the Town Car simply to give Jamie a thrill. If so, it worked. She's checking out every seat, poking into the bar, and examining each and every gadget on the console.

"Wine?" she asks, finding a chilled bottle of Chardonnay in a mini-refrigerator. Shows how much I pay attention. I didn't even know the limo had a fridge. Then again, I was a bit distracted each time I took a ride in it. . . .

Edward takes us out onto I-10 and then heads east, which surprises me, as I'd been expecting us to head for the beach. "Where do you think we're going?" I ask Jamie, who's riffling through the CD collection that I've never bothered to look at.

"Who cares?"

I consider that, and decide she has a very good point.

Fifteen minutes later, it's clear we're heading out of Los Angeles, I'm on my second glass of wine, and Madonna is belting out "Like a Virgin."

"So *totally* retro," Jamie says, half-dancing in her seat. I consider overruling her choice, but it's fun and loud and what the hell.

By the time we pass the windmill farms that mark the desert near Palm Springs, we've played classic rock, classic country, and a varied selection from current artists. We've danced—as much as you can in a limo—and sung and have basically turned the limo into party central. We've laughed so hard we've almost cried, and I think it's the best time Jamie and I have had together since we skipped out of Friday classes our freshman year and drove from Austin to New Orleans.

I am *so* going to show Damien my gratitude when I see him.

Finally, Edward exits the 10 for a smaller highway, then a regular street, then a caliche road. I'm beginning to think that our destination must be a campsite when I see the sunset glowing against the white stucco of a low building nestled near the foothills of the rising mountains. We pass through a security gate, and I realize that what I thought was one building is a collection of several smaller ones, all surrounded by palm trees reaching up to brush the sky.

Jamie and I are pressed to the windows now, and she sees the sign first. "Holy shit," she says. "We're at the Desert Ranch Spa."

"Seriously?" I don't know why I sound so surprised. The Desert Ranch Spa may be one of those insanely expensive resorts where celebrities go for a little alone time, but it's not like Damien can't afford it.

"Are we staying the night?" Jamie asks. "Or maybe we're just here for dinner? God, I hope we're staying the night. I've never stayed in a place like this."

The limo winds its way to the front entrance, and I gulp down the rest of my wine and slide toward the door, so that I'm ready to go the moment Edward opens it. When he does, there's a woman beside him in pencil-thin trousers and a silk tank top. "Ms. Fairchild, Ms. Archer. Welcome to Desert Ranch," she says, with an accent I recognize only as Eastern European. "I'm Helena. Come. I'll take you to your bungalow."

Bun-ga-low, Jamie mouths with eyes wide. We follow her down a landscaped path, me doing my Worldly Nikki routine—

why, of course I get out of limos and go to expensive desert resorts all the time—and Jamie practically bouncing. "For the record," she says as Helena opens the door and we get a glimpse of
the inside of the bungalow, "I am totally in love with your boyfriend."

Boyfriend. I grin. I like the sound of that.

The bungalow is small but exceptionally well-appointed,
with two bedrooms, a kitchenette, a living room with a comfy
couch and chairs, and a fireplace. But the best part is the back
porch, which looks out on the mountains without any sign of the
resort. "You will have dinner in your room, yes? And then tomorrow we begin at eight."

I almost hesitate to ask, but I break down. "Begin what?"

Helena smiles. "Everything."

We're awakened by gentle alarm clocks at seven-thirty, and
it's surprisingly easy to wake up despite having stayed up late
sipping wine and talking after the most amazing dinner of Chil-
ean sea bass and some type of risotto. We mainline coffee, sip
orange juice, and put on the spa robes that we've been told to
wear today.

When our liaisons, Becky and Dana, arrive at our doorstep,
we're eager to see what's in store for us. As it turns out, Helena
wasn't exaggerating. We start with dips in the mineral waters,
then move inside for facials and waxing and—because Becky
whispers to me that Mr. Stark requested it—I even submit to a
little more intimate wax. Not Brazilian, because ouch, but by the
time I leave the waxing room, I have a neat landing strip that
looks more professional than the shaving and Nair job I've managed all these years. My legs are smooth, my brows are fabulously shaped, and we move on to our choice of mud baths or
seaweed wraps.

I go with the mud, because my mother never allowed me to
play in the mud as a kid, and the tubs are outside. Jamie does,
too, and so we lay back in our squishy beds of mud with glasses

of sparkling water in our hands and cool cucumbers on our eyes. We don't talk—by this time we're both limp and relaxed—but it's amazing just soaking up the luxury. So much so that I almost moan in protest when they help us out, scraping the mud off us with things that look like miniature shower squeegees, and then lead us to another mineral spring, which relaxes us even more and cleans us off.

After that, a cold dip wakes us up again, and then Jamie and I are led inside for a delicious lunch. Afterward we get to sit side by side for manicures and pedicures.

The last official spa treatment for the day is a massage. After that, we're told we can go back to our bungalow or look over the activity list. Everything from hiking to horseback riding to yoga to golf. Fresh clothes will be waiting for us. Linen slacks and tops courtesy of the resort.

We part ways to go to our private massage rooms, and the masseuse, a woman with arms so defined I'm sure she must have been a professional athlete at some time, guides me to the table. She picks out an oil with just a hint of spice and I nod agreement. It's unusual, but edgy, and it reminds me of Damien.

Oh yes, he is getting such a thank-you for this surprise.

I strip down and slide under the sheet. The table is the kind with a cutout for your face, and I lay limp, eyes closed, my body more relaxed than it's been in a long time. "Just my back and arms and calves, please," I say. "Not my thighs."

"Of course." She puts on music, and we begin. Her hands are like magic, and as she works the tightness out from along my spine, I'm pretty sure that I've gone to heaven.

Her touch is strong, but not so much as to be uncomfortable, and soon I'm drifting. Not really asleep, but not really there, either. I feel it when she takes her hands off me, then hear the clink of bottles as she gets more oil. I hear another click I can't identify, and I lay still, waiting for her to continue with the massage.

When she puts her hands back on me, they feel different.

Larger. Stronger. My body realizes the truth before I do, and my pulse kicks up. *Damien*.

I smile at the floor but say nothing as his oiled hands glide over me, working the kinks from my body, making me relaxed, making me squirm with desire.

He works my arms, paying attention to each little finger, which turns out to be so desperately erotic that I feel the tug of each stroke between my legs. Then he eases his strong hands down my back and over the towel that covers my ass and thighs. He draws his hands firmly down the back of each leg, then strokes the sole of each foot, and now I do moan with pleasure.

He drives me just a little bit crazy before moving on to each toe and then, finally, turning his attention to my calves. Long, gentle strokes, higher and higher until I feel his fingers grazing the edge of the towel, then easing my legs apart so he can direct his strokes even higher.

I am going completely crazy now, and it's all I can do not to lift and twist my hips. I'm wet and I want him and I'm determined not to say anything but to just lay there and enjoy the moment. But oh, God, I want to feel him inside me.

I'm sure he knows how much he's teasing me, and he pushes the towel up to massage my hips with firm, even strokes. He does the same to my inner thighs, coming so deliciously close to my cunt that I think I'm going to scream with frustration every time he dips near but doesn't touch me.

Then I feel the soft brush of his fingers against my sensitive clit. The firm stroke of his hand over my slick heat. His fingertip dances circles over my clit and I can't help it, I moan with the pleasure of it. And then it's as if the world has slipped away and I'm nothing but this tiny point of sensation concentrated between my thighs, building and building, higher and faster, until I can't take it anymore and I shatter in his hand.

"Damien," I whisper. I am spent. My body is liquid. There's no way I'm ever moving again.

I hear his low chuckle, then feel the press of his lips at the nape of my neck. "I can't begin to tell you how happy I am that you knew it was me."

When I am no longer a limp noodle and can actually compel my limbs to function, I get off the table and back into my robe. Damien and I leave at the same time, and Jamie's door opens as we're passing. She looks between me and Damien, then glances sideways at her masseuse, a tall blond man with large, capable-looking hands.

"You know," Jamie says dryly, "nothing personal, but I don't think I got the same level of service that she did."

To his credit, the masseuse smiles. "Come," he says, gesturing for her to follow.

"That's the problem," she mutters to me as she passes, "*I* didn't."

Back in the bungalow, I start to change into the linen outfit, but Damien has brought a peasant style skirt and matching blouse for me. I put it on, enjoying the way the loose cut of the material feels over my newly polished and primped skin.

He taps on Jamie's door and tells her that he'll be seeing me back to Los Angeles. She's welcome to stay another night. Edward will be back to fetch her at nine in the morning. Jamie's thank-you is so enthusiastic it borders on embarrassing, but Damien just tells her she's very, very welcome.

"What are we doing?" I ask as we walk the path toward the front parking area.

"Celebrating," he says, and I can tell from his enigmatic smile that I'm not going to get more of an answer than that.

I expect to see his uber-expensive car with the odd name, but apparently Damien wasn't kidding about having three Ferraris. A glossy black one is parked right in front of the reception area.

"I thought you might like to take her for a spin," he says.

I gape at him. "Seriously?"

He nods.

"Seriously?" I repeat, and this time he laughs. He opens the driver's door for me and motions for me to slide in. "Just start slow." His grin turns wicked. "But it's no fun if you keep it slow."

The bucket seat hugs me and I sigh as I wait for Damien to get in on his side. "Is she new?"

"No, why?"

"New-car smell. Um, she's not like some rare classic car that's irreplaceable, is she?"

He reaches over and slides the key into the ignition. "Drive, Nikki."

"Drive. Right." I take a deep breath, punch in the clutch, and fire up the engine.

The motor purrs, and it's a sweet, sweet sound. Slowly and carefully, I move the car into first gear and ease out of the drive-way and onto the caliche road leading up to the resort. "Go left when you hit the street," Damien says. "There are no other homes or businesses past the resort. I doubt there will be any traffic at all."

I nod and ease slowly over the caliche. I'm crawling, actually, and I think Damien may be a little frustrated with my snail's pace, but there is no way I'm risking little rocks flying up and chipping the paint on this baby.

And, yeah, I'm freaking nervous.

When I arrive at the intersection, I pause. "You're sure about this?"

"Hell yes," he says.

"What if I strip the gears?"

"I hope you do. I think a striptease would be an appropriate apology for something like that, don't you?"

I squirm, half-wishing he didn't have such an intense and im-mediate effect on me. "Don't talk like that," I say. "I need to concentrate."

He laughs, then takes my hand and puts it on the stick. "All that power in the palm of your hand," he says, and now I *know* he's just trying to make me wet.

"Boys and their toys," I retort, then ease the car left onto the street. "Here goes," I say, and accelerate. It takes me a minute to get used to the steering and the speed, but I have to admit it's exhilarating, and soon I'm all the way into seventh gear— *seventh!*—and the speedometer's hovering over one hundred eighty. The ride is remarkably smooth, and I think I could take it even faster, but the foothills are getting pretty big in the front window and I see the road curving up ahead and I'm still nervous enough that I can't do this on a curve.

I ease up, downshift, and pull over to the side of the road. As soon as the car's off, I peel myself out of the driver's seat and climb over the console until I'm straddling Damien. "That was amazing," I say. "Totally, completely amazing." I kiss him hard and fast, then press his hand to my leg. "Am I trembling? God, I think my body's still vibrating just from the speed of this car."

"*Boys* and their toys?" he says with raised brows. "I think this qualifies as a girl toy, too."

"Heck yeah, it does." I kiss him again, and he opens his mouth, drawing me in. His hands ease up the front of my blouse to cup my breasts, and I moan and reach down for his fly. He's hard—I can feel him against my leg—but he shakes his head, his grin mischievous. "I don't think so," he says. "I think I'm going to make you wait." I run my teeth over my lower lip, because I don't want to wait. And yet there's something tantalizing about the idea of such sweet torture. To be hot and needy and anticipating his touch.

He slides his hand between my legs and strokes me quickly, just one cruel little tease. I buck up and tighten my grip on his leg. "Oh, baby," he says, "tell me you liked our toy."

"Oh, yes."

"I have a new game."

"Game?"

He kisses me. "I bet I can make you come without even touching you."

"Let me drive this car a bit longer, and you won't have to do a thing," I say.

He laughs. "I don't want to make myself redundant. Besides, I brought another toy."

I ease back a bit and eye him. His face is lit with both amusement and passion. He's got the devious look of a man with a plan, but I haven't got a clue what it could be. "All right," I say. "I'm curious."

He reaches into his pocket and takes out a cloth pouch, then pulls a metal egg from it.

"What is that?"

"I'll show you," he says. I'm still straddling him, and he slides his hand between my legs, and as I gasp in surprise, he slips the egg easily inside me.

"What the hell?"

He laughs. "You'll see."

"But—"

"How does it feel?"

"I—it's, um, interesting." I feel full. And very aware. And very turned on.

"Interesting?" he asks, and before the word has even left his lips, the thing inside me starts to vibrate, teasing me from the inside and making me gasp.

"Holy fuck," I say, and Damien laughs. Immediately, the vibration stops.

I gape at him. "Remote control," he says casually, then opens the door and eases me off his lap. He gets out and I take his place. I'm quiet, contemplating this strange, exotic, enticing toy he's brought for us. I have to admit, it feels nice. The idea is weird, but the effect? Well, I really can't complain.

He peels back out onto the street with a hell of a lot more aplomb than I did. I'm pretty sure we cross the two-hundred-mile-per-hour mark before we slow down and get back on the interstate. We drive for about twenty minutes, then exit in a small town called Redlands. "There's a restaurant here I love," he says, and he drives me past restored Victorian homes and into the quaint downtown area. It's eight o'clock on a weeknight, and there aren't many people out. The restaurant itself is only half full. It's in a refurbished warehouse, and has an air of elegance set against brick and stone and iron piping.

"I like it," I say.

"The ambience is great, the food even better."

We're led to a quiet booth in the corner, and I slide in on one side, expecting Damien to sit next to me. He doesn't. He takes a seat across from me. "I want to look at you," he says, but I don't entirely believe him. He has a remote control in his pocket, and I have a feeling that he has plans for this evening.

I lean forward. "Don't you dare. This is a nice restaurant."

But Damien only smirks. And, yeah, he turns it on just long enough for me to jump.

I lick my lips and look around, certain everyone has not only seen me, but knows what we're doing. But there's really no one in our line of sight, and none of the staff are looking our way.

I swallow and shift a bit in the seat. I try to focus on my menu, but it's hard, because any moment Damien might turn that thing on, and I'm both dreading it and anticipating it.

"You're very easy to read, Ms. Fairchild."

I scowl at him and focus on my current conundrum of deciding between a martini and a bourbon, straight up.

The bourbon wins. There's really no contest.

The waitress returns with our drinks and takes our dinner orders—we're both having steak—then leaves us in our little corner.

"You're torturing me, you know," I say.

Damien laughs and holds up his hands as if in self-defense. "Hey, I'm not doing anything."

"Hmmm."

"Anticipation is the better part of pleasure," he says.

"Anticipation is driving me crazy," I retort.

He reaches across the table for my hand, stroking his thumb over mine. "Tell me about the job. What does Bruce have planned for you?"

I eye him suspiciously. "You really don't know?"

He laughs. "I really don't."

I launch greedily into the topic, giving him a rundown of the parameters of my new job. "Bruce seems really cool," I add. "I think I'll learn a lot from him."

"I'm sure you will, but I still don't understand why you don't just dive in and work for yourself. You said you have a product in mind to develop, right?"

"I do," I admit. "Honestly, I think I'm a little scared. I spent five years in school learning all the technical stuff. I trust myself with the science and the engineering. But the business end . . ." I trail off with a shrug. "I feel like there should have been a class on how to find investors or how to raise capital or something." I wave my hand, because I'm sure I sound like a total loser. "I just don't want to jump in before I feel competent. I'm afraid if I do all your money will just slip through my fingers."

"It's your money," he says. "Or it will be soon. But if you need help, all you have to do is ask. I've gotten pretty good at this stuff," he adds with a grin.

"Damien, please. I just—I just feel like I need to be the one who does this. On my own, you know?"

"No one survives in business going entirely on their own."

"Damien . . ."

"Fine," he concedes. "But let me give you some advice. If you're looking to make a splash in the tech field, the time is now. I don't know what ideas you're developing, but I promise that you aren't the only one. Screw around too long, and someone will hit the market first."

"Like what happened to Carl."

"Exactly." He squeezes my hand. "Will you tell me your idea? I'm curious."

I hesitate only a second. I don't want to work for or with Damien, but I do value his opinion. And I'm proud of my idea and want to share it with this man who now fills my world.

"I have several smartphone apps already out there, and they'll be part of the company, of course. But the marquee product will be a cross-platform note-sharing system for use on the Web."

"I'm intrigued. Explain."

I do, roughing out my idea of a web-based software that allows users to leave virtual sticky notes on webpages that their friends and colleagues can see when they access the same website. "That's just the most obvious use. There are all sorts of permutations. But I think it has real potential."

"So do I," he says. "When you're ready, I'll help."

Maybe it's foolish to feel so proud of myself simply because my idea has the Damien Stark seal of approval, but I do. I beam at him and squeeze his hand. "How about you? How was your trip to San Diego? Did you buy a conglomerate? A country? A chain of gourmet cupcake bakeries?"

I'm being a goof, but his reaction doesn't match my words. His face turns cold, the familiar ice returning, and I wonder what I could possibly have said. He picks up his water glass and takes a long drink. When he sets it down, he keeps his eyes on it for what feels like a very long time, but probably is only seconds. He turns the glass, the condensation making patterns on the poly-urethane tabletop. Finally, he looks at me. "I was there to visit my father."

The words come out level. Almost bland. But I realize how much he's telling me. He could have simply told me he had a bad day. I would have believed him. Instead, he's keeping his word.

He's giving me another glimpse into himself—and he has to know how much that means to me.

"How long has he lived in San Diego?" I ask. I keep my tone conversational, as if there was nothing monumental about this exchange of words.

"I bought him the house when I was fourteen," he says. He takes another sip of water. "That was the year I fired him and hired a new manager."

"Oh." I had missed that on Wikipedia, but I hadn't really been paying attention to the mentions of the people surrounding Damien. Only Damien himself. "It was nice of you to visit him. I'm guessing you two don't have the best relationship."

He looks at me sharply. "Why do you say that?"

I shrug; it seems obvious to me. "Him taking such tight control of your career. Making you play even when you wanted to quit and go to the science academy."

"Right." He leans back against the booth, and I'm struck by the odd sense that he's relieved, but that doesn't make sense.

"It was nice of you to go see him."

"An unpleasant necessity."

I'm not sure what to say to that, but I'm saved by the arrival of our waitress with the meal. As we eat, our conversation shifts to a rundown of our spa adventure. "It was amazing," I say, telling him in great detail everything we did. "I've never had a mud bath before."

"I'm sorry I missed it."

"Me, too," I say, smiling from the heat in his voice. My body clenches, and I'm reminded of the little silver egg tucked away inside me. I feel sexy and decadent—and a bit on edge, since I have no clue when Damien may pull *that* trigger.

"Did Jamie have a good time?"

"Are you kidding? She thinks you're the world's greatest humanitarian now. Seriously, it was wonderful of you to invite her. She's been having a tough time of it."

"How so?"

"She's an actress," I say, because that pretty much sums it up in Hollywood.

"Has she gotten any work?"

"A few local commercials and some equity waiver stuff. But considering she's been here for years, she's not exactly making progress. She's frustrated. I think her agent's getting frustrated. And I know finances are a concern. She's not, you know, walking the streets in patent leather, but I think she may have actually slept with a few guys just because she knew they'd feed her well or cover her mortgage for the month."

"And now you're living there."

"Well, that takes the pressure off, sure. But still. She has to find work." I finish my steak and take a sip of wine. "What's so frustrating is that she's genuinely talented, and the camera loves her. If she could just get that break . . ." I trail off with a shrug. "Sorry. I'm rambling. But I love her and I feel bad for her."

"You want to help her."

"Yeah."

Beneath the table his leg caresses mine. "I know the feeling."

The softness of his words takes my breath away, but I can't meet his eyes. I concentrate instead on my wine and am grateful when he changes the subject, telling me how he found this restaurant when he decided to spend a weekend exploring small California towns. By the time the coffee and crème brûlée arrives for dessert, my melancholy for my roommate has disappeared. More than that, I'm having such a good time listening to Damien's stories that I've actually forgotten about the decadent little toy—until it starts to vibrate inside me with no warning at all.

I'm holding a spoonful of dessert, and I gasp a little as it slides over my lips. On the other side of the table, Damien smiles innocently at me. "You're glowing again, Ms. Fairchild. Is that for the crème brûlée? Or could there be another reason?"

"You're a cruel man, Mr. Stark. And I think it's time we get the check."

We've been in the restaurant for hours and the downtown area is dark and abandoned by the time we leave. His car is in a paid lot a few blocks away, and we turn into an alley as a shortcut. There's no one around, and I step to one side, tugging Damien with me. "What is it?" he asks.

"Just this." I kiss him, hard, and ease backward until my shoulders press against the rough brick of the building. "Turn it on," I demand.

"Oh, baby," he says, but he complies.

I take his hand and slide it up under my skirt, putting his fingers right on me. I'm desperately wet.

"God, Nikki, let's get to the car."

"No," I say and unzip his fly. I have my hand inside his jeans, and his cock is steel against my palm. "Now. Please."

He growls, and I know he's fighting for control.

"Now," I repeat. "Leave the thing on. And don't take it out."

That pushes him over the edge and he shifts his jeans to free himself, then slams me harder against the wall. I gasp and curl one leg up around him. "Please," I say. "Please, Damien. Fuck anticipation. I want you now."

I take his cock and guide the head between my legs. My skirt falls over us, the soft feel of the hem moving against us adding to the frenzy. I'm vibrating inside, and that sensation coupled with his deep, penetrating thrusts is enough to send me over the edge in no time at all, Damien right there with me.

"Holy hell," he whispers, clutching me tight. "That was quite a trip."

"Got your vibe on?"

"You're quite the minx."

"I guess so," I say. "I seem to remember someone saying he doesn't have sex in public."

"That's my rule," he admits. "Anyone who works so very

hard to make me break it deserves an equally inventive punishment."

I swallow, my nipples tightening again from his tone. It's low and commanding and I have no doubt that it will be sweet punishment indeed.

"Come on, Ms. Fairchild. I think it's time to get you home."

26

By the time we pull up to my apartment, I am once again liquid with desire. Damien has allowed me to remove the magical vibrating egg, but he makes me sit with my legs spread wide beneath my skirt. That position combined with the thrum of the engine is erotic in and of itself. Knowing that he has a special punishment in store for me is enough to make me almost come every time he taps the brakes or revs the engine.

He parallel-parks expertly and kills the engine. He doesn't, however, get out. I eye him, my teeth scraping over my lower lip. "Are you going to come in?" I'm suddenly afraid that the punishment he has in mind is to not touch me at all.

A predatory spark flares in his eyes. "Oh, I'm coming in, all right."

I exhale in relief, then suck in sharply with confusion as he reaches behind his seat to retrieve a thin leather case, like a briefcase, only smaller. He smiles enigmatically, then exits the car with the case. He's at my side before I can figure out how to work the locking mechanism. He pulls open the door, then takes my hand and helps me out. It's all very proper and polite—and that's making me even more nervous.

What does he have in store for me? What is in that damn case?

My fingers shake as I insert my key in the lock. Damien's proximity and promises have done quite a number on me. I think I'm more aware of my body than I've ever been, and every part of me is taut and tense with excitement, nervousness, and anticipation.

Once we're inside, I stand awkwardly in the room, not quite sure what to do now. It's a strange feeling considering all we've done together, not to mention the fact that he's already seen the apartment. But I feel like a teenager inviting a boy home for the first time.

Jamie is still at the spa, so we have the place to ourselves. Damien shares none of my hesitations; he strides right to the dining table and puts the case down. I look at it, expecting him to open it. He doesn't. He just stands there watching me, his inspection so intense that I feel the urge to fidget.

I don't, though. Instead I stand perfectly still, my chin tilted slightly up. This is part of the game, and right now my role is to wait.

Damien strokes his chin, his head tilted sideways in the manner of a museum patron inspecting a classic work of art. His words, however, lack the sophistication of a museum excursion.

"Take off your skirt." The force and command in his voice is undeniable.

I look down; I don't want him to see my smile.

The skirt has an elastic waistband, and I ease it over my hips, then let it drop to pool around my feet. I step out of it, but I keep my sandals on. Damien hasn't told me to remove those.

"Now the shirt."

I pull the loose blouse over my head and toss it on the table. I'm naked now, illuminated only by the glow of the nightlight burning by the bathroom door.

Damien doesn't shift position at all, but I hear the slow sound of him drawing a breath. And though it may be my imagination, it seems to me that the air between us is heating up. I know that I'm suddenly very, very warm.

"Kick off your shoes, then spread your legs."

I do, then stand still with my legs parted as he walks slowly around me as if I'm some slave girl for sale on a dais. He makes two circles around me, and on the second he pauses behind me. He slides his hand between my legs and cups me from behind. His fingertip brushes my clit, and my flesh quivers in his hand. I bite my lower lip and close my eyes to keep from moaning. It takes every ounce of my willpower for me to remain still.

"Do you want more?" he asks, his finger slowly caressing my sex.

"Yes." The word comes out raw and strangled.

Slowly, he pulls his hand away and circles back to face me. "Go to your room and get on the bed." He leans in close, and his lips brush my ear as he speaks. "No touching. I need your promise, Nikki. And this time I need you to keep it."

I nod. "Okay."

He looks at me, then slowly lifts an eyebrow.

"I mean, yes, sir." I want to ask him when he's coming to the bedroom, too, but I know better. I go, I lie down, and I wait, expecting him to enter with that mysterious case.

I am crazy with need, with longing, with that damned anticipation. I'm flushed and hot and swollen. My breasts and my clit are so sensitive that I think I'll come if the air conditioner kicks on. I want to touch myself with wild desperation, but I remember Damien's words, and I keep my legs spread and my arms wide, afraid that if I don't lay like that I'll be tempted to squeeze my legs together in an attempt to find satisfaction.

The position doesn't help my distress, though. It only makes me hotter. There's something so exciting about being wide open for Damien. My nipples are tight and hard, almost painful. I long to feel his teeth graze them, to feel his hand stroke me, his cock inside me.

Where the hell is he?

And then I hear the television snap on.

I groan aloud, and even though he's all the way in the next room, I'm positive that Damien has heard me—and that he's smiling.

I'm alone, horny as hell, and not allowed to do anything about it. He's out there, undoubtedly feeling smug, flipping channels at random.

This, of course, is my punishment, and by the time he turns the television off half an hour later, I am about out of my mind with the need to be fucked.

Just when I'm starting to fear that he's going to leave, he appears in my doorway and leans casually against the frame. "I like looking at you," he says.

"I like you touching me better." I'm actually pouting. He's reduced me that far. "That wasn't nice."

He laughs. "Sweetheart, that was nothing."

My pulse picks up again as he bends down and picks up the case. It was out of my field of vision by his feet, but now he brings it and sets it on the bed and opens it. The top opens toward me, so that I can't see the contents. His mouth curves down as if he's considering a variety of options, then he pulls out a jewelry case and sets it on the bed.

I frown, wondering what that could be about.

The next item doesn't make me wonder—I get what it's for right away. It's a whip. The kind with several thin bits of leather attached to a thicker handle.

"A cat-o'-nine-tails," Damien says helpfully.

"Um, uh-huh." I bite my lower lip. The rational part of me is thinking *ouch*. My sex, however, is throbbing with anticipation.

He sets the whip down and opens the jewelry box. Inside are

two silver rings, each with two small metal balls on them. They are connected by a serpentine chain. He picks one of the rings up and pulls it apart so that the two balls separate, leaving a gap in the ring. He slides one side of the jewelry box into that gap and then releases the balls. They spring back, clamping to the cardboard.

My brow furrows. I don't get it.

I can tell that Damien sees my confusion, but he says nothing. He just smiles and puts the rings and their chain on the bedside table. He closes the case and puts it on the floor, then he picks up the cat-o'-nine-tails and runs the thin strands of leather through his fingers. After a moment, he sets it beside me, then reaches down to cup my swollen sex. I arch up, silently begging for his fingers inside me, stroking me.

"You've been very naughty. I don't think I should make you come."

"I really think you're wrong about that," I manage, and am rewarded with his laugh.

"Close your eyes. Can you keep them closed, or should I blindfold you?"

"I'll keep them closed."

"Is that a promise?"

"Yes," I say without hesitation. I've already learned that the punishment for breaking a promise isn't really punishment at all. Even so, I'll try to keep my word.

I feel him moving near me, then he tells me to lift my hips. I do, and he slides a pillow under me.

"Keep your legs spread," he says. "Yes, like that. Oh, baby, you're so beautiful. Beautiful and open for me."

He touches me gently, a finger tracing just below my belly button. My skin tightens, and I arch up with desire. Then his touch disappears and I feel the soft flutter of leather across my breasts, my belly. The cat-o'-nine-tails. He's trailing it over me. And then, *snap,* he's flicked it softly over my breasts.

I cry out, surprised as much by the impact as I am by my re-action to it. A slight sting, yes, but then a sweet, spreading heat. *Pleasure mixed with pain.*

"Did you like that?" His palm cups my breast, kneading it, making it grow heavier and so unbearably sensitive.

I drag my teeth across my lower lip, but I can't lie. It's against the rules. More, I don't want to. I am in thrall to this man, and every touch is like a gift. "Yes," I say. "I liked it."

"I told you there might be pain, but only to bring you plea-sure."

"I remember. I—I want more."

"Nikki, oh, fuck, Nikki. Do you know what you do to me?"

"If it's anything like what you do to me, I think I have some idea."

His low laughter is raw, but dies when he closes his mouth on my breast. His teeth graze my nipple as he bites and sucks until my breast is nothing more than a live wire topped by a hard, thrumming pearl. And then his mouth is gone and there's something cold and—"Oh!"—tight and hard.

My eyes flick open.

"No," he says, and I close them again.

The initial stab of pain fades quickly, leaving a low, thick pressure. A tight awareness and an undercurrent of deep, flow-ing pleasure. A moment later, I feel that same sharp stab of ex-quisite pain on my other breast.

"Your nipples are so sensitive," he whispers as his hand slips down to explore my sex. "Oh, yes," he says. "This time I don't think I have to ask if you like it."

I don't remember ever feeling so aware of my body. Even the air is erotic, its whisper touch making me quake.

I gasp as the pressure to both my breasts increases. Slightly at first and then with more force. He's tugging on the chain that connects the two rings, pulling me up, the weight of my own body making the tug on my nipples even more exquisite. Not painful, but tight and aroused and ready.

"Damien." His name is a demand and he answers by closing his mouth over mine. The kiss is hard and needful, and I thrust my tongue in his mouth, desperately trying to claim this moment. He matches me, but all too soon pulls away and then gently eases me back onto the bed. "Keep your eyes closed."

I feel the soft caress of the leather as he trails the whip gently over my belly, then over my legs. I start to squirm, then freeze under his sharp command that I keep still.

Then it's trailing between my legs. My muscles spasm in anticipation and then there it is—*snap,* a light spank on my vulva. I gasp. Never would I have thought I'd feel such exquisite pleasure from getting smacked in such an intimate place, but maybe it makes sense. I imagine Damien pounding into me, fucking me hard. Yeah, maybe it makes a lot of sense.

I wait, my body raw and open. Wanting and needing. But there is no second strike.

"Again," I beg. "Damien, please."

His moan of pleasure tells me everything—he'd been waiting to see if I liked this new play. And I do. So help me, I really do.

Once again the strips of leather land lightly against my sensitive skin. I arch up, my clit feels huge and swollen, and as he smacks me once more, I fear that if one of those straps lands directly on it I'll explode from the combination of pleasure and pain.

"Damien," I say, and that's all it takes. The sensation changes, and it's not the leather on my sex, but his mouth. His hands are on my thighs, and his tongue is inside me, and I can hear his low, hard moans. I'm close, so close, my hips twisting and bucking shamelessly against his face, the scrape of his beard stubble tickling my sensitive skin.

I'm there—right on the edge, when he eases away from me. I

cry out in protest, but my cry changes to a gasp as Damien thrusts inside me. I open my eyes and see him above me. He's looking right at me, his expression one of such intensity that I can't resist drawing my arm around his neck and bringing his mouth to mine.

We kiss, as deep and as hard as he's fucking me, and I'm already so close that I come in just seconds, in what has got to be the most massive orgasm of my life. He's not far behind me, and when he's spent, he eases next to me on the mattress, our bodies still connected. I see the whip where he laid it on the pillow. I look at it and smile. "I think I'm going to like being a bad girl."

He chuckles. "I know you are." After a few minutes, he sits up, then gently takes the rings off my nipples. Immediately, I feel the warm rush of blood. Dear God, I could fuck him again right now.

He kisses the tip of my nose. "A lovely thought, but I need to make a run to the office."

"How do you do that? How do you read my mind?"

A smile is his only answer, but it doesn't matter. I already know how, and it doesn't scare me: Damien Stark can see beneath my mask.

"You really need to go? It's so late."

"I can't stay much longer. I have a conference call scheduled with Tokyo. Unfortunately, I have files in my office that I need."

"I'll see you in the morning, then."

He shakes his head. "Blaine's still in La Jolla. He wants to switch your sitting to tomorrow evening. Why don't you come by around five. I'll take off early and we can have a drink before he arrives."

"What if I'm not thirsty?" I say teasingly.

"I'm sure we can find something to satisfy both our appetites." He holds out his hand. "Come on. Let's get cleaned up."

We take a mostly chaste shower, during which he gently

soaps me down and rinses me off, touching me as softly as if I was fragile and precious. When we return to my room, I pull on a robe, while Damien gets back into his jeans and T-shirt. He puts the nipple rings back in the jewelry box, and then moves to my desk. "Keep them," he says. "Someday, I may tell you to wear them under your clothes."

I lick my lips and nod. He sets the box down, and in the process bumps my laptop. The screensaver dissolves, revealing the image I now use as wallpaper—Damien Stark looking exultant on the beach.

"Well," he says, looking at the screen, his expression odd.

"I love that picture," I say. "You look so happy."

He turns away from the screen long enough to eye me. "I feel very exposed."

I laugh. "Really? More than how I feel standing naked for a portrait?"

His brow rises. "Once again, you've made a good point, Ms. Fairchild."

"Here," I say, grabbing the camera from the drawer of my bedside table. I place it on the desk and set the timer, then I tug Damien's hand and pull him onto the bed with me.

"What are you—"

"Hush," I say. "Say cheese."

"Nikki—" But he's cut off by the intense flash and the click of the shutter.

He cocks his head, and there's censure in his eyes.

"No," I say, before he says a word. "I'm not deleting it, I'm not erasing it, I'm not ignoring it. I want a picture of the two of us together, and you can just deal with it."

The way he's looking at me, I'm seriously afraid I'm going to lose this battle. But then he nods and leans forward to kiss the tip of my nose. "All right," he says when he pulls back. "I want a copy, too."

* * *

I sleep late the next morning, and when I go into the kitchen for coffee, I find a note on the dining table from Damien beside the clothes he's picked out for me: *Wear these. D.S.* Apparently he was doing more than just watching television—he'd also gone through my laundry. He's selected a short denim skirt and a cheap concert T-shirt that really shouldn't be worn without a bra. Not exactly what I would call a stellar wardrobe choice, but I'll wear it. After all, I'm only going to take it off again once I get to the Malibu house.

A wry smile touches my lips. The man sure does love to control every little thing.

After I'm caffeinated, I stand in the shower and let the scalding water pound the life back into me. I am a shell of myself, but it feels so damn good. Yesterday was astounding, like an explosion of the senses. Relaxing, exciting, passionate, erotic, sensual. Most of all, it was fun.

It's a simple thing, but I like seeing Damien happy. And I can't deny the fact that it gives me a special thrill to know that it was me that helped him wipe away the dark remnants left over from his visit with his dad.

I squirt some shampoo into my hand and start to lather my hair, my mind still on the man and his father and their fucked-up relationship. I don't know—because Damien hasn't told me—but I can guess that it is at least as toxic as my relationship with my mother. Even so, it must have been hard, firing his dad as his manager, especially since he was only a kid at the time.

I turn the thought over in my head. There's something about the situation that's familiar. I tilt my head back and rinse my hair, working my fingers through the strands to get the soap out. I can't think what it is, but something is bugging me, dammit, and it's still bothering me when I get out of the shower and pad back to my room.

I'm slipping on the skirt when it hits me. *Control.* Not the fact that he needs it, but the reason driving the need.

I remember so many things that now seem like clues: the way his face looked when he told me that he'd wanted to quit tennis and his father wouldn't let him. His nonanswer when he told me about the new bastard of a coach and I asked if it was the bump up in competitiveness that stole the fun from him. His foundation to help children. Evelyn's reference to secrets swept under the carpet.

And always back to control. In his business. In his relationships. In bed.

I could be wrong, of course, but I don't think so.

Damien was abused as a child.

I poke around some more on the Internet, but I don't find anything to bolster my theory. Even so, it feels right. I don't know if his abuser was his coach or his father or both, but I suspect it was the coach, and that it was guilt from the abuse that drove the bastard to suicide.

The image currently up on my web browser is of a fourteen-year-old Damien after he's won some local tournament. He's smiling and holding up the trophy. But his eyes are haunted and dark. Yes, they are inscrutable.

I need to know the truth, but I can't ask Evelyn. This is the kind of thing that I want Damien to tell me.

I run my fingers through my hair, wondering if I should just confront him. But no. He has to be the one who comes to me. Because this isn't just about what Damien needs. It's about me, too. I need to know that this man I've spilled my heart to trusts me with his secrets.

But until he does, I'll have to be satisfied with my certainty that I understand a little bit more about the man still hidden behind the mask.

* * *

When I arrive at his house at a quarter to five, Damien is outside on the terrace, his back to me, his face to the ocean. He's damp from a recent shower and completely naked. I pass the heap of his clothes on the floor then pause at the threshold. I want to stand there and simply take in this glorious sight. The whole sky looms above him and the vast ocean spreads before him, and yet it is the beautiful, strong body of Damien Stark that dominates the view. There's power in the tension of his shoulders. Confidence in the way he stands. Strength in that back that carries so much.

This is a man who knows what he wants and goes after it.

He wants me, I think. And I feel a sharp stab of something that can only be pride.

"You're early." He doesn't turn to speak to me. I don't ask how he knows I'm there. I've felt the hum of energy between us, too. I don't need to see him to know when Damien Stark is nearby.

"How could I resist an extra minute with you?"

He turns to face me. "I'm glad you're here."

He smiles, but I can see now that the tension in his shoulders is across his whole body.

"Damien? What's wrong?"

"Lawyers and assholes," he says, then shakes his head. "Sorry. It's been one of those days."

"Should I go?"

"Never." He holds out a hand and I go to him. He pulls me against him and I feel his cock harden against my thigh. "Nikki." He sighs, his lips in my hair.

I start to tilt my head up, longing for his kiss, but the sharp ring of his phone interrupts and he gently pushes me away.

"I've been expecting that," he says by way of apology as he grabs the phone off a table. "Is it done?" he demands. "Good. Yes, I understand that, but I also understand that I pay you for advice. The ultimate decisions are mine. Yes, I do. Twelve-point-six? Fuck it, I would have paid more, and you goddamn well know it. I'm damn sure it was the right call; she's not getting dragged into this mess. No—no, it's done. I'm not interested in reevaluating the decision. I made my play, we're running with it."

There is a long pause, then, "Shit, Charles, that isn't what I want to hear. Well, then why the fuck *do* I pay you?"

So he's talking to Charles Maynard. I realize I'm being nosy, but I pay more attention, trying to discern meaning from a one-sided conversation. It isn't easy.

"Right, right. Did your PI locate the man I'm interested in? Oh, really? Well, that's a bit of good news. I'll deal with it first thing tomorrow."

I have no idea what he's talking about. I shift the conversation to the back of my mind and only half listen. Especially since the call seems to go on forever.

"What about London? She's settled again? No, it can't be helped. I'll fly over next week. What? Well, she's not leaving me much choice."

He sighs and paces. "And the San Diego problem? I want someone on that. What? Are you fucking kidding me? Shit, how did they dig that up?"

I pick up Damien's discarded clothes, intending to hang them up for him. But I'm overcome with a devilish little urge, and I give in to it, then tug the slacks over my hips and slip my arms into Damien's sleeves. There's something wonderfully sensual about being clad in Damien's clothes, even if I am technically breaking the rules with the pants.

I'm so preoccupied with the shirt's buttons that I don't even realize the call has ended. More than that, I don't notice Damien's raw temper until I hear the sharp *smash* of plastic and glass colliding with the stonework above the fireplace.

He's thrown his cell phone.

"Damien?" I hurry to him. "Are you okay?"

He looks me up and down, but I'm not sure he's seeing the clothes. Not sure he's hearing anything but the conversation that he must be replaying over and over again in his mind.

"Damien?"

"No," he snaps. "I'm not okay. Are you—oh, God, Nikki."

"Me? I'm fine. I'm—" He shuts me off with a kiss, hard and brutal. Our teeth clack together, and he twists his fingers in my hair to hold my head in place while he assaults my mouth with such force I'm certain my lips will bruise.

He moves us backward, then throws me down on the bed, his hands going to the waistband of the pants. They are loose on me, and he tugs them down, but not off, so they remain on my calves and ankles, like strange ropes binding my legs in place.

He scoots me back and roughly spreads my knees, and I'm wet, so damn wet as he moves to straddle me. Before I know it, he thrusts his cock deep inside me. He pumps, hard and fast and brutal. I watch his face. The face of a man fighting a battle. The face of a man who will keep fighting until he wins.

I reach for him, but some instinct has me dropping my hands. Damien needs this—he needs to take me. To truly *take* me.

And in so many ways, I need to be taken.

He releases a long, slow groan, and I feel it as his orgasm shudders through him. He collapses on me, but only for a moment. Then he pulls himself up and looks at me, and I see pain sharpen his eyes.

"*Shit.*" His curse is little more than a whisper. He pulls out of me, then starts to leave the room. He pauses by the fireplace and turns back to me, his mouth open as if to speak, his eyes full of regret. I wait for the words, but they don't come.

After a moment, he walks away.

I kick the pants off so that I can move properly, grab the sheet and curl up in it, trying to decide what to do. I have no idea what that was about, but it's clear enough that it originated with that phone call. And even though he seems to want to be alone now,

I don't think I'm going with that plan. Tonight, he's damaged. And if I can't fix him, I want to at least hold him.

I strip off the rest of his clothes and pull on my red silk robe, which is where it always is before a session, draped across a stool by Blaine's easel.

Barefoot, I go in search of Damien.

The task is harder than it sounds. The house is the size of a small country, and in the unfinished areas, sounds echo strangely, and it's difficult to tell where to go.

I hear a strange, rhythmic thump, and finally manage to follow it down to the first floor. I find Damien in a huge, unfinished room. It has a treadmill, a basic floor mat, and a punching bag.

It's the sound of his fists pummeling the bag that has led me here.

"Hey," I say. "You okay?"

He throws one last punch and then turns to look at me. He's put on a pair of briefs, but he didn't bother with boxing gloves. His knuckles are raw and bleeding.

"Oh, baby," I say. I look around and see a towel and a water bottle in a plastic crate, along with the gloves he should be wearing. I dampen the cloth and then return to him. "This might sting a little."

"Dammit, Nikki." He pulls his hand away from me and cups my face. The dark wildness that was in his eyes earlier has vanished. Whatever demon he was battling, I think it's been laid to rest. Or at least admitted to ICU. "Are *you* okay?"

"Of course." I take his hand back and gently tend to his battered knuckles. "You're the one I'm worried about."

"I hurt you." There's such pain in his voice that I think my heart's going to break.

"No," I say. "You didn't. You needed me. I *want* you to need me." I smile up at him, trying to be a bit lighthearted. "And I think we've established I can handle a little pain."

From his expression, it's clear he doesn't appreciate my levity.

"Not like that," he says.

"Why not?"

"Dammit, Nikki, I told you I'd never hurt you."

I shrug, tilting my head sideways to look at him. "You spanked me. Hell, you whipped me."

"That turned you on. It was a game. And I did it because I was hot for you and because you got off on it, too."

I'm biting my lip. What he says is absolutely true.

"But what I did just now—" He turns away from me and jabs out two quick punches, pummeling the air. "Goddammit. I was pissed off about something and I fucked you in anger, and I don't do that."

I go to his side, determined to get through to him. "Damien, I'm okay. I don't know what all of that was about, but I do know that you were upset. You came to me. I wanted you to come to me."

"I used you."

"Yes." I want to scream the word. "And I don't care. God, Damien, you're not some stranger off the street. You're the man I—" But I can't go there. "You're the man who's heard all of my secrets. Who's been in my bed and in my head. That's what makes it different. Don't you see that? You can have me however you need me. You can tell me your secrets and it won't change a thing."

He looks at me. "Won't it? I wonder."

His voice is far away, but seems to hold a challenge. I stand there, unsure of what to say.

"I'm going to call Edward to take you home," he finally says.

I find my voice. "No."

"Dammit, Nikki."

"I said no." I move closer to him. "You didn't hurt me." I rise onto my tiptoes so I can whisper in his ear. "I was wet for you, and you damn well know it. So there's no way you can say that you forced me." I hold his arm with one hand to steady myself, but with the other I slowly trace my way over his chest and lower abs until my finger finds the waistband of his briefs.

"No," he says, but I can hear the quickening of his heartbeat, the tightening of his body in anticipation.

"No doesn't always mean no," I say. I ease myself down onto my knees, thankful for the gym mat below me. His cock is straining against the briefs. I find the fly, then tug it out.

"Nikki . . ."

"I'm going to take care of you." I run my tongue down the length of his cock, so hard and velvety. I taste salt. I taste me. And I want to take him all the way in. "Sunset," I say. "It can be your safeword, too."

Before he can say it, though, I rim the head of his cock with my tongue, teasing it as if it were a very large, very decadent lollipop. He gets harder and harder, and when I'm certain that I've brought him close to the breaking point, I draw him in, stroking and sucking and getting myself even hotter in the process.

I can feel the change in his body and I know that he's close, but then he shifts position, pulling out of my mouth and then drawing me up until I'm pressed hard against him. He kisses me, this time softly and sweetly, then eases us both down to the mat.

I open my mouth to speak, but he presses a finger to my lips. "Shhh. No talking."

He unties my robe and leaves it open, laid out beneath us as he climbs on top of me. I spread my legs and draw my knees up, and then close my eyes in pleasure as he thrusts inside me.

He moves in a slow rhythm, the complete opposite of the way he fucked me upstairs. This is making love, and his eyes never leave mine. He takes my hand and slides it between our bodies, and his silent command is easy enough to understand. I'm so aroused my body tingles all over, but I stroke my clit, getting hotter and hotter, my rhythm matching his thrusts until, finally, he explodes, and I do, too, just moments after.

Spent, he lays beside me, sharing the silkiness of my robe.

"I'm so sorry," he says, his fingers tracing a lazy path on my shoulder. "And I'm so angry."

"At me?"

"No. At me."

"But why? I thought we already established that what happened upstairs was okay."

He looks at me, his eyes hot with need. "Because now that I have you, I can't stand the thought of ever losing you."

27

Despite the drama, the evening takes a right turn toward normal. Blaine comes and I pose and he paints and Damien sits quietly in a chair and watches for four solid hours. After that we sit and drink wine and watch the moon on the ocean. Damien offers to let Blaine crash on the mat in the gym, and so we repeat the entire thing bright and early the next morning, finally wrapping at nine when Damien heads out for his office.

When I get home around ten, I find Jamie's note that she's gone to an audition. I cross my fingers for her and settle in for a lazy morning. Damien's in meetings until lunchtime, and though I'd rather be snuggled in his bed, I'm also happy to veg with the television, the newspaper, and Lady Meow-Meow.

I make a pot of coffee, tune the television to a classic movie station, and debate whether or not I should do a load of laundry today.

My Man Godfrey is just about to start, and since that's one of my favorite screwball comedies, I decide that laundry can wait.

The opening credits are still rolling when the phone rings. I see that it's Ollie and snatch it up.

"Can you do lunch?" he asks. "Early, because I have a one o'clock meeting. Like maybe eleven? You could come here? I'll have my secretary order us sandwiches."

"Um, sure. Why the sudden urge?"

"I just want to see you. Does there have to be a reason?"

There doesn't have to be, but of course I know there is. And I'm afraid it's about Courtney. Or worse—about Jamie. I assure him that I'll be there, then set the DVR to record the movie. No time to watch the whole thing now.

When I arrive in Ollie's office just shy of an hour later, the receptionist is expecting me. She leads me to a conference room where Ollie has spread out sodas and Subway sandwiches. Not exactly high class, but it'll do.

He's not there yet, so I sip my Diet Coke and open my bag of chips, all the while reminding myself that I need to be supportive. Lecturing him about how he screwed up won't do anyone any good at this point.

"Hey," he says, pushing into the conference room with a stack of files.

"Please tell me those aren't for me."

For a moment he looks confused, then his face clears. "No, no. These are for my meeting. Sorry. It's been a crazy couple of days."

"So what's going on?" I ask. It must be serious if he's interrupting work insanity to bring me here.

He presses a button on the credenza and the vertical blinds that hang in front of the two picture windows that make up the open sides of the conference room begin to close. A moment later, we have complete privacy.

"You're not going to like it," he says.

I lean back in my chair, already irritated. "Shit, Ollie. Is this about Damien again? Can you please quit playing the role of big brother? I'm all grown up. I can take care of myself."

He doesn't flinch or react. As far as I can tell, he hasn't even heard me. "Do you remember Kurt Claymore?"

I swallow. The infamous Kurt. Of all the things he might say, this really wasn't on my radar.

"Yeah," I say blandly. "I have a vague recollection."

"He's been working the past five years as a manager at a Houston-based manufacturing company."

"So?"

"So your friend Damien had him fired this morning."

"What?" I realize my fingernails are digging into the armrest of his guest chair. "You can't be sure."

"Yeah," Ollie says. "I can. I said I never worked for Stark directly, but I do the work for Maynard. I'm the one who hired the investigator to find Kurt. I'm sorry, Nik."

My heart is pounding painfully in my chest and my skin feels clammy. Damien tracked down Kurt. He got him fired. And he never asked me. Never talked to me. Just did it.

"He's rich and arrogant and as far as he's concerned he owns the world and it damn well better behave the way he wants it to."

"No," I say automatically. My voice is soft. I feel numb. "Damien's not like that. He was protecting me. That was his way of protecting me."

"Protecting you? The way he protected Sara Padgett?"

My head snaps up. "What are you talking about?"

"You know who Eric Padgett is, right?"

My stomach clenches. I'm terribly afraid of what he's going to say. "Yes," I manage. "You know I do. He's the dead girl's brother."

"He keeps threatening to go to the press and say that Stark killed his sister. For weeks we've had all of Stark's resources aimed at stopping this one asshole, and he just keeps pushing back saying he wants his money, and he's going to screw Stark, and there's more dirt out there than just his sister, but it all sounds like the same old smear routine. Just like I told you in Beverly Hills—we figured Eric Padgett was just one more asshole looking for a payday."

"What's happened?" My voice is completely flat. I just want to hear the horrible thing and get out of there. I need to be alone. I need to process this.

"Stark paid him off yesterday. That's right," Ollie adds in response to my openmouthed gape. "The same Damien Stark who wanted a balls-to-the-wall defense against the guy did a complete 180 and paid the fucker off. Forget fighting. Forget all his talk about not backing down, about taking it all the way as far as it would go. He just caved. Quickly and completely."

"Caved how?" I ask, so softly I'm surprised Ollie can hear me.

"Caved to the tune of twelve-point-six million dollars."

"Oh, God." I don't mean to speak, but the words fly out. I press my hand over my mouth and blink back tears.

Ollie is watching me, but I'm not really seeing him. Instead I'm seeing Damien on his terrace pacing with a phone to his ear, talking to Charles Maynard about something I don't understand. And about twelve-point-six million dollars.

"Oh, God," I repeat.

There's no compassion in Ollie's eyes as he looks at me. "Maybe Stark just got tired of the bullshit. But I don't think so. I think he's covering up what he did. He's dangerous, Nik, just like I've been saying. He's dangerous, and you damn well know it, too."

My thoughts bounce randomly through my head as I steer my battered Honda to Damien's Malibu house. Anger, loss, fear, denial, hope. I don't know what I'm thinking or even what *to* think. All I know is that this isn't good.

All I'm sure of is that it hurts like hell.

It's just past noon, but I'm certain I'll find him there. I called his office from the road and his secretary told me he was heading home.

Home, I know, means our third floor studio.

"Hey, Blondie," Blaine says as I step off the landing and into the studio.

"I didn't think you'd still be here."

"Been doing some color studies. Trying to get the damn sky right." He shakes his head. "Getting close, but I'm not quite there yet." Then he gets a closer look at me, and his brow furrows with concern. "Okay, what's wrong?"

I glance at the painting. My image is there on the canvas, more fleshed out, but still unfinished. I look raw, as if the top layer of me has been stripped away, and in that moment I think that Blaine has truly captured me. Because that is how I feel. Like Damien has ripped his way through to see what I kept hidden, and then left me exposed and vulnerable.

Damien steps in from the kitchen. "Nikki." I hear the pleasure in his voice, then the shift as he truly looks at me. "What's going on?"

"I'm going to cut out," Blaine says.

Damien doesn't look at Blaine or answer. His eyes are only on me.

I wait until I hear the door shut, and then I draw in a tight breath. My heart is pounding so hard I can barely get the words out. "Did you control her the way you do me?"

I see confusion in his eyes, and it pisses me off. I hold on to the anger, because it gives me strength. "Sara Padgett," I say. "Goddammit, Damien, do you think I don't know?"

"What is it you think you know?" His voice is as cold as ice.

"I know you need to be in control. Your life. Your business. Your women. Your bed. I even get it," I say. A tear has escaped and is snaking its way down the side of my nose, but I'm holding it together. Right now, it's me who's the expert on control. "You were abused, weren't you? And now you need it. You need to be in control."

I watch his face, looking for confirmation, but there's nothing there. His face is blank and unreadable.

"I do like to be in control, Nikki. I don't think I've ever made a secret of that."

No, he hasn't. But there have been so many other secrets. "Did it start as a game?" I ask. "Did you tie her up, too?" I move toward the bed and take one of the drapes in my hand. "Did you put this oh so gently around her arms? Then around her throat? Did you tell her about pleasure and pain?" The tears are flowing freely now, and my voice is thick with them. "Was it—was it an accident?"

His face is no longer blank. Now it's dark, like a violent storm, and just as dangerous. "I did not kill Sara Padgett."

I manage to look him straight in the eye. "I've got twelve-point-six million reasons to believe that you did."

His face goes white. *It's true.* Oh, dear God, until that moment, I don't think I really believed that it was true.

"How the hell did you hear about that?"

My skin feels clammy and my stomach is roiling. I think I'm going to be sick.

"Certainly not from you," I say. "I guess that's not the kind of thing you were going to try to be more open with me about, huh? Well, I suppose I can't blame you."

"How?" he repeats.

"I overheard some of your phone conversation," I snap. I leave out the rest.

He shoves his fingers through his hair. "Nikki—"

I hold up my hand. "No," I say. I just want to get out of there. I shove my hand into the pocket of my jeans and pull out the ankle bracelet. I take a deep breath and then I drop it onto the bed.

I pause only long enough to look at the raw, unfinished painting. I feel a lump in my throat. Then I turn and hurry down the stairs.

Damien doesn't come after me.

I'm not sure how I get through the next two days. They are a haze of ice cream, classic movies, and really depressing country songs. Twice, Jamie makes me go sit by the pool, saying that the vitamin D will be good for me. But it doesn't feel good. Nothing feels good.

My sleep schedule is all screwed up, and I don't worry about fixing it, because I don't need to get up early since I don't have a job. I called Bruce from the car after leaving Damien's house and told him I couldn't accept the job. I need to cut all my ties with Damien Stark because if I don't, I know I'll get reeled back in. I can feel the part of me that's already tugging in that direction, I miss him so terribly.

My nights are turning into days and vice versa and I'm learning all sorts of things about products that are sold only by infomercial. That's why I know neither what day it is nor what time it is when I'm awakened from a cat nap on the couch by a determined knock at the door. I yell for Jamie to answer it, but of course she's not home. She's had two more auditions and a callback, and while I'm thrilled for her, I'm also feeling lost and lonely.

The pounding continues. I groan and sit up.

Once the blood starts flowing I wonder who could be that persistent. Damien? I doubt it. I haven't heard a word from him. Not to offer me explanations, or even to check on me.

Because you made the right decision. You really were just chattel. He's moved on.

Well, fuck. Now I feel like shit all over again.

The pounding ramps up. "All right! I'm coming! Hang on!"

I stand up and blink. I can feel that my face is puffy and I know that my unwashed hair is a mess. I'm wearing the same ripped flannel pajama pants I've been wearing for two days, and my tank top has coffee spilled on it.

I am pathetic, and I really couldn't care less.

I pad to the door in my fluffy socks, careful not to trip over Lady Meow-Meow, who seems thrilled to see signs of life in me.

I don't usually bother, but I take the trouble to look through the peephole to make certain it's not Damien about to see me like this.

It's not.

It's worse.

It's my mother.

28

"Mother," I say. "What are you doing here?"

She brushes past me, then looks critically around the room, her nose wrinkling. After a moment, she walks to the dining table, then uses the tips of her fingers to pull out the chair. She takes a tissue from her purse, brushes the seat, and sits. She folds her hands in front of her on the table and keeps her back straight.

I follow and flop down in the chair opposite. I prop my elbow on the table and rest my chin on my fist.

My mother smiles at me. The same fake smile she reserves for cashiers and gas station attendants.

I try again. "Why are you in LA?"

"I would think that was obvious," she says. "I came to help."

Granted my brain is a little fuzzy, but I don't know what she's talking about.

"With Damien Stark," she says, and my stomach clenches tight.

"What are you talking about, Mother?"

"I saw the picture, of course. And the caption. Why you didn't tell me a man like Damien Stark was courting you, I don't know. But it's the first good news I've heard about this move to Los Angeles."

I stare blankly at her.

"Well, darling, really. If you're trying to marry a man like Damien Stark, you want to make sure not to disappoint. He can so easily move on to another woman."

Yeah. Easy. As far as I know, he already has.

She looks me up and down, her lips a thin line. "Clearly we have a lot of work to do." She pulls her phone out of her Chanel handbag. "What's the best spa nearby? We'll focus on your makeup first. Thank goodness your hair is still stunning, even if it is filthy. We'll get the ends trimmed, of course. Then a new wardrobe and then this apartment. If Jamie is particularly attached to any of these things, she can put them in storage."

"I broke up with him, Mother."

I swear to God, my mother turns green.

"You what?" From her tone, you would have thought I'd told her that I only had twenty-four hours to live. "Why on earth would you do something so foolish?"

"Why?" I open my mouth, grappling for something to say. "Because he has some truly fucked-up control issues. Does that sound familiar?"

She stands up, her movements slow and practiced the way she always moves when she's angry. A lady doesn't show emotion. A lady doesn't spout off. "You little fool," she says, calmly and coldly. "You always were too smart for your own good. Only Nichole knew best. Only Nichole knew what to do."

"For Nichole, yeah, Mother, that's right. Only Nichole knows what Nichole wants."

Her face is pinched so tight I can see where her makeup is caking and cracking. "You are spoiled and ungrateful. I can't believe I took time out of my schedule to fly out here and see you. I am going to go back to my hotel, and you think about your life. About what you want and where you're going and what you're throwing away. And when you can talk calmly and rationally, I'll come back."

And then she turns on her heel and marches to the door and leaves. She doesn't even slam it.

I sit there, numb. I know I should move, but I can't. I just sit and stare and feel like I'm floating out of myself.

I don't know if it's been fifteen minutes or fifteen hours when my leg starts to cramp and I have to move. I glance down and realize my hand is still in a fist. I open it slowly and see the indentations from my fingernails, some so deep they've almost drawn blood.

I stare at my hand as I get up. I don't realize I'm doing it as I walk into the kitchen. We have a knife block, and I take out a paring knife. I turn on the gas burner, because even in my haze I know I should sterilize the blade, and there's no alcohol in the kitchen and I can't leave the kitchen because then I won't have the courage.

I wave the knife through the flame and then wait for it to cool. I press the blade against the soft flesh of my inner arm. A new place for a new pain. I start to slice—and then I violently hurl the knife across the room. It crashes into the wall, leaving a dent in the drywall.

Everything is blurry now, and I realize I'm crying. I stand up and turn a circle in the kitchen. I'm lost—so fucking lost—and despite everything it's Damien that I want right now. Damien's arms around me, holding and comforting me.

No, no, goddammit, no!

I snatch the kitchen scissors off the drainboard, then retreat to the corner by the dishwasher. I slide down to the floor and without thinking, I take a chunk of hair and cut it off. Then another. Then another until there is a pile of hair around me.

I look at it, run my fingers through it. That hair my mother loves so much. That hair that Damien loves, too.

I pull my knees up to my chest and hug them tight. Then I put my head down and I sob.

I don't remember going to my room. I don't remember getting in bed. But when I open my eyes, Damien is beside me, his eyes sad and soft.

"Hey," he says.

Damien. My heart seems to swell and the blackness that's been clinging to me dissipates.

He reaches out and strokes my hair.

I sit up, remembering. *My hair.*

"It could use some cleaning up," he says gently. "But I think it looks cute short."

"Why are you here? How did you know?"

"Jamie," he says. "I've been calling her for days, checking on you. I thought you needed space. But then this, with your mother . . ."

I nod, vaguely remembering Jamie tucking me into bed and me telling her that my mother had come by. I can't repress my shiver at the thought of seeing her again. "She's still here," I say. "In town, I mean."

"No," he says. "She's not."

I look at him.

"I went to her hotel. I told her she needed to leave. And then I sent her home on the jet." Amusement lights his eyes. "Grayson's been dying to take her out for a long flight, so this was just the ticket. And your mother seemed thrilled by the prospect of a private jet."

I stare at him with awed amazement. "Thank you."

"Whatever you need, baby. I told you."

I shake my head. "No. Damien, I'm sorry. I—we can't."

He stands, and though I expect anger on his face, all I see is concern. "Because of Sara?"

I don't meet his eyes.

"Oh, hell," he says, then sits back down on the side of the bed. He hooks a finger under my chin and makes me look at him. "Do you really believe I killed her?"

"No." The word comes out quickly and firmly and it's completely true. A tear rolls down my cheek. "Damien, I'm sorry. I'm so sorry."

"Shhh." He brushes my tears away. "It's okay. You're right. I didn't kill her. I wasn't even there that night. I was in San Diego. Charles finally got images from the hotel's security camera. I was in the bar most of the night talking with the owner of a company I was interested in acquiring. That's why he was so pissed that I settled. We had what we needed to shut Eric down, and I went and paid him off."

I sit up straighter. "I don't understand, either. Why would you—"

"Two reasons. Maybe I wasn't there, but dammit, I should have shut it down with Sara long before it got out of control. I wanted her interest in the company, and I got it. I bought out some other shareholders, too, which gave me a controlling interest. I edged Eric out and I put people in place who could get the company running again. Turned a tidy profit quite quickly and the value of everyone's stock increased, Eric's included."

I watch him, not sure where this is leading.

"And during all of this I was seeing Sara. I don't usually date, and I didn't love her. But I was busy and she was convenient and more than willing to indulge me in bed. She clung to me and though I didn't admit it to myself at the time, I started to see signs that she was unbalanced. I knew I needed to break it off, but I was focused on some time-sensitive mergers, and I just let it ride. After the deal was complete, I did end it. But that just pushed her off the deep end." He drags his fingers through his hair. "I never expected her to kill herself—and I would never choke a woman in bed—but that doesn't change the fact that I played a role."

"But it wasn't your fault," I say. "And Eric's making horrible accusations. Why would you pay that bastard off?"

"Because of you."

I gape at him. "What?"

"I was willing to fight him until the end of time if I had to. But that was before he approached you at the fund-raiser. I'm not letting him drag you into this, and I'm damn sure not letting him scare you."

I hug myself as goose bumps rise on my arms. I'm in shock; I'm humbled. Damien completely rearranged his plans because of his concern for me. "I—but, Damien. Twelve million dollars?"

"It's the current value of the stock I acquired from Sara, plus the value of Eric's stock. I bought him out. A damn good deal, too. The company's strong. I'll make it back."

"You didn't have to. I can fight my own battles."

He meets my eyes, and what I see in his is so much more than simple desire. It's need and longing. Maybe it's even love. "You can," he says simply. "But this wasn't your battle to fight."

He takes my hand. "Nikki, baby, I can't lose you."

I want to fold myself in his arms, but instead I turn away. "There's other stuff, Damien."

"I know," he says, and I turn back, surprised.

"You know?"

"Jamie told me. Apparently Ollie told her."

"Ollie?" *Shit*.

The corner of his mouth quirks up. "Don't worry. I won't say anything to Charles. Whatever confidences he betrayed, he did it for you. The bastard may have pissed me off, but I understand why he did it. I would have done the same."

"You had Kurt fired," I say.

"Hell yes, I did."

"Damien, you can't just do that to people."

"Actually, I can. He worked for one of my companies."

"But—" I cut myself off. The truth is I don't give a fuck what happens to Kurt, and the fact that Damien had his sorry ass fired doesn't really bother me. Not by itself, anyway. It's the rest of it.

"Nikki?" He's looking at me, his face open and vulnerable.

I reach out and stroke his cheek, the stubble of his beard scratching over my palm. The air between us is thick, and just touching him makes me feel alive. He's like a part of me, I think. Hell, he's like the air I need to breathe. And I need him. I need all of him. But I'm not as certain that he really needs me. "You're wrong about what you said. About me."

"What did I say?"

"You said I wasn't weak." I run a hand over my hair. "I am."

"Oh, baby, come here." I slide into his arms, and it feels like coming home. I press my head to his chest and listen to the rhythm of his heart. "Everyone breaks a little sometimes. That doesn't make you weak. It makes you wounded. And I will always be there to help you heal."

I release a shuddering breath as I pull back enough to look into his face. I can't imagine Damien breaking, but somehow I know that he's speaking from experience. *Everyone breaks.*

"Nikki," he says. "Baby, are we okay?"

I think about what my mother said about what I was throwing away, and I wonder if she's right. For the first time in my life, can my mother actually have something to offer me?

I close my eyes, because I don't want her in my head. When I open them again, I see only Damien. "I want to make this work," I whisper, and the relief that I see in his eyes washes over me like a balm. "Is Jamie here?" I ask, because suddenly I'm thinking about the thin walls of the condo.

I see the hint of a frown. "No." He clears his throat.

I narrow my eyes, confused. "What?"

"This may not be the best time, but I have a confession."

I tilt my head and wait.

"Jamie's going to be getting a call from her agent soon."

"And you know this how?"

"Because it's for a series of national commercials. For a company I have an interest in." He's speaking gingerly, eyeing me as if he's afraid I'll explode.

"You did that for her?"

"For the company, actually. The ad agency presented us with three possible actresses and Jamie was the best of the bunch."

My smile stretches wide across my face.

Damien looks at me, baffled. "Why is that okay, but helping you get the job at Innovative wasn't?"

I grimace, because it's a legitimate point. "Because it just is," I say, then laugh.

He joins me, then brushes a soft kiss over my lips. "Nikki?"

"Yes?"

"I—" He stops, but not before I hear the tenderness in his voice. I close my eyes, imagining that he's told me he loves me. The word sounds right, and not terrifying at all.

"Don't ever leave me again," he says.

"No," I whisper. "How could I? I'm yours."

He rolls over until he's on top of me, then trails light kisses down my neck. "You said I have to be in control."

"Not really an astounding revelation, is it?"

He chuckles. "I'm giving it to you."

"Giving what?"

"Control, Nikki. Tell me what you want. Tell me exactly what you want."

"You mean other than you?"

"Where do you want me to touch you? How slow? Shall I graze my teeth over your nipple? Shall I bite your ear? Shall I dip my tongue into your sweet cunt? Tell me, Nikki. Tell me what you want."

"Yes," I say, meaning all of that. "But start by kissing me."

He does, pressing his mouth softly to mine, then with increasing firmness. His tongue finds mine, stroking and teasing and I'm getting more and more turned on, even though he's doing nothing else. No touches, no caresses.

Damn the man, he meant what he said.

Gently, I break the kiss. "Stroke my breasts," I say. "Then pinch my nipples." I don't think I've ever drawn out a road map to making love, but with Damien I don't feel shy. "Tighter," I demand, then arch up as he twists almost to the point of pain. "Kiss me," I say. "All the way down until you get to my clit. I want your tongue there, and I want your fingers inside me."

He grins up at me. "Yes, ma'am," he says, then begins to slowly, torturously, work his way down my body. I'm trembling now with desire for him. The slightest touch of my body against the sheet brings me even closer to an orgasm. It's as if my entire body is an erogenous zone. And I want him there. I want him *everywhere.*

I gasp with the realization of what it is that I truly want tonight. And even though his tongue on my clit feels so, so good, I ease his head up, then pull him up to kiss my lips. I roll sideways so that we're spooning together, and then I take his hand and guide it to my ass. "Take me here," I whisper.

I feel his body tighten, the raw heat of him increase. "Are you sure?"

"I want to belong to you," I say. "I want to belong completely."

"Oh, baby." He eases me over so that I'm on my hands and knees on the bed. He strokes my cunt, getting his fingers slick with me, then takes a finger and eases it inside my anus. I gasp.

"Tell me if you want me to stop."

"No. No, it feels good."

And it does. His touch sends shocks of pleasure ricocheting through me.

"Have you ever?"

"No," I say. "Only you."

I hear his low growl of pleasure. "Do you have any lube?"

"In the drawer," I say, then feel his weight shift on the bed as he reaches for the small table. He opens a drawer and pulls out the bottle. He puts some on his fingers, then strokes me. I moan from the pleasure of it. "We'll take it slow," he says.

His mouth caresses my back. His fingers play with my clit. His cock teases my ass, and then I feel one finger slip inside me. I tense at first, then relax, overwhelmed by this new sensation.

"Okay?"

"Yes, please don't stop." I was going crazy from the pleasure. From the sensation of being so completely open to him. Of giving him something I'd never given anyone else. "More," I whisper. "I'm ready, but slowly."

Then the bulbous head of his cock is behind me. I feel how hard and stiff it is, and my hips rise without thinking. "Sweetheart," he murmurs. "Oh, baby." Gently, he eases inside me. I gasp, then quickly beg him not to stop.

"Easy," he says. "Slow and easy. God, Nikki, you feel so good." He's inside me now, moving in a gentle rhythm. The sensation of being completely filled with him is overwhelming, and I think I could come just from the feel of him inside me like this.

"Touch my clit," I say because he's taken his hand away. He complies, stroking in easy circles that match the rhythm of his thrusts, and Damien and I are more connected than we've ever been. He moves slowly, careful not to hurt me. His arm is around my hip, his hand stroking my clit, and my climax is building with his.

"I'm close, Nikki," he whispers. "Baby, I'm going to come."

His release is fast and hard, and as he comes inside me his hand presses against my clit, the extra pressure taking me over the brink as well. We collapse together, and he kisses my shoulder, my back, holding me close until our breathing slows. "You're mine," he says.

"I know," I reply, and I mean it completely.

I don't know what kind of favors Damien had to call in, but he gets me an appointment that evening at one of the best salons in Beverly Hills, and so I end up at dinner that night sporting a darling new haircut. Shoulder-length curls that bounce when I walk now that they're not weighed down by the length of all that hair.

I'm showered and shaved and sweet-smelling again. The dinner was to die for, and the chocolate torte is almost as good as an orgasm.

Best of all, I have Damien beside me.

Life is good again.

I take a sip of my white chocolate martini and then kiss the tip of his nose. "Ladies' room," I say. "I won't be long." I start to slide out, but he holds me back, then kisses me so hard and deep I almost melt into the booth.

"Hurry. I want to go home. I have plans for you."

"Get the check," I say.

"Are you finished with dessert?"

I let my gaze glide slowly over him. "Finished? I haven't even started."

I'm rewarded by the heat in his eyes, and I flash a coy smile before turning away and heading toward the back of the restaurant, letting my hips swing just a little as I move. My grin dies, however, when I hit the narrow hallway and see Carl coming.

"Well, if it isn't Nikki Fairchild. Hello, princess. You still fucking Damien Stark? Guess what? So am I."

I'd intended to brush right past him, but that stops me. "What are you talking about?"

"Skeletons," he says. "The kind that live in closets."

"I don't know what you mean." But I feel cold anyway.

"I'm just thinking about how high and mighty our Mr. Stark is. You land pretty hard when you fall from the stratosphere."

"Dammit, Carl, what are you telling me?"

"You? Not a goddamn thing. But tell loverboy I'll be in touch."

He walks away from me. I decide to skip the ladies' room and return to Damien. I give him a rundown of the conversation and watch his face grow hard.

"Do you know what he's going on about?" I ask, thinking about the abuse that he still hasn't told me about.

"No," he says. His voice sounds calm, natural. But there's a shadow in his eyes. That same coldness settles around me, and I'm afraid that he's going to shut down and push me out. But then he draws in a breath and pulls me close. "Probably some shit to do with my father," he says. "Don't worry about it. I don't want either my father or Carl Rosenfeld to ruin our evening."

He pulls me close and kisses me hard, and I nod agreement. Right now, I don't want either of those men between us, either.

Back at the Malibu house, we make love slowly and sweetly, and I lose myself in Damien's touch, letting him erase all my fears and worries. In the shower, he soaps me down, gently stroking the cloth over all of me, then rinsing us both off until we feel clean and new. He wraps me in a towel and leads me back to the bed, then slides under the sheets with me.

He's on his side, looking at me, that enigmatic smile curving on his lips. I curl my fingers in his hair, holding him there, making sure there's nothing for him to see but me. "You're mine, too, you know," I whisper, and only when he says yes do I loosen my hold and draw his mouth down to mine.

I feel the change in his breathing as he falls asleep pressed close against me. I think about the skeletons and ghosts that still hide in the dark corners of Damien's past. I remember Eric

Padgett's words. *Secrets,* he'd said, and I shiver, afraid that Damien's going to have to face that darkness. But I'll be there when he does, and we'll face the darkness together.

I can. Because when Damien's beside me, I'm no longer afraid of the dark.

J. KENNER loves wine, dark chocolate, and books. She lives in Texas with her husband and daughters. Visit her online at www.jkenner.com to learn more about her and her other pen names, to get a peek at what she's working on, and to connect through social media.